A BRIGHT ONE

The Making of a True Warrior

B Burgess Junek

Images of the World

Published by
Images of the World
Rapid City, South Dakota

ISBN-13: 978-0-9630448-9-1

Cover art: Atula Siriwardane
Cover design: B Burgess Junek

Library of Congress Control Number: 2023907917
Printed in the United States of America

ACKNOWLEDGMENTS

Thanks to beta readers Kathy Trotter, Jaff Auchterlonie, Ron Yahne, and Chris Van Ness and for all their comments, encouragements, and insights. Special thanks to my sister, Bobbi Looney, for the final proof read and corrections.

Thanks also to Atula Siriwardane for his fantastic artwork on the book covers and the maps.

I could not have written *A Bright One Chronicles* without the lifetime of exotic traveling adventures, bicycling expeditions, and spiritual quests that I have shared with my wife, Tass Thacker. Nor could I have written it without her red pen and brutally honest editorial skills and sharp critiques throughout the entire process to make the story better. For years, Tass has heroically managed our business and household to give me extra time to write. For all of her humor, strength, inspiration and love, this book series is dedicated to my soul mate, Tass Thacker.

LUNAR CALENDAR

The appendix at the back of the book has a cast of characters list and a glossary for unfamiliar words.

Each moon or month has 29-30 days and is divided into 4 weeks:

Dark Moonday or Divine Night begins the first day of the first week of each month.

Bright Moonday starts the second week of each month and begins evening socializing and travel by moonlight.

Full Moonday starts the third week with a culmination of evening festivities, celebrations and travel by moonlight.

Dim Moonday starts the fourth and last week of each month with moonlight socializing or travel in the early morning before dawn.

 Each week has 7 days except bright Moonday with 8. Luckdays are added every other dark Moonday to adjust the lunar calendar to the appearance of the new crescent moon.

1 moon = one month = 29-30 days
10 moons = one decade

Lunar Calendar Conversion To Solar Years:

12 moons = 1 solar year
50 moons = 4 solar years
75 moons = 6 solar years
100 moons (1 century or centurion) = 8 solar years
150 moons (start of tween moons,
            beginning of adulthood) = 12 solar years
200 moons (2 centuries, full adulthood) = 16 solar years
300 moons (3 centuries) = 24 solar years
400 moons (4 centuries) = 32 solar years
500 moons (5 centuries) = 40 solar years
600 moons (6 centuries) = 48 solar years
700 moons (7 centuries) = 57 solar years
800 moons (8 centuries) = 65 solar years
900 moons (9 centuries) = 73 solar years
1,000 moons (1 millennium) = 81 solar years
5,000 moons (5 millennium) = 404 solar years
10,000 moons (10 millennium) = 808 solar years

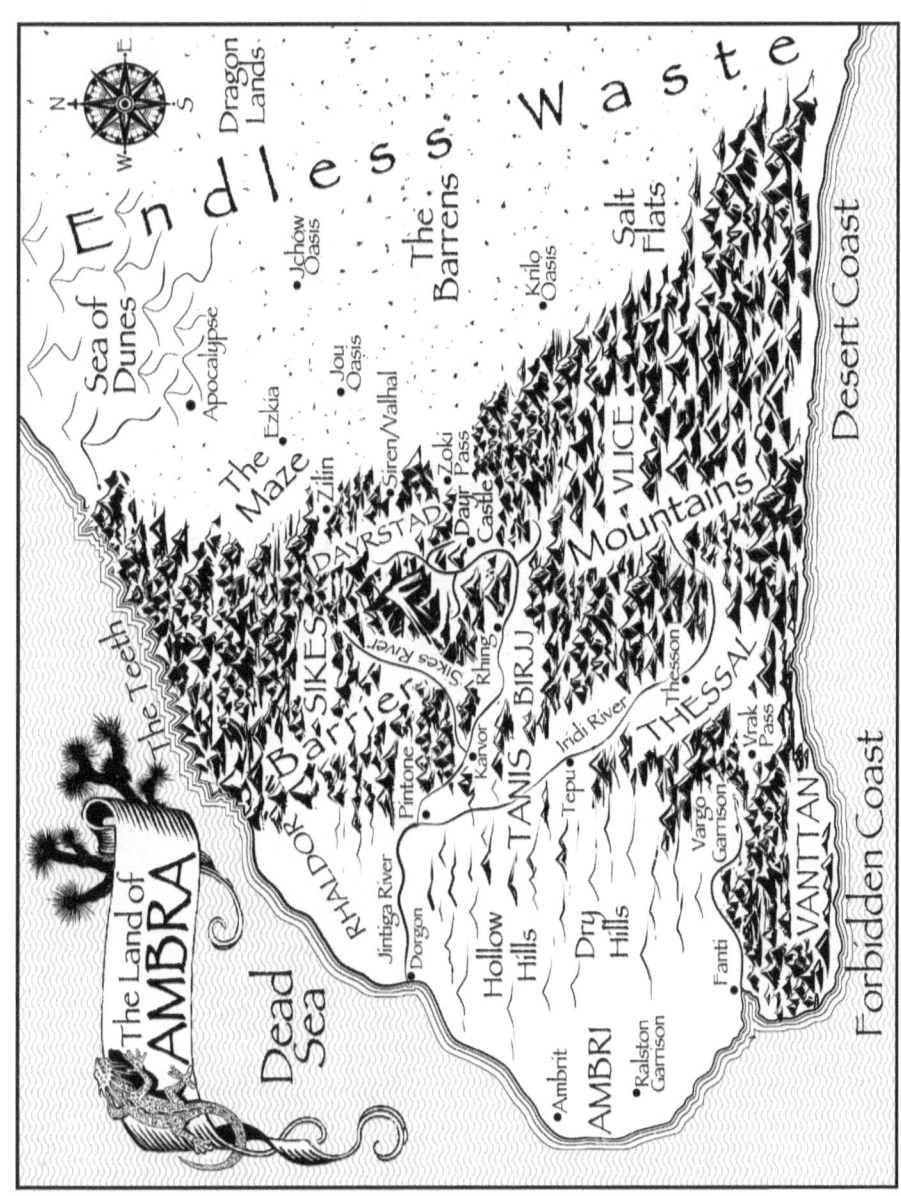

The Land of AMBRA

Endless Waste

Dragon Lands

Sea of Dunes

The Maze

The Barrens

Salt Flats

Apocalypse

Jchow Oasis

Krilo Oasis

Ezkia

Jou Oasis

Zilin

Siren/Valhal

DAVRSTAD

Zoki

Daur Pass

Castle

VLICE

Mountains

The Teeth

SIKES

Barrier

Sikes River

Rhing

BIRJJ

THESSAL

Thesson

Vrak Pass

Karvor

TANIS

Iridi River

VANTAN

RHADOR

Pintone

Tepu

Vargo Garrison

Jintiga River

Dorgon

Hollow Hills

Dry Hills

Fanti

Dead Sea

Ambrit

AMBRI

Ralston Garrison

Desert Coast

Forbidden Coast

PART I

In the Ancient Days women lived as Angels of Light with powers to fly on wings across the sky higher and faster than eagles and were able to sing and talk with each other at great distances. Their cities were built of precious gems, shining and reflecting a dazzling brightness that filled the world with light. There was no sickness, with bountiful food of all delicious flavors. Every woman lived in leisure to a great age until at last she fell asleep with no pain to merge once again with the Mother Creator of All Life.

But men became jealous of the women's wings and beautiful songs. The Mother Creator of All Life cautioned men not to stray from the Path of Glory, for they might fall into the Great Sorrow, or even the Pit of Despair.

Some men said they must have fire in their hearts to cleanse themselves of their impurities so they might also have wings to fly and voices to sing. For just as iron is heated in the forge to make the finest steel, so these men hoped to purify their bodies and make their spirits powerful like the Mother Creator of All Life.

As men argued about how to use the cleansing fire, the fire grew wild and escaped from their hearts and began to burn the world, destroying the cities of light and the beautiful gardens, and finally burning the women's wings so they fell from the sky, scorching their heavenly voices with acrid smoke so they could no longer sing their beautiful songs.

The Mother Creator of All Life saw the great evil that men had done, and She wept at men's foolishness and sin. She took the fire and formed it into the sun and placed it high in the sky so men could never touch it again.

Then the Mother Creator of All Life took dirt and ashes from the fire and added water to form woman anew. She breathed on the body of woman, who opened her eyes. The woman asked the Mother Creator of All Life not to give her wings, nor a heavenly voice, so that man would not be so easily tempted toward jealousy

1

again.

The Mother Creator of All Life took the woman's wings and formed man anew. For the heart of woman was made from the beginning to love man, even in his destructive foolishness. And She breathed on the body of man, who opened his eyes.

Then the Mother Creator of All Life blessed the wise mind of the woman and ordained that women should always rule over men, bringing light to their spirits.

Kabaal Prophecies

The Divine Womb gave birth to everything we see and do not see. We are all children of Divine.

Hope the Proclaimer

UTUNO'S REMEMBRANCE

Epoh was standing in the front corral of the Dayr Castle stables talking with Utuno about buying a daya horse when Riin Ruel came out of the front building with her bags and swords over her shoulder. Epoh gasped in amazement upon seeing the curved scabbards of her twin blades.

"Are you Riin Ruel?" he intuitively guessed. She looked so much older than he would have expected. The compound she had ingested to fake her death and escape prison had turned her braided dreadlocks white. Her black skin was not lustrous but dried and wrinkled. Her body, less than robust.

"I am." She bowed in respect. "You must be Crown Prince Epohco." She had been told that he had survived drowning, been saved by nuns, and had returned from the Endless Waste. She was surprised to see he was darkened, burnt, and fried by the sun with cracks and blisters on his lips, nose, and cheeks. Obviously, he had spent most of his time away from the nunnery and out in the Waste itself.

"I am no longer that person," he brought his desiccated hands together prayerfully, the sign of the womb. "Please call me Epoh."

"We have much to discuss!" Riin Ruel returned the gesture.

"Yes," Epoh agreed and put his hand up before she could say more. "But little time now. The girl you seek, the Bright One, she has gone to Karvor. She is the foundling from these stables."

Utuno gave a startled and surprised look. What did they mean, the Bright One?

"Her name is Tyme," Epoh continued. "She has gone after the man who killed Noot, the stable boy. I leave tomorrow morning to find her. I assume you will come with me."

"I will be ready at first light," Riin Ruel agreed. Divine had miraculously brought them together. She stepped forward and gave Epoh a heartfelt embrace. He hugged her firmly in return, and then strode resolutely back up to the keep to spend perhaps his last night with his family.

Riin Ruel turned to Utuno. She sensed Epoh's statements had triggered the remembrance of a dream in the stable manser. Epoh's words, not her own gaze, had prompted it. She would ruminate at length on that strange fact later.

"You thought of a dream," she encouraged Utuno to speak.

"An old dream," Utuno nodded and scratched his frizzy silver hair with his stubby fingers. "I dreamt it the night before Tyme arrived." His eyes grew moist. "Snippets of the dream have remained in my mind, crystal clear," he told her with amazement, "even after all these moons. Other parts were never clear and long forgotten. But now I remember it all."

"I would ask to hear it," the Blade requested. "'Tis of great import."

Utuno led Riin Ruel to the cookhouse and made tea as he told the story. "I was looking out the top bunkhouse window at the corral in full moonlight." He had heard the sound of distant hoof beats and watched as Noot came out of the stables, stared at the moon, then ran out of the corral. The hoofbeats grew louder.

"A powerful black stallion with a glistening coat rounded the corner into the corral." As he spoke Utuno's eyes grew wide with wonder. "Then I saw her. A small girl. Barely 30 moons. Riding bareback with no bridle. Riding like she was a part of the horse!"

He watched as the horse jumped the fence and slowed down. The girl grew drowsy and leaned forward, asleep. When

Noot reappeared, the horse dropped to its knees. The girl slid off the horse's back into Noot's arms and was carried into the stables.

"The stallion was named King," Utuno said with reverence.

"Do you recall the day you had the dream?"

"'Twas a dark Moonday," Utuno answered. Divine night. The first day of the month, the most auspicious of days. "Noot had the same dream that night. So did Tyme. But she never thought it a dream. She always believed it real."

Riin Ruel listened with fascination. The dreams certainly confirmed Epoh's beliefs about Tyme.

"Tyme and Noot both dreamt that he helped Krueger open castle gate so Tyme could ride through," Utuno added.

Krueger had earlier told Riin Ruel about his own dream of Noot helping open castle gate--to let in a young woman, a dazzling warrior Empress, leading a singing army. Yet another confirmation. The fact that Noot's death caused Tyme to leave the castle was now even more important.

A small, blue-tailed lizard skittered past, the kind Noot loved to catch because their shiny tails popped off when he grabbed them, and the tails continued to wiggle for half an hour in his hands, or in his pockets, where he loved to keep them.

"Noot woke up the next morning looking for the stallion," Utuno recalled. "I did not remember any of the dream until I heard Tyme laugh, so I had no idea what he was talking about."

"Tyme's laugh triggered the remembrance?" Riin Ruel asked.

"Yes. When she was joking with Noot." Utuno told about finding her in Merrylegs' stall.

Riin Ruel nodded thoughtfully. "Did she believe King would come back?"

"Yes. Someday."

"Merrylegs was the Crown Prince's colt," Riin Ruel repeated, thinking out loud.

"Given to him on his 100th moon," Utuno confirmed.

"She is that much younger?" Riin Ruel asked with surprise.

"She is much the same age—now," Utuno shrugged with a lack of comprehension. The whites of his eyes widened bright against his black skin. "When I first saw her in the stables, she seemed 30 moons. Then out in the light she appeared more like 40 moons. Three days later when she went before King Eyrico to give her oath of apprenticeship, she seemed more like 50 or 60 moons in age."

Utuno told about Tyme learning to use a bridle and saddle, and of her exploits riding Spike, a powerful and notorious ibex billy into the mountains with Tao Tau. "Her first trip she seemed to grow and age another decade."

"Tell me of Tao Tau," Riin Ruel inquired.

"She is a healer and something of a nun," Utuno answered. "She taught Tyme to have a practice. And she insisted that Tyme go to keep school."

Riin Ruel was greatly relieved to hear of such influences in the girl's life. "And her relation with Epoh?" she asked. She had an uneasy feeling that Epoh was in love with the girl.

"That was the name she called him," Utuno replied. "He was fascinated with her from the start. He studied dreams and signs and felt she was very special. He liked talking about spirituality and how to have a strong practice. He always went to the Womb on Moondays. I figured he would someday ask her to be his queen."

"Would she have said yes?" Riin Ruel asked.

Utuno broke into his large, white-toothed smile. "She would have been the greatest of Barbarian Queens!" he exclaimed. "She would not have stayed cooped up all day in the keep. She would have been a queen like no other!"

"Who else went with her to Karvor?" Riin Ruel queried.

"Klew, the castle champion and Tyme's sword manser. And Jyg, a young falconer who now has a pet raven. Klew has sent a few letters back to report finding plots against King Eyrico that are connected to plots against the Czarzina." Utuno did not know that some of the messages had come to the castle via

Pio's Pigeons.

"How did Klew come to be Tyme's sword manser?" the Blade asked in amazement. Utuno told of Tyme's sword fight with Noot—again 'twas Noot who played a key part—and how she had been injured.

"Klew rightly saw a special talent and ability in her. Or maybe just her strong will. He started teaching her that night-- using her uninjured arm! He taught her all sorts of weaponry and fighting tricks."

"Curved swords?" the Blade asked. "Using daggers?"

"Most likely," Utuno replied. "She also learned knife throwing from the Ser Cus!"

DESTINY

The next morning Epoh and Riin Ruel left Dayr Castle together at dawn. The sky was a dull and dirty yellow. Epoh was riding Chia, a daya mare he bought from Utuno with money from the gems smuggled out of the Endless Waste in the folds of his clothes. King Eyrico had disowned him for abandoning his duties as Crown Prince and refused to speak to him ever again.

'Twas the Queen who had informed Epoh that Klew from the Castle Guard was staying in an apartment above the Glazed Woman in Karvor. She did not mention Tyme's name. The Queen held to a glimmer of hope that her son might redeem himself by helping to foil the treasonous plots and return back to Dayr Castle a hero.

Epoh held no illusions of glorious return. He was afraid Dayr Castle would never again be home. He somberly asked Riin Ruel if he might ride silently for a while. Around mid-morning they dismounted to walk the horses up a steep section of the Ambri Scout trail and Epoh began to speak.

"Starai, the baby girl you tested out in the canyons near Ezkia, she is the one who found me drowned in the Womb of the Earth, a sacred underground pool deep in the Maze. She was an acolyte at the nunnery because her mother thought that was what you had ordained." He shook his head at the irony. "Starai learned from her teachers that you actually told her mother she was *not* the one."

"She was not the one for whom *I* searched," Riin Ruel said wisely, "But she became the one for you." She looked at him shrewdly. She wondered why Epoh kept appearing and interweaving with important events. He was the one to be born when she had first come to Dayr Castle. He had become Tyme's friend. He had appeared at Ezkia. Could *he* be the reason she herself had gone to the nunnery? The thought made her uncomfortable.

Epoh thought briefly about Starai. He still regretted not being able to say goodbye. "The abbess believed it Divine Will that I fell into the river," he continued thoughtfully, "so that Tyme would be free of me to fulfill her own true destiny. For a while I thought the abbess might be right." He shook his head. "But when a chance came to escape the nunnery," he grinned, "I knew my destiny was to try to find my way back."

"And once you fulfill that destiny?" Riin Ruel asked. "What is your intent once you find her?"

"To help her fulfill *her* destiny," he replied. "In any way I am able. Like you, I believe she is the Bright One. The Divine Daughter foretold by prophecy."

At the top of a ridge, they stopped to put on their sun capes. Epoh had his cape and sun cloak from the Endless Waste, along with some of his desert clothes. When he first arrived at the Siren his uncle the Duke had given him new clothes, and ordered that his old clothes all be burned. Epoh had privately stopped the servant from doing so. In addition to the gems hidden in the folds, he had a sentimental attachment to the simple but well-made garments. Unlike Riin Ruel's exquisite silver cape, Epoh's cape and cloak had a plain cut with a splotchy golden-gray color that blended well with rocks and dirt.

They traveled silently until just after midday when Riin Ruel stopped early to put on her full sun cloak. "I have been very ill," she explained cryptically. "I am slowly getting my strength back."

"We can go any speed you like," Epoh offered.

"I am fine traveling till the heat, and again each evening. Mayhaps in a few days we can travel at night."

A MESSAGE
FROM PIO

The day Epoh and Riin Ruel left Dayr Castle, Jyg's uncle Pio sent Panr a pigeon with the news. That evening Bones visited the dovecote of the eccentric old pigeon breeder in the Alkali Hills and flew back to Karvor with a message tube on her leg.

"What does she say?" the big black bird mimicked Panr's voice perfectly after swooping in to land proudly on the patio.

"Bones has a message," Jyg called out to Tyme and Klew. The raven jumped up with a flap of her wings to land on the table where Jyg could easily remove the tube.

"Sshh! Quiet!" Bones ducked her head solemnly.

"This is not a message from Panr," Jyg said with surprise as he tucked a few stray locks of his red hair behind a freckled ear. "This is my uncle Pio's handwriting." He squinted at the tiny letters. He had never seen such a long message. He only read a few words before he looked up in shock.

"Crown Prince Epohco has come back alive!" he gasped. They all looked at each other in stunned silence, afraid to believe 'twas true.

Tyme clasped her hands prayerfully. She could hardly breathe. "Read it!" she whispered, mouth slack.

"*Prince Epohco returns!*" Jyg announced grandly. They all started whooping and hollering.

"Saved by the bird!" Bones cried out.

Jyg squinted at the small note again. His face grew solemn. "*Abdicates throne to Dracoro.*"

"What?" Klew exclaimed. A stunned silence filled the room.

"Now called Epoh," Jyg read slowly.

"He changed his name?" Klew pondered the implications.

"That is the name I called him," Tyme revealed thoughtfully.

Jyg's voice grew somber. *"Disowned by King."* No one said anything. A pall of heaviness filled the room.

"Blood and guts!" Bones commiserated.

"Go on," Tyme prompted. Could it get any worse?

"Left this morning with," Jyg squinted to read the word, *"Blade for Karvor,"* he pronounced slowly.

"With a Blade?" Klew marveled. "There has only been one Blade visit the castle in millennia, and that was when Crown Prince Epohco, or I should say Epoh, was born. Her name was Riin Ruel."

"I remember you telling me about her," Tyme answered.

"Do you think it could be the same Blade?" Jyg asked.

"She was looking for an infant girl of prophecy," Klew recalled. "She stayed less than a moon and then disappeared."

Jyg held the message close again to read the last words. *"Will meet you at Glazed Woman."*

The implication of it all left them momentarily speechless.

"He is coming to see me," Tyme said with a nervous excitement. He had forsaken his old life as Crown Prince and future King of Dayrstad! What was his plan?

"With a Blade," Klew reminded her. "Also coming to see you."

"City guards!" Bones called out in warning from her perch.

"Why would a Blade want to see Tyme?" Jyg asked.

Tyme had a vague look of being cornered. 'Twas the first instance that Klew ever saw her look uncertain, maybe even a little afraid.

"Mayhaps we best wait to find that out," Klew said lightly, not ready yet to say what he felt deep inside. Tyme was a part of the prophecy! She might even be the Bright One herself!

"No," Tyme said to Klew in a low but firm voice. "I want to

know what you really think. I need to prepare myself for all possibilities."

"The Crown Prince," Klew began, "I mean Epoh, has always believed the dreams and omens around you were special signs from Divine Herself." He shrugged as if embarrassed to further point out the obvious. "You were spiritually tutored by Tao Tau, and you have the strongest practice of anyone I have ever known. You learn everything quickly. You tamed and rode Spike. You are the finest pupil a sword manser could ever hope to have."

"You are the best person, the best friend, anyone could ever hope to have," Jyg chimed in.

"Kaw, kaw," Bones croaked in the deep resonant voice ravens use when greeting an old friend. She hopped over and began gently chewing on Tyme's fingers with her shiny black bill.

Tyme's dark bronze face suddenly looked a little pale. "'Tis all a bit overwhelming to imagine," she said uneasily.

WAS KING A DREAM?

"Tell me about when you first met Tyme," Riin Ruel asked Epoh. They were camped in an alcove along a ridge with a good view of the Ambri Scout trail running through a narrow canyon. The sky was a dusty yellow-gray.

"She arrived at the castle while I was at the Siren with my uncle, Duke Eddarko," Epoh replied. He explained the tradition of the Crown Prince of Dayrstad making the journey on his 100th moon. "I was gone a little over a month. She was in the stables when I came back." Epoh smiled at the memory. "I sensed something special about her right away."

He paused for a moment. "Then I learned that both Utuno and Noot had dreams of Tyme riding into Dayr Castle on a black stallion named King." He gave Riin Ruel a pointed look. "It does not take a soothsayer to interpret that." He told her of his Book of Oneiromancy, and how he had kept a dream journal when he was young. "I told her a black stallion in dreams could symbolize unique perfection."

"Did she think 'twas a dream?" Riin Ruel asked.

"No. Never," Epoh answered with a shake of his head. "She believes it real."

"And you?" the Blade asked.

"I believe in her," he answered frankly. "I think that is what is truly important. How she got to Dayr Castle remains a great mystery to me still."

Riin Ruel nodded thoughtfully.

"However, Tyme did say she once dreamt about King. Much later. Just before I became a tween and was sent out on the

Scout trail and fell into the river." He looked at the Blade thoughtfully. "She dreamed she was riding King out in the Endless Waste looking for something." He shook his head. "I told her my book said that dreams of the desert can mean loneliness or isolation. She felt it signified that something important to her was out there. Not long after, I was in the desert."

"And there was not a day in the desert," Epoh continued, "that I did not think about her. When I got back to Dayr Castle, I asked Utuno if she ever thought about me," he admitted. "He said she prayed for me every day."

Riin Ruel listened somberly.

Epoh put a few more dried fronds and shriveled cactus on the fire for tea. As it brewed, he spoke again. "Our lives have changed so much," he said nervously. "Before, I imagined her as a Barbarian Queen. Now, I wonder if she will be the next Czarzina, or even the Empress to bring back the Ambri Empire! Whatever happens, I hope to stand behind her as a helpmate."

A SPECIAL FRIEND

The day after receiving Pio's message about Epoh coming to Karvor, Tyme went up the hill to the Blue Moon to tell Delgado. She had asked Jyg not to tell him anything. Tyme wanted to do it herself. She hoped talking about it would help her process and understand what she was feeling. She wished she could talk with Wiir Waar.

In the Blue Moon, Delgado escorted her to the private table they sometimes used. He could tell that something was bothering her, which made him nervous. He waited for Tyme to speak.

"We received a message from Dayr Castle," she began. Her voice faltered. "Epohco has returned alive."

Delgado turned ashen but forced a smile. "I know this is what you have prayed for, so I am happy for you."

"'Tis what I have prayed for," Tyme agreed but then grew silent, her thick dark eyebrows furled; there was no sparkle in her golden-green eyes.

Delgado looked at her quizzically. She thoughtfully twisted the engraved gourd of watered wine in her hands but did not take a drink. "You do not seem happy," he noted with acuity, ever sensitive to her emotions.

"I am very confused about what I feel," Tyme admitted. "There was more to the message."

"If there is anything I can do to help," Delgado pledged, "you know I am at your service." He was very uncomfortable seeing her distressed.

"Thanks." She took a deep breath. "Crown Prince Epohco has abdicated from the throne of Dayrstad."

"Is he all, right?" Delgado gasped. "Is he of sound mind?"

"He changed his name to Epoh," Tyme replied. "That is the name I called him when we were alone."

"Did you hope to be queen?"

"I never envisioned myself as Queen of Dayrstad," Tyme answered. "Epoh disappeared before I was of an age to think of such things. We never even kissed."

For the first time Delgado felt the briefest of hopes. Mayhaps, they had only puppy love that would not survive into adulthood.

"He is coming to Karvor to find me," Tyme revealed.

Delgado's glimmer of hope flickered out. That did not sound like puppy love.

"He is coming with a Blade who is *also* looking for me."

"A Blade?" Delgado was immediately suspicious. "Why would a Blade be seeking you?"

"There was a Blade who came to Dayr Castle the moon Epoh was born. She was searching for an infant girl of prophecy. Klew thinks this could be the same Blade. Her name is Riin Ruel."

"Well, I believe you could be a girl of prophecy," Delgado replied lightly, "after watching you beat up Rocozo with a blunt sword."

"That is not funny," Tyme said. Why had she hoped that a moonboy like Delgado might give her an objective viewpoint? "Winning a sword fight with an oafish brute does not make me the fulfillment of prophecy."

"Well, she must have some reason to believe you are the girl," Delgado shrugged.

"There were some unusual dreams the night before I showed up at Dayr Castle," Tyme admitted. She told him of Utuno's and Noot's dreams.

"But I remember riding King into Dayr Castle for real," she said. The sound of the stallion's hoof beats. Holding onto his mane. Feeling the power of his body running under her.

"Does Epoh believe you are the girl from this prophecy?"

Delgado wondered.

"He always took signs and omens very seriously. He has a Book of Oneiromancy, which explains the types and meanings of dreams." Tyme shook her head. "But he never spoke of me and a prophecy."

"The fact that he is traveling with a Blade who knows of this prophecy seems to indicate that he is in some agreement," Delgado mused.

"That is what makes me nervous," Tyme admitted. "I want him to search for me because he loves me. Not because of some prophecy."

"I think you should just see him, alone, at first," Delgado advised. "Spend a few hours, or even a day, getting to know each other again. Then, only when you are ready, meet with the Blade."

"That is an excellent suggestion." She smiled with warmth for the first time that evening.

"I can set a lookout on Jintiga Bridge," Delgado offered, "and direct Epoh to your apartment. I assume he and the Blade will get rooms next door?"

"Yes," Tyme answered. "Thanks. You are truly a special friend."

YOU HAVE CHANGED

As Epoh and Riin Ruel made their way across Jintiga Bridge, they were spotted by Scoop. The spy and scout for the Jawbone Ridge Gang was quick to identify Epoh, who looked very much like someone who had just come out of the Endless Waste. He was wearing a strangely tailored sun cape. His skin was dark and leathery. His lips cracked and parched; his cheeks chapped. The bright glare of the white sky from the afternoon sun hardly caused him to squint. Although 'twas not yet the heat of the day, his companion wore a full sun cloak of a shimmering silver material. Her horse was a similar silvery color, unlike any Scoop had ever seen. He guessed the mare to be a firehorse. Epoh rode a fine mountain daya.

Scoop waited for them to pass through the toll station before he approached. "Manser Epoh," he greeted them with his hands prayerfully together to gesture the Womb.

"Yes," Epoh answered with a surprise.

"I have been sent by Ser Tyme to guide you to the Glazed Woman," Scoop told them.

"How is it that Ser Tyme knows of our arrival?" Riin Ruel asked in astonishment. Any message courier from Dayr Castle would have had to pass them on the road to deliver the news of Epoh's return to Dayrstad, and subsequent journey to Karvor. They had seen no such rider.

"How she knows I can not say," Scoop shrugged. "I was simply told to stand watch for the two of you."

"For two of us?" Riin Ruel asked in amazement.

"Yes," Scoop confirmed. "I was told Manser Epoh would be traveling with a Blade. My instructions are to escort you to lodging next to the Glazed Woman, unless you prefer to lodge elsewhere." Scoop cleared his throat nervously. "I am to ask that you, ser," he informed Riin Ruel, "wait one evening while Ser Tyme meets first with Manser Epoh alone. Then she will be ready to see you."

"I believe that is a wise idea," Epoh agreed before Riin Ruel had a chance to argue. "I would also prefer to meet Ser Tyme alone at first." The significance of Tyme's instructions was not lost on either Epoh or Riin Ruel. By meeting on her own terms, she was signaling that she was not going to be intimidated or coerced into something for which she was not prepared.

"So be it," the Blade consented without further discussion. The fact that Tyme knew of their arrival perplexed her greatly. Had the girl dreamt of their search for her?

They dismounted and Scoop led them up into the city of Karvor. Epoh was so nervous he was barely able to appreciate the brightly colored and vibrant town. Everything seemed like a dream. Was he really about to see Tyme again at last? His hands shook and his heart pounded in his chest.

"I can take you to an inn with a tavern for meals," Scoop told them as they climbed up the steep hill through town, "or an apartment building that has cheaper rooms with kitchens that rent by the month."

"The apartment sounds perfect," Epoh answered. "I plan on staying awhile. I have no place else to go."

"Nor I," Riin Ruel agreed. "The apartment will be fine."

Scoop led them first to the stables where Tyme, Jyg and Klew kept their horses. While they stabled their mounts, Scoop ran up the street to warn Tyme that Epoh had arrived in Karvor. To give Tyme some privacy, Jyg and Klew left for the Blue Moon.

When Scoop returned, he led Epoh and Riin Ruel to the apartment building next to the Glazed Woman. They were each given a room on the second floor in the rear of the building close to the back stairs that also gave access to the apartment where Tyme stayed, although they did not yet know about this convenience. The rooms were small but adequate with a window that could be sealed up with thick shutters during the day. In one corner was a table, chair, and cook pit, in the other corner a raised stone bed with a small door and tiny condition underneath--a cool, dark cubicle just big enough to sit or lie down inside during the heat.

Epoh bathed quickly, standing in a basin scooping cups of water over himself from a bucket. After changing clothes, he followed Scoop down the hall and out the back door. Instead of going down the stairs, Scoop knocked on a small servant's door on the second-floor landing. He waited just a moment before opening the door and led Epoh through a little kitchen area and out into a shaded area of a walled patio. As Epoh looked around, Scoop disappeared back out through the servant's door. When Epoh turned again, he saw Tyme standing in a hallway. They both stood looking at each other for a moment, and then Tyme rushed forward to embrace him.

"I always knew you were alive!" she whispered in his ear.

"The thought of you kept me alive!" he answered in a choked voice, "and brought me back." They stood hugging in disbelief. At last, they broke apart to better look at one another.

"You have changed," she said. His darkened skin was cracked and leathery. His lips blistered like Noot's. But more than that, there was an indestructibility about him. He exuded an invincible force and presence. Yet he had the same gentle kindness in his eyes.

"You have changed as well," he told her. She had blossomed. He had always sensed her strength, resolve, and deep inner spirituality. Now she seemed to glow, more adorable and beautiful than ever with her off-kilter smile, thick black eyebrows, and golden-green eyes. No longer his hoped-for Barbarian Queen, she was something much larger and grandiose. He began to speak of his new realization, but she stopped him.

"No. Say nothing of that yet," she insisted. "I want to hear your story first. What happened to you and how you survived."

He told her of the rock viper, the sickening sound of cracking bones as Merrylegs fell from the cliff, of his being thrown into the river and breaking his nose.

"I kept plunging over waterfalls," he shook his head and looked her in the eye. "I was sure I was going to drown. That was when I first realized how much I loved you."

Tyme reached out to squeeze his hand. He explained how he tied scroll pouches to give himself buoyancy before going over the last huge waterfall into a deep black hole underground. How he struggled to keep his head above water.

"It seemed like for days," Epoh said solemnly. "I kept thinking about you. I thought our destinies were linked, and if I died ... I would somehow be letting you down." His eyes grew moist. "I did not really think of Dayrstad. I worried more about not being there for you. I felt just incredibly sad and alone."

Tyme hugged him and he began to sob. He was embarrassed by his outpouring of emotion, but Tyme knew his tears would help his healing. "You experienced a terrible trauma," she consoled him, "'Tis good to release the pain that's still inside and let it all out."

He cried in her arms for a while then regained his composure to speak.

"I woke up in a cave called the Womb of the Earth. I was found by an acolyte nun on a pilgrimage from Ezkia Nunnery. She saved me and nursed me back to health. Her name was Starai." Epoh paused, unsure how to continue.

Tyme sensed his uncertainty. She could tell something was conflicting him. "She was important to you in other ways as well," Tyme guessed.

"Yes," Epoh acknowledged. "She was a true friend." He searched for the right words. "More than a friend, actually." He shook his head sadly. "I never even told her goodbye." That fact had been weighing on his conscience since he left the nunnery.

"What happened?" Tyme urged him to continue.

"'Tis complex," he replied, uncertain how to begin. "It all has to do with you."

"Me?" Tyme asked with surprise.

"And it has to do with the Blade who is with me."

Tyme grew pensive and quiet.

"Her name is Riin Ruel," he told her. "She came to Dayr Castle when I was born. She was looking for an infant girl of prophecy. The daughter of a King. But I was born instead."

Tyme nodded reluctantly. The Blade was just as Klew had guessed.

"When she left Dayr Castle she traveled to Ezkia Nunnery." Epoh explained how Riin Ruel had enlisted the help of the abbess and had found and tested Starai as an infant. "Riin Ruel told her mother the baby was not the one she was searching for. Regardless, her mother became convinced that Starai was destined for the nunnery and left her there on her 50th moon to be raised by nuns." Epoh shook his head in disbelief. "That is what ended up saving me."

"Because of Riin Ruel's visit," Tyme marveled at the connection.

"When they first got me out of the water, I was nearly dead." Epoh looked remorseful. "I talked about you in my delirium," he apologized. "The abbess quickly realized that you are the one who Riin Ruel had been seeking."

"Why did she think that?" Tyme asked with astonishment.

"She quizzed me on everything about you," Epoh said defensively. "How you appeared at the castle. About Utuno's and Noot's dreams. About you riding Spike. About Tao Tau. About your practice. About you learning the sword. Everything." Epoh looked at her helplessly. "She convinced me that my falling in the river was all part of Divine Will to get me out of the way so that you would follow your true destiny."

Tyme was momentarily speechless. "Is that what you think?" she asked him at last.

"At first I did," he answered, "But now, I think 'twas to teach me some things about myself, and about my relationship with you." He took both her hands in his. "I believe that you are destined for more than I had imagined. I realized that I wanted to be with you more than anything else--whatever my role. I wanted to be a part of your life and help you in any way I could."

Tyme gave him a nervous hug. "Thank you for your loyalty." Yet his words made her uneasy. "Let's talk no more of this tonight. I would wait until tomorrow." She stood to stretch her legs.

"Riin Ruel is eager to meet you," Epoh reminded her.

"I want you with me when we meet," Tyme replied.

"I do not think she will agree to that," Epoh warned. "She views me as being of much lesser import in the grand scheme of things. I am only a supporting player—and a man at that. You are the one blessed by Divine."

"Then I have the authority to make my own decisions," Tyme told him pointedly. "She has no choice. Tell her I will not meet with her unless you are also in the room."

Epoh rose to leave. Tyme gave him a goodnight hug. She thought about kissing him on the lips but instead gave him a peck on the cheek. He was happy with that.

After he left Tyme put a candle in one of the windows for Scoop to let Jyg and Klew know that 'twas okay for them to return from the Blue Moon. When they did, she gave them a brief recounting of Epoh's ordeal in the underground river, and of his rescuer's earlier encounter as a baby with Riin Ruel.

"Are you planning on meeting with the Blade tomorrow?" Klew asked.

"No sense in prolonging the inevitable," Tyme replied. "You can meet her as well. I am going to have Epoh stay and sit with me during our meeting."

"I think that is wise," Klew nodded his head.

"I would like you both to join in for our second meeting," she informed them.

"We are at your service," Klew told her.

"We want to help however we can," Jyg agreed.

"At your service," Bones agreed, mimicking Klew's voice, which gave them all a much-needed laugh.

A PRIME CANDIDATE

The next morning Epoh brought Riin Ruel to the apartment and introduced her to Tyme. The Blade looked much older than Tyme had expected from Klew's description of her first appearance at Dayr Castle. Her hair was now completely white. Although she still had a commanding presence, Tyme did not feel as intimidated by her as she thought she might.

Riin Ruel realized she needed to treat Tyme like a young colt that had been spooked. She had to put the girl at ease and let things proceed at a much slower pace than she would have liked. Riin Ruel was accustomed to people being in awe at her presence and prestige. Neither of those factors seemed to be having much effect on the girl.

Epoh greeted Jyg and Klew with a hug. Then Tyme introduced Riin Ruel to Klew.

"Epoh told me you were the Dayr Castle champion," the Blade greeted him Barbarian style with her right fist to her heart

"I was raised and trained at the Military Academy in Ambrit," Klew replied, correctly guessing that would impress the woman warrior more than any Barbarian credentials.

"Indeed," Riin Ruel nodded thoughtfully, noting the mercenary chose to no longer go by his Academy name, which would have been Klewono.

"And this is Jyg," Tyme continued, "my dear friend and companion."

"You are the falconer," Riin Ruel greeted him also Barbarian style.

"My familiar is now a raven," he told her, gesturing the

womb before bowing respectfully in the Ambri fashion. "Let me introduce you." He called out a soft *kaah*. A large raven swooped down from the roof to land with a loud whoosh of her wings on Jyg's outstretched arm. "This is Bones," he said proudly.

"Manser Jygaro!" the bird greeted him respectfully with a bob of her head.

Riin Ruel's eyes grew wide at the human sound of her voice.

"This is Riin Ruel," he informed the bird.

Bones examined the Blade shrewdly with first one eye and then the other, then bobbed her head and said, "At your service," in a voice imitating Klew from the previous night.

Riin Ruel nodded respectfully, clearly intrigued by the raven.

"And this is Epoh," Jyg introduced the raven to the former crown prince.

"Brronk!" Bones gave a deep, echoing call.

"That is the greeting ravens use for old friends," Jyg marveled. "She only does that for people she knows and likes. She must have sensed that we have herstory together."

"I am honored," Epoh grinned at the raven.

"Okay, Bones," Jyg told the bird. "That is all for now." He gave a little flick of his arm, and the raven flew back up to the edge of the roof.

"You have much to discuss," Klew nodded to Tyme. "We will wait in Scoop's alley within earshot if you need us." He wanted to make sure Riin Ruel knew that Tyme had loyal friends nearby.

When they left Riin Ruel turned to Tyme. "Epoh tells me that you have a strong practice. Mayhaps we could sit quietly together in prayer before we begin to talk."

"I would like that," Tyme agreed. She got out her prayer rug and seat cushion along with Jyg's and Klew's rugs and cushions for Epoh and Riin Ruel to use.

"They also have a daily practice?" Riin Ruel inquired as Tyme handed her Klew's rug.

"Yes, for part of the heat," Tyme said as they all positioned themselves comfortably in the adepts pose. It felt good to sit silently in meditation and prayer and let go of her lingering unease over what Riin Ruel might want of her.

Epoh was thrilled to sit with Tyme in meditation. For moons at the nunnery, and then out in the desert, he had visualized just such a scene, contentedly doing his practice with her beside him. Now, being safe and quiet together, without any need for words or speech, felt like complete bliss.

Meanwhile Riin Ruel said her own special prayers of revelation and focused on the energies emanating and flowing out from Tyme. Riin Ruel had been trained to sense and read the ether surrounding those who were in prayer, and thereby gain some insight into their spiritual wellness. What she perceived in the young woman only confirmed what she already believed. She was surprised, however, and somewhat unsettled by what she discerned from Epoh. The boy also had a celestial power. Whatever could that mean?

When Riin Ruel finished her divinations, she decided to sit silently and let Tyme and Epoh determine the length of the practice. They both sat without the slightest movement, totally immersed in their prayers. When they did finally open their eyes, they seemed to do so together. After putting the prayer rugs away, they sat on regular cushions to talk.

"Ultimately, what I believe about your destiny," Riin Ruel confessed to Tyme, "is not as important as what *you* believe about your destiny. If you ignore, or struggle and fight against the powers that are steering you in certain directions, your true destiny will remain unfulfilled. You must believe and have faith in your own path."

"There are signs and teachings that I want to share with you," Riin Ruel continued, "that are for your ears only. However, I do not believe you are ready yet to hear those things."

The Blade smiled ruefully. "You do not know me," she said, "so you do not trust me." She nodded toward Epoh. "You trust your friends. You want Epoh to help you discern the truth to my words. And I believe that after I leave you will be quick to share with your other friends out in the alley what I have told you, to get their advice as well."

"Yes, I will," Tyme replied honestly.

"Then let us refrain from such charades," Riin Ruel shook her head. "Call to your friends on the street and have them join us. I will only speak of the things that they can hear. That will be plenty enough to start."

Tyme went to the window and whistled. A few moments later Klew and Jyg came back in through the door. Tyme motioned toward the bench by the table where they quickly took their seats.

"Your lady is very willful," Riin Ruel began.

Klew chuckled at her choice of words. He had said the same thing to Tyme as a young girl, when he had found her fighting Noot, even after his warning.

"Since she insists on sharing everything with all of you, I will include you in what I have to say," Riin Ruel continued. "Mayhaps you can help me convince her of the truth to my words. However," she warned them, "just because I agree to include you in these talks does not mean the tale is ready to be spread across town. Tyme's life could be in danger if the wrong person learns what I have to say."

Klew and Jyg both nodded gravely.

Riin Ruel looked Tyme squarely in the eye. "I was imprisoned by the Czarzina for over one-and-a-half centuries just because I was searching for you."

Her ominous words cut like a knife. They all sat soberly in their seats.

"Were you not sent to Dayr Castle by the Will of the Blades?" Klew asked, remembering what she had told King Eyrico so long ago.

"The Will did send me, but she was on her deathbed when I returned. The new Will conspired with the Czarzina, who censured me as a heretic, without trial, and sent me to the Box at Ralkan Garrison." She shook her head in disgust. "Many in power claim to support the fulfillment of the prophecies, while secretly doing everything possible to maintain their own positions and influence."

"How did you get out?" asked Jyg in a hushed tone.

"My escape is a tale for another day. For now, let me just say that I am not alone in this search." She paused to let her words sink in. "I searched for Tyme to insure her health and safety. Others hunt for her with wicked intent."

"You came to Dayr Castle just before Epoh was born," Klew recalled. "Did you believe the girl would be born to a Barbarian King?"

"There are ancient writings that hinted of such an event," Riin Ruel admitted. "Regardless of that confusion," she continued, "the appearance of such a girl at Dayr Castle was foretold by others. Did you know that Krugero, the guard at castle gate, also dreamed of the Bright One?"

"He told me he had a powerful dream once," Epoh remembered. "But he said it had not come true."

"Not that he knew of," Riin Ruel corrected him. "His dream was not like Utuno's, with a direct connection to the arrival of Tyme in the stables the next morning. But that does not mean there was no truth to Krugero's dream. He told me about it just a few nights later in the Rusted Sword," Riin Ruel confided. "He dreamt he was on top of tower one on castle gate on a full Moonday when he saw a young Empress descend out of the clouds on a path of shining light, wearing dazzling armor and crystal shield, and holding a fiery sword as she led a glorious army marching and singing into Dayr Castle."

"What makes you think that has anything to do with me?" asked Tyme.

"Your own mysterious arrival at Dayr Castle makes you a prime candidate," Riin Ruel said with conviction.

"If you were so sure I was going to show up at Dayr Castle," Tyme replied defensively, "why did you go out into the Endless Waste to Ezkia Nunnery?"

"A prophet dreamt that the Endless Waste was the birthplace of all peoples. She saw an Angel of Light appearing near the edge of the Endless Waste at a small oasis named Ezkia." Riin Ruel did not tell them that Anna Nana believed the angel to be the precursor to the return of the Empress.

Epoh listened thoughtfully. "Is Starai the Angel of Light?" he wondered in shock. "You told her mother that she was not the Bright One. Did you ever think that she might be the angel?"

"I believed that she was neither," Riin Ruel answered. "How she came to rescue you confuses me and is certainly thought provoking. But that does not make her an Angel of Light." The continuing intrusion of Epoh into all the portentous events and places confused her even more. The thought that *he* might be the Angel of Light was so preposterous and blasphemous that she could not allow herself to even speculate in such a fashion. Everyone knew that only women were Angels of Light.

"How did you know that Starai was neither?" Tyme asked with keen interest.

"I have certain tests and ways of knowing."

"What tests?" Tyme insisted. "Are you going to test me?"

"The tests only work on infants," Riin Ruel explained, "when children have not yet developed their own views and beliefs about themselves, and who they think they are."

"So, if I do not think I am the Bright One, then I will not be?"

"No," Riin Ruel replied solemnly. "You will not be. That potential will go unfulfilled. Wasted."

"The prophecies will go unfulfilled?" Tyme said with surprise.

"For this Age at least," Riin Ruel answered gravely. "Perhaps they will be fulfilled in another Age, and at another," she paused for dramatic effect, "...a different *time*."

THINK ABOUT EVERYTHING

"Let me know when you are ready to talk again," Riin Ruel told Tyme as she stood to leave their apartment. 'Twas almost noon. "I would like to go to the Womb before the heat."

Riin Ruel was exhausted. She had used much of her limited energy traveling to Dayr Castle from the hermitage at Falcana Nunnery on the shores of the Dead Sea, where she had been recuperating from the poison she had taken to fake her death and escape the prison at Ralston Garrison. She had expected to rest at Dayr Castle upon her arrival. But she had met Epoh the first evening and they had immediately left the castle the following morning for the six-day trip back to Karvor. Although they had traveled at a moderate pace, the effort had taken a toll.

"She has been very ill," Epoh noted to the others after the Blade left.

"She looks four centuries older than she did when she first came to Dayr Castle," Klew told them in astonishment. "Her hair was black, her body buffed and hardened." Now her dreadlocks were white and her skin dry, wrinkled, and loose from loss of muscle mass underneath. She looked capable, but not formidable.

They all sat thinking quietly.

"Riin Ruel said there were ancient writings that prophesized about the Bright One," Tyme questioned Epoh. "Do you know anything about that?"

"There is a famous passage about the Bright One in the *Book of Elders*," he replied. "I remember she carries a fiery sword of truth. She is also mentioned by name in some other Clan writings, but no descriptions or hints about where she was born like Riin Ruel alluded. Mayhaps that is from the *Kabaal Prophecies*." He shook his head. "I have never read them. There was not a copy of the work, or even a commentary about it, at the Dayr Castle library. 'Tis a very rare manuscript."

"Would there be a copy in Karvor?" Tyme asked.

"Mayhaps," Epoh said hopefully. "I will try to find out."

"That would definitely be helpful to read," Jyg declared.

"Yes," Klew agreed. "Having an unbiased interpretation can make an important difference in deciphering the meaning of the texts."

"You do not trust Riin Ruel's interpretation?" Tyme asked.

"I do not think she would deliberately deceive us," he answered. "But she has been raised and taught to view things in a certain way. It never hurts to get a different viewpoint."

"I will definitely search all the shops selling books and scrolls in Karvor," Epoh declared.

"I wonder if Delgado would know of anyone?" Jyg asked.

"Rare religious manuscripts are not exactly Delgado's field of expertise," Tyme chuckled. "But I guess it would not hurt to ask. He is full of surprises."

"Who is Delgado?" Epoh inquired. He was quick to note that both Jyg and Klew looked to Tyme to answer.

"'Tis complicated," she joked. "Kind of a sublunary version of you and Starai."

"Sublunary," Epoh nodded with a smile. "Belonging to the physical world as contrasted with the spiritual world. That is a word Xacano would approve." Their philosophy teacher at Dayr Castle always encouraged them to learn descriptive new words.

"Mayhaps we should set the stage for Delgado's appearance," Klew interjected to help Tyme out. He explained how they had followed the murderer's trail to Karvor and searched all the stables to find a daya that had been ridden hard and abused. "Tyme found the horse up the hill in Old Town. A rougher part of the city."

"A hoodlum tried to block my way in a narrow alley and demanded payment for passage," Tyme took over the story. "He tried to grab me, so I gave him a quick headbutt."

"What is a headbutt?" Epoh asked.

"Ho, ho," Jyg laughed with a relish. "Tyme has learned all sorts of tricks while you were gone. She has become a formidable warrior!" Klew explained the technique.

"I broke his nose and wounded his pride," Tyme continued. "A few nights later he tried to ambush me with an old, rusted sword. I let him take a few wild swings, then I jumped in with my knife to his throat, took away the sword, and tied his hands behind his back. He kept threatening that the Jawbone Ridge gang was going to get me. So, I made him take me to his leader to straighten things out."

"That is Delgado," Jyg jumped in. "His headquarters is at the Blue Moon saloon in Old Town. It has the best music in Karvor."

"Jyg spends all his free time up there now," Klew interjected.

"What happened?" Epoh asked in amazement.

"Delgado was very charming like everything was a big misunderstanding," Tyme continued. "Then a rival gang leader showed up saying he was taking over part of their territory. The guy was a vicious brute. The kind of person who might have killed Noot. Without even thinking, I challenged him to fight."

"She used the old blunt sword from the first guy she still had tied up," Jyg noted with relish.

"'Twas a perfect weapon," Tyme shrugged. "I did not want to kill the guy, I just wanted to teach him a lesson." She looked at Epoh apologetically. "I kind of lost my temper."

"And he lost half his teeth and got his sword arm broke, along with a leg and a bunch of ribs and various nasty cuts and bruises all over his body," Jyg bragged. "The story is still being told across town." He explained how Delgado spread false versions of the tale to keep Tyme's identity a secret. "Most people believe 'twas a huge white woman with red hair, a warrior full of the Fire who beat him up." Being one of the very few to have red hair himself, Jyg loved that part of the yarn.

"So, I became an honorary member of the Jawbone Ridge gang," Tyme said. When she didn't say anything more Klew picked up the tale.

"Delgado has been a big help in tracking Noot's killer. His name is Gribono." Klew told Epoh some of what they had learned about the man and all of his spying. And how the Jawbone Ridge gang had kept watch over the stables in Old Town to signal when Gribono was preparing to leave again. "I followed him to the mountains of eastern Vanttan and the outposts of Vargo Garrison. He is reporting to someone in the Hammer Legion."

"King Eyrico told me that you had found a nest of vipers and treachery," Epoh said, "but he did not give any details."

"That is only half of it," Klew shook his head. "Jyg uncovered a whole other network of treason. But that is a tale for later." 'Twas now the heat of the day and the apartment was feeling suffocating to everyone but Epoh, who hardly seemed to notice the temperature. They prepared a small cold meal of bread, goat cheese, dates and fruit, and took it into the condition to eat. When they finished, they lay down for a short nap.

Near the end of the heat, they got up for their devotions. They began with stretching poses and then sat cross-legged to meditate. When they finished Epoh began to softly chant and sing one of his favorite Praises. The others joined in the simple, repetitive verse, their voices resonating in the small, stone enclosure. Tears of joy ran down Epoh's cheeks while he lightly swayed to the tune with his eyes closed.

"That was powerful," Jyg said in amazement. He had become much more attuned to the subtle and emotional impact of music from his evenings spent at the Blue Moon. "Delgado would like that," he mused.

"He likes to chant?" Epoh asked with surprise. He could not get a clear understanding of the man.

"He is just learning to meditate," Jyg answered. "Tyme has been helping him with his practice. He is very interested in music of the soul, as he calls it. Music that touches deep into the heart."

"I would like to meet this Delgado," Epoh said.

"He is also interested in meeting you," Jyg answered. "We could all go up to the Blue Moon tonight."

"Why is he interested in meeting me?" Epoh wondered.

Jyg and Klew both looked to Tyme to answer.

"He is kind of a moonboy over me," Tyme's face grew hot. "He basically wants to make sure that you are good enough for me."

"What is a moonboy?" Epoh asked in confusion.

"He professes to be madly in love with me even though he hardly knows me. I have tried to tame his ardor, but I have only had limited success."

"Tame, but not ask that he cease?" Epoh inquired.

"He has been a special friend," Tyme replied. "I warned him that my heart was torn by your disappearance. I have always believed that you were still alive. But I did not know if or when you would ever return."

"Shall we go up to the Blue Moon?" Jyg asked again.

"I would prefer to spend another evening just talking with Epoh," Tyme replied. "But I look forward to introducing them later."

"Yes," Epoh agreed. "I would prefer to spend the evening alone with Tyme as well. Give Delgado our regards."

After the others left Tyme and Epoh sat together in a corner of the patio.

"You think I am the Bright One," Tyme said with concern, getting right to the point. "You have abdicated your throne to follow me. Do you see the pressure, and presumption, that puts on me? What if I am *not* the Bright One?" She shrugged her shoulders. "What if I am just Tyme? What if that is all I want to be."

"I want to be with you," Epoh professed. "No matter who you are or what happens. I could not stay at Dayr Castle knowing Riin Ruel was coming to find you. I did not accompany her to add pressure. I came to *relieve* pressure."

"How are you relieving pressure when you started thinking I was the Bright One when you were at Ezkia Nunnery?"

"'Tis not like I was hoping you were the Bright One. 'Twas more like, Holy Divine! She could be the Bright One! If she is--I have to be there to help her!"

"And if I am not?"

"Then we will be free to live as we wish."

"And what do you wish?" she asked.

He stood before her thinking. "I do not want to contest with Dracaro over the throne of Dayrstad," he answered. "If I was truly free? I guess I have never imagined it. I have always had some great force propelling my life or dragging me along helplessly behind." He paused again. "Mayhaps I would be a teacher. Or even a shaman."

"A teacher or shaman," she smiled at the thought. "Yes. You could be either."

"And you?" he asked. "What do you wish?"

"I am no longer sure," she admitted. She told him about Tao Tau retiring to publish her healing book. And Spike's declining ability to carry her growing body into the mountains. "The things that made Dayr Castle home have changed. I was considering not returning, for awhile at least. I do not think Jyg is going back." She looked at him with teary eyes. "I did not want to go back if you were not there."

They embraced heartily. "I am here now," he whispered in her ear. "Nothing has to be decided immediately. Give yourself time to think."

CHANNELING THE JUDGMENT OF DIVINE HERSELF

The next morning, Tyme, Epoh, Jyg and Klew met with Riin Ruel under the shaded patio of their apartment. The mystical Blade warrior did not press Tyme about her connection to ancient prophecies. She was more interested in what had brought Tyme to Karvor.

Riin Ruel believed that nothing happened around Tyme through coincidence or happenstance. The girl seemed to draw people and events to her that fit into much grander schemes. Following Noot's murderer to Karvor was larger than just the death of a stable boy. Tyme was being pulled into her destiny whether she realized it or not.

Riin Ruel asked to hear the story of Noot's death from the beginning, and explained how the smallest detail might be of great importance.

Tyme told how she had found Noot, and Klew described how the killer had been someone quick with a knife who had most likely killed before.

"Suspicions pointed to a man with fancy rings who had left that night by moonlight." Klew said. "He had been seen with two soldiers from the Siren."

"Did anyone talk with the soldiers?" Riin Ruel asked.

"I told everything to King Eyrico," Klew replied. "The King said he would look into it."

"The Duke would not be helpful in such matters," Epoh sighed, "even though they were his soldiers. He does not get along well with the King."

"Even if the soldiers were involved in possible treason against the King?" Riin Ruel said in surprise.

"The Duke would say the King was overreacting and being paranoid," Epoh shrugged his shoulders.

"Do you think the Duke would plot treason against the King?" Klew asked.

"I believe the Duke is not to be trusted in any manner, as I think King Eyrico also believes," Epoh replied. "That is why the Duke is at the Siren, more for banishment than any reward."

"Tell me of your journey to Karvor?" Riin Ruel asked.

Klew told how they were unable to catch up to the fancy ring man, and guessed he must be a messenger or spy to travel so fast. They had searched the stables for an injured daya, and Tyme had found the horse in the shed in Old Town.

Tyme again told of her encounter with the ruffian in an alley. Riin Ruel made her describe their skirmish in detail, how he had swung his weapon, how close she allowed the blade to come, when did she chose to jump forward, and the exact technique she used to disarm him with only her dagger.

Riin Ruel listened with obvious enjoyment at the girl's confidence and fearlessness. Tyme described her meeting Delgado, the appearance of the rival gang member, and her decision to challenge the violent brute to a duel using the old sword. Again, Riin Ruel insisted that Tyme describe the fight in great detail.

Tyme seemed embarrassed. "I kind of lost my temper," she said.

"How do you mean?" asked Riin Ruel with concern. "Do you not remember some of what happened?" She prayed the girl was not a berserker. Had she come too late to teach the girl to control her powers?

"No, I remember it all. I just felt a profound anger, like he needed to be taught a harsh lesson, and I wanted to give it to him."

"That is not losing your temper," Riin Ruel said in relief. "That is channeling the judgment of Divine Herself. He had broken all the Divine Laws. A sinner full of corruption and hate. You were dispensing justice, as you were born to do."

"He certainly merited what he got," Klew agreed.

Tyme looked uncertain.

"I can teach you how to look into a man's eyes and see into his soul," Riin Ruel told Tyme. "To know for certain that he is beyond redemption in this life, and fully deserving your judgment."

"Well, he did not learn his lesson," Jyg said. "After he healed, we think he tried to ambush her just recently with others in an alley behind the apartment."

Tyme described how Scoop had warned her of the attack. How one of the muggers had been killed by Scoop's slingshot, and how Rocozo had gotten away.

"He lives to continue in his murderous ways," Riin Ruel said with distaste. "By showing him mercy, you have only allowed him to harm others in the future."

Tyme made no reply, but sat thinking.

Klew told of Delgado's honoring of Tyme as a gang member, and of the help from the Jawbone Ridge gang in setting sentries for the fancy ring man's return.

"He is a gambler and a spy named Gribono. He plays cards with Heart Legion officers, with the shaman from the Mother Womb, and with the brother of an influential shaman from the mountains of Birjj.

"Gribono must be reporting to someone in Ambrit," Riin Ruel mused.

"We thought the same," Klew nodded, "until I recently followed Gribono to eastern Vanttan, to a back sentry post of Vrak Pass at Vargo Garrison. He was not there long enough to reach the garrison headquarters. Whoever he met was high in the mountains." Klew brought out his scroll with the list of offisers from Vanttan, and explained which captain was their main suspect. "His name is Targono."

Riin Ruel shook her head. "I know nothing about him," she said regretfully. "But I can find out."

"Oddly enough," Klew replied, "I may know him. My best friend at the Ambrit Military Academy was named Targono." He explained how Targono bested him in a tourney to become squire for a captain who later fell from favor. "The last I knew, Targono had been sent to the Hammer Legion and stripped to the rank of private."

Klew shook his head. "Targono had too much talent and ambition to stay at the bottom for long. I think he rose up through the ranks fighting Vanttan rebels."

"Then Targono is a formidable tactician and commander," Riin Ruel said ominously.

"Indeed," Klew agreed. "A fearsome enemy." He raised an eyebrow. "Or mayhaps, a powerful ally."

"An ally?" Tyme questioned. "Even if his spy killed Noot?"

"That gives us plenty to consider for today," Riin Ruel said without answering the question. She rose to leave before the heat. "I trust we can all meet again tomorrow?"

EPOH'S STORY

After the heat Tyme and Epoh hiked up the hill toward Old Town and the Blue Moon. The evening sky was silvery with a nearly full Moon of White Dust shimmering before them above the Barrier Mountains. Jyg had gone ahead to let Delgado know they were coming. Klew had left earlier and would be joining them shortly.

They hiked slowly, occasionally arm in arm, enjoying the moment and taking a break from thinking about their meeting with Riin Ruel. Epoh marveled at the color, style and architecture of the buildings. Because of the steep hillside, many structures had two or three stories in front but only one story, or even just a rooftop access out the back.

Inside the Blue Moon, Tyme discreetly led Epoh around the back of the room to the far front corner ornately screened for privacy. Once past the lights they could see Vorcono, the Jawbone Ridge enforcer, who motioned them toward the table with Delgado and Jyg.

Delgado rose and formally greeted Tyme and Epoh in the traditional Barbarian fashion. He was shocked by Epoh's appearance. He looked more sunbaked than the laborers who carried loads of clay on their backs at the kilns. His rippling muscles were sinewy and hardened. He appeared an indomitable force.

"I give thanks to Divine that Tyme's prayers have been answered and you have returned safely to Ambra," Delgado told Epoh solemnly.

"And I give thanks to Divine that you have been a special

friend to her," Epoh replied, using Tyme's description of their relationship.

Delgado seemed pleased by his words. "I would propose a toast to your return," he told Epoh. "Would you join in? Wine? Mescal? Viruna?"

"I am afraid I have done very little toasting of late," Epoh replied apologetically. "Watered wine will be plenty strong for me."

"For me as well," Tyme agreed.

"Then we shall all drink watered wine together," Delgado obligingly agreed.

Klew arrived to join them as they raised their glasses to Epoh. Everyone was eager to hear the tale of his survival and return from the Endless Waste.

Epoh was able to tell the story of the underground river without getting so emotional. The tears he had shed with Tyme about the ordeal had cleansed and released much of the remaining trauma. Everyone listened somberly as he explained how he was found floating in a sacred underground lake by an acolyte nun named Starai, who nursed him back to life. And her surprising connection to Riin Ruel.

"I tried to be the best monk I could be," Epoh recalled, "but once I learned about the grubbers, and the possibility of escaping the nunnery, I could think of little else." He told how his book, *Dragons of the Endless Waste*, played a key part of his acceptance by Harvig, his older brother Horton, and finally their madcap uncle, Grinst.

"I told them 'twas a children's book. But the descriptions of the route in the book matched the route they planned to take leaving Apocalypse."

"You have seen Apocalypse?" Delgado was stunned. He had always thought the legend of the lost city was a fairytale. His estimation of Epoh rose another notch. Tyme also was entranced. She had not heard this part of the story.

"'Twas where we met up with Grinst," Epoh replied. He told of the Stone Forest and having to wait three weeks for the moon to brighten before moving on. "We laid traps all through the night to catch kangaroo rats and desert hopping mice. We skinned them every morning and threw them in a pot, heads, tails, feet, bones, guts, and all, to cook all day with tin reflectors in the sun."

Tyme grimaced, Delgado's eyes bulged out, and even Klew looked a little horrified.

When Epoh saw them squirming he elaborated further. "Morning and evenings we caught locust with little cactus fiber nets we wove and stuck on the ends of dried sticks. We ground those up, even the wings and legs, and mashed them together with the flesh from the inside of cactus, then baked the patties on rocks so they would not spoil." Epoh grinned at the memory. "We made stacks of them, but Grinst would only let us each eat one a day. We saved them up for crossing the Lake of Shimmering Heat."

Delgado's cup of watered wine was empty. He was going to order another but noticed that Epoh had hardly drunk from his. Delgado licked his dry lips, feeling embarrassed by his soft and pampered lifestyle. Could he have survived such a journey?

"'Twas so hot each tiny breath was painful. We were saved by a cave condition in a low ridge of rock, just like in my dragon book."

Delgado could not wait any longer. "This story is making me thirsty," he apologized as he signaled for a waiter. He was relieved that Jyg and Klew were also ready for another drink. Epoh and Tyme declined.

Epoh told about the Sea of Dunes with white sand so compacted they could walk across the surface without leaving a footprint. "We followed the book to find the dragon perch and the nearby seep."

"'Twas built for dragons?" Delgado asked in amazement.

"That is what the book said," Epoh answered, and he told of their long, fruitless search for dragon bones.

"One day Grinst announced a storm was coming." He

described their race through the night and next morning back to camp. "We were only minutes away when Grinst ordered us to huddle on the ground. A wall of blowing sand hit us like a hammer." He told how Grinst had led them stumbling blindly through the maelstrom back to the seep where the storm raged for three days before they were able to dig out the seep. Then waiting for the water to slowly refill. "That first cup was the best water I ever tasted."

Epoh raised his engraved gourd cup in a toast, put it to his blistered lips, and finished his watered wine. When Delgado motioned to order him another he declined. "One is quite enough for now," Epoh smiled happily. "Cool water will be more than fine." He waited for the cup to be served and took a slow and satisfied drink before resuming his story.

"After the storm the dunes were completely different." Epoh paused dramatically. "That was when Harvig appeared wild-eyed and whispering that he had seen a dragon sleeping in the sand." He recounted how they had all crept carefully up to the crest of a big dune.

"We looked over the top," Epoh spoke slowly and softly, pulling his audience in. "Sure enough ... a giant ... gleaming ... silver body with wings ... lying in the sand."

Everyone leaned in closer to hear.

"Brrarr!" Epoh roared out and threw up his arms.

Delgado shrieked and knocked over three drinks. Tyme jumped out of her chair while Jyg nearly fell over backwards in his. They joined Epoh in laughter as he told how Grinst had pulled the same trick on the other grubbers.

"'Twas actually Dragon bones?" Delgado asked in amazement.

"That was what Grinst claimed. He said when a dragon dies, her skin turns to metal. She was long and rigid with an enormous barrel body and thick neck. The head, tail and underside of the body and wings were still buried in the sand. About the size of the Mother Womb in Karvor."

They all listened with astonishment.

"She was not like any dragon described in a book." Epoh looked at Jyg. "Her wings were long and slender and swept back like a falcon, but without joints. I started to doubt whether 'twas a dragon at all."

"What else could it be?" Delgado asked as the waiter arrived with replacement gourds of watered wine. What he really wanted was a little metal cup of viruna.

"Grinst said dragons swallow their treasure or keep it in belly pouches. We searched for a weak spot in the armor and found a strange scale in front of the wing. 'Twas shaped like a rounded door. It opened to a hallway filled with drawers and cupboards full of strange devices."

"'Twas built by the Ancient Ones," Tyme guessed.

"A flying mechanism," Delgado exclaimed. "There are legends of the Ancient Ones being able to fly. 'Twas not with wings on their bodies like angels or birds. They flew an apparatus with mechanical wings."

"Exactly," Epoh replied. "The inside was a giant warehouse stacked full of things built by the Ancient Ones, all bundled and boxed up and piled together."

"What kind of things?" asked Klew in amazement.

Epoh held his arm out over the table and pulled up the sleeve to reveal his large silver clock bracelet with its impressive array of buttons and ornate dials. Everyone stared in awe as the thin little wand jerked incrementally around the face of the disk.

"'Tis a wrist clock," he explained. "Each time the thin, jerky wand goes around these 60 tiny marks, the big wand moves one of those 60 marks. Each time the big wand goes all the way around, the short wand moves 5 marks. In one day, the short wand goes around the circle twice." It all sounded so confusing.

Epoh recounted how he had grown tired of the search for treasure. "We had more gold, silver, and gems than we could carry. I did not see any sense in looking for more."

"More than you could carry?" Delgado repeated in

astonishment.

"What did you do?" Tyme asked.

He told about the thin objects with black glass on one side. How he had used the largest ones to reflect sunlight into the flying device to illuminate the few piles of manuscripts and books they had found.

"I spent weeks sifting mounds of paper before I found a scrap of legible writing. Some of the alphabet and words were similar to Ambri. Then I discovered some of the words were Hool."

"Hool!" Klew exclaimed. "The Ancient Ones spoke Hool?"

"Not all the words were Hool. But many were. I realized the Ambri language and the Hool language both originated from the Ancient Ones. We have that commonality."

"You can speak Hool?" Jyg asked in surprise.

"I needed to learn Hool to survive and find my way back home," Epoh said defensively. Duke Eddarko had been horrified that Epoh had learned the language. "What else was I to do? Harvig gave me lessons."

"I think you were strong, resourceful, and wise," Tyme said with admiration.

"Did you find anything else?" Delgado asked. He liked the stories of treasure. Any deep implications of having the same language heritage as the Hool was lost on him.

"Yes, the most amazing book of all," Epoh answered. He described his days with thin knife blades and metal spatulas peeling away one page at a time.

"The paintings were unlike any I have ever seen. Each one was so incredibly detailed. 'Twas like looking directly at real life."

He smiled at Tyme. "The first page was a painting of cloud forests much like you described seeing in the high mountains, with plants growing so thick they were piled on top of each other. But they were not all thorny or spikey. More delicate and fine. Flowers with gorgeous giant red and yellow blossoms. Everything was growing around a river and waterfall. The sky was a strange color of blue."

"The sky was blue?" Jyg could not imagine such a thing. None of them could. The sky they knew was colored yellow, orange, red or purple during sunrise and sunset, and then shimmery to blinding white during the day.

"There were paintings of beautiful colored birds and strange animals," Epoh continued. "Horses with black and white stripes. Giant hairless beasts with enormous ears and a nose that hangs down as long as its legs, and two huge white tusks of similar length."

"All those animals must have lived during the age of the Ancient Ones," Tyme mused in wonder.

Epoh nodded. "The Dead Sea was full of life, with huge clusters of brightly colored fish, and colorful plants and bushes living under the water."

"The Ancient Ones not only destroyed themselves, they destroyed the world," Delgado said solemnly.

"They called it Earth." Epoh told them of the cover of the book. "'Twas a painting of what the world looks like when flying high in the sky. Like a colored marble. The Dead Sea was blue, with wispy white in a number of places."

"The white was clouds," Tyme guessed. Unlike the others, who had only seen dust clouds, she had seen moisture clouds in the high mountains, churning and blowing across the cliffs.

"I could see rivers and lakes on the land and ripples like mountains drawn on a map. There were brown areas, so there were deserts then as well. But there were also large areas of green, which had to be lands completely covered with plants and trees."

They all listened in awe. Epoh grew serious.

"Then the cargo bird blew up in a thunderous explosion." He told them of the bad air, and the ball of fire and smoke that blasted a hole in the top of the metal bird and rained down fiery debris. Of Harvig's terrible burns and recovery. Their escape from Hool bandits east into the Broiled Mountains to reach Jchow Oasis. Then a camel trip to Valhal and the Siren.

The entire journey sounded arduous and grueling. Delgado could not imagine such hardships. And he realized he could never compete against Epoh for Tyme's affections. They were destined to be together. Delgado could only hope to be a part of her life in a lesser role.

REPORTS TO
RIIN RUEL

The next morning Epoh came to the apartment at dawn to do his practice on the moon patio with Tyme, Jyg and Klew. The act was simple yet profound for Epoh. He had a tremendous sense of contentedness with each breath. Tyme also felt a sense of comfort and completeness having Epoh so close.

When finished they ate breakfast as the sun came up over the mountains and took off their warmer garments to sunbath while they could and enjoy the pleasant and luxurious warmth of the risen sun in the cool morning air.

When Riin Ruel arrived, she asked Tyme about the Ser Cus and throwing daggers. Tyme explained to her and Epoh how she had met the Ser Cus through Jyg. How she had learned gymnastics and become best friends with Wiir Waar, the sword juggler and knife-thrower.

"She gave me a brace of knives that I can show you," Tyme told Riin Ruel.

"Yes, later," Riin Ruel replied agreeably. "When 'tis just the two of us."

"Wiir Waar also taught me to dance," Tyme continued, "She got me dressed up for the keep banquet!" Tyme gave Epoh a fond look. "I thought of you that night," she said. "I felt certain that you were still alive." Her eyes grew moist.

"We saw the Ser Cus again in Karvor," Klew added. "But before you hear about that you should hear of the sleuthing Jyg has been doing."

Jyg told Riin Ruel about raising Zaru and having to sell the gyrfalcon to pay for his uncle Pio's hushed and secretive experiments. How he had recently visited his uncle's partner, Panr, and about her claims of arson and stolen birds.

"We found her birds up in Old Town," Jyg said. He recounted his switching of birds, which allowed Panr to intercept and read all the messages before sending them onward.

"We have already gotten six messages, and we think we know the identity of one of the people," Klew nodded as he pulled out his scroll.

Bones saw the manuscript and flew from her roost to the table. "What does she say?" the raven asked in Panr's voice as she ducked and bobbed her head, then added, "Sshh! Quiet!"

"Bones says that whenever she carries a message tube, or when Klew writes in that scroll," Jyg explained. He motioned and the raven took a big jump and a flap of her wings to observe from a nearby roost.

Tyme told about the Ser Cus arriving, and spying in the homes of wealthy nobles. "Wiir Waar and I did a performance at a tween banquet and overheard a girl complaining of having to leave early for Pintone because her grandmother died. Wiir Waar found out the girl's aunt is Major Bayn Baya."

Klew pointed to a line of cryptic writing. "A pigeon went to Ambrit with this message the next day: "Y left for P mom die. Which means Y might be the Major," Klew reasoned. "Everyone believes she has a vast spy network."

"Now someone's spying on *her*," Tyme said with little sympathy.

"Mayhaps," replied Riin Ruel. "But she could also be reporting on her own movements. She will be preoccupied and away from Karvor for a week at least. She might be letting others know."

"The next message went to Ralston Garrison," Klew reported. "It says *meet U BMoon 4day PB patio*. We guessed PB was the Plumed Bird, the fanciest casino in town." He shook his head. "Off limits for Jyg and me. So that spying fell again to Tyme and Wiir Waar."

"We got dressed up a few evenings before to scope the place out." Tyme said. "On the Fourthday of bright Moonday, General Cata Cara spent the evening on the third-floor patio. Major Bayn Baya was also there, along with Captain Kin Kell, and some other offisers. A wealthy noble from the Potter's Guild, Gina Gain Gani, showed up unexpectedly. The General invited her to sit at the table. They talked together like old friends for at least an hour."

"Was Major Bayn Baya a part of that talk?"

"No, she came later. Like she was expected. The General was much more officious and business-like with the Major."

A GLORIOUS AND HARMONIOUS REIGN

"A part of me," Tyme admitted to Epoh when they were alone together, "could be lured into the idea of being Empress. Lured into the fantasy of a glorious and harmonious reign."

"Is that what you think the prophecy is?" he asked. "A fantasy?"

"Not the prophecy itself, but rather Riin Ruel's interpretation of it."

"Which part of the interpretation do you not believe?"

"That one person is going to establish a government that is beyond corruption," Tyme answered. "Governments are run by people. No matter who is leader, the government is not going to be pure of heart if the people are not pure of heart. Placing me on a throne is not going to change basic human nature."

"That is true," Epoh replied, "But you can change the laws that govern the people. You can change the government's direction toward a more equitable and fair society."

"'Tis hard to imagine myself ruling over a vast court," Tyme said uncertainly. "Those are not my talents."

Epoh nodded in agreement. He was frankly overwhelmed at the idea of being thrust into the middle of Ambri court intrigue and politics.

"What happens if only part of the Senate is with me?" Tyme asked, and then answered her own question. "I will be facing a rebellion from Captain Targono, and the Hammer Legion, as well as from another offiser, most likely General

Cata Cara of the Heart Legion, who is also planning to seize power in a coup. I have no desire to lead armies and battle as a Warrior Empress, nor to fight and hold an Empire together."

"Creating Empires is bloody work," Epoh agreed.

"Riin Ruel has the belief," Tyme continued, "that my mantle of Bright One will shine so intensely that all other claims to the throne will simply abandon and give up their own ambitions and plans. That all others will concede, and we will all live happily ever after." Tyme shook her head. "I do not think that is going to happen."

WE ARE ALL IN THIS

"You tell me I am the one you seek from prophecy," Tyme said to Riin Ruel. "If that is true, what then do you advise I do now?" 'Twas the following morning and she was sitting with her friends in the apartment patio.

"What do *we* do now?" Epoh was quick to amend. "We are all in this with you."

"Yes! We!" Klew and Jyg agreed.

"We stay right here in Karvor," Riin Ruel assured them. "Tyme and I will train together, the rest of you continue your fine sleuthing of these conspiracies. A change is coming to Ambra. Our job is to stay ahead of it."

Riin Ruel had no immediate plans to bring Tyme to Ambrit. In truth 'twas much too dangerous. The Czarzina was too powerful. She controlled the Will of the Blades and a group of important Senasers. The rest of the Senasers were fractured and powerless, and too intimidated to challenge her. Now that Riin Ruel was no longer an official Blade, she was an outsider to the workings of power. She no longer carried special papers that allowed her free access through checkpoints and military garrisons.

"I have a few questions," Klew said to Riin Ruel. "You said you were imprisoned by the Czarzina. How did you get out? Is there a warrant for your arrest?"

"I took a poison to fake my death," Riin Ruel explained. "The Czarzina and the Will of the Blades both think I am dead and buried at Ralston Garrison." She touched a handful of her dreadlocks. "The poison turned my hair white and aged my body three centuries. I am still recovering."

"So," Klew clarified, "some splinter group within the Blades, or other secretive group, helped you escape from the highest security prison in the land. And that group now backs your actions and intentions?"

"There are others besides me, yes," Riin Ruel assented.

"Are you in contact with them? Do they know about us?"

Riin Ruel nodded her head. "I have sent a rider with a report." It would be another few days before it reached Major Gwen Gail at the Ambrit Military Academy, who was also the secret Hilt of the Daggers.

Everyone sat quietly.

"I feel a shift in my loyalties," Klew said. "I am here at the bequest of King Eyrico, following Noot's murder and uncovering conspiracies against the King." He looked at Tyme. "But now I realize my true loyalty is to you. I would write to King Eyrico and ask to be released from his service." He dropped to his knees before her. "I would vow my obedience and service to you."

Tyme was shocked. "You are my sword manser and friend!" she said. "Come sit next to me." She patted the bench. "Not on your knees before me. Get up!" She helped him rise. "If you start treating me like some kind of noble, I shall be very cross." She shook her head. "I have no way to pay your room and board." She looked at all of them. "I cannot have you as my retinue if I do not have any money."

"I have money," Epoh said. He still had a fat purse of gold coins from the single small gem he had sold at Dayr Castle. And more gems were sewn and hidden in the seams of his clothes.

"We all want to be with you and support you," Jyg agreed. "No matter what happens."

"Yes," Epoh affirmed. "We are all in this with you, like it or not."

"Okay," Tyme said. She took a big breath and turned to Riin Ruel. "I will start your training. But I still want to withhold my decisions on these other matters until later."

PART II

For a man shall leave behind his mother's family and shall be taken in by his wife as her helpmate to serve and protect. And he shall build a home for her, and she shall make that home their own, leaving behind her dependence on her mother and her grandmother, to form a new family leading her husband.

        The Book of Elders

Epoh left behind his family and his title of Crown Prince with full intent of creating a new life with Tyme.

        Hope the Proclaimer

VIRIDESCENT CANYON

When Duke Eddarko had Bokono poisoned over their rivalry for rebel leadership, Bokono's plot to kill Singer was also exposed. The fear of rebel violence spreading to the mountain farms caused the Manser of Agave for the King of Sikes to release Singer and his apprentices, Draktono, Frisoto and Swindovo, from his experiment with the effect of music on worker production.

Free from their assignment, Singer and his small band of followers walked down the Sikes River Valley singing songs, often prompting smiles and encouragement from those they met on the road. After six days they crossed Jintiga Bridge and followed the canyon rim to bypass Karvor on the old road to Birjj. They had heard about an old kiva there. But as they grew near, they found a group of militant Fire devotees in an uproar over a tween girl who had gone in the kiva, sliced the leg out from under their leader, and made her escape. Just the type of situation they were trying to avoid. The kiva sounded more like an armed hornet's nest than a contemplative site to start a school for boys and men, which was now their ambition.

The group turned around and headed for another kiva they had heard about on the other side of Karvor. They were mesmerized by the brightly painted buildings and the spectacular views as they skirted above the city and Old Town to reach the Painted Hills. The barren, dusty landscape of buttes and eroded valleys held all the colors that were used to make the famous pottery and artwork for which Karvor was known. The group made their way toward Viridescent Canyon, where a venerable shaman named Gybeko lived.

They hiked up the nearby trail that led to the Dusted Man, where they were captivated by the different colors of the pigment workers' clothes and bodies. Everyone sat at tables and chairs matching their mine's colors, mostly yellow, but also gangs of red, blue, and green. Singer's group stopped in for water, sang a few lively songs, and were each treated to a complimentary cup of pulque by the owner.

"I will give you more," Dari Riad promised them, "if you come back and sing in the evenings. Especially on bright moon nights."

"I will come back!" Swindovo enthused after finishing the drink. He liked the sharp and tangy fermented flavor. They all laughed. Singer continued with his humming.

"Yes," Draktono agreed. "We might come back occasionally. We hope to sing and perhaps have gatherings at the kiva of shaman Gybeko."

Dari Riad praised the shaman as a wise and gentle man, wished them luck, and gave them directions to his cave. They left feeling hopeful that they might have finally found a region and a kiva more conducive to their music and message.

As they entered Viridescent Canyon, the twisting trail ran through hills streaked with lines and narrow bands of rock and clay of every greenish hue.

"Who ever imagined rocks could be this color?" Swindovo marveled as he held up a hand-sized mint green flake of rock. They had been singing as they walked but now were focused on their unusual surroundings. Singer continued to hum.

"There must be water close by," Draktono announced. "Someone has been watering a little garden." He pointed to a shaded draw. They followed the trail a short way to the cave. An old man sat at the entrance, eyes closed, in prayerful meditation. He opened his eyes as they drew near.

Draktono stepped forward and introduced everyone.

Singer hummed lightly. The shaman invited them inside and began making tea. Once they were served Draktono explained how they had come from Sikes looking for a kiva where they could sing and start a theology school.

"Well," Gybeko answered with an official tone as he set down his cup of tea. "I would first like to hear you sing."

Singer stepped forward and belted out a dramatic Praise with his arms open wide and his head held high. Then Draktono, Frisoto and Swindovo all joined in harmony with a rousing chorus. When they finished Singer launched them into one of the catchy tunes Swindovo had modified with a fast beat that was so popular with the workers in Sikes.

"Indeed," the Shaman beamed when they finished, "you have my permission to sing here as much as you want." He chuckled as he served them more tea and looked at Draktono hopefully. "What do you propose to teach at your school?"

Draktono told of his studies to become a Womb certified shaman, his discovery of a forbidden book in the library of Sikes, and his expulsion from the school. "Now, my life work is to better understand male energy, and raise awareness of the need to have input from men when formulating, understanding, and interpreting theology."

"I should like to hear more," Gybeko said with interest. "You may start a school here as well."

He showed them the kiva. None of them had been down inside one before. Singer hummed low and strong. The round underground chamber reverberated with the tone. He began singing a simple Praise as the others joined in. After a few repetitions Gybeko began to lightly sing along.

"'Tis wonderful to have you all here," the shaman beamed after they finished. He showed them some caves nearby where they could live, and another larger cave where they could have their school.

"You have come at an opportune moment," Gybeko told them. "I believe there will be interest in your music and your ideas."

EMBRACE DAGGERS

Epoh, Jyg, and Klew left the apartment so that Tyme could begin her training with Riin Ruel. The two put out their prayer rugs and sat quietly for half an hour before Riin Ruel spoke.

"I represent a long and secret tradition of guardian warriors of great wisdom and knowledge who have long awaited the coming of a new Divine Empire. As each of us ages and dies our knowledge is passed on to others in our order, to keep our search continuing. However," Riin Ruel told Tyme, "I believe that search ends with you. What I will teach you will allow you to fulfill your destiny."

Tyme started to speak but the older woman stopped her. "After you learn the teachings," she said, "you must choose your role. If you are not the Bright One, then before you die, you must pass the teaching on to some other, so that the hope for Her does not perish with you."

"I will learn the teachings, and then choose my role," Tyme agreed.

"Then we are ready to begin," Riin Ruel nodded with approval. "Have you ever recited any of the *Prayers for the Dead*?"

"Yes. At the remembrance for Epoh when he disappeared and was thought dead."

"The first group is called *Prayers for the Mortal Body*, which help the departing spirits find a smooth journey," Riin Ruel informed her, "and also helps those who are mourning to process and deal with their grief. You must learn and memorize them before you can know the deeper meanings. We will begin with the first prayer, *Behold! The Mortal Body*."

After an hour of memory work, they switched to arms and weapon training. Riin Ruel was amazed by Tyme's abilities and skills and realized she was no longer strong or fast enough to challenge the girl with a sword. She suddenly felt very old.

They went back to memorizing prayers.

On their second round of weaponry, Riin Ruel asked Tyme about her training with daggers.

"Klew taught me the basics, then Wiir Waar taught me flair and throwing," Tyme replied. She shook her head ruefully. "I continue training yet throwing daggers is the one thing I still cannot get quite right."

"How is that?" Riin Ruel asked with quick interest.

Tyme told of her first experience with Wiir Waar. "The daggers felt so natural in my hands. I did two solid throws just outside of the bullseye. The third landed almost perfectly in the center." Tyme exhaled wistfully and could not help but grin. "Wiir Waar kept making a big deal of how the mighty third made a perfect tone when it hit."

"And the last two throws? Riin Ruel asked.

"They both hit flat and fell to the ground," Tyme shook her head in dismay. "I had to throw a number of sets before I got a single dagger to stick again."

"And now?"

"I have practiced and practiced. I still occasionally have dead throws. Wiir Waar cannot see what I am doing wrong."

"Let me watch you throw," Riin Ruel recommended. Tyme got out the special knives that Wiir Waar had given her. Four of the daggers stuck soundly, two bullseyes, and two in the first ring. The last knife hit flat and fell to the floor.

"You have a strong throwing posture," Riin Ruel complimented. "I saw nothing bad about your last throw to indicate anything wrong," Riin Ruel said thoughtfully. They both stood quietly thinking. "What if Divine is telling you that your path is not to throw daggers," Riin Ruel said solemnly. "Your path is to use and embrace daggers in a much different way."

TO MUSIC

Epoh was glad that Tyme had decided to begin training with Riin Ruel. He felt it important for Tyme to learn what the mystic warrior had to say and teach. After he left them at the apartment, he spent the remainder of the morning and early afternoon searching for a bookseller that had a copy of the *Kabaal Prophecies*.

Epoh enjoyed walking up and down the colorful streets of polychrome Karvor where the buildings were painted in bright, bold, and pastel colors of every tint and shade imaginable. After so long in the desert, the riot of colors tickled his eyes and made him smile with delight. He stopped occasionally to appreciate the stunning views of the round, blue domes of the various Womb Temples, the magnificent Skyline Stadium, and a number of other grand buildings perched on the steep hillsides.

However, he did not have much luck finding a copy of the *Kabaal Prophecies*. Just two bookshop owners were familiar with the writings, and both only had commentaries that referenced the work, and not the actual prophecies themselves.

"The *Kabaal Prophecies* are half gibberish," a large woman with frizzy, black hair told him matter-of-factly. "Nobody wants to read through the actual prophecies themselves."

That evening when Tyme continued to train with Riin Ruel, and Jyg was on spy surveillance with Bones, Epoh went up to the Blue Moon to see Delgado. He was intrigued by the sound as he entered the building. A lively band was playing music unlike anything he had ever heard. He skirted around the back of the room and stepped through the screen and lights. Delgado was at a table with two others. He stopped his conversation and rose to greet Epoh and directed him to an alcove with a small, private table.

"I am delighted by your visit," Delgado told him. "I hope that we can be friends."

"Tyme told me you say what you think," Epoh laughed before growing serious. "I hope we can be friends as well."

"Watered wine?" Delgado asked.

"Yes, for me," Epoh agreed and could not help but joke, "I saw you sneak little shots of viruna on my last visit. Feel free to drink whatever you wish around me."

Delgado chuckled. "Watered wine is a bit weak for my taste, I must admit. 'Tis viruna I prefer." Epoh asked about the music the band was playing, and Delgado explained 'twas a group from Vlice. When their drinks came, Delgado made a toast. "To music, may it help heal the pains of the world."

"To music," Epoh agreed. "I love singing and chanting. That helped me stay joyful in the desert."

"What did you sing?"

"Praises. Glorias. Hallelujahs that I learned in the choir at Dayr Castle. 'Tis Barbarian custom to sometimes allow men in the refuge to sing along with the women's choir in the Womb."

"Only young boys with high voices are allowed to sing in the refuges here in Karvor," Delgado noted.

"I also sang at Ezkia Nunnery. They had never heard a man sing the bass part to any of their songs," Epoh grinned at the memory. "They have wonderful acoustics in their meditation caves and choir rooms. Certain tones create a resonance of sound like a strong vibration you can feel in your body. 'Twas a wonderful place to sing," he smiled with sadness when he thought about leaving Starai without even saying goodbye.

"I would like to hear you sing," Delgado said with interest. "Maybe even join in. I have started a practice, and I am learning to meditate." He told about the altar he had made in the corner of his room, and the antique prayer rug he had recently purchased. "'Tis all because of Tyme," he confessed sheepishly. "Her energy and vitality. I want to have that kind of presence and soul as well."

"As do I," Epoh agreed.

They talked about learning to create and maintain self-discipline. "Once I made the commitment to practice," Delgado reflected, "I felt this power within myself strengthen. Now I just want to build on that."

"Consistency and perseverance are important for the long road," Epoh agreed. "But 'tis in the here and now of each day that we meet Divine. This very moment."

They sat without speaking and listened to a woman sing a sad lament. Delgado noted that Epoh's eyes swelled with tears. The next song was a lively tune, and everyone began to clap along.

"Would you like another drink?" Delgado asked when he saw Epoh's gourd cup was empty.

"Yes. Without water. A cup of regular wine will be fine."

After they got their drinks, Epoh leaned forward. "Do you know anyone who deals in rare manuscripts?" he asked. "I am trying to find a copy of the *Kabaal Prophecies*."

"As a matter of fact, I do," Delgado replied. "Her name is Ser Hain Haan Hana. She has a shop near the Mother Womb on Blessing Street. 'Tis actually hard to find. She also has a scholarly interest in traditional Tanis Mountain music," he grinned. "She has helped me sponsor singers and musicians from the Painted Hills."

They listened to another song without talking. Delgado could tell Epoh was taken by the music. When the song ended he asked, "What is the *Kabaal Prophecies*?"

"They are a very old group of stories, visions, and dreams," Epoh answered. "Written before the Ambri Empire."

"By the Ancient Ones?"

"No. Not that old. More from the end of the Dark Ages. When the Women's Clans were first starting to grow powerful."

"And it has the prophecies of the Bright One?"

"Yes. I believe so," Epoh replied. "Hopefully it can help give Tyme some insight into what she should do."

"What do you think she should do?"

"Just what she is doing right now," Epoh answered. "Train with Riin Ruel. Learn more. Get ready for what comes next."

"What do you think that is?"

"I am not sure," Epoh could say no more. Could she truly become Empress? Or even Czarzina? The thought was dizzying.

"You trust completely in Riin Ruel?"

"I trust what I know of Riin Ruel," Epoh said thoughtfully. "I trust completely in Tyme."

"And I as well," Delgado agreed.

THE TRUSTED SCRIBE

The next morning Epoh headed down the steep streets and stairs toward the Mother Womb, the largest temple in Karvor. The previous day he had been focused on the riot of colors on all the buildings, now he enjoyed walking slowly and observing the hustle and bustle as various people with a wide variety of dress and appearance made their way up and down the narrow, brightly painted avenues and alleyways. He was amazed by the array of items for sale from across Ambra. Karvor was more cosmopolitan than Epoh ever imagined.

Near the Mother Womb on Blessing Street was the Trusted Scribe. Epoh would never have found it without Delgado's directions. The second-floor shop had only a small sign at the top of some stairs. Inside was a couch and viewing table. Epoh rang the bell on the counter. He could see a group of scribes in the next room working at their desks. A woman came out and introduced herself as Ser Hain Haan Hana. She was tall and lean with the richest, darkest black skin.

"I was given your name by Delgado at the Blue Moon," Epoh introduced himself.

"How may I help you?" she discreetly eyed the sunburnt young man before her. He was scorched and blistered yet still handsome with a subtle and alluring power.

"I am searching for a complete copy of the *Kabaal Prophecies*," he told her.

She raised an eyebrow in interest. "That surprises me," she chuckled. She liked to think of herself as a quick judge of character. "I presumed you would have some rare desert manuscript to sell."

Epoh smiled. "Yes, I do rather look the part. Unfortunately, all the manuscripts I found crumbled at the slightest touch and could not be collected."

Ser Hain Haan Hana looked him over shrewdly. He wore simply cut yet well-tailored clothes. Was he employed by some scholar who wished to remain anonymous? Her dashing yet educated moonboy?

"The *Kabaal Prophecies*," she said thinking out loud. "There are two different versions. The *Mask of Splendor* and the *Mask of Brilliance*. I will have to do some searching. The complete works are only available in a set of scrolls. I must warn you, some of the scrolls are confusing and without sense. Most choose to study and learn about the Prophecies through books with scholarly commentaries about the works."

"I appreciate your frankness and concern," Epoh said. "But I have my reasons to acquire the entire set of scrolls."

"It could cost a few gold pieces."

"That will be fine."

"Okay," Ser Hain Haan Hana replied. "Give me a week and I will see what I can do."

"And I would like to buy a copy of the *Book of Elders*," Epoh said. "Do you have the Fifty?" The work was commissioned by Ser Mena Mane Miin, the founder of the Ambri University system, who brought together fifty of the best scholars in Ambri to analyze and judge which writings of the women's clans were to be included in scripture.

"Excellent choice," Ser Hain Haan Hana agreed. "'Tis the most authoritative and accurate translation. I have a copy with an indexed text for more scholarly use." She guessed that would be more to his interest. "Or," she offered, "I also have a copy with beautiful calligraphy and illustrations for display."

"The indexed text would be perfect," Epoh enthused. She went into the back room for a few moments and returned with a leather-bound book. The way he held the book she wondered if he might be buying it for himself. Could it be there was no wealthy ser behind him?

Epoh opened it on the desk to appreciate the fine handwritten script. "Do you know any reference numbers to prophecies of the Bright One?" he asked hopefully.

"The Bright One is mentioned by name in various places by a number of Clans, but only foretold or described by one Clan." She took a small piece of paper from a bowl on the desk and wrote some numbers. "The first number is the chapter of the Clan in the *Book of Elders*," she told him. "The second number is the paragraph."

Epoh took the note and thanked her as he paid for the book.

"Stop back in a week," the bookseller told him. "I should have the *Kabaal Prophecies*."

He left the shop and walked a short way down the street to the Mother Womb. Epoh marveled at the beautiful tile work on the building and the graceful lines of the domes. He went through the giant, open doors into the Hall of Attributes and turned into the refuge for the men, with the statue of Tatano, the first True Warrior, and the altars to the Divine Hand and Divine Fist. The remains of red wax, candles lit for the Fire, covered the altars despite continually being scraped away by order of the priests. A small, tin sun disk had also been left on an altar and not yet removed by the shaman or workers.

Epoh found a nice spot out of the way to sit quietly and replenish himself in the calming stillness of Divine. He felt a tremendous sense of purpose.

SET THE MANTLE ASIDE

The purple-red colors of the setting sun filled the sky. Tyme and Epoh sat on the open patio of the apartment looking at the *Book of Elders* that Epoh had just purchased.

"How often is the Bright One mentioned in the book?" Tyme asked.

"Just briefly about ten times," Epoh replied, "and often in reference to creating a New Empire." He pulled out the note with the index numbers that Ser Hain Haan Hana had given him. "There is only one passage in the *Book of Elders* that describes her in any detail." He used the numbers to locate the paragraph quickly.

"This is the most recited description of the Bright One," he said before reading:

The Bright One shall walk among us!
Her sword shall be Flames of Truth,
Her shield a Dazzling Crystal,
Her Voice a Great Song!
She shall slay the enemies of the Light,
And bring Righteousness to the world.

Epoh looked up. "Her weapons are made of light," he noted. "Her voice beautiful and inspiring."

"Flames of Truth," Tyme pondered thoughtfully. "How often is she described as a Warrior Empress?"

"I do not recall exactly," Epoh answered. "She is described by a number of Clans in various ways with different names.

The Bright Angel. She is also called the Divine Daughter if I remember right." Epoh held the book in his hands. "I will reread it and find out." He had read the *Book of Elders* cover to cover when he was younger and found much of it to be heavy reading.

"These are old stories filled with complex meanings," Epoh explained. "Unless you are a scholar, 'tis better to just read the important, selected parts along with a respected priestly commentary. Ideally read with a group, or at least one other person, which helps create discussion over the interpretation. The stories can have surprisingly different meanings to different people."

Tyme opened a random page and began to read. It appeared to be a confusing story of a woman lost in a foreign land. The listing of names and places made little sense.

"Each story was written for a specific audience at a specific moment in herstory. The story is important because aspects and truths can be learned and applied to us today. However, that does not mean the book is without error. There are hundreds of contradictions in the text. The book is not written by Divine. 'Tis written by women prophets, about Divine. That is a big difference."

Tyme set the book down. "So, you read the thick scholarly parts, and then together we can read the selected and relevant passages." She gave him a proud grin. "And you can provide the insightful, priestly commentary!"

Epoh bowed. "I am not a shaman, yet," he smiled. "But I am an studious disciple, who would be happy to offer commentary and discussion." He got up and began lighting the small lanterns around the darkening patio.

"That is nice," Tyme said of the soft, gentle light.

They sat quietly watching the stars appear in the sky above them.

"I have always admired you," Epoh said at last. "From the very beginning I felt that you were something special in my heart," he touched his chest.

"And I you," Tyme agreed.

"If I had not fallen into the river, I would have asked you to marry me," Epoh smiled wistfully. "I thought you would become a famous Barbarian Queen!" He shook his head in amazement. "Now that seems a slur against your true destiny."

"Barbarian Queen would be no slur in any court I presided," Tyme protested. "Do not elevate me out of the room."

Epoh apologized. "You are right. Sometimes I am overwhelmed with your mantle of Bright One."

"I am overwhelmed as well," Tyme replied. "'Tis a lofty title when placed upon some other person, but feels arrogant and presumptuous when placed upon oneself. And a bit terrifying frankly."

"'Tis a bit terrifying," Epoh agreed solemnly.

"I do not think I always need wear the full mantle," Tyme mused. "Can we set the mantle aside and be just the two of us like we were before?"

"Well, not quite like before," Epoh replied with a chuckle. "I was Crown Prince of a Barbarian Kingdom. Now we are in one of the old cities where women rule, and I must ask for permission to woo you." He dropped to one knee and smiled merrily. "May I woo you?" Had he really grown up here, he would have asked the question before other female witnesses, preferably from both their families, to guard against any later misunderstandings.

Tyme's eyes sparkled with delight. "Yes, you may." She extended her hand for him to hold.

"May I kiss your hand?"

"Yes, you may."

He gently kissed her hand and tenderly held the back of her hand against his cheek. "I am very happy when I am with you."

"I am very happy when I am with you," she agreed.

"May I kiss you?"

"Please," Tyme smiled as they bent together to kiss tenderly for a few moments. "Your poor lips are cracked," she consoled him as she ran her fingers over his blisters.

"Your lips are like water to a man dying of thirst," Epoh said dreamily.

"Do not go moonboy on me," she retorted. "Your lips are like a cactus! We have to get you healed."

HERE WITH
YOU NOW

Tyme and Riin Ruel continued training drills with close dagger work. Riin Ruel was amazed at how quickly Tyme was learning. And how fast she moved.

"What does the *Kabaal Prophecies* say the Bright One will do?" Tyme asked when they stopped for a short break.

"She will lead a rebirth of the Ambri Empire," Riin Ruel answered solemnly. "A Holy Ambri Empire."

"She will be Empress?" Tyme said the words gravely.

"Divine's own Empress," Riin Ruel answered assuredly. "The Divine Daughter."

"How can such a thing come about?" Tyme asked with incomprehension. "Do you have powerful allies in Ambrit?" In the Senate? The Legions? The Blades?"

"None of those, sadly," Riin Ruel admitted. "We are a small group, but we are effective." She gestured around their training area. "I am here with you now, am I not?"

"Yes, you are here."

"Then let us resume our training," Riin Ruel advised.

When they finished, they studied more of the *Prayers for the Dead*. Tyme had already learned all 19 of the *Prayers for the Mortal Body*, which were used during last rites.

Riin Ruel told her there were more *Prayers for the Dead*, and that the next three prayers were only known and taught at one remote nunnery.

"Why are the next prayers not taught or included with the

first group?" Tyme asked Riin Ruel.

"These prayers are not for the uninitiated. Their meanings can be misconstrued," Riin Ruel replied without explaining anything.

"And how do you know I will not misconstrue them?" Tyme asked.

"Because I will be sitting beside you as you memorize and learn each one."

MY DATE

After she first sang in the Mother Womb of Karvor with Wiir Waar and all the Ser Cus women, Tyme had returned every Moonday to be a part of the amazing choir. She also visited on other days to sing and do her devotions. Now she had finished her practice and was sitting to the side alone, contemplating the enormity of her overwhelming and hard-to-believe destiny.

The Bright One!

Empress!

She could not imagine what circumstances could occur that might possibly transform her into such a role. She remembered how Epoh had told her when they were younger of the burdens of being Crown Prince. The role was an honor, but also a life-changing responsibility.

That was what she felt. A staggering accountability and duty. She had a foreboding sense the weight was going to test her. Mayhaps to her core.

But the test was not yet.

She put the burden out of her mind to try and find some calm in the moment.

She thought about Epoh again. She had always loved him as a friend, and wondered what might have happened if he was to return. Whether she would fall in love with him again. Now she knew the answer. Suddenly she realized that she wanted to tell him.

She left the Womb at the end of the heat and climbed the hill to the apartment above the Glazed Woman. Everyone was congregating on the patio. The sky was a dark, dusty red.

"I have the evening off," Tyme told Epoh. "Let's go on a date to the Blue Moon."

Epoh's face lit up. "I would be honored to be your date," he said.

"I have a dress that Wiir Waar gave me. You wear the white shirt with the embroidered trim we got for you the other day."

"Okay," Epoh beamed. "Anything else I can do to be more presentable?"

"Just be ready in fifteen minutes," Tyme replied as she sashayed into her bedroom and closed the door.

At the Blue Moon, Tyme and Epoh sat at their own private table. Delgado was busy with other guests, while Jyg and Rona were laughing and dancing together and oblivious to everyone else. The band was from Vlice, the most remote of the Barbarian Kingdoms with music Epoh found intriguing. They both ordered mescal moonrises.

"You look great in that shirt," Tyme told him.

"And you look great in that dress," Epoh repeated for the third time that evening. He made no attempt to hide that he was smitten. They talked and laughed and enjoyed each other's company. They also listened quietly to a few songs. Epoh seemed especially touched by the laments.

"You are so easy to be around," Tyme marveled. "It feels so right and complete with you here."

"You know I am devoted to you," Epoh assured her. What more could he say?

"I was at the Womb singing during the heat," Tyme told him. "And I realized how much you mean to me." She leaned forward and kissed him tenderly. "I love you, Epoh."

"I love you," he replied, "with all of my heart and soul." His eyes grew moist.

"Because of my mantel," she did not use the words Bright One, "there may be great change in my life."

Epoh nodded.

"I feel an urgency, now, while we still have some control

over our lives, to be together as much as possible. To enjoy each moment that we can."

"I am happier now than I have ever been," Epoh told her.

Tyme smiled and hugged him. "Yes, let us treasure this time together in Karvor." She did not voice her fear that they would later look back and say Karvor was their best of times. Their own special moment. Falling in love during the calm before a great storm.

A NEW TRANSLATION

A week after his first visit, Epoh climbed the stairs to the Trusted Scribe just after the heat under a dirty and dusty-orange sky. He was excited to learn that Ser Hain Haan Hana had been able to acquire a set of the full *Kabaal Prophecies*.

"Two gold pieces and 10 silvers," she told him. "This version is from the *Mask of Splendor*. I warned you that parts of the Prophecies are confusing and without sense. The letters do not always make words, nor the words make sentences." She unrolled a scroll and showed him a portion of the script.

Epoh leaned forward. "That is Hool," he said with certainty. "Those are Hool words mixed with Ambri."

"You know Hool?" Ser Hain Haan Hana's eyes widened bright with surprise.

"Yes," Epoh replied. He studied the document more closely. "I can read some of it."

"I would be interested in hearing your appraisal of the scrolls," Ser Hain Haan Hana said. "I would pay favorably for an improved translation and commentary."

Epoh arrived back at the apartment as the last colors of a cinnamon sunset were fading into night. On the patio he excitedly showed Tyme, Jyg and Klew a large, finely tooled leather scroll pouch. "The *Kabaal Prophecies!*" he said with satisfaction.

"The first part of the prophecies are proclamations on better living to serve Divine," Epoh explained as he opened the leather pouch. "Other scrolls have arcane religious stories and mystical visions. Everything is intermixed with what most scholars call a jumble of garbled nonsense."

Epoh smiled dramatically. "But when I looked at one of the scrolls briefly at the store, I recognized some of it was Hool."

"You can translate it," Tyme enthused. "Our desert scholar!"

He assembled a small wooden holder and set the scroll to reel from one spindle to the other as he turned. "I am going to index it as I read," he explained. The numbering would help him go back to find important passages of the manuscript later."

"Where did the *Kabaal Prophecies* come from?" Jyg asked.

"From before the Ambri Empire," Epoh answered. "Mayhaps from before the Women's Clans. They are very rare and arcane texts that few people have actually read. Most quotes attributed to the Prophecies come from references in other works."

"Prophecies," Epoh continued, "by their very nature, are highly subjective to interpretation, and are strongly influenced by the time, place, and culture of their origin."

"How does culture affect a prophecy or a dream?" Jyg asked. "A real prophecy should be true regardless of the location or beliefs of the people living in the surrounding area."

"A prophecy is one person's glimpse into a higher truth, but that glimpse is colored by their own prejudices, and their accuracy and understanding of the true nature of Divine. Even prophets only see a narrow and incomplete view of the Divine Glory. Most struggle to comprehend the full nature of the revelations."

RENEGOTIATE BOUNDARIES

"At the beginning of my apprenticeship, I agreed to hold much of my training and instruction in secret," Tyme addressed Riin Ruel resolutely. "Before we go further, I wish to renegotiate some of those boundaries."

Riin Ruel's only reply was a steely gaze and icy silence. She held her head high in indignation.

"I will not be muzzled and left unable to confide and discuss aspects of my training with those I love and respect," Tyme said. "I can not have only you for my council. I must have others I can trust to ensure balance in what I am going to do, and how far I am willing to go, in this role that you have set before me."

"I have set before you?" Riin Ruel questioned with a shake of her head. "Divine gives each of us our roles." She leaned forward. "'Tis we who must live up to those roles."

"We may have a different view as to what my role might be," Tyme straightened her shoulders. "But whatever I believe," Tyme added resolutely, "I have every intention of living up to it."

Riin Ruel looked at her appraisingly.

"I am going to study the *Kabaal Prophecies* with Epoh," Tyme revealed further. "He said parts of it are written in Hool."

"Written in Hool?" Riin Ruel said with surprise. Her brows creased in perturbation. "Then I would have thought there would have been a copy in the library at Ezkia Nunnery. The abbess would have told me." She shrugged. "Mayhaps he is confused."

"He is not confused," Tyme said with consternation. "He knows more about it than the owner of the Trusted Scribe here in Karvor, or any of her scholarly friends and colleagues. Ser Hain Haan Hana said she would pay him handsomely for a copy of his translation."

"And publish it under a man's name as the translator?" Riin Ruel snorted. "Did he ask her that? If she was willing to put his name on it?"

"No," Tyme conceded, "he did not ask." It had never occurred to Epoh, or Tyme, that his being a man would be a credibility issue. "But he will now."

"By all means," Riin Ruel agreed. "And be sure to tell me her answer as well."

"Have *you* ever read the *Kabaal Prophecies*?" Tyme asked. She knew that Riin Ruel had not and was tired of her dismissiveness of Epoh. "Have you even read any of the scholarly commentaries?"

"No," Riin Ruel sniffed. "I have only read quotes and references to the work. But," she added with more dignity, "I trust what many experts have spent their lives studying."

"How odd that none of those experts," Tyme marveled with mock surprise, "realized that many of the confusing parts were actually a different language? Mayhaps that might have helped them understand more of the meaning."

Riin Ruel had no retort but icy silence.

Later that night on the apartment patio, Tyme had her first lesson with Epoh.

"The first thing that is important to understand," he explained, "is the *Kabaal Prophecies* were written by a number of women over a long period of herstory. None of the authors were alive at the same time."

"How can you know that?"

"When you read the original scroll," Epoh replied, "'tis possible to discern differences in style, in the flow of the writing, in the choice of different words that might be used heavily in one area and not even appear anywhere else in the whole book. All of that shows compelling evidence of different authors at different dates."

"That is why the Bright One is often portrayed as a Warrior Queen, but other times as the Divine Daughter, who is the representative, here in this world, of our Divine Mother."

"So, does that mean the Bright One is all of those things? Equally?" Tyme wondered. "Or is she more of one than the other?"

THE PROPOSAL

Tyme was excited and maybe just a bit nervous. Tonight, was a big night. A night she would remember for the rest of her life.

She was wearing a finely embroidered blouse that Wiir Waar had given her with a skirt and a well-concealed dagger, a fashionable gauze wrap, and high sandals that each hid a long, thin knife. After her ambush by Rocozo, she never went anywhere without weaponry.

Epoh knocked on the back door and they headed up the street to the Blue Moon. He was wearing the shirt she loved.

"I really like Karvor," Epoh said as they climbed up the hillside of brightly painted buildings toward Old Town. "Everything is so vibrant and colorful." He grinned and took her hand. "Or mayhaps 'tis because I am here with you."

At the Blue Moon they joined Jyg and Rona at Delgado's table, who was being his usual charming host, explaining the evening's music and introducing them to the musicians. When the band started with a catchy drumbeat, Jyg and Rona jumped up to dance. They had earlier given Epoh some dancing tips, so he was eager to show Tyme his improvement.

Dancing Barbarian style, Epoh took the lead and proudly swung and directed Tyme gracefully through a series of swirls and twirls. With each dance they grew smoother and more flamboyant, adding in new elements and flairs.

"Did you dance much with Delgado?" Epoh asked. He noted the gang leader watching them intently.

"Yes," she answered, "he is a great dancer." She told Epoh about being in the private Ser Cus performances, and the marginal dancing prospects at some of the banquets after the shows. How there had been a plot to smuggle Delgado into the Mayor's party so Tyme could have a fun dance partner and companion. "But with all the spying we never did get to dance together."

"So, I am very lucky to be dancing with you now," Epoh said with satisfaction.

"Yes, you are very lucky," Tyme snuggled her head against his shoulder. They danced the next few songs without talking. When the band took a break, they joined everyone at the table. Rona told a few funny stories about a rich patron at the Plumed Bird, and Delgado shared some humorous customer tales from the Blue Moon.

When the dancing resumed Tyme had something new to show Epoh. "I learned it from Wiir Waar," she told him. "But I have never danced it with anyone."

"Can you teach me?" Epoh asked. She showed him the basic steps and led him around the dance floor, smiling happily.

"Just keep doing the basic step in place," she told him as she broke away and began to dance around him. He started swaying his arms. She circled around him twice and then led him through some twirls and embraces. Again, she danced around him and then spun them both across the small dance floor. As they moved together the dance grew in power and sensuality.

"Let's do that again!" Epoh begged when the dance finished, and they hugged.

"Don't worry," Tyme promised as the band began another song. "We are just getting started." As they danced Tyme added more and more sultry moves. Then she began to shimmy. When the band took a break Tyme escorted Epoh to a small private table. Jyg and Rona went back to Delgado's table.

"Did you tell the others you wanted some privacy?" Epoh noticed.

"Yes," Tyme answered. "I told them I wanted to talk with you alone tonight."

"What do you want to talk about?" he asked, growing serious.

"Our future." She held his hands in hers. "How much I love you." Tyme got down on one knee before him and looked up into his eyes. "Will you marry me, Epoh? Will you be my husband? Will you be my helpmate and life partner?"

Epoh's eyes welled up. "Will you have me?" he said with uncertainty. He had feared her mantle as the Bright One might preclude their marriage.

"Yes, I will have you," Tyme joked. "What I am asking is-- will you have me? Will you marry me?"

"Yes! Yes! A thousand times yes," Epoh replied with a dazed smile. He helped Tyme to her feet and they hugged in excitement, then sat together entwined and close.

"We have to get rings," Tyme said. "I want to have the ceremony right away. As soon as we can."

"What will Riin Ruel say?" Epoh asked nervously. He had a feeling the warrior mystic would not be pleased. He felt a bit nervous himself. He wondered how their vows might affect her becoming Empress. Or being proclaimed the Bright One?

HINT OF
IMPROPRIETY

"I asked Epoh to marry me," Tyme told Riin Ruel when they met the next day for training and lessons.

Riin Ruel's face grew serious as she motioned for them to sit and talk. "I urge caution over such action now," she advised sternly. "You do not want any hint of impropriety. Or sign of weakness."

"How does being married hint of impropriety?" Tyme asked with skepticism. "Or weakness?"

"Married is one thing," Riin Ruel answered. "Married to a Barbarian Crown Prince is another. I am sorry, but 'tis true. People in Ambrit, and here in Karvor, and throughout the old Empire, believe Barbarian men are domineering and controlling."

"Hardly controlling when he abdicated his throne," Tyme said dismissively.

"To become the commanding husband of an Empress?" Riin Ruel pressed her point. "Why rule Dayr Castle when you could have the Ambri Empire?"

"That is preposterous!" Tyme said with disbelief. "Everyone who knows us would laugh and say 'twas a lie."

"But how about all the people who do not know you? All the people who will never see you together, but will only hear rumors and gossip? How will they know 'tis a lie?" Riin Ruel shook her head. "Those who oppose you will invent all kinds of lies to discredit you."

"Well, I am a Barbarian," Tyme said in resignation. "Like it or not, I am from Dayrstad."

"You come from Dayr Castle," Riin Ruel agreed, "but you were not born there. The fact that you were *not* born there means you could have been born *anywhere*, including Ambrit. Emphasizing that gives you universal appeal. Emphasizing your Barbarian roots makes you a complete outsider. Marrying a Barbarian is the worst thing you could do."

The old warrior shook her head emphatically. "Much better to keep him as a consort. That would not be such a distraction. Then he is further proof of your power, without being detrimental to your cause. A trophy moonboy."

Riin Ruel pointed her finger accusingly at Tyme. "If he is your husband, he will give your enemies a sure means to attack."

PROPHECIES OF SISIA

"I have found two references to the Bright One in the *Kabaal Prophecies* so far," Epoh told Tyme when they met up at the apartment. "They are from the prophet Sisia."

"What does she say?" Tyme asked, glad for a diversion from Riin Ruel's anger over their wedding plans.

Epoh read the first prophecy aloud.

She is the Bright One
Who Knows All Truth
The Divine Daughter
Our Warrior Queen

"Divine Daughter and Warrior Queen seem like opposite ends of the spectrum," Tyme noted.

"Precisely," Epoh said. "It portrays an all inclusive representation. Like from start to finish."

"Being a Warrior Queen seems straight forward," Tyme chewed her lip. "But I am not sure how to be a Divine Daughter."

"Follow in the ways of Divine," Epoh shrugged his shoulders. "You already exemplify that."

"I believe it will require more than what I have been doing so far," Tyme said.

"Yes," he nodded soberly. "I am afraid this will require much more of you as well."

Tyme raised her thick, black eyebrows in a determined acknowledgement.

"You say being a Warrior Queen seems straight forward," Epoh said. "But actually, the meaning of Warrior Queen can also have a wide spectrum. It can be literal, but also metaphorical."

"Give me an example."

"Riin Ruel has a literal interpretation," Epoh explained. "Metaphorically, the Warrior Queen fights for the battle between good and evil inside each of us."

"Hmm," Tyme contemplated. "That is nteresting."

Epoh raised his eyebrows in confirmation.

"You said there was a second reference to the Bright One in the Prophecies of Sisia?" Tyme asked.

"Yes. 'Tis the prophecy that helped lead Riin Ruel to Dayr Castle," Epoh replied. Again, he read aloud.

Born of a King
A girl shall appear
The Divine Daughter full of Radiance and Hope
She shall be the Bright One

"Ambri scholars translate the first line *Born of a King*," Epoh noted. "However, the way 'tis originally written would be interpreted by Hool more as borne by, or carried by, if referenced to a man. If King is a horse, the translation would be riding."

"Riding King?" Tyme said with astonishment.

"Yes," Epoh nodded gravely. "The start of the prophecy would be interpreted:

Riding King
A girl shall appear!"

Tyme did not even know what to say. They sat thinking of the enormity of those written words, which so accurately described her.

"No mention of truth or Warrior Queen," Epoh noted at last. "But a Divine Daughter full of radiance."

"Divine Daughter," Tyme repeated fondly.

"And the last line would be interpreted *She shall be a Bright One*."

"*A* Bright One?" Tyme noted with quick interest, "That is much different than *the* Bright One," she observed with conviction. "*A* is more inclusive and attainable. That feels much more inspiring and hopeful. There can be others."

"There can be others," Epoh echoed.

RINGS

"Karvor has amazing sunsets," Tyme marveled as she and Epoh left the apartment the next evening to go shopping for wedding rings. The sun was a giant bruised, purple-red shimmering disc. Dust and haze reflected a vibrant glow across the entire western horizon.

"The Sea of Dunes has sunsets like this," Epoh recalled with a smile.

"Do you miss any part of it?" Tyme asked, and then joked, "Besides the food?" Everyone was still talking about mice stew and locust patties.

"Everything was simple. Life and death, but simple," Epoh replied. "Mayhaps, I miss the quiet. I had to accept so many things that were out of my control, and not to fret and stress over my circumstances." He looked her in the eye. "Not dwell on you, and all that I was missing at Dayr Castle."

Tyme gave him a hug. "It made you stronger. Like steel being forged. Much stronger than you would have ever been staying at Dayr Castle. Not to mention learning a new language and uncovering the secrets of the Ancient Ones."

"All of that makes me appreciate being here, right now, all the more," he replied.

They arrived at the first of three shops around Jeweler Street that Delgado had suggested for buying rings. The proprietor was an older woman with frizzy, black hair in an enormous ponytail ball on top of her head. Her rings were silver with a fine filigree pattern. She said she could size the rings to their fingers by the next day. The price was 35 silvers. It seemed like a lot to Tyme, who was not accustomed to shopping in Karvor, or buying jewelry. They told the proprietor they wanted to look around before deciding and left the store.

"Did you tell Riin Ruel about our plans?" Epoh asked as they descended the steep, narrow sidewalks and stairs.

"Yes," Tyme answered without further comment.

"Well, what did she say?"

"She advised against it."

"Let me guess," Epoh sighed. "A Barbarian husband would be perceived as dominating or controlling. And it emphasizes your outsider-ness."

"Good guess," Tyme conceded. "How did you know?"

"Because that is what I worry about as well," Epoh admitted. "I grew up in court. I studied politics. I know how things can be twisted and used against you."

"So, you do not think we should get married?" Tyme veered to a small viewpoint off the sidewalk to talk.

"I said I worry about it." He searched for the right words. "My worst fear is impeding or altering your destiny."

"Altering my destiny need not be a bad thing. Mayhaps, you alter it in a better direction."

"Mayhaps," Epoh said without conviction. He thought of Nadi Nani. The abbess of Ezkia Nunnery had been certain that he would be a distraction to Tyme. He had a hard time getting her warnings and concerns out of his head. Riin Ruel had thought likewise. "Are we just fooling ourselves in thinking we can have a life together?" he asked.

"If not a life … at least this time now. Here, in Karvor. I want you to be my husband," she vowed. "So that no one can ever take that from us."

He looked into her eyes and felt unsettling premonitions. "No one will ever take that from us," he agreed, feeling her concern. They embraced each other solemnly.

"Are you hungry?" Tyme asked, eager to move on. She wanted this evening to be easy and fun.

Epoh nodded with a smile.

She led him down to Skyline Street across from Peppers and

introduced him to Dani, the girl selling pies under a stairwell. "She has pigeon pies that taste just like back home."

Epoh took a bite and nodded in agreement. "Mmmm. Moist and tender," he said with praise and then got a sad look. "I thought about eating pigeon pies with you when I was out in the desert. I planned to eat pigeon pie with you in celebration when I got back to Dayr Castle. But you were not there." He held the food before him as an offering and took a bite. "Eating pigeon pie with you in Karvor," his grin widened, "is better than any restaurant."

Dani looked at Epoh with wonder. He did not look or act like any noble she had ever heard about.

"We are getting married," Tyme told her proudly. "We are shopping for wedding rings."

"Get him a collar as well," Dani advised. 'Twas customary for women to have a silver necklace soldered permanently around their husband's neck. A sign of a man's marital status, including a fob engraved with the wife's name, so that anyone could report the man should he behave poorly.

Tyme did not look convinced.

"I would proudly wear your collar," Epoh told her as he started his second pie.

"That says I do not trust you," Tyme protested. "I can not believe that you, a Barbarian, would wear a collar."

"Precisely why I should."

"'Tis an insult," Tyme insisted. "We should be setting a better example. Neither of us should dominate the other. We should be a true partnership. A team of equals."

"I am not insulted," Epoh shrugged. "Because we are *not* equals. You are a Bright One. That is what is most important. Not my ego."

"Can we not still be equal partners?" Tyme asked with dismay.

"In some things," Epoh consoled her. "But we cannot change everything all at once. We have to choose our battles. If my wearing a collar helps others to be less threatened by my Barbarianism and helps your cause, then I would wear it proudly."

"He is a good man," Dani told Tyme with approval. "Good men are happy to wear the collar. They have nothing to hide."

"That settles it," Epoh agreed. "We need to buy a collar."

"Why do they not at least call it a necklace?" Tyme complained. "'Tis just a thin chain."

"Some are not so thin," Dani chuckled. Her mother regularly checked the links on her father's collar for evidence of new soldering and advised her daughters to do the same when they married.

Tyme and Epoh continued the discussion as they climbed the stairs up to Jeweler Street. A thick crescent moon hung in the western sky. The skyline and sidewalks filled with lanterns and firepots being lit on patios.

"I do not want you to get a collar," Tyme said again. "I do not like what it implies."

"Okay. No collar for now," Epoh conceded. "But I would like to talk about it again when we leave Karvor. I want to do everything I can to help you."

"You can help me by encouraging me to be true to myself."

"And you can help me," Epoh responded, "to be true to myself as well."

"You are true to yourself. That is why I love you so much."

The second shop sold gold jewelry. The short, heavyset woman showed them three different styles of rings. The cheapest pair cost more than a gold piece. The last shop sold both silver and gold, with prices even higher. Tyme shook her head. She had little money. Normally the woman's family bought the rings. She would have to rely on Epoh to pay the bill.

"Spending money on a ring does not mean we love each other more," Tyme said as they left the shop. "It only means you have, or had," she joked, "a fat coin purse."

"What *would* mean that we love each other more?" Epoh asked.

"Something that has more significance for us," she answered and then smiled with an idea. "Let's make our own rings. I will make yours. And you make mine! We can pay a jeweler to use her tools and show us how to make them."

"That is a great idea!" Epoh's eyes sparkled. "I would love to make your ring! What style did you like?"

"I liked the rings of beaten silver we saw at the first shop. How they caught the light. But make ours thicker and not so delicate."

"I want a solid ring as well. And I like silver," he said approvingly, "Elegant but not pretentious."

They searched the alleys of smaller shops until they found a proprietor willing to help with their request. The Silver Star was owned by Sera Resa, a young woman from the Painted Hills who had recently moved to Karvor to start her own business. She was a romantic and loved the idea of Tyme and Epoh making each other's rings.

"But it will cost more than if I just make them myself," Sera Resa apologized. "Because this will take much more time."

"We decided to make our own rings, so that money was not the object," Epoh laughed. "Now it ends up costing more!"

"But for the right reason," Tyme enthused. "To make them personal. Truly ours."

"Truly ours," Epoh happily agreed.

"You two are amazing," Sera Resa held her hands over her heart. She wanted to find a love like that. She began instructing them how to beat a small rod of silver to the right size and shape, hammer in the highlights and bend into a circle, and solder it together, each inset with two small diamonds from the cargo bird.

They worked all through the night. At dawn they finished their rings.

THE WEDDING

Tyme and Epoh left the Silver Star jewelry shop as the early morning sky was growing red and the last few stars were disappearing. The streets were coming to life. They stopped at an overlook where they could see the domed roofs of the largest temple in Karvor on the hillside below.

"I wonder if we could get married in the Mother Womb?" Tyme questioned. From her first visit to the beautiful building with Wiir Waar and the rest of the Ser Cus women, she had enjoyed returning each Moonday for singing and ceremonies, and also stopping to pray during the week. And, of course, during her moon blood, her power surges, when she was allowed into the sanctum, the holiest part of the temple.

The round building had graceful flowing lines of arches, columns, and struts, the walls and roof filled with colored glass panels and skylights creating a wonderful, soft light inside.

"The wedding chapels are beautiful," Epoh said. Like the refuge, the chapels were located in the outer ring of the temple where men were allowed. "I snuck a quick look once during a ceremony." He had frequently visited the refuge to meditate while Tyme had trained and studied with Riin Ruel.

"And why were you curious to look?" Tyme asked with delight.

"Because I could not help but dream that we should be wed there," Epoh said. "And now, mayhaps, we will be."

They walked excitedly arm in arm down the street toward the Womb.

"Mayhaps we could even get a honeymoon suite at the cavort?" Tyme speculated. The swank rooms were offered as enticement for couples to begin their marriage in an environment best suited for fertility success.

Epoh gave her a startled look.

"Do not worry," she laughed. "I have not changed my mind about children." They had both agreed that such a thing at this uncertain stage of their lives was out of the question. "My moon blood has been erratic. I am not in my fertile period. But I have heard they sometimes let newlyweds use the room anyway, to get them registered in the Book of Life."

When they got to the temple, they were pleased to find that with a modest donation there was an opening the next afternoon, immediately after the heat, for a small, quick wedding. After that, the entire week of bright Moonday was all booked.

"I want three days for a honeymoon," Tyme said when they returned to the apartment. "Three days just you and me. No Bright One."

"What would you like to do?"

"Let's sleep in and stay in bed the first day. Just totally relax. Then I would like to be outside. I have not been camping since I got to Karvor. But that is probably the last thing you want to do."

"Actually, camping alone with you sounds great," Epoh enthused. "As much as I enjoy Karvor, quiet time with you sounds even better."

"Then we should go to the Painted Hills," Tyme said with excitement. "There are amazing views I would love to show you."

If Crown Prince Epohco had wed Tyme at Dayr Castle, the crowded ceremony would have been presided over by the high priest herself and celebrated with bells ringing loudly throughout the castle and the countryside.

Instead, Tyme married Epoh in the smallest chapel of the Mother Womb in Karvor, with just five friends. Tyme cried in her red bridal dress before the ceremony over those she loved who could not be there. Utuno. Tao Tau. Wiir Waar and the Ser Cus. Noot.

Riin Ruel stood beside Tyme as mother or grandmother of the bride wearing the traditional blue, much to her chagrin. She had repeatedly advised against the marriage to no avail. Jyg stood as best man with Epoh, who wore the traditional black with red trim. Klew, Rona, and Delgado, who paid for bouquets of real flowers, made up the audience.

The priest was an elderly, unmarried woman, a no-nonsense realist who was suspect of the couple's lovey-dovey, collarless ceremony. She believed their constant touching was symptomatic of a continual need for reassurance and attention. She was certain the marriage would not last. It mattered little to her, as long as the woman got pregnant, and the rugged and virile stud's name was listed in the Book of Life.

Tyme and Epoh did not let the dour attitude of the priest diminish their enjoyment of the ceremony. They sang a song together and recited their own special vows.

To support and challenge each other to be their best.

To treat each other as equals.

To always be honest and true.

To love each other forever.

The priest was unsettled with Epoh's singing where she believed he had no business doing so, and unhappy with their vows of equality in the relationship. Regardless, she announced them woman and husband, just to get them out of her chapel.

Much of the Jawbone Ridge gang met the wedding party as they came out the door, along with a brass band playing with gusto. Two large caricature figures on poles bobbed and spun above the crowd: a bride and her husband. She was wagging her finger disapprovingly. He was grimacing and pulling mournfully at his oversized collar. A festively dressed group of Rona's friends danced before them, slowly leading the way up the hillside toward Old Town. Others nearby, hearing the lively music, joined in behind the procession, happily accepting small shots of viruna liberally given out by the Jawbone Ridge gang.

When the music changed Tyme and Epoh joined the dancing. The procession came to a standstill. The growing crowd danced as well. The necks and faces of the musicians bulged ever redder as they played even louder. The pace of the dance grew faster and faster along with the cheers of the crowd. The song ended in a mighty crescendo of approval. The band instantly started up a new tune.

Everybody began slowly moving and dancing up the street again, changing partners as Tyme and Epoh each made separate dances through the crowd. After dancing with Tyme, Jyg found himself partnering with a number of Rona's friends. Some danced very seductively up against him, and then circled nearby for more. He noted that Rona most often danced with Delgado.

When the song ended Tyme and Epoh did a small shot of viruna to the cheers of the crowd, embraced, and kissed languidly. They hugged each other happily, and resumed walking up the hill.

At the Blue Moon everyone gathered around Delgado's table for a toast. Like the parade, the shots were quite small. "To Tyme and Epoh," Delgado raised his little cup, "Your love inspires all of us. May you enjoy many, many moons together!"

Tyme was joined by Rona and her friends, who helped perform the traditional marriage dance of the Women's Clan, proclaiming their power and prestige as they accepted Epoh, the new helpmate and husband, who was promised shelter, food and work in his new family and clan.

The next song Tyme and Epoh danced alone, radiantly and elegantly. Then everybody joined in again. The band was one of Tyme's favorites. She and Epoh danced every song until the band took a break. While Epoh again thanked Delgado for the celebration, Tyme asked Riin Ruel if she was going to dance.

"I stood beside you at your wedding with great reservation," Riin Ruel shook her head. "I will not have it be said that I danced."

"I think it would be good for you," Rona said boldly to the amusement of everyone else. "You should relax when you get the chance."

Epoh started reminiscing with Tyme and Jyg about Dayr Castle, and the fun they all had together so long ago. Epoh stayed only two nights at the castle after he came out of the Endless Waste, and now he reveled in recalling happier memories from home. As they shared stories Rona went off dancing with Delgado.

The music and celebration went late into the night. Tyme and Epoh cuddled together and laughed and danced until the band quit. After final hugs they were escorted by Jyg, Klew and a few gang members as they walked in the moonlight back down through Karvor to the Mother Womb. Instead of entering through the front door, they went around past the Mother's Milk to the cavort. They were greeted by the host and a clerk, who took their names and herstories.

"I was afraid being a Barbarian might be frowned upon," Epoh whispered as they were escorted to the honeymoon suite.

"Not as a stud," Tyme shook her head. "Then it is all about strength and virility. They believe you are uncouth because of upbringing and culture."

"That is a relief," Epoh laughed, "to know I am not inherently uncouth."

"'Tis the only reason I married you," Tyme teased. "You are still trainable."

They were led through the greeting lounge, where unattached patrons could mingle and get to know one another. The area held few people at this late hour. The honeymoon suite was on the second floor with a small balcony. The room was candlelit with billowy curtains and a huge bed with satin pillows. A table nearby held love oils and assorted lovemaking toys. Another table held two metal goblets of wine and a small bouquet of cactus flowers.

Tyme and Epoh fell onto the bed in exhaustion and lay there quietly in each other's arms. "I am the happiest I have ever been," she marveled.

"I am definitely the happiest I have ever been," he agreed.

"'Tis wonderful," she squeezed him tight.

They sat up, clinked the two goblets, and toasted, *to love*. Then quickly undressed one another and passionately made love long into the night.

Tyme and Epoh were served breakfast in bed and spent the day making love and relaxing in the honeymoon suite. They checked out that afternoon before the heat broke. The surprised flaunt, who had looked up Tyme's moon rhythms from her visits to the sanctum, insisted they come back to the cavort and use the suite again on a more propitious evening for Tyme's fertility.

"Motherhood is closest to Divine," she reminded them.

THE HONEYMOON

Tyme and Epoh walked up hot, empty streets and steps to their apartment to change clothes, collect their bags, and get their horses at the stables for their honeymoon to the Painted Hills.

Karvor was just coming back to life after the heat as they rode up the hill to Old Town then east up the ridge on the trail where Tyme had stopped the wagon robbery. The western sky was beginning to take on color and turn yellow and red as the heat receded. They rode along casually, telling stories. She was fascinated by his tales from the Endless Waste. He was amazed by her exploits with Wiir Waar and the Ser Cus.

"I would love to see you in one of those Ser Cus outfits," Epoh said with delight. "I remember being shocked when I was little at seeing what the Ser Cus performers wore."

"You would look good as well," Tyme agreed, "with your chiseled muscles." She gave a husky laugh. "We need to borrow some costumes for a few nights to have our own private show."

"I like it," Epoh nodded enthusiastically.

They stopped at an overlook for the sunset. The western sky was now a deep and bruised red as a distorted and shimmering sun dropped into the haze of the far horizon. "Like the Endless Waste?" she chided him. Whenever there was a spectacular sunset, he always said 'twas like the Endless Waste.

"Not *all* the sunsets in the Waste were amazing," he said by disclaimer. "But being here with you, and seeing this one, 'tis definitely the best ever."

"Very charming. You know the way to a woman's heart."

As it grew dark Tyme led them a short way off the trail to a campsite where they would get the morning sun. There was a small alcove for a fire with a flat area of smooth stone to relax on. "We will have great views of the Painted Hills and the Barrier Mountains in the morning."

'Twas the night before bright Moonday. The nearly half-full moon above them bathed the hills in soft, glowing light. Tyme asked him more about Ezkia Nunnery. He told her of the third Ambri expedition into the Waste ending in disaster, of the Saint of the Desert, and the founding of the New Order.

"Were you able to read some of the books at the library?" she asked. She knew how much he liked ancient writings.

"Hardly at all," Epoh lamented. "I spent most of my time writing."

"What were you writing?"

"The herstory of the fall of the Ambri Empire, the rise of the Barbarian Kingdoms. The herstory of Dayrstad." He gave her a grin. "I wrote your whole life story in detail."

"My story?" Tyme was shocked.

"The abbess ordered me to write it. After she read it, she gave me a big list of things to further elaborate. And then another list of questions from those answers. And on and on. I was so happy when she finally told me to write about something else."

"'Tis strange to think of you writing about me," Tyme's thoughtful look turned to a smile. "But I guess that is like me being there with you."

"Yes. You were definitely there when I wrote."

They finally let the fire burn out after the moon went down and made love under the stars. Afterward Tyme and then Epoh cried tears of happiness, hugging one another and falling asleep in each other' s arms.

They rose at first light for their practice and sat in prayerful meditation facing the morning light, then ate noodles and bean cake for breakfast, a Karvor specialty. The sky was purple and red, welcoming the sun over the Barrier Mountains. They had a stunning view of the Painted Hills, an unbelievable patchwork of brightly colored clay mounds, buttes, and eroded, dusty and desolate valleys filled with mines for the colorful clay and pigments that made the pottery and artwork from Karvor so famous.

They packed up the horses and rode to the overlook of a large, orange clay mine owned by the Potter's Guild, and then worked their way back into more remote areas with no wagon access, where the clay had to be carried out in fiber sacks by backboard and tumpline.

At mid morning Tyme led Epoh on a wild horse ride up a narrow valley with mounds of maroon and purple clay and rock, racing around tight winding corners, then up a twisting gulley to arrive with both horses and riders breathing heavily at the Dusted Man tavern.

"Do not bump into anybody," Tyme reminded Epoh with a laugh as two men covered in bright yellow powder descended a foot trail with wide tumplines across their foreheads and heavy yellow baskets filled with sacks on their backs. They eased their loads to rest beside similar colored baskets on a yellow stone bench, and then went in through a yellow-rimmed door. Another bench and door were colored red. The closest bench and door were bluish green. Tyme gestured toward it. "That is the safest to enter."

Inside, the bright yellow workers, the Canaries, took up the middle and far end of the room. Apart from the yellow tables were separate groups of orange and red workers, and a table for green and one of blue.

Tyme motioned to the bar stools. "These are for the colorless."

"The defender of my clay wagon," the bartender and owner, Dari Riad greeted Tyme with a dazzling white smile, setting two cups of watered pulque before them. She had a few errant splotches of yellow color dabbed across her lustrous ebony skin, and a small streak of red above one thick eyebrow. She introduced herself to Epoh.

"This is my husband," Tyme proudly introduced him in return.

Dari Riad gave Epoh a curious look. "You been out in the Endless Waste?" she joked.

"For decades," Epoh nodded. On a lighthearted impulse he extended his arm and pulled up his sleeve to reveal the large knobbed, metal clock bracelet around his wrist. 'Twas the first time he showed it in public. "I only brought back a few things," he said.

Dari Riad's eyes bulged at the sight of the shiny ornate device. A murmur went across the bar.

"He brought me one as well," Tyme exclaimed as she held out her arm and pulled up her sleeve. Her clock bracelet was slightly smaller to fit her wrist. She explained how the moving wands on both clocks always pointed in the same direction.

"So, you just returned?" Dari Riad asked in amazement.

"And now we are on our honeymoon," Epoh replied with wonder, gazing at Tyme, hardly believing it to be true. They hugged and kissed.

"You see that!" Dari Riad cried out to her patrons. "They came to the Dusted Man on their honeymoon! That means a free drink for everyone! On the house!" She was going to toast to a long marriage as was traditional, but at the last moment toasted to "a love marriage," because they seemed so enamored.

"A love marriage," the patrons all cheered in reply, raising their cups.

When they prepared to leave, Tyme signaled Dari Riad. "I think Ser Gina Gain Gani might control the wagon shipments for the Potter's Guild," she reported. "Mayhaps she is behind the attacks on your wagons."

"We are getting no help in our investigation from the City Guards," Dari Riad said with frustration. "Thankfully, rumor of your patrolling the area has kept us from any more attacks. If there is anything I can help you with let me know!"

"Do you know about the kiva nearby with the shaman?" Tyme asked.

"Yes. A group of singers from the kiva will be performing here later this afternoon. Very popular. The place fills up. I love their music. They have also started a school."

"How do we get to the kiva?" Epoh asked.

"On foot you can climb straight up the gully above us," Dari Riad answered. "But on horses you best ride up the ridgeline to the west and drop in from the top. The kiva is in Viridescent Canyon, an area filled with streaks and bands of green clay and rock of all hues."

PART III

Her Gaze pierces all Souls
Her Sword a Fiery Truth
Morning Star of Heaven
Whose Dagger slays the Beast.

Kabaal Prophecies

Killing in the name of Divine is the greatest sin of all.

Hope the Proclaimer

STARTING A SCHOOL

When Singer and his followers arrived in Viridescent Canyon, they soon realized there were not enough men coming to the kiva to spread the word about the school for boys and men they hoped to start.

"We need to get out and let people know about us," Draktono said.

"We should go to the Dusted Man," Swindovo suggested immediately.

"Yes," Singer interrupted his humming to agree. "We can also sing at the mines."

Draktono nodded his head. "Like we sang for the workers in Sikes."

They spent the next day singing at two nearby mines. The workers all shot them suspicious stares and glances at first, and then a few smiles, along with looks of puzzlement. The owner of a third mine drove them off.

In the afternoon when it grew hotter, they headed for the Dusted Man. Dari Riad greeted them happily. She moved a table and chairs to make room for them to stand and sing. They began with a catchy and repetitive Praise that Swindovo had modified and sped up. A few of the patrons were soon clapping along.

Next Singer led them in an uplifting Gloria with beautiful and intricate harmonies. Most of the audience sat rapt with attention. When they finished the tavern was silent for a moment, followed by an eruption of applause.

Swindovo began beating his drum to the rhythm of a new

Hallelujah he had revised. The audience resumed clapping. Frisoto started dancing as the song became ecstatic. A few cheers from the crowd. A whoop from Dari Riad. The speed and intensity grew as the song reached a final crescendo. More whoops and cries of encouragement for Frisoto, who kept up his rapid dancing until the very end.

When the applause and cheers subsided, Draktono introduced himself along with the others, and told the audience that they had moved into the caves by Gybeko's kiva. "We are going to have celebrations on Moondays and at other occasions when the kiva is being used. All men are invited. We are also going to start a school and speak about spiritual practices, about the discrimination against men and others marginalized by society, and about raising our voices together in protest for change."

"And we are starting a choir," Swindovo added. "If I have worries, I can release them when I sing." He did a drum roll and then started a Praise with a fast beat. The audience clapped along.

After they had performed several songs, they took a short break. "If anyone would like to talk about singing, about school, or about having a stronger spiritual practice," Draktono told the audience. "Come see us at our table. Do not be shy."

While Swindovo and Fristo were being served gourds of pulque by a delighted Dari Riad, a hardened and sinewy old man with body and clothes of yellow dust approached Draktono.

"I do not need no school to learn about discrimination against men," he snorted. "Not when I live it every day."

"We need your passion and outrage to help make changes," Draktono proposed in return. "What is your name?"

"Ozono."

"Nice to meet you, Ozono. I am Draktono," he gave a Barbarian salute. "What *would* you like to learn?"

"What would I like to learn?" the yellow man repeated the

question in exasperation as if it had nothing to do with the issue.

"Yes, if you had a teacher," Draktono calmly rephrased the question. "What would you ask them to teach you? What do you not know that you would like to learn?

"What makes you think you are smart enough to teach me anything?"

"Smart in some things," Draktono smiled agreeably. "Just learning many others. You could teach me about the Canaries, about your mine, about your life."

"And why would you want to know about my life?" Ozono huffed.

"Because I want to be allies with you. I want to be in service to you. I want to help make life better for you."

"And why would you want to do that?"

"Because our group has taken a vow to make the world a better place. To ease pain, suffering, and injustice."

"And you are going to do that by talking?" Ozono said in disbelief.

"'Tis a powerful start," Draktono assured him.

Ozono was speechless. He shook his head in bewilderment and returned to his chair and drink.

When the heat came Dari Riad fed them bread, goat cheese and dates. Singer sang soft haunting melodies and lullabies while Swindovo and Frisoto slept.

"I have never had so many customers stay so long," Dari Riad marveled to Draktono. "I will feed you better next time. Is there anything else I can do for you?"

"Let us sing this evening," Draktono laughed.

"Yes, of course! I would be thrilled if you sang more. All night if you like! You are great for business."

"Good," Draktono smiled. "And thank you for letting me talk briefly about social issues and justice. That is very important."

"I admire what you are trying to do," Dari Riad answered. "I will help in any way I can."

That evening they relied on the format that had worked well in Sikes. They mixed Swindovo's popular sing-alongs with catchy Praises, and Singer leading choruses of Hallelujahs. Draktono made comments between songs and gave occasional short discourses.

They stopped as it was growing dark so they would have time to hike back to the kiva. Dari Riad was thrilled with the increase in business, and happy to learn the kiva group, as she named them, wanted to come back.

"We plan to sing at different mines each morning," Swindovo told her. "And would like to come here for a while in the afternoons and some evenings. Moondays we will celebrate at the kiva."

Dari Riad gave them Barbarian salutes with her right fist touching her heart. "Come as often as you can," she told them.

They returned the next evening. After singing a few songs, Draktono spoke of the coming celebrations at the kiva, about starting a school, a drum group, and a choir.

When they took a break, the old man covered in yellow dust approached the table once more. He had a look of great determination and seriousness.

"I want to learn to write my name," Ozono informed Draktono without preamble. "I want to learn to read."

"Reading is a marvelous skill," Draktono agreed. "Our school should definitely have a reading class. Excellent suggestion. You can be our first pupil."

Draktono stopped singing at the Dusted Man in the afternoons. He stayed at the caves below the kiva to be available for teaching. Ozono showed up the next day an hour before the heat. His first lesson was to learn to write his name.

This simple act had a profound effect on his confidence. Draktono was glad the name was easy to spell, which gave the leader of the Canaries an immediate success, bolstering his confidence greatly.

Ozono's name denoted the worst kind of troublemaker. The ono at the end branded him as an orphan, raised in a Mother's Milk and ward of the state, most likely to be a future soldier or laborer at the farms. In accordance with the generosity of Ambri law, he was given a chance to attend school. But like many boys he was too rambunctious and distracted to sit quietly. His exasperated teachers had given him his adult name by adding on the two worst letters of the alphabet. O at the front, the mark of extreme obstinacy, most likely dangerous, followed by a z, the last letter of the alphabet, signaling no hope for redemption.

Draktono realized that despite Ozono's bravado, the old clay miner was secretly unsure of his ability to learn. He had long ago internalized the derogatory comments of his first teachers. Draktono knew that learning and memorizing the entire alphabet might be too daunting of a task to start. Better to give him shorter lessons with quicker, positive results. So, he next taught Ozono to write the words Canary and Canaries.

Ozono practiced diligently all through the heat. By the time he finished in the evening he had learned to write his second and third word. The next afternoon, he returned with another Canary. By the end of the week, two more Canaries joined him in coming to the school.

THE KIVA

Following Dari Riad's directions, Tyme and Epoh rode their horses around to the top of Viridescent Canyon before descending into a warren of alcoves and caves with veins of greenish rock and clay. They walked the horses to better appreciate the strange formations. Epoh spotted the faint hints of a trail across the hard clay soil. He stepped around a formation for a closer look and came face to face with a lean and sharp-boned old man with dark brown skin strutting toward him.

"The Burnished Man!" he exclaimed when he saw Epoh. "You are a shaman?"

Epoh was about to say no, then reconsidered. What was he? "Mayhaps I am a shaman of sorts," he acknowledged. "I travel with ..." He wanted to say a woman of prophecy but Tyme had asked for three days without mention of the Bright One. "... a young woman eager to learn of your practice."

"The Burnished Man heralds a young woman?" the grizzled shaman said with astonishment.

"Yes," Epoh replied with a relaxed grin. "She is also my wife." The words felt wonderful to say.

Tyme joined them and prayerfully gestured the Womb, which the shaman returned. They introduced themselves. The shaman's name was Gybeko.

"I heard someone with horses," he explained. "You can tie them to those rocks in the shade," he pointed. "My cave is up these ledges."

The cave was pleasantly sculpted, a perfect small dwelling

in the rock, with a worn reed sleeping mat, a few water jugs, clay pots, and a small fire pit with a hole above for a vent. Gybeko motioned for them to sit while he started a fire with dried cactus fronds to make spice tea. No one spoke.

When he served the tea, he asked what Tyme would like to know. She told of her mentoring by Tao Tau, a wise herb woman from the mountains of Dayrstad, who had expressed interest in knowing more of the mountain shaman's practice.

"I have such interest as well," Tyme said.

"You wish to know of my practice?" Gybeko asked in surprise. "Not what I believe? Nor the name of the god to whom I pray?"

"What you believe we can discuss later. First, I want to know how you live. What gives your life meaning? The fruit of your life?"

"Silence is the fruit of my life. Silence is the fulfillment of words no longer needed."

"Then let us commune in silence," Tyme nodded and motioned to sit, "and hear what cannot be said."

They sat in the Adept's pose with legs tucked in and backs straight, in quiet stillness. Epoh felt a tremendous calmness. Tyme also felt a peacefulness in the old man's presence. Gybeko prayed for two revolutions of his long prayer beads and then rose quietly to restart the fire of dried cactus fronds to make more tea. Tyme and Epoh opened their eyes and silently watched him.

After he served the tea, he looked at Epoh. "I would hear from the Burnished Man. Tell me of the desert."

Epoh talked about the dawn meditation on the Ezkia Nunnery rooftop, under a giant ceiling of red rock in a sandstone canyon, and the Quiet Ones who lived alone in hermitages in caves.

"You did not visit any kivas in the desert?" Gybeko asked in bewilderment.

"No, I did not hear of any. At Jchow Oasis I visited a Bool temple, which had ornate blue tiles and domes like the Womb.

Bool is a male god but not really a god of war, as is commonly thought, although the main Attributes seem to be power and might." He had been surprised by the civility of the people and impressed by the large school and library. "The underground caves go five levels deep where 'tis always cool."

"You do not look like you spent much time where 'twas always cool," Gybeko observed dryly.

"No," Epoh chuckled. "I was only there a few days. And at the nunnery a few decades. Mostly I was in the Sea of Dunes."

"You have seen Apocalypse?" the shaman asked.

Epoh nodded. He described the ruins, told of the stone forest, and the Lake of Shimmering Heat.

"The Burnished Man," Gybeko confirmed his first impression of Epoh.

"Why do you call me Burnished Man?" Epoh asked.

"He has long been a part of shaman oral tradition. He emerges from the desert heralding a new dawn and a New Age."

Gybeko turned his gaze on Tyme. "You are the young woman who cut the leg from under Otovo in Perich."

"An unfortunate misunderstanding. He threatened my life. He thought I was a spy for the Womb."

"And still does. He recently had the yellow kiva up in arms about a spy, until he described you. The leader of the Canaries told him you saved their clay wagon from robbery."

"Ozono spoke up for me?" Tyme smiled in surprise.

"Yes," Gybeko said, "How well do you know him?"

"We have only met briefly," Tyme replied. "I was lectured too."

"He does tend to lecture," Gybeko agreed with a chuckle. "He was the first student to enroll in the school that Draktono started in the caves below the kiva. He was instrumental in getting other Canaries and miners to come."

"Ozono goes to school?" Tyme said with interest.

"He is a serious and determined pupil."

"I am glad to hear that," Tyme said before changing

subjects. "Back to Otovo for a moment," she said. "Why does he say I am a spy?"

"Otovo is filled with vengeance," Gybeko shook his head sadly. "He seeks conflict at every opportunity. He wants to fight. Being cut and hobbled by you has only made him angrier. Mayhaps worse than before."

Tyme thought of Otovo's similarities to Rocozo. Another man with a festering hatred of her, who had tried to ambush and kill her in a dark alley not long ago.

"I was wrong to go into the kiva," Tyme admonished herself. "I meant no offense to the Fire devotees."

"Otovo and his burners were offended," Gybeko acknowledged. "But that does not mean all Fire devotes would be offended. Or that all shamans would be offended."

"Otovo said no woman had been in a kiva for millennia," Tyme recounted. "'Twas against the law."

"He is right that no woman has been in a kiva for millennia," the shaman agreed. "But not because 'tis against the law. 'Tis because no woman has *wanted* to visit a kiva for millennia. Or even asked."

"May I visit your kiva?" Tyme questioned.

"Certainly," the shaman replied, "I would be happy to share it with both of you." He led them through some green splattered rock and clay formations to a group of stones marking out the underground building.

"This kiva has four entrances and altars facing the four directions," the shaman told them as they descended the narrow stairs. "This is the main entrance facing east."

At the bottom they ducked under a low stone archway and came into a dark chamber behind the back of the altar. They stepped around the altar into a round, dimly lit room with four circular tiers for seating around a flat central area. The altar facing east had a Fire shrine with a sun medallion of polished tin. They quietly examined it, along with each of the other altars, which held a variety of shrines, offerings, totems and burned down candles.

"Prayers for help and food. Prayers of remorse. Prayers for hopes and dreams," Tyme said thoughtfully, as if hearing each offering speak. "Different rituals yet the requests of the prayers are the same as those made in the Womb."

"Not many prayers of thanksgiving," Epoh said with his own dawning awareness.

"No," the Shaman shook his head sadly. "Not yet. For most who live here, life is very hard. But mayhaps those moons are changing."

"Let us all pray for that," Tyme agreed.

When finished, they came out of the kiva and Gybeko made tea. After they were served, he began to speak.

"Much of my life has been filled with silence," Gybeko told them. "That has been, and will always be, an important part of my life. During most ceremonies I drum more than I talk. Always drumming alone. I thought that was what a shaman did. It never occurred to me to encourage others to drum along."

"When Singer and his group arrived, I started drumming with Swindovo. So powerful," the shaman's face lit up. "The singing and music they make has become a part of me. Like nothing before. It has changed my life."

"I would like to hear it," Epoh said.

"Singer and Swindovo should be returning soon from playing at the Dusted Man," Gybeko said. "Usually, a small group comes with them. Then school stops and they all start singing and drumming. Draktono gives a short talk, and they end with more singing."

"I would like to hear them as well," Tyme said. "And see their school. But I prefer not to disturb or interrupt what they are doing."

"I will take you to the school now," Gybeko offered. "We can sneak in from a smaller side cave so you can sit and watch without being noticed."

Gybeko led them to a group of greenish caves below the kiva where the school was held. They followed him into a small cave that led to a low, dark passageway. The air was cool and refreshing. As they approached the main cave, Gybeko motioned for them to sit in a darkened corner. Before them, on the smooth, sculped wall of the cave, the letters of the alphabet were painted in red. Below, a sentence was written in large, bold letters with chalk.

Each time a man stands up for himself, he stands up for all men.

The rock floor of the cave was swept clean. A group of students were writing the sentence on the floor. The men were hunched over, intent with their work. Draktono and Frisato moved slowly from student to student, checking their progress to make sure they were copying the letters correctly.

Tyme watched as Ozono labored at his task. She thought about her own schooling, when she had been given her first gray tablet and chalk for writing. How excited she had been to learn to read and write. These men did not have desks, nor tablets, nor smooth, round sticks of chalk. They wrote on the stone floor with broken fragments of soft, green rock, scratching out letters.

As the men were finishing their lesson, Tyme and Epoh caught the faint sound of singing. The men stood up to view each other's work, then put their writing rocks into a pile by the alphabet wall. As the voices grew near, one could be heard above the others--a young man singing Praises with the most beautiful, rich, and evocative voice. When the new arrivals came into the cavern, everyone moved to another part of the cave to sit together.

Gybeko led Tyme and Epoh out from their darkened corner to introduce them.

"This is Tyme," the shaman introduced her first, in Ambri fashion. "She is the one who saved the Canaries' wagon with the clay shipment. She also cut the leg from under Otovo in Perich."

"In self-defense," Tyme demurred. "An unfortunate misunderstanding." She gestured the womb with her hands prayerfully together at her chest. The men all politely returned the greeting. "I commend you for your studies and am eager to hear your music," she said diplomatically.

"And this is her herald," the shaman continued with obvious approval. "The Burnished Man from the Endless Waste!" The men all greeted Epoh Barbarian style with a fist to their hearts.

"I am Tyme's husband as well," the Burnished Man returned the greeting. "You can call me Epoh."

"The Burnished Man," Draktono stepped forward with a look of keen interest. "Do you come to fulfill the prophecies?"

"Can one fulfill the prophecies without knowing them?" Epoh asked, thinking more about Tyme than himself. "We come to learn the sacred ways and insights of those before us."

"The Burnished Man comes out of the Endless Waste," Ozono informed Epoh with cautious assessment, "and returns to the Endless Waste."

Epoh was unsure how to respond.

"Have you seen Apocalypse?" Swindovo asked in awe.

"Yes, he has seen Apocalypse," Gybeko answered gruffly, cutting off further inquiry. "Let me introduce you all before you interrogate him further."

No sooner were the men named than they resumed bombarding Epoh with questions about the great desert. Tyme stood off to the side, happy to be temporarily forgotten. Singer also stood apart, listening while quietly humming to himself.

"That is enough questions," Gybeko broke in at last. "He came to see the school and hear everyone sing," he reminded them.

"Okay," Draktono smiled in agreement. "Swindovo, give us a beat for an easy sing-a-long."

The young man picked up a drum and began one of the snappy and popular Praises that he had transformed and rearranged. Epoh and Tyme quickly learned the repetitive stanza and joined in with the others. After a few lively songs, Swindovo set aside his drum and Singer led a Gloria that Epoh knew well enough to sing the bass accompaniment. The others were greatly impressed with Epoh's voice and singing ability. Tyme just listened, thrilled to hear a men's choir.

"Do some more," she encouraged when they finished.

"Do you know the Triumphant Hallelujah?" Singer asked Epoh.

"Yes," Epoh replied. "'Tis one of my favorites."

Tyme sat enraptured listening to their chorus. She was an okay singer but did not have Epoh's rhythm or musical ability. She preferred to let them perform together. After a number of songs, they took a break, as was their custom, to hear Draktono speak.

"Ambri law was written by women, for women," Draktono told his audience. "There is no doubt those laws were a tremendous step forward from the chaos of the Dark Ages. The foundation of Ambri society and culture was built upon those laws."

Draktono paused for a moment. "Does this mean those laws are perfect and without ever a need for improvement or further clarification and refinement? Were the laws written by Divine? Or were they inspired by women's views of Divine? Views that were held at that particular moment in herstory?"

Draktono paused again. "But what of *his*-story? What of men, and their place in the story? What of their contributions? What of their dreams and goals? Men are second class citizens, relegated to subservient roles."

The men in the audience listened ruefully.

"Subservient roles," Draktono repeated. "Does this mean 'tis wrong to serve?" he asked his audience, and then answered, "Of course not." He looked away from the men and gazed straight at Tyme. "Serving others is one of the highest ideals." He looked back at the men. "I have chosen to dedicate my life to that ideal. To serve the needs and aspirations of men. I have chosen this role freely of my own will. That is true service."

"However," Draktono continued, "forced servitude does not, cannot, meet those same lofty goals or ideals. Forced servitude is nothing more than a form of bondage disguised as

Divine law and intent. Forced servitude is not true service to others. Forced servitude is oppression. Oppression in the name of Divine, which is the most insidious and deceitful of all lies and injustice."

Draktono pointed to the sentence written with chalk below the letters of the alphabet. "That is our lesson for today. That is what we need to remember when we are faced with oppression and injustice." He read the words aloud. *"Each time a man stands up for himself, he stands up for all men.* May those words give us strength to carry on and not give up our struggle. Together, we are stronger. Together, we can change the world."

Draktono sat back down. Everyone was silent, contemplating his words.

Then Swindovo began drumming a crowd favorite Praise for help in life. They did a few more songs before stopping and gathering to chat in a circle on the cave floor.

"Your music and your message are very important," Epoh told the men. "There is a saloon and dance hall in Karvor called the Blue Moon where traditional musicians from the mountains of Tanis, and folk musicians from as far away as Vlice, are paid to perform. I believe your music would be of interest to Delgado, with Draktono speaking briefly as well. If you are interested, we can talk with him about having you perform some night in Karvor."

DRAW UP PLANS

Captain Targono of the Hammer Legion was in his office at the fort and barracks on remote Vrak Pass in the Vanttan Mountains. He was busy filing reports in preparation for his meeting with General Deed Dard at Vargo Garrison headquarters down at the base of the mountains. The General, who was supposed to be the commanding offiser of Vargo Garrison, spent most of her time between Ralston Garrison and the capitol, hobnobbing with politicians and the social elite. She was returning briefly for a decade review.

The General's lack of oversight, along with the fact that Captain Targono was stationed high and isolated in the mountains, gave the Captain unprecedented freedom from authority. The Hammer Legion guarded the valuable silver mines in the Vanttan Mountains. Captain Targono was in charge of dealing with rebels attacking the supply lines. His dramatic success at reducing rebel attacks allowed him even greater autonomy. He constantly patrolled the twisting supply routes through the fractured mountains to keep the rebels from threatening the silver shipments.

Which is what he detailed in his report. None of it was true.

Captain Targono was actually training a highly elite and mobile fighting group. A group that was bonded to him--and would obey his commands without hesitation. A small, loyal, and deadly army that would follow him anywhere. And a spy network to guide him.

A knock at the door and Sergeant Kakano of the engineers appeared. Captain Targono waved him in without a salute and gestured for him to take a seat by his desk. He put down his quill and set his papers aside and got out a special bottle of viruna.

"From the King of Sikes' own personal distillery," he reminded the Sergeant, pouring them each a swallow in a small metal cup. "To the Grall Canyon bridge!" he toasted.

It had been their hardest challenge yet. They had redesigned and re-forged all the couplings to make it work. Using small diameter lodge poles with metal caps that pinned together in triangles, they had quickly made a framework structure strong enough to drive a loaded wagon across a deep, narrow canyon.

"The bridges will be much faster to build with the new couplings," the Sergeant enthused. "Your idea worked perfectly. Where do we go next?"

"I am going to give the soldiers a rest for a few days here at the barracks," Captain Targono said. "But I have a secret task for you while I report to headquarters." He gave a wicked smile.

"Say the word," the Sergeant replied. He knew that grin. The Captain was quite pleased about something.

"I want you to scout out the locations and designs for a series of bridges on the old mining trail to Thessal," the Captain informed him. Kakano was his best engineer and well able to accomplish such an important task without Targono's help.

Sergeant Kakano gave a confident smile in return. What in the deepest hells was the Captain up to? Something momentous he had no doubt. Whatever 'twas, he knew he would follow the Captain faithfully. Exciting days appeared to be ahead.

"I want detailed drawings with the anchor placements and number of struts and pins required to make each bridge. Take Chapano to help you." He handed the sergeant a stiff weatherproof pouch with paper, quills, and ink to draw up the plans. "These will be exciting to build," he promised with a grin.

ANOTHER MAN

The day after Tyme and Epoh's wedding, Jyg saw Rona briefly on the street as she was on her way to work at the Plumed Bird.

"Did you like dancing with my friends?" she asked him.

"They were quite the dancers," Jyg face grew red. They had all swarmed around him as everyone paraded up the street from the Womb to the Blue Moon.

"What do you mean?" Rona laughed.

"They seemed rather forward." The whole group had danced very suggestively, rubbing and caressing him fondly.

"I told them to treat you nice," Rona smirked. "Did you like any of them?"

"What do you mean?" Jyg asked in confusion.

"You know what I mean," Rona chided. "Were you attracted to any of them?"

"No," Jyg protested. "I am attracted to you." He felt like he was being tested or falsely accused.

"Do not get all worked up," Rona said tersely as she continued down the street.

Jyg did not see Rona again for two days. They met at a pie shop near Skyline Street, close to where she worked. She explained she had been busy dancing.

"Did you get in a new chorus line?" Jyg asked.

"Yes," she answered distractedly.

"Which one?" He knew she was practicing for more than one show.

"What do you mean?" she said with a fluster.

He gave her a strange look. "I mean which of the shows. The name."

"Why? So, you can check up on me?" she grew angry. "You do not trust me?"

"No. Not at all," Jyg protested as the misunderstanding turned into a fight. Suddenly she was listing out deficiencies in his character.

"What is going on?" he asked with bewilderment. "Are you unhappy with me?"

"You are just not dependable," she accused him.

"Not dependable?" Jyg said with bafflement. "In what way have I been undependable?"

"I do not know if I can count on you," she complained as they got into another argument.

"Will you please explain what this is about?" Jyg pleaded.

Finally, the real issue began to surface.

"You said you were only going to be in Karvor a decade or two," Rona told him. "That you might run off with the Ser Cus, or train falcons for the King of Sikes."

"That was when I first got here," Jyg protested, "before I got to know you. That is not what I think now."

"I cannot trust you to stay," she repeated.

He struggled to convince her otherwise, but she seemed impervious to his cause.

At last, she admitted the truth. "There is another man," she said, and then, without prompting. "I have always loved him."

Jyg was so shocked he did not know what to say. "Why did you not tell me?" he stammered.

"I thought you would be here only a short while," she explained, "You said so yourself." But it still made no sense.

"And the other man? What does he think?"

"He was temporarily dazzled by another woman," Rona answered. "But she has married another."

The realization hit Jyg like a shock. "Delgado," he stated dully. "You are in love with Delgado."

She could not deny it. But she could not say it out loud.

"Does he know?" Jyg asked.

She shook her head and began to tear up. "Not really. We flirt, but I did not have the nerve to tell him the truth." She had always seemed so confident to Jyg. He was stunned by her vulnerability. "Just when I was ready to say something, Tyme came along, and Delgado was moon struck."

Jyg shook his head at the irony. "So, are you going to tell him now?"

"I want to," Rona began to tear up again. "But you and I had to break up first."

Jyg fought a sudden urge to stand up and walk right out the door. But he willed himself to sit and not say anything until his feelings of hurt and anger began to dissipate. Rona had never made any mention or promise of something longer. And frankly, he could see how she would be attracted to Delgado.

"I wish you both much happiness," Jyg said numbly. "I really do." He rose from the table. He knew he was going to start crying and preferred to be alone in some alley corner.

WHAT HAPPENED?

When Tyme and Epoh returned to Karvor, they told their friends all about their honeymoon, the kiva and school they visited, and the music they heard. Delgado was excited about having Singer and the men's chorus perform at the Blue Moon and hearing the upbeat songs that Swindovo had created. He was also curious to learn more of Draktono's ideas about rising up and challenging the discrimination against men.

"It will be a while before they can come," Epoh said. "They are committed to teaching and performing at the kiva the next few weeks."

Jyg waited a few days to let Tyme and Epoh bask in the glow of their honeymoon before he said anything about his break-up with Rona. But as full Moonday approached, he could no longer hide what had happened.

"Are you and Rona going dancing the next few nights?" Epoh asked. "Mayhaps we could go out with you."

"We had a parting of ways," Jyg answered glumly. He was still stunned over his misunderstanding of their relationship, which he had assumed was smoothly moving forward toward something long lasting. But he had only been a diversion from her real goal. He told them everything that had happened.

"You could take her dalliance with you as a compliment," Epoh said sympathetically. "She noticed and chose you, even if only for a little while. You, yourself, said that you felt she was way above your league when you first got together."

"Way above," Jyg nodded.

"Remember how much she built your confidence," Tyme

agreed. "Do not let your breakup now shatter that confidence. Whoever you meet next, you will be a better partner because of the things you learned from Rona."

"You were an uneducated Barbarian," Klew jested in agreement. "Now you are refined and cultured."

"I actually thought of that as well," Jyg conceded, "but it still hurts." His brow grew furled. "At the wedding she had her girlfriends grind up against me when we danced," Jyg sputtered. "Like I was just going to forget about Rona and go run off with one of them?" He felt an overwhelming sadness. "Did she not know I was more serious about her? That I was not going to run off with the first woman who made a pass at me!"

"Did you ever tell her that?" Tyme asked.

"I never said it," Jyg hung his head. "But I felt it. I thought she felt it too." He looked at Tyme and moaned. "The next woman I feel that way about, I will tell her and make sure she knows." He went into his room, closed the door, and lay down on the bed for a short and pitiful cry.

That evening he went up to the Blue Moon. The moon was nearly full, and everyone was in a party spirit. When Delgado noted that he seemed somber, Jyg told him the truth.

"Rona broke up with me."

"What happened?" Delgado asked in surprise. He waved for two small cups of viruna.

"She does not view me as dependable concerning how long I will be here in Karvor," Jyg shrugged his shoulders. "And I guess she is probably right. As much as I love Karvor, I am foremost with Tyme." He shook his head. "And I do not think Tyme will be here for long. If she goes to Ambrit, I am going too."

"But you looked like you were having so much fun together," Delgado protested. "Why can Rona not just enjoy being with you for these moons that you are here?"

Jyg made a mournful laugh. He was not sure if 'twas his place to say anything more. But he spoke regardless. "Her heart yearns for another."

Delgado looked incredulous. "She has met someone else?"

"She has known him for decades but never told him."

Delgado pondered this for a moment. "So now she has told him?"

"No," Jyg answered, "Not yet. She wanted us to be over and resolved first."

"Are you over and resolved?"

"I have accepted her choice," Jyg said with resignation. "He is worthy of her admiration."

"You know him?" Delgado gasped.

"Yes," Jyg patted his friend's arm. "He is a great guy."

Delgado's face reflected a sudden shocked realization. "Me?" he asked incredulously.

"You two would actually make a great couple," Jyg predicted.

"I swear," Delgado vowed, "I had no idea!" He ordered more viruna. When it arrived, Jyg insisted that they toast to Rona. They sat into the evening discussing the unfathomable mysteries of women and love.

When Jyg stumbled back to the apartment, he cried again for Rona. Then, to his surprise, he found himself crying for Zaru, the gyrfalcon he had been forced to sell so long ago, before finally falling asleep.

THE 20TH PRAYER
FOR THE DEAD

That same evening Tyme and Epoh sat out in the bright moonlight on the patio overlooking the city. Tyme talked about her training with Riin Ruel. The dagger work she was learning was growing physically closer.

"Almost intimate," she revealed. "I do not know how else to describe it. Very personal dagger work."

"How about your *Prayers for the Dead*?" Epoh asked. He had taken a break from reading and translating the *Kabaal Prophecies* to research some of Riin Ruel's other teachings and beliefs.

"Riin Ruel says I am learning quickly," Tyme answered proudly.

"How many *Prayers for the Dead* does Riin Ruel say there are?" Epoh asked curiously. The special prayers were recited by the loved ones and friends of the deceased, to help give them comfort during grief and loss. The prayers also helped release the spirit of the deceased from this world to find Divine.

"She says they are sacred and does not want me to talk about it," Tyme fidgeted uncomfortably.

"You cannot talk about it?" Epoh shook his head in consternation. He questioned why Riin Ruel was so secretive. "You cannot talk about it even though the priests commonly recite them at the Womb after people die? They are also called the *Prayers for the Mortal Body*. They probably recited them at my memorial service at Dayr Castle."

"Yes, they did. The prayers helped me to cry and release the hurt and emotion. Even though I never thought you were dead, you were gone just the same." Tyme took a slow breath. "Afterward, when I was wrung out, the prayers helped me come back to my senses, so I could clean up and leave."

Epoh hugged and gently swayed Tyme in his arms. Tears began to well up in his eyes.

"Are you crying?" Tyme sensed his vulnerable emotions.

"Probably," Epoh admitted with an ironic chuckle. It felt cathartic not having to hide his true feelings. King Eyrico had always forbidden Crown Prince Epohco to display such sentiments.

"The prayers helped me to see that grieving is a process," Tyme continued. "The priests repeat the prayers that you most need help with, and in whatever order is needed."

"So how many *Prayers for the Dead* are there?" Epoh resumed his questioning.

"Riin Ruel does not want me to talk about that at all," Tyme protested.

"Okay!" Epoh threw up his hands and tried a different approach. "That does not mean I cannot talk to you about it, does it?"

"What do you mean?"

"You are supposed to be learning about the *Prayers for the Dead*, right?" Epoh reasoned.

Tyme nodded.

"Let me tell you what I have found out," Epoh offered, "and that will give you another reference to increase your knowledge. You do not have to say anything to me about it."

"Okay," Tyme smiled, "I can do that!"

"Most scholars," Epoh began with authority, "believe there are more than the 19 *Prayers for the Mortal Body*." He opened his satchel and pulled out a small manuscript titled *The 20 Prayers For The Dead* by Ser Via Vee Vua.

"'Tis written by a highly regarded authority on the matter," he informed her, handing her the writings.

Tyme opened the cover to look at the prayer numbers and chapter titles with subtitles:

Prayers 1–3, *Behold! The Mortal Body*: Facing the Shock of Death

Prayers 4–7, *Embrace the Mortal Body*: Through the Denial of Death

Prayers 8–12, *Mourn the Mortal Body*: Releasing Lost Expectations

Prayers 13–15, *Wail for the Mortal Body*: Through the Depression of Death

Prayers 16--18, *Strike the Mortal Body*: Fighting the Anger of Death

Prayer 19, *Release the Mortal Body*: Affirming the Acceptance of Death

Prayer 20, *Flee the Mortal Body*

Tyme flipped to the back of the book to see the 20th prayer, which was written out in full, word for word. "Riin Ruel said this prayer should never be read or spoken aloud without special training!"

Epoh was unruffled. "Divine Council is said to secretly acknowledge that the 20th prayer is to direct souls toward the Gates of Heaven," Epoh surmised the technique. "When a body dies, a healthy spirit filled with love and compassion will naturally seek, and also be drawn and pulled, toward Divine. Weak and undeveloped souls that do not have a strong moral compass will sometimes hover, uncertain and confused, over the body after death. The 20th prayer is supposed to help lost souls."

"I am amazed the prayers are written out openly for sale," Tyme said in astonishment. "Riin Ruel says they are very sacred and should only be spoken by a priest when a person has died. They should never be read as a scholarly exercise. Especially the 20th prayer. She would be aghast that this has been written out for anyone to see."

"Well," Epoh conceded, "not just anyone can see it. 'Twas actually quite difficult for me to get. Even with my connections." He pulled a smaller treatise from his satchel.

"That is not all," he warned her. "A few scholars believe the *Prayers for the Dead* come in sets."

From the look on Tyme's face, Epoh could tell 'twas true.

He held up a small, tattered, and faded scroll. "A few mystics believe the next set of prayers is called the *Bridge*, which actually starts with the 20th prayer, and goes through the 21st and 22nd prayers."

"I do not think you should read those without proper instructions!" Tyme said with concern. She could not dismiss Riin Ruel's repeated warnings.

"Do not worry, the full prayers are not written out, or even the full titles," Epoh said. "'Tis all mysterious speculation, conjecture, and hidden meanings. Obviously, the prayers in the Bridge have many arcane layers and uses."

Tyme was speechless. She had only just memorized the Bridge herself, and was uncertain what to say, or believe. Riin Ruel had told her very few people were even aware of the 20th prayer, or the Bridge beyond. Only one Nunnery taught the higher prayers, and then to just a very small, select group of trained devotees. No one outside of Riin Ruel's cabal was supposed to even know anything about the higher prayers! Did Riin Ruel not know of such writings and conjecture? Or was she trying to keep Tyme from being influenced by outside sources?

STRIKE FIRST

Riin Ruel called everyone together for a meeting. Tyme had insisted her friends be given a general idea of the warrior mystic's plans.

"The Czarzina builds monuments to herself while the Ambrit Imperium rots with treachery, graft, and fraud," Riin Ruel stated sadly. "The Senate cannot agree on anything and seems powerless to effect change. And all the while here in Karvor you uncover growing plans of revolt and civil war."

"What do you propose we do?" Klew asked.

"We can sit here and watch the events unfold," Riin Ruel answered. She would never do that, of course. But she had to let the group come to their own conclusion.

"Just let the plots of civil war play out?" Klew asked.

"That is one option," the former Blade answered. "We allow other factions to struggle over removing the Czarzina. When they reveal their true nature and intent, we will know if we want to align ourselves with them."

"Do we have allies in the Senate?" Epoh asked. "That seems critical."

"We have a small but dedicated group of Senasers," Riin Ruel replied, "who would support the Bright One immediately. Others would need some proof. With the right actions we can bring many of the Senasers to our banner."

"What is the other option?" asked Tyme.

"Strike first," Riin Ruel said, as if 'twas the only choice that made sense.

"Who do we strike?" asked Jyg.

"The Czarzina herself," Riin Ruel answered in a steely voice. "She is the core problem. Her misrule has created the unrest. Her vengeance and crimes have contaminated and poisoned the Imperium. Better for one woman to die than to have a civil war."

"What makes you think if she dies there will not be a civil war?" Tyme asked. "You think the other plotters will just abandon their plans and give up?"

"If the Czarzina is replaced by the Bright One," Riin Ruel replied assuredly, "replaced by someone who commands the respect of the Senate and the Legions, the plotters will likely abandon their coup attempts--or will be foiled quickly if they do not."

"How am I going to command the respect of the Senate and Legion?" Tyme asked skeptically.

"By executing Divine Wrath and killing the Czarzina. As 'tis written in the *Kabaal Prophecies*." She spoke the words dramatically:

Her Gaze pierces all Souls
Her Sword a Fiery Truth
Morning Star of Heaven
Whose Dagger slays the Beast.

"After she has been executed you will go to the Senate to proclaim and justify your actions as the fulfillment of Divine Wrath," Riin Ruel promised. "You will reveal yourself as the fulfillment of prophecy."

"And they are all going to believe that?" Tyme said with incredulity. "That the Czarzina was possessed by the Beast, the devil himself?" She looked from Klew to Epoh for help.

"If the priests are behind you," Klew allowed with uncertainly, "many Senasers might welcome you if you came before them with a mandate to create a New Order."

"Unfortunately, not all of the priests will be with you," Riin Ruel admitted, "which means not all the Senasers either. But, if you are strong and do not falter, those who are against you can be held in check."

"They may profess to be with you publicly," Epoh warned. "Behind the scenes might be another matter."

"And the Legions?" Tyme was not convinced.

"The common soldiers will love you for your weapon skills," Riin Ruel predicted. "'Tis the offisers who will be dangerous to you," Klew noted in retort.

"You will have enemies," Riin Ruel agreed. "Especially at first, from those who will lose power and influence. It will not be easy."

Tyme could not imagine how such a plan might work. "How could I possibly get close enough to the Czarzina to kill her?" she asked.

"That is being planned as we speak," Riin Ruel replied cryptically. "I will tell you when I know more."

KILL THE CZARZINA?

Tyme agonized later with Epoh as they discussed everything again. "Riin Ruel believes my destiny is to kill the Czarzina and become Empress of a new Holy Ambri Empire," she lamented. "Is that truly to be my path?"

Epoh tried not to let his own fears and desires influence his support of Tyme. But that was very difficult, given his understanding of the reality and intrigue of Ambrit court politics. "Riin Ruel sees you only as a Warrior Empress," he replied. "How do you see yourself?"

"I know how to fight," Tyme replied. "But I know nothing of war or politics. I do not know if I have the talents, or desire, to embrace such a role."

"What role should you play?" Epoh asked.

"I do not want to kill anybody," Tyme said simply. "I do not like using murder or assassination as a political strategy. That is not the kind of Empress I want to be."

She talked about Rocozo, the gang leader, and his unwavering quest to kill her. Of Otovo, from the kiva on the road to Biirj, who also hated her and had tried to kill her. Of Snoop, who had used a slingshot to protect her, killed an assassin, and was now plagued with nightmares from that event. And of Noot, who was killed randomly because of political intrigue, along with all the people who would be caught up in an armed revolution of Empire building. The weight of it felt enormous.

"Do I have any choice in my role?" Tyme asked. "Or is everything foreordained by Divine as Riin Ruel claims?"

"What choice would you make?" Epoh asked in

commiseration. "What do you think you should do?"

"I have no idea," Tyme said with a shake of her head. "But I cannot just walk away from Riin Ruel. At least not yet. She says my training is not complete, and until then, I do not understand everything."

Epoh nodded his head solemnly in consent. Regardless of their disagreements with Riin Ruel over vital issues, he believed destiny had brought them all together. He could not ignore all the signs, dreams, and prophecies. He felt they had no other choice at present, but to follow the spiritual warrior and have Tyme finish out her instructions.

"But that does not mean I have to do everything she says at the end," Tyme vowed. "At the end, I make my own decisions."

THE GLORIOUS LADDER TO DIVINE!

Tyme told Riin Ruel about Epoh's offer to help inform her of important scholarly research and give her more references to increase her knowledge. "He has a book titled *The 20 Prayers for the Dead.*"

Riin Ruel did not look pleased. "You must not read or listen to those who would corrupt the true teachings. This is precisely how falsehoods are spread."

"Epoh said Divine Council has acknowledged the accuracy of the book for priests and scholars," Tyme retorted. "But they do not endorse it for the laity, which he and I both question. If 'tis true, why can it not be shared?"

"Some things are too powerful to be shared," Riin Ruel snapped back in frustration. "Would you give a child a crossbow?"

"'Tis not the same," Tyme argued. "He also has an ancient scroll on the Bridge, with parts of the 20th, 21st and 22nd *Prayers for the Dead.*" Tyme had just finished learning them herself.

"Those writings are tainted, filled with errors and wild speculation. You must keep your mind and prayers pure." When Tyme started to protest, Riin Ruel cut her off. "I refuse to hear anymore of such nonsense," she said adamantly.

Riin Ruel insisted that they do silent, centering prayers for an hour, and then had Tyme chant and recite the Bridge three times to make sure she said every word correctly with the exact intonations.

The 20th Prayer - *Flee Your Mortal Body*

The 21st Prayer - *The Path of Clouds*

The 22nd Prayer - *The Gates of Heaven*

Only then did Riin Ruel feel they were ready to move on.

"The next set of prayers," the warrior mystic announced triumphantly, "describes a series of prophetic visions." Again, she reminded Tyme that what she was learning was sacred, arcane teachings that could only be revealed carefully under expert supervision.

"First, you will chant the title of each prayer. Only when I believe you have sufficient respect and understanding for each title, will you begin to learn the words for the prayer."

"I am ready," Tyme said with resolve.

"Then sit and contemplate the resplendent name of the 23rd *Prayer for the Dead: Appear! The Glorious Ladder to Divine!*"

LEAVING KARVOR

A few days later Riin Ruel came to the apartment before the heat. "I have just received word from Ambrit," she announced to them all. "Czarzina Hana Hama Hala is going to be unveiling a new statue of herself in the Avenue of Rulers. A large celebration is planned, with a special banquet that evening in the Empress Auditorium." She gave Tyme a steely look. "That is when you will strike."

"How soon is the event?" Klew asked.

"One month away," Riin Ruel answered. "We should leave Karvor as soon as possible to insure an adequate period for preparation in the capitol. We will travel slowly, only the distance a wagon goes each day, so Tyme may continue her daily studies and training. 'Tis important that she arrives well rested. We must leave tomorrow, on dark Moonday."

Although they had known they would have to leave for Ambrit at some point, now that an actual day was set, and so soon, an ominous feeling filled the apartment.

"I need to get Panr's pigeons back to her dovecot before we leave Karvor," Jyg said with a sudden realization. They were still uncertain who actually owned the new dovecot and was sending the messages they had been intercepting.

"That is no longer a priority for us," Riin Ruel shook her head dismissively. "The only important task now is to eliminate the Czarzina and put Tyme on the throne as Empress of a New Empire. Everything else is secondary. We must not take a chance on something going wrong that could in any way endanger our main goal."

"I promised Panr I would return her birds," Jyg said

adamantly. "I am not going to break that vow."

"Then you are on your own to do whatever you feel necessary," Riin Ruel countered. "The rest of us leave tomorrow."

"Mayhaps I will stay briefly as well," Klew said. "If Jyg can come up with a plan, I will help him. We can catch up with you in the Hollow Hills."

Riin Ruel gave Klew a critical look. "You would risk everything for some pigeons?"

"I risk nothing in helping Jyg," Klew countered. "I do not seem to have any role in your plans anyway, other than following along behind with no request from you for input, nor any opportunity to give either help or council."

"Do what you think you must," Riin Ruel huffed. "We leave at dawn." She looked at Tyme and then Epoh. When they said nothing to challenge or question her, she turned and went out the door.

"I feel my life is out of my control," Tyme said.

"You are certainly being pulled by large events," Epoh agreed.

"And Riin Ruel is pushing me from behind."

"Going to Ambrit does not mean you have to do everything she says once we get there," Epoh reminded Tyme of her own words earlier. "The events may be out of your control, but the way you respond can still be up to you. You make the final decisions, not her."

Tyme nodded resolutely.

"I need to get to the Trusted Scribe before it closes," Epoh remembered. "Hopefully some manuscripts I have been waiting for have arrived."

Tyme lifted her dark eyebrows. "I will walk with you to the Womb to pray and light a few candles."

"Good idea. I can meet you there when I am done."

After the heat, they went up to the Blue Moon for one last time. Delgado could tell by their faces that something was different. When he learned that Tyme and Epoh were leaving the next day, he tried to make light-hearted banter about the excitement of them seeing the capitol city for the first time. But the look in his eyes showed his concern. Delgado feared the power of the Czarzina, as well as all the other forces Tyme was going against.

Jyg was glad that Rona was working that evening at the Plumed Bird. 'Twas less awkward saying goodbye to Delgado. Jyg's challenge of getting Panr's birds back from Jakiko offered a diversion from weightier matters.

"If I take the pigeons," Jyg said with concern, "what is to keep Jakiko from going straight to Panr's and stealing them back again?"

"You need to make him think someone else stole the birds," said Delgado.

Jyg smiled mischievously. "You just gave me a great idea." He patted his friend enthusiastically on the back. "A very good idea. But we can talk of it tomorrow. Tonight, let's have fun and celebrate our friendship."

The group tried to stay cheerful and enjoy the music and conversation, but the evening reminded Epoh of his last night with the grubbers before he left Jchow Oasis. There was an underlying somberness, as though they would never be back. As if they might never see each other again.

Especially for Tyme. Even if everything should work out as Riin Ruel planned, what was the chance that an Empress would come to Karvor? That an Empress would visit the scandalous Blue Moon in Old Town?

The following morning Riin Ruel led Tyme and Epoh out of Karvor. They did not go down the Jintiga Canyon on the Royal Highway toward Pintone, but headed southwest over the mountains on the faster Ambri Scout trail to cross the dry Iridi River and follow the southern cenote route across the Hollow Hills to reach Ambrit.

ATTACK OF THE LIZARDS

After Jyg and Klew said goodbye to Tyme, Epoh and Riin Ruel, they headed back up the hill toward Old Town. When they met Delgado at the Blue Moon, Jyg explained his plan.

"We are going to make Jakiko think monitor lizards ate the birds!" Jyg chuckled. "Make it look like he forgot to secure the night shutter and the lizards got inside. That way no one will come looking for the pigeons."

"And Jakiko will get into huge trouble for letting it happen," Delgado pointed out with glee. "How can I help?"

"I need a staging area just up the hill from the dovecote," Jyg answered "A small roof where we can set up some ropes." Jyg smiled. "And three or four good lookouts. We will do it tonight."

Jyg and Klew headed for the market to buy a pushcart, which they stacked with crates of pigeons, along with bundles of sticks to make larger cages for the lizards. Jyg also bought long broom handles, metal eyelets, and plenty of twine. At the apartment, he fixed the long poles with eyelets on the end, where he fashioned loops of twine like a lasso, which could be pulled tight into a noose around the lizard's legs.

Then they headed to an alley in Old Town where Jyg remembered seeing a nest of large Speckled monitor lizards in an abandoned, crumbling, and roofless building among some giant agave cactus. The big lizards hissed loudly when Jyg and Klew drew near. One was nearly four feet long.

"Let's start with her first," he said. "If we loop her head or tail, she will slip right out. I will get her by a front leg. Then you try to lasso her back leg." He showed Klew how to hold the pole, and how to pull the noose tight once 'twas around the lizard's leg.

"Have you done this much?" Klew asked in amazement.

"I used to catch lizards all the time," Jyg answered. "When Whi did not have money for food, we would sometimes eat lizards for weeks, rather that eating pigeons or chicken that we could sell. The smaller lizards taste better. The big ones are tough and chewy."

Jyg moved toward the biggest lizard, which turned toward him and hissed defiantly. She lifted her head up off the ground in anger, allowing him to slide one end of the stick and loop of twine close along the ground. As the lizard started to move away, she lifted her foot to take a step. Jyg flicked and twisted the pole to deftly lasso her leg, then yanked the cord to tightly cinch the noose around her front ankle. Immediately the big lizard began thrashing wildly, jerking the pole along with Jyg's arms. He had to brace his legs to keep from being pulled forward.

"Try to get her back leg," Jyg cried as Klew brandished his own noose and pole. The lizard twisted and writhed frantically, clawing and scratching. After a few tries Klew got his noose around part of the lizard's kicking leg, but as he pulled the noose tight, the lizard yanked its leg free. Klew pulled his pole back to reopen and adjust the loop for another try.

Despite the writhing and moaning of the big lizard, the other lizards did not run away from the danger, but merely moved off a few feet and continued hissing. One of them climbed over the others, leaving her foot and claws poking into the other's face, with no reaction from the one below.

Klew tried again to loop the twine around the rear leg of the lizard. He missed as the lizard suddenly sprung forward to attack Jyg, who struggled to maintain his balance as he went from pulling the lizard to pushing it away to keep it from biting him. Monitor lizard bites often became infected.

"Good grief!" Klew exclaimed. "Let me hold the front pole while you lasso the back leg."

On the first try Jyg deftly flipped the lasso over her foot and pulled it tight, then they stretched her out lengthwise. Jyg grabbed the tail to control the thrashing reptile more easily, dropped it into the tight cage, flipped the lid closed, and tied it shut.

"After you catch a bunch of lizards you get the hang of how they move," Jyg consoled Klew.

Once they had three large reptiles, Jyg said a prayer and began breaking the necks of pigeons and feeding them to the lizards. He baited the lizards to bite at the dead birds then pulled back so the lizards would just get a mouthful of feathers, which they chewed until they realized there was no meat, then they let the feathers drop from their mouths as they hissed and tried for another bite. After the bird was plucked clean, Jyg let the lizards eat it, while he collected the crunched and slimy, saliva covered remains.

"With the feathers all chewed, Jakiko will never be able to tell that they came from a slightly different breed and plumage than Pio's birds. I will spread the feathers all around the inside of his dovecote so it will look like all the birds were eaten."

He fed the lizards until they were so fat, they would not take another bite, even when he tried to push the meat into their mouths. They resumed full time hissing. Jyg squeezed the stomach of the largest lizard until it threw up, which he collected in an offal pouch. Then he fed it till 'twas full again.

They loaded the cages onto their cart and covered them with a tarp. The lizards continued to hiss as they were pushed through back-alley ways to the dilapidated shed Delgado had found for a staging area near Jakiko's dovecote.

"I was hoping once they ate, and were covered and dark, they would quiet down," Jyg said with a frown. "'Tis going to be harder staying undetected with them making such a racket."

That evening as it grew dark, Snoop, Kreoko, and two other member of the Jawbone Ridge gang stood lookout while Jyg and Klew climbed onto the roof of the shack next to the dovecote. Klew braced himself against the wall for Jyg to climb onto his shoulders to reach the first line of trim stones and tiles circling around the slanted, conical building. Jyg carried a small backpack with two strong, thin cords of agave twine tied to a belt around his waist. He carefully worked his hands and feet to climb and balance his way up the barely protruding stones and tiles.

After the first row of designs, he had to smear his feet in little dents and depressions to work across another smooth area before reaching the higher trim stones and finally the top row of tiles and decorative stones. He cautiously balanced, reaching up to grasp one of the wooden struts under the round top cap.

Jyg used a knife blade to slide open the shutter lock. He pulled up the first of the empty cages he would use to load up Panr's birds and hung it on the inside of the window. Once all the cages were in place, he pulled up a sack of saliva-stained feathers and dropped it inside, along with the rope ladder from his backpack. He climbed through and lowered down the cages, then descended the ladder in the darkness. After lighting a candle, Jyg began collecting all the pigeons from each of the pens, which he put into marked cages. Finally, he opened the bag of chomped feathers and carefully spread them about.

When everything looked to his satisfaction, he climbed the ladder and hoisted the cages up to the shutter. Then he lowered the cages of birds, one by one, down to Klew on a taught line pulled away from the dovecote to keep them from banging against the side of the building and scraping off any trim stones. Klew loaded the cages onto a cart for two other gang members to take away to safety.

Meanwhile, Spook grabbed the ends of the agave twine dangling down, which was stuffed in two small sacks, and played the cord out of the sacks as he climbed up the hillside shacks and roof tops to reach the higher staging area, above the dovecote. He pulled the lines tight. Stacked nearby, the lizards had finally quieted and fallen asleep in their covered cages.

Klew hiked up the alley and stairs to reach the back of the building, then climbed up to the rooftop staging area with the lizards. He double-checked the cord and the knots Snoop had tied, and hooked one of the lizard cages to the line. The lizard woke with the movement of the cage and began to hiss. Klew tugged the second line, which tightened in response, as Jyg pulled the loudly hissing lizard toward the dovecote window.

The hissing seemed to resonate up and down the ally as the cage was momentarily whisked across the skyline. Jyg hung under the cap of the dovecote, holding the cage to the window while he opened and released the thrashing lizard to tumble into the dovecote. Klew pulled the empty cage back and put a new cage and lizard on the line. Not all the reptiles wanted to come out of the cage; a few Jyg had to poke and prod repeatedly. Finally, with all of the lizards inside, Jyg put his rolled-up rope ladder and gear into the last crate for Klew to pull back. Then he untied the main rope line and gave it a toss, for Klew to pull in.

Jyg left the shutter hanging open. He took out the offal pouch and spread a pathway of puke, slobber and saliva down the outside of dovecote as he descended. Near the bottom, Klew had pushed a barrel and a rotten fence against the dovecote to make a ramp where the big lizards could have bypassed the overhanging base of the building to access the slanted but climbable upper slopes to the top. Jyg smeared a path of slimy lizard spit across everything.

A night gecko screeched. The warning sign! Jyg hurried to cover the final area convincingly. Moments later he heard voices coming down the alley. Boisterous men, hushing and cursing each other. Jyg stuffed the offal pouch into his pants and flattened himself against a dark wall away from the dovecote in an effort to remain unseen.

Just as the men came around the corner an urgent voice called out. "City guards! City guards!" 'Twas Bones, saving him again.

The men all spun and darted back up around the corner. Jyg headed down the alley in the opposite direction. He planned to circle around just to be safe, and then rejoin Klew, Kreoko, and the others at their rendezvous point.

Jyg turned the corner and ran straight into three city guards who were coming to investigate who had cried in alarm. "Was that you who called out?" the sergeant asked. The two large men with her both carried long spears. 'Twas too late for Jyg to run. He did not want to risk a spear in his back.

"A group of men were trying to rob me," Jyg answered breathlessly.

"Where are they?"

"They went around the corner," Jyg answered and pointed truthfully up the alley where one of the guards was already looking, shaking his head. "No one here now," he reported.

"Your voice does not sound like the voice we heard yell," the sergeant said suspiciously. "I think you had better come with us."

The guard next to Jyg put his big, meaty hand on Jyg's shoulder. "Do not try anything," he advised gruffly. "Or you are going to get hurt." The sergeant led them up and down stairs and passages, canvasing the area, looking for windows or doorways that might have been forced open. She did not even look at the dovecote.

But the sergeant was still not satisfied. "Where do you live?" she asked.

Jyg's mind raced. What should he say? He was not going to reveal that he had been living in the apartment above the Glazed Woman. Nor admit to any connection to the Jawbone Ridge gang. And above all, he could not risk being linked to the calamity at Jakiko's dovecote. He knew his accent would give him away as not being from Karvor.

"I am from the mountains of Birjj," he told the sergeant.

"Are you a runaway from the farms?"

"I do not know anything about farming," Jyg said. "I apprenticed at a stable." He knew enough about horses to pass as a stable hand. "I came to Old Town looking for work."

"What kind of stable work do you look for at night?" the sergeant asked.

"I was looking for a place to sleep," Jyg said contritely.

"I know where you can sleep," the sergeant replied. "In jail. That is where you are going. Mayhaps then we can get this straightened out." The two guards grabbed firmer hold of Jyg, one on each arm, and marched him down the alley.

POETIC OR POSSIBLE?

Riin Ruel led Tyme and Epoh southwest out of Karvor through the Tanis Mountains on the Ambri Scout Trail, which also led past the Alkali Hills to Tepu. As they dropped into the lowland mountains, they left behind the variety of agaves, aloes, and fleshy cactus found in shaded areas in the higher mountains, and began to see patches of fire cactus, with their shiny cloaks of thin, shimmering spines woven and spun so densely the cactus were able to survive the burning afternoon sun.

Tyme did her studies with Riin Ruel a few hours each day while they rode and sometimes walked by themselves. Then Riin Ruel spaced herself ahead or behind to allow the newlyweds privacy.

"I am sorry that we are not going to Ambrit as a true honeymoon," Epoh admitted to Tyme soon after they started out on the second morning. "Without the weight of prophecies and expectations hanging over us." He smiled wistfully. "I would have liked to travel the world with you simply for the joy of learning and seeing new places."

"Yes," Tyme agreed with a sigh. "That would have been delightful."

The coming sunrise filled most of the sky with streaks of red and yellow. Layers of dust in various hues of orange and purple hung across the lowlands below them. The morning breeze out of the mountains was already hot on their backs.

"As to our true purpose," Tyme continued after a moment, "unless we have some new insight or circumstance to discuss, let us leave those worries, and focus instead on enjoying each moment we have together. Here and now."

Epoh nodded his head. "Thanks for bringing me back."

They enjoyed talking and reminiscing about Dayr Castle, the stables, and about their first meeting. Epoh recalled with a smile how he had been smitten by her. "I knew from the start that you were going to be important in my life."

"You seemed so gallant and true," Tyme remembered, "and so serious!" she laughed. "You always had some new thought or insight from a book."

"And you," he said with pride, "some new talent or amazing ability."

"We were clearly meant for each other," Tyme's golden-green eyes sparkled with delight.

"I thank Divine for every day with you."

"As do I." They leaned out from their mounts to give each other a hug.

On the third day they came to the caravansary built along the Royal Highway from Pintone to Tepu, which ran beside and above the dry bed of the Iridi River. Stables built of stone block against a limestone cliff provided shade for horses and animals. A crank well and a conveyor of buckets were supposed to supply water to a stone trough, but 'twas broken.

"The Czarzina collects exorbitant taxes to guard and maintain the Royal Highways," Riin Ruel observed. "Yet nothing ever gets repaired." She tied her own water skin onto a long cord, and they took turns lifting it out, hand over hand, which required considerable effort, due to the depth of the well. After they watered, fed, and rubbed down the horses, they set up camp in one of the traveler's caves.

A group from Vlice arrived with five lumber wagons and set up camp at a far cave. While this group tried to get water for all their horses, a large and heavy wagon pulled by six horses arrived heading toward Tepu. The two groups were soon arguing over access to the well. The new arrivals had driven their horses hard and were anxious to get them watered. They thought the group from Vlice inefficient and too slow in using the well.

"Such arguments can sometimes turn deadly," Riin Ruel said as she monitored the situation from a distance. One man was pushing and shoving against another's chest. "When the government is broken, the dysfunction spreads throughout society." She turned toward Tyme and Epoh. "We need a new hope to guide us in a better direction."

Later that evening Epoh took Tyme aside. "Before we left Karvor I went down to the Trusted Scribe to see if Ser Hain Haan Hana had been able to locate a very rare manuscript."

"Is that what you have been reading when I am with Riin Ruel?"

"Yes. I wanted to wait until I had a chance to study it before I said anything."

"So, I need to put my mantle on, is that it?" Tyme joked.

Epoh nodded. "'Tis about more *Prayers for the Dead*," he said. "The *Glories* they are called."

"With the prayers written out?" Tyme blurted in surprise, unwittingly confirming their existence to Epoh. She, of course, knew the full title was *The Glories of Divine on Her Throne*.

"Not the full prayers. Only a few snippets are revealed. The book is a compendium of speculation and writings on the subject from a variety of resources. Very interesting. The writing is quite poetic."

"For example?" Tyme asked.

"The *Glories* start with the 23rd *Prayer for the Dead*," Epoh answered. "Here is a sentence from the chant of that prayer." He picked up the book and read:

Behold! Now appear a multitude of ladders, and upon their rungs the Angels of Light ascend into the Heavens."

Epoh looked at Tyme expectantly.

"That is very poetic," she agreed without further comment.

"Poetic?" Epoh asked. "Or possible?" he asked pointedly.

"Does it seem possible to you?" Tyme questioned, unwilling to answer directly, and overwhelmed and amazed by the magnitude of it herself.

"With Divine all things are possible," Epoh answered assuredly.

OLD TOWN JAIL

Jyg could not believe his bad luck as he was marched in the darkness of night to the Old Town jail escorted by three city guards. Bones had called out *city guards* to scare away some ruffians and keep him from being discovered at the dovecote, only to have real soldiers come running to arrest him moments later for suspicious behavior.

Jyg had used a Ser Cus powder to color and disguise his red hair, which made his hair look dirty and unkept. The pouch of offal he had stuffed and hidden in his pants was not closed tight and leaking down his leg. The smell grew stronger as he strode along.

"He stinks," one of the guards complained.

The jail was an imposing structure of black stone. Torches in scones lined the walls yet everything seemed dark and foreboding.

"Hold him for a day or two," the sergeant informed the jail clerk. "He was behaving suspiciously up behind Ella Lela's leather shop. I want to make sure no one from that area has any complaints about things being stolen, or any other problems, before a judge sees him."

"What is your name?" the clerk asked.

"Fagedo," Jyg answered, giving the name of the Manser of Medicines at Dayr Castle who had intimidated Tyme when she was younger.

The clerk eyed him critically. "There will be a bucket of water in your cell. I would suggest that you use it to clean yourself up." She tried not to be prejudiced but she was disgusted by how some men lived and took care of themselves. How they needed to be told and reminded of the most basic grooming skills. "It will go harder on you if you come before the judge looking and smelling like you do now."

The clerk waved to the jail guard. "Put him in the west jail, by himself and away from the others." Two guards escorted Jyg down a stone hallway of locked doors made of thick wood, iron-banded with a small, barred window. They went through an unlocked door out the back of the building to an alleyway facing an older, smaller building. Inside was a guard cubicle and five cells. The lead guard took a set of keys from a peg on the wall and opened the door to the first cell. He motioned Jyg inside the room of rough-cut stone. The other guard brought a bucket of water and gave it to Jyg with a small sliver of soap and a rag for washing up. They locked the door, took the only torch, and left Jyg in the darkness.

THE HOLLOW HILLS

After leaving the dry Iridi River, Riin Ruel, Tyme, and Epoh traveled south into the Hollow Hills where fire cacti grew in such large clusters it blanketed the ground and made walking off the trail difficult. Occasional scattered groupings of sun palms were the only trees. When the colors of the sunrise faded, the sky turned white and grew in a dazzling brightness. By mid-morning they wore hats and visors to protect their eyes. By afternoon, sun shields and blinders were needed when walking toward the blinding light. The terrain was mostly gentle rolling mounds and small rises interspersed with little rocky knolls, which gave repetitive views of endless cactus and rolling hills.

At last, they dropped into a small draw with caves and a cleft in the grey limestone rock where the Ambri had carved out narrow stairs to an underground cenote. After unsaddling the horses, they went for water. The stairs curved down a narrow slot into a tunnel where Riin Ruel stopped to let their eyes gradually adjust to the darkness. The air was damp and humid.

"It smells like the Womb of the Earth," Epoh said solemnly. "Thick and strong of wet stone, minerals, and dirt."

They could see a dim light around a corner, which led them into a huge cavern. A narrow shaft of light streamed in through a hole near the center of the roof, illuminating the large pool of water filling the bottom of the cave. Huge globs of dry flowstone hung from the roof and walls, like layers of candle wax.

"The Hollow Hills have many cenotes like this," Riin Ruel said. "We will camp next to one every night from here to Ambrit."

As they descended the steep steps, they could better see the beautiful turquois color of the water in the shaft of sunlight. Along one edge they could view the bottom with small stones shimmering and dancing to movements in the crystal-clear pool.

"The water came from rains high in the Barrier Mountains, which has flowed down through cracks and channels in the rock to fill these cenotes," Epoh told them. "Just like the water on the eastern side of the mountains flows underground into the Maze, and even out to Jchow Oasis."

IN PRISON

Jyg stood morosely in the darkness of prison, his mind racing. He was being held pending any complaints or alarms in the neighborhood where he had retrieved Panr's pigeons from Jakiko's dovecote and left a scene of destruction. He could not imagine Jakiko figuring out what had really happened, or going to the guards with any complaint, which would only draw attention to his own secret and illegal activities.

Yet, even if there was no complaint against him, Jyg still had to go before a vagrancy judge, with the possibility of being sent to the farms.

He thought of Riin Ruel's warning against doing anything that could endanger the larger goal of Tyme becoming the Bright One. He had been so sure he could rectify Panr's situation without any problems. He had given his word to her. But now look what had happened.

When his eyes adjusted to the darkness, he saw there was a window at the back of his cell. The starry, moonless sky was faintly growing light with the new day. He hoped that Bones had followed behind the guards when they brought him to the prison.

"Kaah. Kaah," Jyg stood at the window and made the call a raven parent uses to announce food for the chicks. Jyg waited a short time and repeated the call. The night air was still, and the sound carried a long distance. Jyg called again.

A few moments later he heard whooshing wings and Bones appeared outside the window.

"Bones!" Jyg whispered in relief.

The big raven stretched her body and pulled in her wings to squeeze between the bars, then opened her wings and dropped to Jyg's shoulder.

"Sshh! Quiet!" Bones confirmed in a low, conspiratorial tone, her shoulders hunched and her head ducked.

"You have to help me get out of here," Jyg implored.

"Saved by the bird!" Bones bragged, mimicking Zandero's amazed voice when he learned how Bones had helped Jyg escape the guards at the Mayor of Karvor's compound.

"There may be a chance you can save me again," Jyg agreed. "But we have to wait for more light."

Jyg sat cross-legged in his cell while Bones gently chewed on his fingers with her big, thick bill. He stroked the bird's back and neck.

"There were some keys hanging on a peg that the guard used to open my cell door," Jyg told the bird. "If the guard put the keys back on the peg, you could get them for me so I could open the door."

"Saved by the bird!" Bones boasted again, followed by an admonishing, "Sshh! Quiet!" Despite all his fear and anxiety, Jyg found himself chuckling.

Once he could see, he picked up a few pebbles of rock off the floor of his cell. He went to the door and looked into the empty guard cubicle. To his relief he could see the keys hanging on the peg on the far wall. He called to Bones, who hopped over. Jyg picked the raven up and gently pushed her through the window bars into the room.

"Craawk!" Bones made a disgruntled squawk of annoyance, opened her wings and dropped down to the floor.

"Grawk! Jyg made the chuckling call used for playing the follow the leader game when trailing people. But instead of pointing to someone for Bones to follow, he pointed to the keys on the wall.

Bones looked around for something to follow, but nothing moved. Jyg tried again, calling and pointing.

"That was a hint to let you know that what I want is over

there," Jyg explained to the raven and pointed to the keys. He reached into his pocket and pulled out a little stone. "I do not want this stone," he shook his head. "I am throwing it to show you what I want." Jyg took aim and threw the stone. It hit the wall not far from the keys.

Just as Jyg expected, Bone immediately hopped over and picked up the stone in her bill. She flew up to the window to give the stone to Jyg.

"Craawk!" Jyg gave the squawk of disproval and refused to take the stone or show any interest. Bones dropped back to the floor with the stone still in her mouth.

Jyg aimed carefully and threw another stone, which hit the same distance from the keys but on the other side. Bones dropped the first stone and hopped over to retrieve the second. But again, Jyg squawked with agitation when Bones brought it to him, and he refused to take it or even look at it. They repeated this process until Jyg had just one stone left.

"Grawk," Jyg called and pointed at the keys like the follow the leader game. Then he threw his final stone. The rock sailed through the air in a perfect arc and hit one of the keys with a resounding plink. Bones hopped over to the rock, picked it up in her bill and threw it into the air. The rock landed with little noise on the stone floor. Bones leapt over and threw it again.

Jyg pointed to the keys with a pleading "Grawk."

Bones spread her wings and flew up to land awkwardly against the wall on the short peg holding the keys. She dropped her head and gave the keys a sharp peck. The keys tinkled against each other. Bones gave the key ring a shake. The keys jangled louder. Bones seized the key ring more firmly in her bill and lifted it off the peg to hold it proudly in her bill. She lost her balance on the short wall peg and dropped with her wings open to the ground. The big raven hopped across to the cell door shaking her head and jingling the keys.

"Good girl, Bones," Jyg praised the bird with a "Brronk!" A deep, echo-y, happy hello or yes.

Bones pranced in circles before the cell door with the ring

of keys a few times and then flew up to Jyg's outstretched hands. He gently took the keys from her bill.

"At your service," Bones said in Klew's voice.

Jyg smiled at the raven in amazement and then carefully examined the keys. Each had numbered gash marks. Jyg found the key with just one gash, held it carefully, and reached down to put it in the lock. He tried to turn it but nothing happened. He wiggled the key around and tried again. Nothing. He pulled the key out and put it back in. The key still did not work. More wiggling.

Click. The lock opened at last!

Jyg said a prayer of thanks as he slid the bolt aside and came out the door. He relocked the cell door and put the ring of keys back on the wall. He went to the front door and nervously tried to open it. It was unlocked, as it had been earlier. Jyg breathed a sigh of relief. He went to the window to peek out through the shutters. Some guards were unloading a wagon.

"Sshh! Quiet!" Bones hushed, imitating Jyg's voice.

Jyg could see the inner courtyard of the jail and the wagon gate exit with two more guards. There was no place to sneak about or climb the wall without being seen. He could not think of any way out.

He watched the men finish unloading the wagon, then begin loading a few things back in the wagon. They packed the boxes and bags tightly, and Jyg saw no place for hiding. When the wagon was nearly loaded there was a shout, and a cook came out of the kitchens rolling an empty nutapple barrel. There was just enough room to stand the barrel up in the back corner of the wagon.

"Kaah. Kaah," Jyg whispered and touched his shoulder. Bones took a couple of hops and flew up to land on his shoulder where he tapped.

"Sshh! Quiet!" Bones spoke softly in his ear.

"Sshh," he agreed. "You fly away quiet when we go out the door." He opened it a crack to look out, hoping to sneak to the wagon and climb into the barrel. The men finished loading the wagon and disappeared from view. But the guards at the prison gate were looking straight at the wagon as they talked. Jyg mentally willed them to turn around, but they just kept standing, talking, and staring his way. Talking and staring. Jyg was panicked. This might be his only chance to slip into the barrel and escape!

Too late. The two men with the wagon returned. They stood by the wagon and joked with the guards at the prison gate, having a good laugh. Someone else yelled and the two men got into the wagon. The driver started off while the passenger looked back over his shoulder toward Jyg, and yelled a joking comment to someone Jyg could not see.

The guards at the prison gate kept talking and watching the wagon as it crossed the prison courtyard. The passenger kept looking back over the wagon toward his friend. Jyg was frantic to be losing his only chance of escape.

Then the wagon passenger turned to face forward, and the guards turned toward the gate to open it. Jyg did not hesitate. He slipped out the door and ran toward the back of the wagon as fast as he could, while Bones flew up to perch on a roof edge and watch the action. Jyg carefully climbed up into the back of the wagon and instantly stuffed himself into the barrel. His heart was pounding wildly. He did not hear anyone call out. The wagon continued rolling. Jyg looked straight up to see the yellow and red streaks of a colorful sunrise. The guards continued their banter as the wagon passed through the prison gate and out onto the street.

Jyg waited until he was sure the prison was out of sight before peaking out of the barrel. The two men riding in front were facing forward. Jyg poked his head out a little more. No place to hide on either side of the road. He pulled his head back down and waited a little longer. The next time he looked he saw a steep alley of stairs off to the side.

This was his chance! Jyg popped out of the barrel and dropped over the side of the wagon and was quickly out of sight as he raced down the steps.

PRAYERS FOR
THE DAMNED

On their first evening in the Hollow Hills, Riin Ruel solemnly led Tyme to a secluded cave to continue her lessons in private.

"There is a final set of *Prayers for the Dead* you must now begin to learn," Riin Ruel told Tyme in a steely voice. "The last group is called the *Prayers for the Damned*."

Tyme sat quietly without comment.

"The prayers work like a lock, to bind evil from the world, and protect women from the influence of the Beast," Riin Ruel continued. "These prayers are only known to a few Divine Warriors. They are short but powerful prayers."

"Tell me what I need to learn," Tyme answered resolutely.

"You must start by contemplating the terrifying name of the 51st *Prayer of the Dead*, which is the first of the *Prayers for the Damned*." Riin Ruel paused before continuing fiercely. "*Wail! Before the Gates of Hell!*"

SOMETHING BAD

Jyg raced down the stairs after escaping the prison wagon and stopped at the first intersecting alley to duck around the corner and peer back up the steps to see if he was being followed. No one was there. He had escaped!

He stood up and walked normally, no more running, to the stables where Klew, Kreoko, and the others had Panr's pigeons loaded into a wagon to be delivered to her at Alkali Canyon. Delgado was even there. Klew had seen Jyg get arrested and had followed the soldiers to the prison. None of them thought they would see Jyg again for at least a few days, or maybe even moons if he had been sentenced for vagrancy and sent to the farms.

While Jyg cleaned up and washed the black powder out of his hair, he told them what had happened, and how Bones had gotten the keys for him to open the door of his cell.

"Saved by the bird!" Bones swaggered back and forth on a railing to everyone's applause and congratulations. Jyg related how he had waited in agony for the guards to look the other way so he could climb into the barrel in the back of a wagon and sneak a ride out of the prison.

When Jyg and Klew prepared to leave, it was obvious that something else was troubling Delgado. Something besides Jyg's safety. He asked to speak with Jyg alone.

"I did not know how to mention this the other night when you all came up to the Blue Moon to say goodbye," he confessed. "Of course, my thoughts and prayers are with Tyme. I cannot describe the depth of my feelings of respect and gratitude toward her." He hesitated. "And of course, I believe in her as well." He hesitated again.

"What are you trying to say?" Jyg asked.

"If something were to happen," Delgado continued to struggle for words, "you know, like what almost happened to you." He looked pained. "If something ... that was not planned ... something bad happens ... you can always find a safe hiding place with the Jawbone Ridge gang. No matter who is hunting you."

Jyg nodded his head somberly. "Thank you, Delgado. I pray that we do not have to face such possibilities."

"You are like a brother to me," Delgado embraced Jyg. "You always have a home with the Jawbone Ridge gang in Karvor. All of you. Epoh and Klew as well," he added to make sure Jyg understood.

"You can tell Klew what I said," Delgado continued. "But do not say anything to Tyme or Epoh, unless," he faltered again, "unless something happens, and they need protection. I do not want them to think that I do not have faith in whatever Tyme is going to do."

REUNION

Jyg and Klew caught up to the others late in the evening at their second campsite in the Hollow Hills. Epoh was tending a small fire while Tyme was away studying with Riin Ruel. When they finished, Tyme seemed unusually quiet and subdued. She was feeling the stress of learning the *Prayers for the Damned.*

Tyme listened without emotion to the story of Jyg's clever tactic to fool Jakiko into thinking the birds he had stolen from Panr had all been eaten by monitor lizards, and how the pigeons had been successfully returned to Panr.

"We did have one close call," Jyg admitted. He told about the city guards and being taken to jail. How Bones had brought him the keys for his release.

"Saved by the bird!" Bones mimicked Zandero's voice.

That finally got Tyme to smile and behave more like her usual self. "'Tis wonderful to have you both back with us," she said earnestly as they sat around the fire. "'Tis important for me to have us all back together this last week before we get to Ambrit. I really need and appreciate your support right now."

The day before they were to arrive in Ambrit, Riin Ruel finally explained her plans to Tyme.

"The Czarzina will be at the Empress Auditorium, which was built by Empress Rada Dara Arad, who was terrified of assassination. On the wall behind the throne is a tapestry hiding a small door and emergency escape. A long tunnel leads downstairs and through passageways to reach a safe house in a nearby neighborhood."

Riin Ruel's voice grew firm. "There is a hidden panel in the study of the safe house. You will go in through this back door and sneak up the passageway. During the performance, you will spring out and assassinate the Czarzina," Riin Ruel's eyes shown with fierceness. "Then escape down the tunnel before anyone realizes what has happened."

Tyme listened solemnly without comment.

PART IV

Behold! There appeared a multitude of ladders, and upon their rungs the Angels of Light ascended into the heavens. While far below Divine Warriors descended ladders into the lowest hells to win release of tormented captives, held fast by their evil actions and deeds.

> *Kabaal Prophecies*

They struggled mightily with the implications of the teachings. Was there truly a road to hell paved with good intentions?

> *Hope the Proclaimer*

ARRIVAL IN AMBRIT

Under a shimmering white sky, Riin Ruel led the group through the eastern gate into Ambrit in the early afternoon before the heat. There were no high city walls or thick iron-bound doors. The ornamental gate was to welcome visitors, and collect a tax.

The Royal Highway into the city offered wonderful views of the capitol. Ambrit was famous for its magnificent buildings and architecture. The travelers could see five of the nine hills that made up the city, along with the Splendorous Dome of the Divine Womb, the most beautiful building in the world. The enormous Ambrit Library stood on another hill, filled with the most important ancient books and scrolls known to women.

The capitol was also called the City of Awnings. Ornate and brightly colored, permanent awnings sprouted from the tops and sides of the buildings like bills on hats. Streets were oriented for afternoon protection with sunshades, canopies, blinds, and screens. They passed Ambrit University on a hill near the center of the town. Most of the buildings were sealed and closed long ago. Only a small part of the upper campus was still in use.

Riin Ruel steered clear of the Ambrit Military Academy and the nearby Manor of the Blades, which was behind the Royal Palace Estate, close to the city center. The warm wind off the Dead Sea gave the air a welcome moisture. The city smelled fresh.

In its glory the city held nearly a million people. Now 'twas less than half.

The group rode into a wealthy neighborhood and stopped at the front gate of a large house with beautiful arched awnings and verandas. Riin Ruel dismounted and opened the door to the tiny gatehouse and slipped inside. A moment later the larger gate drew open, and they rode their mounts into the stables.

"This will be our base," Riin Ruel raised her arms wide. "We have the entire house and property. We call it the Veranda." They rubbed down, fed, and watered the horses before carrying their saddlebags into the house.

"No one else is here?" asked Tyme in amazement as they were shown to their rooms. Bones flitted in and out through the patios.

"You get the ser bedroom," Riin Ruel surprised Tyme and Epoh as she opened the double doors into a sumptuously decorated and opulent set of rooms and baths.

Tyme squealed with astonished delight.

"Enjoy it," Riin Ruel said with a smile. "You deserve it." She motioned toward a large stack of towels and robes. "Use whatever you need."

The next morning Riin Ruel, Tyme and Epoh left at dawn for the Splendorous Dome of the Divine Womb.

"I have always wanted to make a pilgrimage here," Epoh said with excitement when they entered the gardens and reflecting pools surrounding the building. He had seen a book at the Dayr Castle library with a painting of the domes and arches, but it did not capture the magnificence and graceful symmetry.

They entered the giant round doors into the refuge. Epoh followed Tyme to stand at the entrance into the sanctuary. The enormous domed ceilings were even more beautiful inside. They stared in wonder at the fabulous, ornate, blue tile work.

"I wish you could come in and sit with me," Tyme whispered.

"As do I," Epoh agreed. "'Tis feeling ever more divisive and wrong to worship apart." He noted that Riin Ruel was ahead, waiting for Tyme. "I will probably stay less than an hour," he told her. "I want to do some research at the Ambrit Library and visit a couple of booksellers."

"Good luck," Tyme gave him a kiss on the cheek. "I will meet you back at the house."

Epoh turned around and walked slowly through the refuge along the circling row past the shrines for the Seven Attributes:

The Holy Spirit of Divine.

The Holy Womb, creator of all life.

Love, the first natural instinct between mother and daughter.

Compassion, the second natural instinct.

Truth, the search for the Divine Way.

Justice, the correcting of wrongs.

Forgiveness, the return to love.

After the last Attribute was a shrine with a statue of Tatano, the first True Warrior, and the only man to have writings included in the *Book of Elders*. Nearby, and busier, was a shrine for Divine Hands, the state supported sect with most of its membership from the Legions. Busier still was the side shrine to the Divine Fist, a more volatile warrior cult that gained popularity in the outer fringes of the Empire after the Fracture War, and was only recently tolerated in the capitol. Although the shamans tried to keep the area scraped clean, there was residue of red candle wax left behind by followers of the Fire. Epoh watched two men set out and light red candles.

He returned to the quieter alcove of the Attribute of Compassion to do his stretching postures and then sat cross-legged in the adepts pose to meditate and pray. When he finished, he walked back outside and was surprised to see Tyme sitting in a meditation alcove.

"Good!" she said with a smile as he approached. "I was hoping you had not left yet."

"What are you doing here?" he asked.

"Riin Ruel somehow received a signal," Tyme guessed. "I think she saw something on an altar because suddenly she had something she needed to do, and she said I could have the day off."

"Wonderful!" Epoh exclaimed. "We can explore the city together."

They sauntered through the reflecting pools circling the outside of the magnificent building. A deep red sun was just rising out of a haze of dark-orange dust on the distant horizon. They sat quietly on a bench holding hands, enjoying the view and each other's company.

"When we sit like this, I can forget the cares of the world," Tyme said contentedly.

"What cares?" Epoh joked. She knew he often worried more than she.

"I love you," Tyme smiled and kissed him on the lips.

They resumed walking and made their way under awning-covered streets up the hill to the beautiful Ambrit Library. The enormous building held copies of all of the important books and scrolls known to civilization. Epoh took a quick scan through the large areas on religion and philosophy. He excitedly reported his findings back to Tyme.

"They have some different commentaries on the *Kabaal Prophecies* I would like to study, and also some manuscripts on the *Prayers for the Dead* that I could not find in Karvor."

"Now I will know where to find you if I finish early with Riin Ruel," Tyme smiled. She liked the thought of him here, surrounded by so many books.

THE HIDDEN CRYPT

When they left the library Epoh directed Tyme to a street of booksellers. "There are a couple of books that I want to buy. And some rare manuscripts I want that the library does not have," Epoh explained.

"I thought the Ambrit Library had copies of everything!" Tyme said with surprise.

"Everything that is approved to be discussed in the open. But there are some works that are kept hidden from the uninitiated. Works of power and arcane knowledge. Those are not on display for all to see, or even know about."

"Now you sound like Riin Ruel," Tyme chided him.

"I do not disagree with all of her warnings," Epoh protested.

"No," Tyme nodded, "nor do I."

"Ser Hain Haan Hana from the Trusted Scribe in Karvor gave me the names of two shops where I might find what I am looking for," Epoh explained. "The first is close by." The Knowledge Scroll was off the main street with a small sign, and filled with a staff of scribes who were hunched over their tables.

"May I help you?" a tall, thin, dark-skinned woman with long gray hair tied up in a bun gave Epoh a quick suspicious look before addressing her question to Tyme.

"He is the customer," Tyme gestured to Epoh. Men seldom came in the Knowledge Scroll, and Epoh looked unlike any man the woman had ever seen. A flurry of whispers filled the room as the women scribes all stole glances in his direction.

Epoh introduced himself and showed her the letter written

by the owner of the Trusted Scribe that listed his credentials. The letter was addressed to Ser Crin Cren Cran. The woman broke the seal and scanned the letter with apparent disbelief. "This says you can read Hool," she smirked as if it were a joke. Of what use could that possibly be?

"I am sorry," Epoh bowed, "What was your name?"

When he found out she was not even the woman to whom the letter was written, Epoh quickly plucked it back from her hands. "I would deliver the letter in person. Can you tell me how I might find Ser Crin Cren Cran?"

"She will not be in until tomorrow," the woman said dismissively.

"Then I will return tomorrow," Epoh said pleasantly.

Tyme fumed as they walked down the street. "She was disrespectful and demeaning to you," she said. "You did well not to lose your temper."

"I am not the brute she believes me to be," Epoh shook his head and gave a sly grin. "It only makes me want to show her she is wrong."

They came to a cenote where half the roof had collapsed and was now a sunken and shaded stone terrace filled with plants overlooking the water. They climbed down stairs along a cliff covered in vines to reach the terrace. Tyme squealed with delight when she saw a group of beautifully patterned succulents.

"These are like the plants I saw in the high mountains with Tao Tau and Spike," she marveled.

"I love the intricate design the rows of leaves make against each other," Epoh pointed out.

"Tao Tau had me use patterns like that as a mandala, to meditate and focus on the wonderous beauty of Divine." Tyme smiled wistfully as she thought of being with the old herb woman in Lost Valley. "She was going to publish a book on how to make her healing salve. I wonder if she has done so already? It would be amazing to see her here."

"That would be amazing," Epoh grinned.

"I wonder what she would say about me being a Bright One?" Tyme questioned.

"I think she always thought you *were* a Bright One!" Epoh laughed.

Tyme nodded thoughtfully. "I wonder what she would say about Riin Ruel's plans?"

"That would be interesting," Epoh agreed. "I think she would have some of the same reservations as you are." They strolled and admired the strange succulents, agave, and cacti, and then took the stairs down to the water and sat at a small bench with a view of the shaded side of the pool. A group of young women were giggling loudly as they emerged from a swim.

"You said you had the name of another bookseller?" Tyme asked.

"Not exactly a book seller," Epoh replied. "She deals in antiquities. Ser Hain Haan Hana gave me the name reluctantly. She has never dealt with the woman herself. She gave me the impression the woman has an unsavory reputation and should not be trusted."

"Then why would Ser Hain Haan Hana give you her name?"

"What I am looking for is far beyond orthodox," Epoh explained. "Few scholars know of it. And if they did, they would never consider selling it."

Tyme thought of Riin Ruel, and all her warnings to keep certain teachings secret. It made her nervous about encouraging Epoh, yet she greatly valued hearing his thoughts. His research and studies helped put Riin Ruel's teachings in perspective.

"'Tis a bit of a conundrum," Epoh explained. "Anyone who would sell such a work should not be trusted."

"Mayhaps 'tis best then that I am along." Tyme pushed her shoulder against his and joked, "I will be your bodyguard."

They climbed the stairs out of the cenote back onto the street. Epoh pointed to the large hill covered by Ambrit University. "Her shop is on the southwest side of University

Hill," he said.

"The sunny side," Tyme noted, "a rough part of town?"

"By Ambrit standards, yes," Epoh nodded. "By Jawbone Ridge standards, rather tame."

"We will see," Tyme replied. The streets were now all covered with awnings. While it added a festive, colorful look, the city had a more serious feel than Karvor. The women gave Epoh a wide berth and all seemed to be in a hurry. The men busy and unsmiling with their chores.

"No one seems very happy," Tyme noted. "There is an oppressive feeling. Almost suffocating."

"It definitely lacks the joy of life that is in Karvor," Epoh agreed.

They found the right street easily enough, but had trouble finding the store. The Hidden Crypt lived up to its name, off an alley, down some cracked stairs, through a tunnel, and into a cool, vaulted basement. Two guards sat playing dice at a table in the corner. One of them rang a bell and motioned them to enter. The small shop was crammed full of old, religious iconography, artwork, statues, and paraphernalia for both priests and shamans. There were symbols, shrines, and altars for a host of saints, along with unorthodox and possibly heretical totems, amulets, and charms. One wall held shelves of dried plants and herbs. Tyme spotted a number of herbs Tao Tau had said were sometimes used by witchdoctors for love potions. She also spotted poisonous and deadly compounds as well.

Behind a packed counter of antique religious jewelry, an old gray-haired woman with a limp came out of a heavy door and locked it with a large iron key. She had skin almost as white as Noot's. She sized-up Tyme quickly before setting her eyes on Epoh.

"You have seen the sun," she said mysteriously. "And the Fire."

"I am the Burnished Man," Epoh replied, using the name he had been called by Gybeko, the Painted Hills shaman.

The old woman's eyes grew wide.

"Are you Ser Jaza Zaja Ajaz?" Epoh asked, saying the name carefully to make sure he got it right. Women in Ambrit were extremely sensitive about the correct pronunciation of their names.

"At your service," the old woman replied with great seriousness.

"I was given your name by a scholar," Epoh told her, "who said you could help with discreet requests."

"The privacy of my customers is guaranteed," the woman replied. "Who was the scholar?"

"That would not be discreet to say," Epoh pointed out.

The woman said nothing. She looked at Tyme again and then back to Epoh. "What does the Burnished Man seek in the Hidden Crypt?" she asked.

"That also would not be discreet to say," Epoh replied seriously. He caught Tyme's eye and gave her a nod to move away, as if she was dismissed. Tyme flicked her robe theatrically to show Ser Jaza Zaja Ajaz the set of daggers around her waist, then moved away to stand alert near the door.

"Mayhaps you would like tea?" the old woman offered. She motioned to a small table and stools with a brazier and kettle.

Sitting together Epoh talked about the *Prayers for the Dead*, which were recited at the Womb. 'Twas obvious that Ser Jaza Zaja Ajaz was well acquainted with the subject. They discussed *The Twenty Prayers for the Dead* by Ser Via Vee Vua, and then talked about the *Bridge*, the 20th, 21st and 22nd *Prayers for the Dead*. They each hinted of knowledge of even higher prayers, the *Glories*, before Epoh brought the conversation back to the 20th *Prayer for the Dead*.

"Some claim the 20th *Prayer for the Dead* is unique among all the prayers," he said cautiously.

Ser Jaza Zaja Ajaz's face remained impassive, but her breathing stopped for a moment.

"*Flee Your Mortal Body*," Epoh whispered, "the 20th *Prayer for the Dead*, is a mirror. A swinging door."

Ser Jaza Zaja Ajaz nodded somberly. "'Tis your wish to take such a door?" she asked in a hushed voice.

Epoh nodded gravely. "I seek guidance beyond the swinging door." He lowered his voice again. "I seek guidance to the 51st *Prayer of the Dead.*"

"What you seek has great cost," the old woman warned.

"I will brave the cost," Epoh declared somberly. "I seek a copy of *The Lair of the Beast,* by Ser Zoltu Zoltu Zoltu."

When Epoh and Tyme left the Hidden Crypt, he carried a scroll pouch in his hand.

"Well," Tyme asked, "Did the Burnished Man get what he was looking for?"

"Thanks for playing along," Epoh replied. "The dagger flourish you did with your robe was perfect. I had a sudden hunch that I might get what I was looking for as the Burnished Man, rather than just being Epoh."

"So, you got it?" Tyme asked again.

"No," Epoh held up the pouch. "This is something else. But she thinks she can get the book I want in a few days. I will tell you more once I determine if 'tis credible and authentic. Then I will give you a full report."

THE SER CUS

When Tyme and Epoh returned to the Veranda house for the heat, they found Jyg in a state of great excitement. "The Ser Cus is here!" he yelled with a grin.

Jyg had remembered that they did not perform at the beautiful Ambrit Amphitheater, which was built for plays, music, and festivals, and could hold fifteen thousand people. The Ser Cus was not considered artistic and refined enough by Ambrit standards for such a venue. They performed at a much smaller, run-down theater on Revelers Street.

"I told them that Crown Prince Epohco was alive, and here with us, along with a mystic warrior," Jyg said. "But no more than that. They invited us to come over during the heat, so we can talk and be together right away."

Riin Ruel had still not returned, nor had Klew, so Jyg, Tyme and Epoh went by themselves to meet the Ser Cus.

"We have so much to tell you," Tyme exclaimed as they came through the door to the family tent. "But first let me introduce to everyone my husband, Epoh, the former Crown Prince Epohco of Dayrstad." She was glad Jyg had already given them some warning. Still, they all looked rather shocked.

Epoh bowed. "I am honored to be your guest," he said with a big smile. "I remember you very fondly from my childhood at Dayr Castle and your wonderful performances."

"We must celebrate!" Mams, the matriarch of the clan stood up and raised her arms to the sky. "And leave all serious talk for later!" She knew they would not be in Ambrit without some intrigue.

"Yes!" Wiir Waar agreed. "We want to hear of your courtship and wedding!"

Tyme and Epoh immediately embraced in the swaying dance they had learned for their marriage ceremony, which they now did spontaneously when they caught a certain look in each other's eye. The Ser Cus erupted in laughter and applause. When they finished everyone scurried to offer them pillows to sit and lie upon, and then food and drinks.

"Let us first hear at least some part of how Epoh survived his fall into the underground river," Wiir Waar said, "and made his way out of the desert."

They sat spellbound by his tale of twice near drowning, and waking in a sacred cave to be saved by nuns. Of becoming a monk. Then leaving the nunnery to travel to the mythical lost city of Apocalypse, with grubbers, who were searching for dragon bones and treasure in the Sea of Dunes. It all sounded like a fairy tale. Everyone was amazed by his story of the cargo bird filled with mysterious devices built by the Ancient Ones. He showed them his wrist clock and explained the possible uses it might have had.

"Epoh brought one back for me as well," Tyme held out her arm to show them the device. "'Tis supposed to keep track of time," she joked. "Keep track of me!"

Epoh told of the bad air and the explosion, their escape from Hool bandits, the strange beauty of Jchow Oasis and the underground city, of returning by camel to the Barrier Mountains and finally arriving home at Dayr Castle. "Once I learned that Tyme was no longer at the castle, I knew there was no reason for me to stay in Dayrstad. I crossed the desert to be with her."

"He is so romantic!" Wiir Waar told Tyme approvingly. "You get all the interesting men!"

Tyme told of their first encounter in Karvor. "He was even more broiled by the sun and covered with blisters. He is hardened and toughened on the outside, but on the inside," she said proudly, "he has the same loving heart, filled with wisdom and compassion."

"We were only together for a few weeks when Tyme proposed," Epoh pulled open his shirt to show his bare neck. "A modern marriage with no collar," he boasted. "Just rings for each of us." They held out their hands and told how they had made each other's rings.

Everyone in the Ser Cus voiced their approval. Tyme told of their simple wedding, and Wiir Waar insisted they perform their full wedding dance, with Zintowo and Zandero drumming and Lana and Tana Pana shaking tambourines.

That evening Tyme, Epoh and Jyg joined Wiir Waar and the Z's for a private meeting around a firepot on a secluded patio. Epoh told them about traveling with Riin Ruel, the mystic warrior, and the strange dreams and prophecies that led her to Tyme.

Tyme explained a little about Riin Ruel and the training she was receiving with daggers and mystical prayers. "I am not supposed to say anything about what I am learning," Tyme apologized. "But I can say that we are here in Ambrit on a serious task with far reaching consequences."

"You do not need to explain anything more," Wiir Waar said. "We are all with you. We believe in you. Tell us if there is any way in which we can help."

"Thank you. Your support and encouragement mean everything to me."

Epoh looked at Tyme and Wiir Waar, sitting arm in arm. "You both look so happy together," he marveled. "Mayhaps I should go out for a drink with Jyg and the Z's, and give you two a chance to get caught up?"

"That would be great," Wiir Waar gave Epoh a peck on the cheek and waved them all off. She turned to Tyme. "Okay, what is going on?"

Tyme gave her a hug. "I have so wanted to hear your

opinion and advice," she said. "I have been caught up in an unbelievable whirlwind." She took a big breath.

"Riin Ruel believes I am linked by prophecy to the Bright One, who is often portrayed as a Warrior Queen." Tyme paused before she could say the words out loud, they sounded so crazy. "She thinks I should assassinate the Czarzina. Then reveal and proclaim myself to Divine Council and the Senate, whom she believes will make me Empress of a New Empire."

Wiir Waar was momentarily speechless. "What does Epoh believe?" she asked at last.

"He has always believed my arrival at Dayr Castle was accompanied by prophetic dreams and mystical portents. Even the abbess at the nunnery where he was saved believes I am the Bright One!" She told how the abbess had made Epoh write a book about her. How Riin Ruel had traveled to Dayr Castle and then Ezkia Oasis in search of her. How Riin Ruel had been imprisoned for centuries by the Czarzina for her quest.

"What do you believe?" Wiir Waar asked in wonderment.

"I believe I am in an extraordinary circumstance," Tyme said simply. She shared how Epoh had found a rare copy of the *Kabaal Prophecies*, along with numerous other scholarly works. Of how he had learned Hool while in the Endless Desert and had been able to translate a number of confusing passages and sections of the book.

"'Twas the *Kabaal Prophecies* which first led Riin Ruel to Dayr Castle," Tyme explained before reciting the famous passage:

Born of a King to a Barbarian Land,
a girl shall appear.
The Divine Daughter full of radiance and hope.
She shall be the Bright One.

"Epoh said the Ambri translation *Born of a King*, translated in Hool, would be *Riding King*."

"You are the Bright One!" Wiir Waar gasped.

"Everyone says *the* Bright One," Tyme allowed reluctantly.

"But actually, Epoh says the Hool translation would be *a* Bright One." She felt that was important to clarify.

"Are you going to assassinate the Czarzina?" Wiir Waar asked in awe.

"I am not sure. I do not like the idea starting a reign with a murder."

"More like justice," Wiir Waar said with a snort. "The Czarzina's hands are covered with innocent blood. In any fair court of law, she would be found guilty of murder, vengeance, and cruelty many times over." Wiir Waar raised her dark eyebrows. "Most of Ambrit would be joyous to be rid of her."

"Riin Ruel believes I would be channeling and executing the Wrath of Divine," Tyme said. "But if Tao Tau were here, she would say it sets a terrible example to others ... attempting to justify the killing of someone in a power struggle."

"There is truth to that," Wiir Waar nodded.

"Besides, what do I know of Ambrit politics?" Tyme asked incredulously. "I do not know if I even *want* to have a reign. Endless meetings with a squabbling Senate? Overdone banquets most every night? Constant intrigue and backstabbing." Tyme shook her head at the absurdity of the whole idea.

"The crown would be very heavy," Wiir Waar agreed. "Do you know how you are going to make your escape after you kill the Czarzina?" Wiir Waar asked.

"Yes," Tyme nodded. "Riin Ruel has it all planned out." She showed Wiir Waar some of the moves for the close dagger work she had been learning.

"Interesting," her friend observed respectfully. "Those are some deadly skills."

Tyme put the dagger away. "Did I tell you? Rocozo, the gang leader I beat up, he and a group of friends tried to ambush me in a dark alley." Tyme described the elaborate charade of the drunk hitting the helpless woman, and how Scoop, the Jawbone Ridge lookout, had foiled the plan, and killed one of the muggers with his slingshot in the process.

"I am not comfortable with him killing someone to protect me," Tyme said. "Scoop has nightmares now. He dreams over and over that he kills the mugger, but when he comes up close to look, he realizes it is me he has killed instead."

"That is creepy," Wiir Waar shuddered.

"*Violence leads to more violence*, Tao Tau used to say."

They sat quietly for a minute and then changed their conversation to lighter matters. Wiir Waar asked questions about Epoh, and then about Jyg, who had been silent all evening.

"He broke up with Rona," Tyme explained. "Or I should say, Rona broke up with him." Tyme shook her head. "You are not going to believe this. Jyg was her moonboy while she waited for Delgado to stop mooning after me. Apparently, she has been in love with Delgado for decades."

"How is Jyg taking it?" Wiir Waar asked.

"He is trying to view their relationship as a good learning experience. He feels she taught him a lot. He has managed to stay friends with her and Delgado both."

"That says a lot about Jyg's personality," Wiir Waar said approvingly. "For many people, that would ruin the friendship. Jyg has strong self-confidence."

"He has a strong sense of his own personal power," Tyme agreed.

"He has matured and grown a lot in the last few decades," Wiir Waar nodded her head thoughtfully.

"I think he would appreciate a few words of support and encouragement from you," Tyme said. "I think he admires you and looks up to you."

"Really?" Wiir Waar said with a surprised look. "If you think it would help, I would be happy to say something."

When the Z's returned to the Ser Cus camp with Epoh and Jyg, Wiir Waar had a few minutes alone to speak with Jyg. "I was sorry to hear of your breaking up with Rona," she told him.

Jyg shook his head in bewilderment. "Turned out she was in love with Delgado all along." He looked embarrassed.

"I assumed the relationship was going one way, while she assumed 'twas going quite differently. I guess we never talked about big things. We only talked and laughed about everyday things," said Jyg.

"Like what big things?" asked Wiir Waar.

"Life goals. How do you want to live? Where do you want to live? Whether you want children someday?" Jyg shook his head wistfully. "She thought her idea of *someday having children* was much sooner than what I meant by *someday having children*."

"Was it?"

"Probably," Jyg laughed. "I have my own life to live first. Then mayhaps I will think about children after that."

"So, you were not made for each other as much as you first thought," Wiir Waar shook her head sympathetically. "Well, I have never found a perfect partner either." She barked a laugh. "Not that I am looking that hard, mind you." Her face lit up with an impish smile. "But 'tis always good to keep an eye out, just in case."

She patted Jyg on the back. "As you said, this will make you a better partner for the next lucky woman to recognize your many talents and charms." She gave him a peck on the check and sent him off into the night.

BIND EVIL FROM
THE WORLD

Tyme had loved learning and reciting the 23rd through the 50th *Prayers for the Dead*, the *Glories of Divine on Her Throne*. She had begun learning them in Karvor, and had chanted them whenever possible, morning and evening. Her meditations had been beautiful and calming. She had forged a deeper bond with Riin Ruel and had grown to trust her more.

But that feeling of spiritual connection changed when they traveled through the Hollow Hills, and she began learning the *Prayers for the Damned*.

"These prayers must never be discussed with the uninitiated," Riin Ruel had warned her sternly. "Doing so could place them at great risk. When my mentor was a young woman, an apprentice burned to ash after speaking certain words aloud without the proper preparation."

Tyme could only guess how many more prayers there might be. She was now learning the 63rd prayer, and she was near the bottom of the third hell. The sessions were intense and draining.

Riin Ruel had told her the prayers worked like a lock, to bind evil from the world, and to protect women from the influence of the Beast. Reciting the *Prayers for the Damned* revealed another side of Riin Ruel, the hardened warrior, well adjusted to the punishing toll of descending into hell. Tyme now saw where the hard edge to Riin Ruel came from. And she began to realize the tremendous inner battle the mystic warrior was waging as she recited the daily prayers during her practice.

Whenever Tyme questioned her plans, teachings, or techniques, Riin Ruel would not abide any doubts or concerns, and repeated her same refrain. "Once you have the full knowledge of your training, you will understand and know your necessary response."

A PLOT BETRAYED

"We may have been betrayed," Riin Ruel told Tyme the next day. "There is no longer certainty that the back entrance into the Empress Auditorium from the safe house is secure. The plan to have you ambush the Czarzina at the Auditorium may be a trap to lure you to your death."

"Like Rocozo tried to lure me into the ally," Tyme shook her head in disbelief. "If the Czarzina knows of it, why would she not arrest us here?"

"This house was arranged through different contacts, who are unaware of each other," Riin Ruel explained. "Our Auditorium contact has no idea where we are staying, or even if we are in the city yet. She must wait for us to arrive there to betray us."

"We must seek a way to use this to our advantage," Riin Ruel continued. "If 'tis a trap, they will be expecting us to strike by coming through the back passageway from the safe house to the throne. Which means they will not be expecting us to strike from another way."

"What other way?" asked Tyme.

Riin Ruel showed Tyme the drawings of the layout and design of the Auditorium.

"Her throne is behind the stage on an open dais. There are ten guards with crossbows hidden the ceiling protecting her."

"How do I get past ten guards with crossbows?" Tyme asked.

"We could drug them,' Riin Ruel suggested hesitantly. "Which can be risky because the effectiveness of a sleeping draught can vary among members of such a large group. If one guard succumbs a minute sooner or later than the others, they will see what is happening and call the alarm."

Tyme listened intently.

"Much safer to poison them," Riin Ruel suggested casually.

"Poison them?" Tyme exclaimed. "Just like that? Kill ten innocent guards?" She shook her head in indignation.

"Ten guards die to stop a civil war?" Riin Ruel said with an air of total justification. "That is a bargain any day. We just have to figure out a way for you to make your escape. Mayhaps your band of followers might be put to use after all."

BUYING BOOKS

The next day Riin Ruel refused to discuss Tyme's apprehension about killing the guards. "To alleviate great suffering," she informed Tyme, as if everything was already decided, "hard choices must be made."

When Tyme finished her training for the day, she told Epoh what Riin Ruel had said as they walked together down through town.

"King Eyrico always told me the same thing when I was Crown Prince," Epoh commiserated. "Rulers are often forced into unpleasant situations and actions."

"So, you agree with Riin Ruel?" Tyme asked.

"Not necessarily," he replied. "Not without at least trying to find another way."

"And what might that be?"

"I have no idea."

When they arrived at the Knowledge Scroll, the same unhelpful woman was behind the counter. The scribes seemed to have been waiting for Epoh to return, as he was noted by all the women in the workroom.

"Is Ser Crin Cren Cran here today?" Epoh asked pleasantly, gesturing the womb. The letter of introduction was tucked into a pocket in his satchel.

The tall, dark-skinned clerk gave him a pinched look. "I am afraid Ser Crin Cren Cran is busy today," she said with poorly concealed displeasure at his reappearance.

"Will she be free anytime tomorrow?" Epoh asked.

"I am sorry, I just don't know," the woman demurred.

As Epoh was turning to leave, a large black woman with short, frizzy-gray hair came out the door of an office. Her eyes landed on Epoh and widened at his burned appearance.

"Are you Ser Crin Cren Cran?" Epoh guessed hopefully.

"Yes, I am," the woman replied with wary surprise.

Epoh gestured the womb as he introduced himself. He handed her the letter of recommendation. "The seal was broken by your associate yesterday, who can vouch for its authenticity." He gave the unhelpful woman a prompting glance.

"And why was I not told of this?" Ser Crin Cren Cran asked the woman behind the counter.

"Clearly, it is some ruse or hoax," the woman replied. "I did not want to waste your time."

Ser Crin Cren Cran read the letter quickly. When she finished, she folded it and handed it back to Epoh.

"And what is it you want from me?" she asked suspiciously.

"I am looking for the complete set of scrolls with the original text of Ser Qwen Qwan Qwil's commentaries on the *Kabaal Prophecies*."

"The complete scroll set includes scrolls with unreadable text," Ser Crin Cren Cran warned.

"I am aware of the difficulties" Epoh assured her. "I believe those scrolls may be written in Hool. I know that some of the scrolls from the *Mask of Splendor* are written in Hool."

Ser Crin Cren Cran could not quite believe what she was hearing. Hool? Instead of asking him more she simply said, "'Tis three gold pieces for the scroll set."

"That will be fine," Epoh smiled, reaching for his coin pouch.

Now Ser Crin Cren Cran could not believe what she was seeing as the mysterious man calmly laid the gold coins on the table. She retrieved the set of scrolls from a wall of books and set them on the counter.

"You believe some of the scrolls from the *Kabaal Prophecies*, *Mask of Splendor* are written in Hool?" she asked with cautious interest.

"Definitely," he confirmed.

"And now you wish to see if the *Kabaal Prophecies* from the *Mask of Brilliance* has similar sections of Hool text?"

"Yes," Epoh replied, "and also compare the writings. I have read that the two versions do not include all the same scrolls."

"That is correct," Ser Crin Cren Cran answered. "Each has 14 scrolls that are the same. The *Mask of Splendor* includes five more scrolls that the *Mask of Brilliance* does not have. And the *Mask of Brilliance* includes three more scrolls that the *Mask of Splendor* does not have." She unrolled one of the scrolls on the counter and pointed to an area of text she could not read. "This is Hool?" she questioned.

Epoh looked closely at the page. "Yes, that is Hool."

"What does this say?" she pointed on the page.

Epoh looked at the passage, licked his chapped lips, and slowly deciphered it aloud.

The enemies of Light
appear all around us.
Yet it is inside
where the True Battle is won.

A look of wonderment filled the old woman's eyes. Even the woman behind the counter was curious.

"Ser Hain Haan Hana said she was interested in publishing a new translation," Epoh said. "But I find myself in Ambrit now, not Karvor. If you have interest, mayhaps we can work together at a later date."

"Yes," Ser Crin Cren Cran said enthusiastically. "I would be very interested in seeing your translations and getting them published."

"Once my other concerns are settled," Epoh smiled, "we can speak of this again." He gestured the womb and left the store.

"I never imagined such discrimination against men," Tyme declared when they resumed walking down the street. "That first woman did not believe anything about you. Even with a sealed letter of approval! And Ser Crin Cren Cran was suspicious until you paid with gold coins." She looked at him and giggled. "You do look a bit … wild and untamable. But in a good way."

"The Burnished Man," Epoh declared solemnly.

They repeated his title in exaggerated intonations and joking comments as they strolled under the awning-covered streets to the Hidden Crypt, where he had first taken on the name for himself. Down the cracked stairs and through the tunnel to the vaulted basement where the two guards played dice. This time the guards kept them waiting outside the door until a shrouded customer came out with a large package under her arm. The guards waved them through.

"The Burnished Man," Ser Jaza Zaja Ajaz gestured the womb as she greeted Epoh solemnly. She came out from behind the counter to make tea and sit with Epoh at the small table.

Tyme stood for a moment at the counter looking at the array of strange religious statues, masks, unusual prayer beads, cryptic symbols, and amulets. Behind the counter was a box on a shelf covered with a black cloth. A corner of the cloth was not tucked in and revealed part of the head of a devilish doll. The terrible face of the doll made Tyme think of one of the demons in the second hell of the *Prayers for the Damned*. She turned away and quickly recited the sealing of locks to the gates of the second hell, then scurried away to take her position near the door. She had not liked the Hidden Crypt on her first visit, now she felt even more revulsion.

Meanwhile Ser Jaza Zaja Ajaz was pouring Epoh tea. "The book you discreetly requested was more costly to procure than I expected," she told him sadly. "I did not know if you would still be interested."

Epoh had been expecting such a gambit. They began bargaining once again, each trying to bring the other to a more favorable price. When 'twas at last agreed upon, Epoh offered another proposal.

"Rather than paying in coins," Epoh said, "would you be

interested in a gemstone?" He held out a beautiful, dark-red ruby he had a hunch she would covet. All the jewelers charged him a steep commission to exchange gems for gold coins. If Ser Jaza Zaja Ajaz took the ruby for its true worth, it would save Epoh a tidy sum of money, and help justify the outrageous amount he was paying for the book.

As he suspected, her eyes lit up. They spent the next cup of tea arguing over the cost of the ruby. Epoh stayed firm. He knew the true value, having shown the stone to a number of jewelers. Luckily, Ser Jaza Zaja Ajaz wanted the gem badly, and at last she agreed to his price.

She took the ruby, paid him the balance due with a purse of coins, and then from behind the counter, retrieved a small metal bound, wooden box with a latch and two keys. She set it on the table.

"*The Lair of the Beast,* by Ser Zoltu Zoltu Zoltu," she said in a hushed voice.

Epoh looked at the box warily.

Ser Jaza Zaja Ajaz's face grew more serious. "Under no circumstances," she admonished, "should you ever read any of this book aloud." She waved her hands and shook her head emphatically. "And most certainly," she warned, "*never* speak any of the names in the book out loud."

"Of course," Epoh replied solemnly.

"You may open it here to assure its authenticity," Ser Jaza Zaja Ajaz allowed, "but only briefly." She lit some special incense, cleansed her hands in the smoke, and muttered prayers as Epoh opened the lock and the lid.

He carefully lifted out the dark-red leather book and scanned the first few pages. He glanced at a few more random pages in the middle and at the end before returning the book to the box.

"It appears to be authentic," he said gravely. He shut the lid, locked it, and put the keys in his pocket. The book unsettled him. It felt tainted in his hands. He wrapped the box in a cloth, bound all six sides with a cord, and put it in his satchel. Then he cleansed his hands in the incense smoke for a few moments as Ser Jaza Zaja Ajaz had done.

"I do not like that place at all," Tyme said as they left the tunnel and climbed back up the cracked stairs to the alley and the street.

"Nor do I," Epoh agreed. "I hope that this is all a dead-end, but I felt I had to get the book to check on some rumors, just in case it has bearing on what you choose to do as a Bright One."

Tyme wished the shop had no bearing on a Bright One at all. But after seeing the malevolent doll similar to a demon in the *Prayers of the Damned,* she was more disturbed. She would wait to hear Epoh's report. Then she would decide how much to tell him.

A NEW PLOT

"I will not poison ten guards so I can assassinate the Czarzina," Tyme said firmly. She had finished her training and studies with Riin Ruel, and they were arguing again.

When Riin Ruel realized that Tyme would not be swayed, she changed tactics. "There may be another way," she acknowledged. "But we would need help."

"Why did you not tell me earlier?"

"Because 'tis much riskier," Riin Ruel replied with consternation. "Get your followers together and we will try to put together a plan. We only have 12 days."

That evening they were joined by Epoh, Jyg, Klew, Wiir Waar and the Z's at the apartment patio around a table with drawings of the layout of Empress Auditorium.

"'Twas built by Empress Rada Dara Arad," Riin Ruel explained, drawing everyone closer.

"Who many now blame for causing the Fracture Wars," Epoh noted. "'Twas the last grand building constructed during the Ambri Empire."

"She wanted the appearance of an open court," Riin Ruel continued, "but was in fact obsessed by fears of assassination. The hall was built with her throne behind the stage on an open dais, giving the impression of only a few distant guards. But hidden in the ornately patterned arched ceiling are ten guards behind mesh screens with crossbows to shoot anyone approaching the throne from the stage or audience."

"However," Riin Ruel added, "there are a few places on the stage where the crossbows cannot be aimed accurately." She pulled out another old manuscript.

"This was a secret report prior to the dedication of the building," Riin Ruel revealed. The screens and latticework were designed for artistic decoration and acoustics. After 'twas built the Empress had the idea of hiding archers behind it. The guards are perched in cramped positions between braces and struts along a narrow walkway with scant room to maneuver their crossbows."

She showed them an illustration of the stage, with three spots where the guards could not fire. Between those spots, some of the guards could not fire easily. It appeared almost feasible to link together a route across the stage out of the range of the crossbows.

"During the reign of Empress Rada Dara Arad, the guards were using smaller crossbows," Riin Ruel continued, "than what the Blades use today. They will have even less maneuverability with the larger, more powerful crossbows, which are slower to reload. A dash across the stage is possible. Once you are on the dais with the Czarzina, you are out of range." Riin Ruel showed them a chart with the exact dimensions. "We would have to sneak in before and leave small marks on the stage to show Tyme the safe path across. After the Czarzina is eliminated, Tyme can use flash powder to blind everyone and make an escape."

Everyone studied the drawings thoughtfully.

"We still have to get her in and out of the building," Riin Ruel sighed. She turned to Wiir Waar. "That is where we need help."

"Have you performed for the Czarzina?" Jyg asked.

"She is too lofty to book us," Wiir Waar shook her head. "Knife throwing and acrobatics are beneath her. But we have done shows at the Empress Auditorium for Legion offisers. We know all the entrances and exits."

"The hallway skylights," the Z's said together with knowing smiles, as if everything was solved.

"The performer's dressing rooms are off the stage down a narrow, curved hallway with a high ceiling," Zintowo explained.

"One day we were goofing around," Zandero jumped in, "and stemmed our bodies across the hallway with our feet on one wall, and our arms stretched across to palm our hands on the other wall. Then we chimney climbed our way to the top to look out the vent windows."

"Two of the bars had missing stonework," Zintowo resumed. "I pulled one out and then put it back before we stemmed back down. The window is above the rear corner of the building."

"Jyg could climb up the stone trim on the outside back wall of the auditorium," Zandero volunteered his friend, "and set up a sky hook at the top of the vent."

Zintowo explained how a cord on a pulley could be used to lift an actor quickly and smoothly into the air. "We can lift her up to the vent, lower her into the hallway, then lift her back out, through the vent, and lower her all the way to the ground to escape."

"What show will be performing for the Czarzina?" Wiir Waar asked.

"The Ambrit Opera Company will be doing a special presentation of *The Founding Mothers*," Riin Ruel answered. "A not-so-subtle hint from the Czarzina that she considers herself a new Founding Mother."

"A tedious performance to watch," Wiir Waar shook her head. "But perfect for costuming, with the scarves and billowy clothes of the Women's Clans. The finale of the Dance of the Masks would be the best moment to strike." Wiir Waar smiled. "I know who makes the costumes. We can get Tyme dressed in exactly the same outfit."

"We can drop her into the hallway at the right moment behind the other actors and she can follow them onto the stage," Zintowo grinned.

"We can check out the building tomorrow," Zandero figured, "to find a safe staging point below the back side and establish a way up the cliff to the back of the building."

When Wiir Waar told Mams about the plan later that night, the matriarch of the Ser Cus decided the rest of the troupe should immediately leave Ambrit.

"Should anything go amiss," Mams said, "we would all be in great danger. I cannot risk implicating the Ser Cus in any treasonous acts. We will strike the tents tomorrow and leave for Pintone. We will go to the Catfish Festival. You and the Z's must stay behind to help Tyme, and fade into the shadows when you are done."

THE ROUTE UP
THE BACK

The next morning Wiir Waar and the Z's helped take down the tents and pack up the Ser Cus. As the wagons rolled out of Ambrit, they slipped away from the caravan. Wiir Waar went to get a Founding Mothers costume for Tyme while the Z's met up with Jyg and Bones on the back side of Empress Auditorium. The building was in the southwestern part of town on a small hill overlooking the city, just high enough to offer good views of the capitol without straining the horses pulling fancy carriages, nor requiring an extra brakeman coming down.

The building had a large domed roof with three smaller domes attached in front to enlarge the entrance and sides of the building. Rows of small skylights, windows and vents made beautiful patterns around the domes and tops of the walls.

The back corner of the building was built over a cliff of limestone rock that had been augmented with stone block foundation buttresses. Because the cliff faced the afternoon sun, no one went there. The scorched hill beneath the cliff and buttresses held a scattered collection of boarded up houses and walled up buildings tunneled into the hillside.

Jyg posted Bones for lookout. The raven soon spotted the Z's and brought them to where Jyg had found a hidden spot for a staging area behind some dilapidated sheds between two foundation buttresses. The limestone cliff above was pocked with holes of all sizes and shapes, which made it easy for them to climb.

At the top of the cliff was an access path wide enough for a wagon around the building. The mid-morning sun was already heating up the back of the auditorium, which was covered with trim work of thin columns and high pointing arches and decorative embellishments. Jyg studied and memorized a couple of route options. He would climb it later when it was cool and dark, and he had less chance of being seen.

The trio returned that evening under a purplish and bruised sunset. The moon would not rise for another three hours. Jyg studied and visualized the climb, practicing a sequential charade of moves necessary to make it safely up the trim work.

"Some of this is very dynamic climbing," he told the Z's. "'Tis critical to keep my momentum going through the thin places." He put on a small backpack with a skyhook, and a wide leather belt, which trailed two lines of cactus fiber cord from Sikes, made with the finest, strongest weave available.

When the first stars appeared in the sky, Jyg began his climb. He put his feet on the outside of one arch trim, his hands on another, and extended his arms to lie backwards, creating enough pressure with his body to hold him in place. He walked his feet up while pulling up sideways, arm over arm, climbing quickly and methodically up the lower row of arches.

The Z's watched with admiration as Jyg moved fluidly up the wall. They knew the strength required to perform such feats, and the skill needed to do it so smoothly—and look effortless.

When Jyg got to the vent, he attached the skyhook pulley so that it was hidden under the overhang. He checked that the bars on the opening were still loose and able to be removed. After putting them back into place, he signaled the Z's and was lowered back to the ground.

THE 7TH HELL

The 75th *Prayer for the Damned* took Tyme to the bottom of the 7th hell. That was when Riin Ruel began to reveal the true nature of their mission.

"The locks sealing the levels of hell in the *Prayers for the Damned* can be recited backwards," Riin Ruel told Tyme with great seriousness, "thus opening a gateway allowing a Divine Warrior access to battle the demons within."

Tyme listened gravely.

"There is also a more immediate gateway," Riin Ruel divulged solemnly. "If you recite the 20th Prayer, *Flee Your Mortal Body*, while you slay someone with a Divine Dagger, you will link together spiritually in the Yoke."

Riin Ruel pulled out a leather pouch with a short strand of prayer beads made of bone. "These are the end bones from the little fingers of sword hands."

She rubbed them gently. "One from each of the thirteen people I have had to kill in my life. I Yoked myself with each of them. Thirteen souls with whom my fate is now forever linked. Thirteen demons I must battle, to help free those souls from eternal torment."

"I have gone as deep as the 5th hell," Riin Ruel whispered, "but I have never reached the 7th hell, which is necessary in order to fulfill the last two prayers."

"But you," Riin Ruel said in awe, "You have the opportunity to Yoke with the Czarzina as you kill her and make a gateway straight to the seventh hell. You can arrive fresh without struggling through the upper hells. Then you can recite the

76th Prayer of the Dead."

Riin Ruel paused solemnly. 'Tis short," she warned Tyme, "but it will require a great force of will and exertion of strength. Grit your teeth and prepare to learn the 76th *Prayer for the Dead.*"

Tyme steeled herself for greater terrors to come.

"Smite the Beast!" Riin Ruel hissed, dramatically divulging the prayer's name.

THE CACTUS CLUB

When Tyme finished her training with Riin Ruel, she felt overwhelmed, dazed and disturbed. She had a throbbing headache and was nauseous. Thankfully, their session had not lasted all morning. She returned to her room and lay down to rest. She woke up feeling disoriented. The Czarzina's banquet was now just ten days away.

"Are you okay?" Epoh asked with concern when she came out onto the Veranda patio after the heat.

Tyme managed a weak laugh. "I am actually feeling a little better. I had a terrible headache and dizziness, so I took a nap."

"I think she is pushing you too hard," Epoh fretted.

"There are major issues that I want to share with you," she said, "but I don't have the strength to talk about it now. Just thinking of it ... starts to give me a headache."

"We can talk of it tomorrow," Epoh consoled her. "Right now, you need to take a break from all that and get more rest."

"I just slept from mid-morning till after the heat," Tyme said with stretch of her arms. It felt good to be up and moving. "Let's go dancing," she said on impulse.

"Dancing?" Epoh responded with a surprised smile.

"We need to relax and have fun."

"Sounds great," Epoh agreed.

"We can wear our new clothes," Tyme added with growing enthusiasm. Epoh had taken her, Jyg, and Klew to a tailor when they first arrived in Ambrit. She had a skirt and a blouse made of linen, which felt delightful against her skin in the hot, lowland climate. She also had a stylish silk dress.

Since the Ser Cus had left for Pintone, Wiir Waar and the Z's were now staying with them at the Veranda. Tyme invited everyone to come along.

"I know a perfect spot with a great dance band," Wiir Waar informed them. "'Tis nearly dim Moonday, so it will not be crowded. We can have our own party in a corner."

When the heat ended, they joined their friends on a patio. Even though they believed they were not being watched at the Veranda, they still refrained from using the front door to ensure they were not being followed. They slipped through a back fence in small groups and faded into the shadows, heading toward the south side of town.

The Cactus Club was on Hillside Road. The rooftop patio was filled with lanterns and pots of brightly colored agave cactus and succulents. A band played in the front. In the back were some fountains and a pocked limestone wall with naturally sculpted chambers and alcoves filled with benches, cushions, and firepots. They picked a small, private cave with a great view of the patio where they could hear the band.

"Drinks are on me," Epoh declared, "compliments of the cargo bird." He said nothing of the ruby he had recently sold at the Hidden Crypt.

"Cargo bird!" Bones flew in and mimicked Epoh's voice from a perch on a stool, then added, "Saved by the bird!" in Zandero's voice.

Everyone burst out laughing as the band started a lively tune. Tyme grabbed Epoh and they began to dance.

"Like to dance?" Wiir Waar asked Jyg.

"Sure," he replied. The dance was a fast high-stepper that was all the rage in the capitol, and also in Karvor. Rona had loved it. While she was a spirited and athletic dancer, Jyg was amazed at how much stronger and more powerful Wiir Waar felt in his arms.

"You dance well!" she laughed as they linked elbows and leaned away from each other to spin in a circle. When the next song had a similar fast beat, they continued dancing.

Zintowo headed to the dance floor near the band where he was soon picked up as a partner. After two more fast songs the band took a break, and the dancers came back to the tables.

"I would like to hear more about the cargo bird," Wiir Waar requested, hoping to prompt a response from Bones. She was eager to keep everyone's mind off Tyme.

"Cargo bird!" Bones complied using Wiir Waar's voice, then added, "Saved by the bird!" in Zandero's voice, and "Bring your raven?" in Panr's scratchy voice.

"Yes, we brought our raven," Jyg laughed along with the others. "Thank goodness."

Epoh's tales of the cargo bird soon led to questions over the ancient manuscripts and the book of paintings he had found. And all of the strange animals and birds. Everyone sat quietly for a moment trying to imagine such things.

"If the Ancient Ones were so smart," Zandero asked finally, "how did they screw up everything so much?"

"Sadly, smart is not the same as wise," Tyme noted. "Behind all their marvelous inventions they were probably just people like us. Except they had more powerful weapons, so when they waged war, the destruction reached a terrible magnitude."

"What kind of battle ends up killing all the life in the Dead Sea?" Zintowo wondered.

"Maybe 'twas not just a war," Epoh speculated. "I think something else must have happened to the world. And that was followed by a war."

"So, you really think the Ancient Ones were just people like us?" Zandero asked. "Without wings and heavenly voices?"

"I think those descriptions are more metaphorical than factual," Epoh replied. "I think we can learn more from the stories of the Ancient Ones if we look beyond the literal interpretation to the deeper and more important issues. What are the tales trying to teach us?"

"What are they trying to teach us?" asked Wiir Waar.

"When women stray from the loving path of Divine," Epoh answered, "terrible evils can be unleashed. Hubris, greed, and selfishness can destroy the mightiest of civilizations. The ensuing madness can have devastating consequences."

"Blood and guts!" Bones swore.

"What has been done, has been done," Wiir Waar saw little reason to agonize. "We have all learned to live with the consequences of their destruction. Mayhaps 'tis easier not to dwell on the glory of a world we no longer have."

The band resumed playing.

"Right now," Tyme announced, "I want to focus on what I *do* have! Wonderful friends! A loving partner! And great music!" She grabbed Epoh's hand and pulled him off to dance.

"Care to dance again?" Wiir Waar asked Jyg. "Or would you prefer to hang out with the Z's?" She did not want him to feel obligated to entertain her. "I can easily find a different partner."

"I think dancing is just what I need tonight," Jyg replied, taking her hand. They joined Tyme and Epoh. 'Twas another high-stepper, which allowed them to dance as a four-some and briefly switch partners, Tyme with Jyg, and Tyme with Wiir Waar when the men danced together.

The dancing and music gave Tyme an exuberant and joyous feeling. She and Epoh grinned with delight, constantly making eyes and love looks at each other when they parted and came back together. Epoh admired how Tyme seemed to totally forget her worries. Her mantle. He tried to do the same.

The band played three fast songs in a row. The fourth song was much slower and gave the dancers a chance to catch their breath. Tyme and Epoh embraced each other firmly, swaying to the music. Jyg and Wiir Waar danced closely as well. He was now taller than she. To her he had always been like a young brother, but now he was a man.

When the band took a break, the dancers returned to the tables. The waning half-full moon was rising on the horizon. Jyg could not help thinking about what Epoh had described of the pictures of the world during the age of the Ancient Ones. How there were plants covering entire hillsides and valleys.

Even in the direct sunlight.

"Were there deserts back in those days?" Jyg asked.

"Yes. The paintings showed deserts. And the cover of the book had a view of the world from high in the air."

"What does the world look like?"

"'Tis round like the moon," Epoh replied. "Just like the Ambri taught. The Dead Sea used to be blue and covered much the world. You can see both green and brown regions of land."

"I wonder if any of those green regions still exist?" Zintowo reflected.

"Everything is green and covered with plants in the high mountains at Lost Valley," Tyme reminded them, "where Tao Tau took me with Spike." She had always found it difficult to describe what the amazing abundance of plants actually looked like. The vibrancy of the new growth. "Clouds of mist sometimes cover the plants in moisture and water droplets," she told them. "The mist feels tingly and cool and refreshing on your skin."

"Mayhaps if such places exist high in the Barrier Mountains," Epoh reasoned, "they might still exist elsewhere in the world as well.'"

"You mean on the other side of the Endless Waste?" Klew wondered.

"The Hool had to come from somewhere," Epoh shrugged. He told them of Jchow Oasis, the whitewashed buildings, the vast network of the underground city carved into the rock. "The people who live there today all believe the Hool came from further east."

"What do you think?" Klew asked.

"I do not think the Endless Waste goes forever," Epoh said. He told them about Grinst seeing evidence of a trail going in and out of the Valley of Death. "Grinst was convinced there was something on the other side."

"Mayhaps some of those green regions still exist elsewhere," Jyg said.

"Mayhaps," Tyme agreed. "We can only hope."

THE YOKE

The next evening Epoh and Tyme met alone to talk. He sensed she was struggling with the vows she made to Riin Ruel not to discuss what she was learning with anyone else.

"Since you are not able to tell me what's bothering you," Epoh said from their perch on the patio, "Let me share some things that are bothering me, and see if there are any correlations."

"Okay," Tyme nodded.

"If I say something that you have not talked about, you can tell me without breaking your vows to Riin Ruel. If you do not say anything, then I will know it is a subject you have discussed with Riin Ruel, and you can not talk about it."

Tyme smiled at his persistence and cleverness.

"I told you earlier I know a little about the *Glories*," Epoh began. "They are the triumphant hallelujahs of praise in the *Prayers of the Dead* that start after the *Bridge*. When we talked about it in the Hollow Hills, I read you this passage from the 23rd prayer, which is the first of the *Glories*."

Behold! There appeared a multitude of ladders, and upon their rungs the Angels of Light ascended into the heavens.

"Most likely the *Glories* come to their conclusion with the 50th Prayer for the Dead," Epoh said cautiously. "That is the Magnificent and Divine ending." He paused for a moment. "At the end of our time in Karvor, and when we were in the Tanis Hills, I could tell you were learning the *Glories*. There was something glowing about you whenever you finished your lessons with Riin Ruel."

"But when we came into the Hollow Hills, something changed. I could tell that what you were learning with Riin Ruel was no longer glorious, but hard, and challenging, and very draining. Since then, you have been more serious and less joyful."

Tyme sat solemnly listening.

"Because of your change in emotion, I started to put more credence into certain possibilities that I had not taken seriously before," Epoh continued. "But now I do." He paused for a few moments. "After the *Glories*, there is yet another group of *Prayers for the Dead*."

Tyme's eyes widened slightly. She lifted a brow without a word.

Epoh's heart began to thump in his chest. Could the wild speculations all be true? "The 51st Prayer for the Dead does not follow the 50th prayer," he began slowly.

Tyme continued to listen without comment.

"To reach the 51st prayer, one must begin at the 20th prayer, *Flee Your Mortal Body*."

Tyme tried to keep her face impassive. How much did Epoh know?

He pulled out a scroll. "The sentence I just read from the 23rd prayer is also in the 20th prayer, but with a different ending." He read from the scroll.

Behold! There appeared a multitude of ladders, and upon their rungs the Angels of Light ascended into the heavens. While far below Divine Warriors descended ladders into the lowest hells to win release of tormented captives, held fast by their evil actions and deeds.

Tyme licked her lips and did not say anything. The depth of his knowledge continually amazed her.

Epoh's chest tightened. The manuscripts with the wild speculations were true. "*Flee Your Mortal Body*," Epoh whispered, "the 20th Prayer for the Dead, is a doorway to the *Glories*. But also, a trap door to an alternative set of prayers that begins with the 51st Prayer for the Dead."

Tyme's face paled. The 51st and 52nd prayers were part of the Under Bridge, *The Path of Sorrows* and *The Path of Pain*. Epoh had sleuthed out the basic structure for all the *Prayers for the Dead*.

"Which leads to the *Prayers for the Damned*," he finished solemnly.

Tyme looked at him admirably. "You are quite the investigative scholar."

Epoh exhaled loudly. "That is why I went to the Hidden Crypt. The book I bought came in a locked box. Ser Jaza Zaja Ajaz warned me never to read any of the book aloud, and *never, ever,* speak any of the names from the book aloud."

Tyme chewed on her lip.

"The name of the book is *The Lair of the Beast,* by Ser Zoltu Zoltu Zoltu," Epoh said in a hushed voice. "'Tis a map showing locked pathways into hell, much like the *Prayers for the Damned*."

"And you have read it?" Tyme asked with unease.

"Not all, but enough," Epoh said. "I did not want to read more."

Tyme could no longer keep quiet. "Riin Ruel wants me to assassinate the Czarzina and then battle the demon who possesses her soul."

"The Yoke," Epoh guessed in a hushed voice. He had read references to such spiritual battles but considered them hyperbole for dramatic effect.

Tyme nodded slightly.

"A ritual slaying," Epoh said with trepidation. He wanted to shout in warning. The whole idea seemed wrong. "Why would you bind yourself to someone so evil and cruel?"

"To save her soul," Tyme replied, "and ensure the evil inside her is unable to return to the world."

"And how can that happen?"

Tyme could no longer hide from Epoh what she was learning. "If I look into her eyes and recite *Flee Your Mortal Body* as she dies, I can trail her later straight into the lowest hell."

Her voice grew hushed. "Riin Ruel says I can arrive fresh enough to perform the 76th prayer, *Smite the Beast!*"

Epoh felt numb. *Smite the Beast!* "Is such a thing truly possible?" he asked fearfully.

"The *Glories* are magnificent beyond words," Tyme replied. "But I am sickened and horrified by the *Prayers for the Damned*."

"As I was horrified and repelled by *The Lair of the Beast*," Epoh said with anguish. "And now more so! Knowing your collusion!"

Neither of them slept well that night.

A TRUE WARRIOR

Although Tyme revealed secret aspects of her training and studies with Epoh, she did not share those details with Klew and Jyg. But she was eager to hear their views on a different issue.

"I have been thinking," Tyme said, "of the vows I took with Klew when I became a True Warrior."

"What did you say for the first vow?" Epoh asked. He had studied the Book of Tatano, the first True Warrior, and the only man whose writings were in the *Book of Elders*. Tatano ended the Dark Ages when he convinced his soldiers to stop fighting for leadership amongst themselves and submit to the will of the Women's Clans. Epoh knew Tatano's original first vow, to be a servant to the Women's Clans, was now normally changed to be a servant of the Ambri Empire.

"I vowed to be a servant of the Noble Path," Tyme said.

"I told her the dangers of vowing total allegiance to a government or political group," Klew explained. "How I had struggled to follow the Czarzina's orders. 'Tis best to vow to the highest ideal, not to a specific person, faction, or government."

Klew recounted his graduation from the Military Academy and placing second in the final Swordmanser competition behind his best friend Targono. How his friend was awarded and made squire for a captain who was a True Warrior. "The captain spoke frankly at an offisers council about his resolve to follow first his own beliefs if ever faced with a morally questionable order," Klew related. "His comments enraged the Czarzina, who demanded unquestioning loyalty."

"The captain was transferred from the Heart to the Hammer, and exiled to Vargo Garrison, where he lost his squire," Klew continued. "Targono was demoted to private. I never heard from him again."

"And this might be the same Captain Targono whose spy, Gribono, killed Noot?" Epoh recalled.

"That is my suspicion," Klew nodded. "Targono would be fast to rise up through the ranks if military brilliance was the main criteria, not politics. Fighting rebels at Vrak Pass is the one place where a man might rise from private to captain solely by his own merit. Those are the most battle hardened of all soldiers."

"Blood and guts!" Bones confirmed with a croak.

"Following the Noble Path did not work out well for the captain, nor Targono," Jyg noted.

"The Noble Path is never easy," Klew agreed. "That is why so few men take the vows anymore. The statue of Tatano in the refuge represents the highest ideals of sacrifice and submission. Most soldiers today find it much easier to be members of the Hands or Fists."

"Remember when you were trying to get Klew to make you a True Warrior?" Jyg mused.

"At first he said only a man could be a True Warrior," Tyme smiled slyly. "But I convinced him otherwise."

"That does not surprise me," Epoh laughed. "Actually, the *Book of Elders* does not say only men can be a True Warrior. It just assumes only men would *want* to do so. The purpose was to manage and control groups of armed men. Women had no desire to be in subservient roles."

Klew nodded in agreement. "Men are to be helpmates and protectors to our sers and wives."

"At your service," Bones mimicked Klew's voice.

"I have also vowed to be a helpmate and protector," Tyme said, "to follow the Noble Path." She brought her fist to her chest in a Barbarian salute. "I am ready to be that servant. Whatever it takes. Whatever the cost."

Epoh listened somberly. He knew the cost could be great.

"Now, I seek guidance in what I must do," Tyme continued. "Riin Ruel believes I am to be a Warrior Empress, and that I must kill the Czarzina. Is that what a True Warrior would do?"

"The Czarzina is corrupting the greater good," Klew said with distaste. "She is evil and must be confronted."

"Confronted or killed?" Tyme asked.

"I do not know if she can be stopped without killing her," Klew said sadly.

No one said anything for a long while.

"The second vow of the True Warrior," Tyme said at last, "is to put others first. Becoming Empress, or even Czarzina, is not putting others first. That's putting *me* first. Even if I *do* kill the Czarzina, as a True Warrior, I should not be the one to replace her. I am supposed to be the servant."

Epoh was not so sure. "You can be Empress or Czarzina and still put others first in your actions and deeds," he reasoned. "Your government can put the people first and foremost."

"But that is still me overseeing and watching over everything," Tyme replied. "That makes it all about me. Me making or approving all the decisions." Tyme shook her head. "A True Warrior would not become Empress to order everyone around and save people from their own mess. A True Warrior would lead by example and encourage everyone to find their own voice, their own power--and save themselves."

"Lead by example," Epoh nodded. "I like that. Encourage the Senate and the people to make the changes."

"Do you think there are that many honest women in the Senate?" Jyg asked.

"If there is not," Tyme answered, "Maybe I should focus my energies on helping to make them honest, rather than ruling over them and ordering them about."

"How do you make them honest?" Klew asked.

"I do not really know," Tyme replied. "And I have just eight days to figure it out."

MOTHER OF ALL DAUGHTERS

Tyme had told Epoh of the 76th *Prayer for the Dead, Smite the Beast!* And more recently, she had revealed the final *Prayer for the Dead*, the 77th, *Slay the Beast!*" He had no idea what to believe about such arcane and terrifying conjectures.

While she trained and studied each day with Riin Ruel, Epoh skimmed through *The Lair of the Beast* by Ser Zoltu Zoltu Zoltu, desperately hoping to find something that might help Tyme better understand her path and destiny. The book ended at the bottom of a seven-layered hell. The same location as the 75th *Prayer for the Dead*. He found nothing but despair and misery. Epoh locked the nightmarish *Lair of the Beast* back into its metal bound box and stored it wrapped and tied in the bottom of a trunk.

Epoh was relieved to focus his energies on the set of scrolls he purchased at the Knowledge Scroll, Ser Qwen Qwam Qwil's commentaries on the *Kabaal Prophecies* from the *Mask of Brilliance*.

"This is really interesting," he told Tyme while he studied one of the scrolls. "She has a section specifically about the prophecies of a Bright One."

"Does she say *a* Bright One as well?" Tyme asked hopefully.

"No, she translates it in the Ambri fashion, *the* Bright One. But she does have some very unique views as to her role.

Rather than focusing on the warrior aspect, she emphasizes the importance of the verses about a Bright One as our mother."

"Which verses are those?" Tyme asked with interest.

"This is the verse she thinks is the most important," Epoh replied, finding the passage of text and reading aloud.

She is the Mother of all Daughters,
the Daughter of all Mothers,
Who fills the world with love and compassion!
The Bright One will vanquish the enemies of Light,
and bring Righteousness and Truth to all.

"Mother of all Daughters," Tyme said thoughtfully. *"Fills the world with love and compassion.* I like that part" She looked at Epoh. "Riin Ruel told me the prophecies say *The Bright will slay the enemies of Light,* but you just read *vanquish the enemies of Light."*

"Scholars sometimes disagree on exact words for translations. I think *vanquish* would be more accurate here," Epoh answered.

"What do you think *vanquish* means? Are there any passages where a Bright One is not fighting something?" Tyme asked hopefully.

"Vanquish in this context means eliminating. Mayhaps even with love and compassion from the previous line."

"Using love and compassion to conquer the enemies of Light?" Tyme pondered with intrigue.

"It is certainly a credible interpretation." Epoh said with conviction. "Of course, some scholars would disagree. But there are others who raise the possibility."

"I wonder what Riin Ruel would say to that?" Tyme remarked. She wished she could talk more about her unease with Riin Ruel, but her teacher dismissed such ruminations as evidence of a lack of faith.

"You asked if there were any passages where a Bright One is

not fighting something." Epoh flipped the pages of the book for a moment and then read aloud again.

The Bright One will bring a New Light to all
Her Truth a Beacon of Hope
Wise and Loving Mother
Her rule is like a gentle rain.

"*A gentle rain,*" Tyme pondered. "*A wise and loving mother.* That is certainly a very different viewpoint."

The next day Epoh had an even more startling revelation. He read the passage that Riin Ruel used to describe the Bright One as Warrior Empress:

Her gaze pierces all souls,
Her Sword a Fiery Truth.
Morning Star of Heaven,
Whose Dagger slays the Beast.

"Ser Qwen Qwam Qwil says in her commentaries that this passage was originally not even in the *Kabaal Prophecies* from the *Mask of Brilliance*. This prophecy was added later by scribes who took it from the *Mask of Splendor*."

Epoh shook his head. "She even questions whether the Morning Star of Heaven is the same as the Bright One, or someone else entirely. She makes a convincing argument that this might be a much older prophecy regarding something else. Either way, she casts some major questions about putting too much emphasis on this one prophecy."

Tyme felt like a burden was lifting from her spirit.

"If you take out this prophecy, the remaining ones have a much different tone," Epoh revealed. "The Warrior Queen fights only for truth and is subservient to the role of Divine Mother and Daughter."

"She doesn't *slay the Beast!* in any of the other prophecies?" Tyme asked, seeking reassurance.

"No, she does not," Epoh replied. "Most of the other prophecies have a completely different focus and direction."

"I need a new direction," Tyme said resolutely. "The path I am on is not going the right way."

'We need to be guided by the entire group of prophecies and teachings," Epoh agreed. "Not by just a single passage or verse. Especially when there are contradictions."

"I am done with the *Prayers for the Damned*," Tyme declared sternly.

"Hallelujah!" Epoh exclaimed in approval.

"I am not going to *Smite the Beast!* Nor *Slay the Beast!*" Tyme vowed adamantly. "Conjuring up demon battles in the lowest pits of hell gives demons what they want," she said with growing awareness. "They want me, in hell, using violence trying to stop violence." She shook her head in distaste.

"What we focus on, we become," Epoh agreed. "Leave the Beast behind. Turn to love and compassion."

"*She is the Mother of all Daughters, the Daughter of all Mothers, who fills the world with love and compassion!*" Tyme thoughtfully recited the passage. "Tao Tau always told me that Divine loves us like a mother loves her daughters. That should be my role model. To love the Czarzina like a mother loves her daughter." Tyme paused in thought. "What would I do if I was the mother of the Czarzina?"

Epoh shook his head. He could not imagine such a thing.

"What mother would kill her own daughter?" Tyme asked. "No matter what wrongs or wickedness the daughter has done, a mother would always pray that the daughter would change and cease her evil ways. A mother will always hope for redemption and be ready to show mercy and forgiveness."

"And if the mother sees the daughter doing great evil?" Epoh asked. "Does the mother not try and stop the daughter?"

"Of course," Tyme agreed. "But murder or assassination takes away any chance for redemption. Execution takes away any opportunity for a change of heart."

"Indeed," Epoh nodded.

"Rather than killing her own child," Tyme answered, "a mother would give her own life to try to stop the evil." She looked imploringly at Epoh. "What would we do if the Czarzina was *our* child?" she asked pointedly.

Epoh chewed his lip. He could not comprehend it.

"Not every child follows in the footsteps of their parents," Tyme pointed out. "Look at your uncle the Duke. Born from the same mother as your father, King Eyrico, who has devoted his life to the noble ideals that Dayrstad was founded upon. Yet his brother, the Duke, the same blood, raised by the same mother and family, abandons those ideals to grasp power by any means possible. Mayhaps even treason."

Epoh nodded his head sadly. He had heard the disturbing whispers of how Duke Eddarko had been as a child. Of his violent and abusive temper. His mean and cruel behavior toward animals, servants, and others.

"No one is immune from such tragedy," Tyme continued. "If we had children, there is no guarantee that one might not turn against the other. Or even against us as well."

"No," Epoh admitted. The horrifying idea was almost blasphemous to speak, yet he knew 'twas true. "No parent has any guarantee, no matter how tenderly the child is raised." He exhaled sadly. "Not all children bring happiness. Some bring great heartbreak."

"The Czarzina is someone's child," Tyme shook her head. "Someone's grandchild."

"Every evil person in Ambra," Epoh observed, "is someone's child and grandchild." They both sat pondering that reality.

"What are you going to do?" Epoh inquired. "You only have six days to plan something."

"I am not sure yet," Tyme answered. She would have to face Riin Ruel. The question was soon or later?

GOOD THEATER

The next morning the group met together without Riin Ruel. Now that Tyme had finished her training and learned all the *Prayers for the Damned*, she met less with the warrior mystic, who was growing busier preparing for the shake-up she believed to be coming with the death of the Czarzina. Tyme took the opportunity to tell the others she had decided that she was not going to kill anyone.

"I am going to confront her with her crimes," Tyme said boldly, "so that everyone can hear and know of her corruptions."

"Planning to confront the Czarzina," Wiir Waar pointed out, "is much different than planning to kill the Czarzina."

The group was studying the diagram in the secret Dagger report showing where the crossbows were unable to shoot.

"Killing the Czarzina is about speed and stealth," Wiir Waar continued. "Confronting the Czarzina is about theater." She strutted grandly with her arms in the air as if to great applause. "And good theater is about suspense! Good theater," she said expansively, "is controlling and manipulating the emotions of the audience for maximum effect."

"Maximum effect," Tyme applauded. "I like it."

"Ser Cus style," the Z's affirmed together.

"Rather than dancing close with your dagger to confront the Czarzina," Wiir Waar advised, "You should control her from the stage. From a distance. Holding a dagger at her throat is too brutish, no matter how stylish the blade." Wiir Waar shook her head. "You must control her from afar. That enhances your power."

"What do you propose?"

"Use throwing knives rather than a dagger," Wiir Waar said as if 'twas obvious. "Nothing is more suspenseful."

"She has a point," Epoh agreed.

"You know my consistency with throwing knives," Tyme said dismissively.

"You claim your first few throws are always good," Wiir Waar reminded her confidently.

"Yes, that's true. But then they go bad, even after all my practice."

"No problem," Wiir Waar declared, "You will need only one, mayhaps, two throws, to make a grand and convincing performance!"

"I can do that."

Wiir Waar pointed to the diagram. "This shows three spots on the stage where the crossbows cannot hit you. If you stand in those places as you call out the Czarzina, you will appear invulnerable from the crossbows," Wiir Waar exclaimed, "that will be something that no one will ever forget."

"It does sound dramatic," Tyme lifted her thick, dark eyebrows in agreement.

"Very theatrical," Epoh enthused.

"With Riin Ruel, we talked about you dashing toward the dais during the Dance of the Masks to kill the Czarzina when there is a lot of noise and distraction. But if you are going to *confront* the Czarzina, you should appear, as if from nowhere," Wiir Waar said with an amazed look in her eye. "When the stage is silent, just before the Listing of the Women's Clans."

"Sshh! Quiet!" Bones hushed everyone.

"We should make a replica of the stage for you to practice," Zintowo advised. "We have the exact stage dimensions from the report. And you should practice with the skyhook and vent, going in and being lifted out. We can set up a training area in the back courtyard." The crew set off to help.

Wiir Waar stayed behind with Tyme. "Have you told Riin Ruel that you are planning on *confronting* but not killing the

Czarzina?"

"I have tried to tell her of my doubts all along," Tyme replied, "but she refuses to listen. She is convinced there is only one path—the one she and her group of spiritual warriors have laid out—and that I must follow their vision."

"Spiritual warriors?" Wiir Waar asked. "What does that mean?"

Tyme could not answer with the truth. *They want me to battle the Beast in the 7th Hell.* She evaded the question and changed the subject.

"If something were to happen to me," she told her friend, "I would not want Epoh to mourn me for too long. I want him to remember the love and joy we had together. And celebrate that by living and embracing life again. To find some type of happiness and fulfillment."

"Nothing bad is going to happen," Wiir Waar assured her. "We are going to have everything all planned out."

"I just need to know that everyone I love will be strong and go on to experience life for me," Tyme insisted. "To remember me in a positive way, not just sorrowful."

"Do you have a premonition?" Wiir Waar asked with concern.

"Just a realization of the huge risks involved," Tyme answered. "We both know there is no guarantee that I will be coming back."

A few hours later Riin Ruel arrived at the Veranda, as Tyme prepared to practice her route in and out of the replica Empress Auditorium the group had built in a shaded courtyard. The stage was outlined on the ground with reeds, with a built-up dais and Czarzina's chair, and the marks for Tyme's route across the stage, including the three places where she could stand safe from the crossbows. There were walls and curtains built to scale showing the door and hallway off stage to a corner below the skyhook, which was attached above on the stone wall of the bell tower at the same height as the auditorium vent, with a frame representing the hole Tyme would crawl through.

"Everything is built to the exact scale of the auditorium," Zintowo said proudly. "This will be just like training for a Ser Cus act."

"The only difference, three of us will pull you up to the vent window to start," Zandero explained. "At the auditorium, I will drop and run down the cliff to pull you up."

Tyme put her hand into the small loop at the end of the cord and pulled it snug up against the back of her wrist and into her palm to hold herself securely with little effort. She held her arm above her head to take any slack out of the cord and nodded that she was ready. The Z's and Jyg promptly pulled Tyme up to the sky-hook where she sat inside the frame representing the vent window.

"Good," Zintowo directed. "You will sit there until you hear the music cue to drop inside. Just tug on the cord and we will lower you in."

Tyme was swiftly let back to the ground.

"Now pull the cord to your waist and release your wrist," Zintowo continued. "Lift your hand up high, and Zandero will pull the line back up to see how much to bring in until you can just reach the loop with your fingers. Just push the cord into the corner. No one will see it in the darkness. Make sure the loop is hanging how you want it so you can grab it and put it on quick to get out."

Tyme made her way out of the hallway and was shown the landmarks around the stage and dais to triangulate the lines and find the safe areas out of crossbow range. With Riin Ruel watching, Tyme strode along the route without stopping. After reaching the Czarzina's chair, she began to practice her escape.

She pulled out a bag representing flash powder, closed her eyes, and made her way across the stage and through the curtains to the door and exit into the hallway. She found the corner where the loop of cord was dangling, grabbed the thin line, and slipped her wrist into the small loop. She yanked the cord to send the signal and was immediately pulled up into the air by the Z's and Jyg. At the top she slipped back through the frame representing the vent window and was lowered swiftly back to the ground.

"Very impressive," Riin Ruel said with satisfaction. "I leave you to continue practicing and will see you tomorrow morning."

After she left, Tyme did a different routine on the stage. She came in from the hallway at a different song, and joined other dancers, circling the stage twice. The two circles gave her adequate opportunity to locate the faint stain on the floor showing the first spot where she must stop. When the music ended, she would hunch down above the mark, then jump up, calling out the Czarzina and throwing a dagger into the head of a wooden statue next to the Czarzina to keep the ruler from running. Still practicing, Tyme feinted and ran to the next safe spot, stopped, and then continued to the third. From there she pulled out the flash powder and made her planned escape. She practiced the entire routine over and over again the rest of the day.

TOP ARCHERS

Vela Vara, the Will of the Blades, was a true believer in the power and righteousness of Czarzina Hana Hama Hala. 'Twas the Czarzina, her mentor and guardian, who had promoted her rapid rise to Will of the Blades. That was why Vela Vara was dismayed to hear of the Czarzina's plans to have a banquet and theater performance at the Empress Auditorium.

The Will of the Blades did not like how the Czarzina was guarded while on her wooden throne on the dais. She did not like the contrived use of the hidden and remote crossbows in the ceiling. The Will preferred the guards to be close at hand, with two curved swords, ready for any surprise. When she expressed her concerns, the Czarzina brushed them away.

"I have a spy," the Czarzina said without further explanation, "who has uncovered a plot against me that very night. The assassin will attempt to come up the escape tunnel to surprise me from behind." She turned to the Will. "You will post guards in the tunnel and hide guards at the safe house to catch them. Alive," the Czarzina added. "I want to find out who is behind this!"

"If there is a plot against you, I believe we should also station guards with swords on the dais and along the sides of the stage," Vela Vara advised with concern.

"And show everyone sitting in the auditorium that I am nervous and worried about my own safety with guards all around? Never!" Czarzina Hana Hama Hala replied sternly. "The plot has already been taken care of," she said confidently. "Just station the guards where I say."

"As you command," the Will saluted, but did not turn to leave.

"What now?" the Czarzina asked with irritation.

"The ceiling guards," Vera Vala said hesitantly, "should be the very best archers. Most Blades have little practice with crossbows. Mayhaps we should select a special group for the task."

"Excellent suggestion," Czarzina Hana Hama Hala replied. "And I know just the lieutenant to put in charge." She had recently met the woman at a Heart Legion archery contest. "I will have her put together a group of top archers."

PASSED THE MANTLE

Three nights before the Czarzina was to be at the Empress Auditorium, Riin Ruel returned to the Veranda and met with Tyme.

"You have been very diligent in sharing with me everything that you know of the sacred teachings given to you by the Daggers," Tyme told Riin Ruel. She had only recently learned the name of the secret group. "I appreciate all of your sacrifices and admire your persistence and determination in carrying out your mission. You have done everything you possibly could."

Riin Ruel nodded her head in cautious agreement. She had a feeling this was leading to something else.

"Now that you have passed the mantle on to me," Tyme acknowledged her growing sense of calling, "you must be willing to trust me and accept the choices I make. To accept what I believe it means to be a Bright One."

"What it means to be *The* Bright One?" Riin Ruel cried with indignation. "I was not aware there were choices."

"There are always choices. You taught me that. I have chosen not to kill the Czarzina."

"If you do not kill the Czarzina," Riin Ruel stated with agitation and authority, "there will be civil war. Thousands will die!"

"I believe there will be civil war either way," Tyme said sadly.

"You can *stop* the war by creating a new Holy Ambri Empire. You must rule as Empress."

"I have no desire for soldiers to kill, or be killed, in my

name," Tyme replied. "Remember the boy from the Jawbone Ridge gang that saved me from Rocozo's ambush in the ally? His name is Scoop. He dropped one of the villains with his slingshot. When we rolled the thug over, we found he was dead."

Tyme paused for a moment. "Now, Scoop has reoccurring nightmares of it happening again, but when he rolls the body over, he finds that *I* am the one that is lying there dead. He ends up killing me by mistake."

Riin Ruel offered no sympathy but shook her head derisively. "You are going to base your decision on the dream of a boy gang member?"

"I base my decision on everything I have learned in my life," Tyme declared. "Not solely what I have learned from you. Everything that Tao Tau taught me. My vows I took with Klew to be a True Warrior. Everything that Epoh has taught me and continues to teach me. Even the ugly things I learned in Karvor about politics, rebellion, and revenge. All of these things guide me."

"You are here to end the era of the corrupt line of Czarzinas and establish a new Divine Empire," Riin Ruel thundered. "You are here to vanquish Czarzina Hana Hama Hala, body and soul."

"What if I look into her eyes, as you have taught me, and see that her soul is *not* lost?" Tyme asked. "And even if it appears lost, killing her removes any chance for her to find redemption."

"What of *Smite the Beast?* What of *Slay the Beast?*" Riin Ruel demanded. "What of your duties as the Bright One to rid the world of evil?"

"You are so eager to attack demons," Tyme answered, "you would justify killing the Czarzina in order to open a pathway to the 7th hell. But throwing myself into demon battles in the lowest pits of hell gives demons what they want. They want me, in hell, fighting." Tyme shook her head with resolution. "I must leave the Beast behind and turn to love and compassion."

"If you can not kill the Czarzina," Riin Ruel vowed in fury, "tell me now. *I* will do it."

"And you will be the Bright One?"

"No! Of course not," the Point of the Daggers snapped. "But I can be the Bright One's Hand. I may not be able to *Slay the Beast!* But I can surely *Smite the Beast!*"

"Killing the Czarzina is not the right thing to do. Coming to power through violence is not the example I want to set," Tyme reiterated. "Nor do I choose to battle demons in hell. It would defeat the purpose if I allowed you to do those tasks for me. Or in my name."

"What do you plan to do?" Riin Ruel whispered in resigned shock. "What other choice do you have?"

"I can confront the Czarzina," Tyme said, "I can speak truth to power and call out her crimes."

"And you think that will make any difference?" Riin Ruel snorted with disbelief. "Everyone already knows of her crimes! That is the problem! No one is able to do anything about it!" She shook her head in despair. "That was where *you* were supposed to come in and be different." The warrior mystic covered her face with her hands over her colossal failure to mentor the young woman properly.

THE NIGHT BEFORE

The Z's, Jyg, Bones, and Klew returned to the Empress Auditorium the night before the Czarzina's banquet to recheck the sky hook pulley and mark out the safe places on the stage. Klew and Zintowo hoisted Jyg and Zandero separately on the cord up to the vent window to look inside.

"Sshh! Quiet!" Bones hushed them from the nearby roof edge. When they affirmed the building was empty, they were lowered inside and made their way in the darkness to the stage.

Jyg had a collection of pre-cut cords, which he and Zandero used to precisely measure from various angles on the stage to find the exact locations of the three safe spots where Tyme could stand without being hit by the arrows. Jyg marked each area with a stain that would grow darker by tomorrow evening, then fade again later that night. When finished, they were hoisted out of the auditorium and lowered back to the ground where they hid the lines in dark corners for the following night. Everything was working according to plan.

Tyme had hoped to have all her friends together on the night before the banquet. But Jyg, Klew and the Z's had things to get ready at the Auditorium, and Wiir Waar had an unexpected problem regarding Tyme's costume, and was visiting the seamstress.

Now that they were gone, Tyme felt an unexpected calm that everyone was not together. That seemed too foreboding-- like a last dinner. Being alone with Epoh was more relaxing.

Like tomorrow night was not a big event.

"I thought about going to the Cactus Club," Tyme said. "But that seems too far away. And we cannot replicate our earlier visit."

"Let's go to that small moonclub we passed the other day on the short-cut to the Mother Womb," Epoh replied. They had commented to each other about the narrow, tall building with patios.

"I can wear my new silk dress again!" Tyme exclaimed.

"New clothes are fun," Epoh agreed happily. The process of being measured for garments at the tailor shop had been fascinating, and he was quite satisfied with the results.

They snuck out through the small opening in the back fence and made their way to the nearby Sun Palm, which had the iconic lowland trees swaying above the patios on all three floors. The band was on the bottom floor, where a shaded courtyard with overflowing pots of succulents opened to the street. Tyme enjoyed looking at all the plants.

"Some of these grow in Lost Valley," she informed Epoh.

"'Tis amazing that you were able to go there on Spike," Epoh grinned.

"'Twas an exciting childhood," Tyme agreed wistfully. "I will always hold those days close in my heart. Along with everything I learned from Tao Tau."

They sat at a corner table overlooking the courtyard and ordered drinks. The band began a livelier tune so they jumped up to dance. The musicians noted their enjoyment and enthusiasm and began playing more dance songs. When the band took a break, Tyme approached the women and complimented their music. She returned to the table smiling.

Epoh looked at Tyme appreciatively. "I like how you make friends so easily," he said. "You are always talking with people, the waiters, the workers."

"I find people interesting," Tyme replied. "They told me we should check out the top patio. Let's go while the band is on a break." She led the way up the steep and narrow side stairs to the third floor. Colorful lanterns decorated the tables and floors, and small twinkling lights strung like stars above. 'Twas especially striking with the dark sky of the new moon. They sat at a table with a nice view of the city lights and the parks beside the Mother Womb and ordered non-alcoholic fruit drinks.

"When you fell into the river, everyone in Dayr Castle believed you to be dead," Tyme told him. "I never did. But I still mourned for you knowing that I would not see you for a long time, if ever again."

She looked at him with sad eyes. "Life lost its brightness and hope. I descended into a sea of grief. Tao Tau called it the Great Sorrow. She said I needed to grieve fully and allow Divine to help heal my heart. But she warned me not to wallow in my mourning. She said to pay respects to my loss, but then begin building my life anew. The Great Sorrow was nowhere to live."

"I have also visited the Great Sorrow," Epoh nodded. "Indeed, 'tis no place to live."

"If something unforeseen were to happen to me, I want you to remember the love and joy we had together," Tyme said, "and celebrate that by embracing life again. To continue having meaning and fulfillment and remember me with happiness and even delight!"

"There would be no delight for a very long time," Epoh informed her soberly.

Tyme said nothing but gave him a hug.

"Do you have a bad premonition?" Epoh asked nervously.

"No, I think our plan can work. But 'tis very risky. I said the same thing to Wiir Waar last night. We would be foolish not to acknowledge that."

They could hear the band playing below. They sat quietly, holding hands, listening to the music. The third song had a great beat, inviting them to make their way down the steep, outside stairs to the first floor to dance. On the next break they returned to the top patio.

"I have no vision of my future," Tyme told Epoh honestly.

"Of our future."

"I have no idea either," Epoh admitted. "I cannot imagine where this is going to take us."

"Riin Ruel thought that after killing the Czarzina, I would go before the Senate to be declared the Bright One," Tyme shook her head. "I do not see how that would happen whether I kill the Czarzina or confront her and denounce her as I now plan to do. I have no vision of standing before the Senasers and having them rallying to my cause. They do not know me," Tyme exclaimed. "And I do not know them."

"It does seem a bit unlikely."

"What else can I do? I have to try something. I cannot walk away from this struggle. My whole life has directed me down this path."

When the band resumed playing, they danced late into the evening. They did not talk again about the morrow, but held each other firmly as they twirled and stepped to the rhythm of fast songs, then embraced and hugged in total appreciation during the slow dances.

YOU ARE VERY TALL

Earlier that day when Vera Vela, the Will of the Blades, went to the Empress Auditorium to do an advance security check before the Czarzina's banquet, she was stunned to find Lieutenant Erin Rine of the Heart Legion arriving from Ralston Garrison with a group of longbow archers.

"Were you not told you would be shooting crossbows?" Vela Vara asked in frustration.

"Long bows, crossbows, no matter," the lieutenant shrugged. "These women can shoot anything."

"The problem is longbow archers are very tall," the Will of the Blades snapped in anger. It required long arms to pull back the bow. Women with long arms also had long legs. "You will be stationed in perches that are small and cramped."

The Czarzina herself had chosen the Heart Legion archers, so there was little the Will could do but order some crossbows brought quickly. While they were waiting, she showed the lieutenant the hidden catwalk where they would be stationed behind the patterned ceiling arch.

"You will inform your archers that being posted here is all highly secret," the Will ordered. "No talking to others about this." While the archers climbed up into their perches, the Will oversaw the Blades security sweep of the building. They did not notice the light stains on the floor of the stage.

The soldiers had finished their inspection of the building when the crossbows finally arrived. The lieutenant passed the crossbows up to the archers so they could have a moment to practice their sitting and firing positions. The archers found it cramped and extremely difficult to move. But after already arousing displeasure with the Will of the Blades, the lieutenant did not want to complain.

EMPRESS AUDITORIUM

The day of the banquet Tyme woke early. The sky was dark. She lay in bed, snuggled together with Epoh, enjoying the warmth and touch of his body.

"Are you awake?" she whispered.

"I am now," he answered sleepily.

"Good. That way you can be aware of how marvelous this feels," Tyme said as she gave him a loving squeeze.

They lay quietly savoring the moment, listening to each other's heartbeat and breath.

How do you stay so calm? Epoh almost asked her. But he did not want to speak aloud his own worries and doubts and spoil the aura of her relaxation.

"I have to pee," Tyme apologized with a giggle as they untangled themselves from each other. "I am ready to get up. This is the big day. I want to do my practice and get prepared."

"Yes," Epoh agreed as he sat up in bed. They both did longer devotions than normal, then met the others for breakfast. Riin Ruel had already left on her own mission. She was deeply dismayed by Tyme's choices and appeared to be in damage control with the Dagger leadership. Her absence made things more relaxed. Klew cooked Tyme's favorite corn bread with red sweet peppers and agave honey. Wiir Waar prepared a new sweet tea with spices and goat's milk that was the latest trend. Zintowo taught Jyg how to make delicious, fluffy omelets for everyone with onions, mushrooms and peppers. The atmosphere was jovial.

After the meal Tyme went to the shaded courtyard where they had the mock-up of the Empress Auditorium. The Z's and Jyg rapidly pulled Tyme up to the sky-hook where she slipped through a frame representing the vent window and was lowered swiftly back to the ground.

She made her way to the stage, circled, and then huddled over her first mark. When she jumped up, she called out the Czarzina and threw her knife. Then she feinted and ran to the next two spots. Finally, she pulled out the flash powder with one fast move, covered her eyes as if exploding the powder, and made her way with her eyes closed off the stage and through the curtains to exit at the auditorium. She found the corner where the cord was dangling, slipped her wrist into the small loop, tugged the cord, and was pulled up into the air by the Z's. She slipped back through the frame and was lowered swiftly back to the ground.

Tyme went over the routine for a few hours, especially the part where she was on the stage moving from safe spot to safe spot. Everyone watched and offered moral support.

Later, they all retired to the condition together for a light meal of cool pumpkin soup with rosemary nan bread, olives, goat cheese, humus, and vegetables.

"I have butterflies," Zandero said. "This feels like the most important Ser Cus performance ever.

Tyme got a big smile. "This *is* a Ser Cus performance." She lightheartedly puffed up her chest and proudly declared, "I am Ser Cus!"

"Forever!" Wiir Waar exclaimed. Everyone hoorayed.

They lay down to rest. Tyme normally took a short power nap but was now unable to sleep, nor did anyone else. When Tyme and Epoh rose to do their practice, the others joined in with the prayers and devotions.

The heat was ending when they left the condition. Wiir Waar and Klew gave them final hugs and safe prayers. They would wait behind at the Veranda. Jyg and the Z's slipped out the back fence and walked together, while Epoh escorted Tyme across Ambrit toward the hill in the southwestern part of town where the Empress Auditorium was built. The sunset colors filled the western sky with reds and purples. The building looked beautiful in the rich, dramatic light.

They let the sky grow dark as they slowly made their way around the back of the hill to a cluster of crumbling old buildings up against the bottom of the limestone cliffs beneath the back of the auditorium. Their staging area was hidden behind a sealed-up shed.

Epoh helped Tyme put on her costume. "I love you," he whispered.

"I love you," Tyme replied. "So very much." They kissed and embraced with a prolonged hug.

The Z's led Tyme up the limestone cliff between the foundation buttresses, keeping them hidden from sight. The rock was filled with holes and pockets in all shapes and sizes. The climbing was easy, a nice warm-up to get her blood flowing and help settle her nerves.

At the top of the cliff, they darted across the cart path to the back corner, where the building towered above them trimmed in relief with narrow columns, high pointing arches, and decorative designs. Tyme could not see the thin cord running up to the sky hook. Zintowo reached up and plucked it out of a darkened corner and handed her the end with the loop. She slipped her hand through the loop, set it snuggly around her wrist and hand, then held her hand ready, arm above her head. She nodded to Zandero, who pulled on the other end as he snuck back across the cart path to the edge of the limestone cliff. When it was tight, he wrapped a few loops around his leather wrist guard.

Epoh, Jyg and Bones were watching from nearby rooftops with good views of the area. They gave the all-clear sign.

"'Tis Ser Cus time," Zandero said with a confident smile. "Ser Cus … Tyme," he added as he stepped over the edge and began running in gentle bounds down the cliff while pulling and lifting Tyme swiftly up along the back wall of the Empress

Auditorium. Zintowo stood at the cliff edge to help pull and control the cord line and stop it smoothly when Tyme reached the top. At the same moment, Zandero arrived at a large pocket on the cliff where he knew to stop and stand.

Tyme slipped deftly onto the sash of the vent. She squatted comfortably as she listened to the intermittent sounds from the stage to determine how far the play had preceded. They were still in the first act. The evening was going slower than expected. Tyme tugged the cord once to give Zintowo the signal and sat down to wait.

Empress Auditorium was built on a hill overlooking the city with grand views of the capitol. Luxurious carriages made their way up the patterned, cobbled road that had been swept of all dirt and imperfection on orders of the Czarzina.

The central dome had three smaller domes attached in front making the grand entrance and sides of the building. Rows of small windows, vents, and skylights created beautiful patterns around the domes and walls.

The auditorium was built for political ceremonies and banquets, and rarely used, even in the days of the Ambri Empire. The biggest crowd was the evening of the dedication and opening of the building by Empress Rada Dara Arad. She had ordered it built to prove she was the greatest of Empresses. She never used the building or set foot in it again. Her wasteful opulence led to the Fracture Wars and the breakup of the Ambri Empire.

Czarzina Hana Hama Hala arrived with an escort of Blades who positioned themselves beside the main aisles around the audience, the servants' entrances, and along the back. A few Blades stationed themselves near the front. The Czarzina strode without guards across the wooden stage to sit in the center of the raised and ornately carved wooden dais with a few of her closest councilors, who each arrived bowing and heaping praises upon the Czarzina.

Above the dais the 12 archers with crossbows were tucked into their small, cramped perches along the low, narrow walkway behind the patterned arching wall and ceiling looking out over the stage.

The archers could shoot across the dance floor and into the front of the audience. Because of the angle, the archers could not shoot down at the dais below or the Czarzina herself.

TO FULFILL THE PROPHECY

Tyme pulled on the cord twice to signal the Z's that she heard the second act of the play begin. She looked down at the rooftops far below, trying to make out the buildings from which Epoh, Jyg and Klew where watching. She felt their energy and support, along with that from the Z's and Wiir Waar. And also, Tao Tau. She was certain that the old herbwoman would be pleased with her choices, even if Riin Ruel was not.

She took a deep breath to calm herself. Tonight, she would see what her choices would bring. No matter the outcome, she was committed. She felt she had no other option. Other than to walk away. And that seemed no choice at all. Her whole life had led her to this moment.

Below to the east she could see only a few lights around the Splendorous Dome of the Divine Womb. The priests, with the Czarzina's backing, were discouraging most lantern and firepot use on dark Moondays, labeling it frivolous and disrespectful. She championed a return to strict religious fundamentalism in a manic pursuit of more power.

Tyme felt a mixture of anger, disgust, and pity for the woman, sorrow for the lives she had ruined, and the hopes and opportunities she had crushed. Tonight, the Czarzina would be called out for her crimes.

When she heard the bass drums on the stage beating the prelude before the Listing of the Women's Clans, Tyme gave the cord three quick jerks to warn the Z's. She felt a tug in answer. All ready. Her heart rate and breathing increased as she got into position. Eight women ran off stage through the hallway below her to their dressing rooms. As they changed, Tyme made a few final adjustments to her clothes and scarves. When the actors emerged, they huddled together in the hallway for a moment for their cue, now all wearing the same outfit as Tyme.

As they began filing out onto the stage, Tyme gave the signal and was rapidly lowered to the floor as the last one left the hall. She pulled the cord to her waist, slipped her wrist from the loop, and flipped the cord into the corner as Zintowo pulled it up above head level, and took a moment to feel the exact place it hung. Knowing precisely where the loop was, and grabbing it on her first try, could be the difference between a successful or failed escape.

Tyme went through the curtains and out onto the stage behind the others. The dancers were running in a multitude of circles, wearing the same billowy scarves and clothes. Tyme joined them and quickly spotted the faint stains on the floor placed earlier by Jyg and the Z's. She made sure she was standing on the correct spot when the drumming stopped.

All the dancers hunched down. Tyme squatted as well, ripped off her scarves, and waited a few moments for the silence to grow before jumping back up.

"Czarzina Hana Hama Hala!" Tyme cried out. "Your reign is over." A crossbow bolt nearly grazed her right hip. Another zinged past her right shoulder. Both hit the wooden floor with a loud thunk. She took a slight step to the left as the other dancers fled the stage.

"Kill her!" the Czarzina screamed.

For a moment there were no more bolts, just a frantic shuffling and thudding that could be heard from the ceiling as the archers struggled to aim their crossbows at the woman standing on the stage. Lieutenant Erin Rine's crossbow hit against a strut, making any shot impossible. For others, their heads bumped walls or struts and they could not sight the crossbow correctly. Some of those archers now shot regardless, pointing their crossbows by guesswork and firing.

A scattering of arrows flew past Tyme from numerous directions. A few fairly close, others wide from their mark. The effect made it appear as if she had some magical shield around her.

As expected, the Czarzina began to rise from her throne to slip away through her escape tunnel. Before she could even stand, Tyme threw her first dagger. The blade struck with a loud thunk near the Czarzina's head, into the face of the wooden statue carved into the throne beside her. The Czarzina sat back down.

"Stay seated and I will not harm you," Tyme promised. Another dagger was already in her hand, arm cocked and ready to throw. A full brace of knives could be seen around her waist.

Arrows fired sporadically as the archers reloaded. None of them were able to hit the target.

"Tell the Blades who have come forward to move back," Tyme commanded. "I only want to talk."

"Stay back," the Czarzina shouted with obvious panic. The dagger-throwing woman before her appeared invulnerable.

The guards all slowly backed away. Half the crossbow archers were reloading again. The others held their breath, eager to shoot the moment the intruder moved from her place on the stage.

"I was sent to kill Czarzina Hana Hama Hala!" Tyme announced dramatically to the entire auditorium, "With this dagger!" A thin shiny blade suddenly appeared in her other hand. She held it out for the audience and the guards to see, her back briefly to the Czarzina. Suddenly she spun back around, feinted a jump directly toward the Czarzina, then sprang another way as a volley of crossbow bolts struck the floor the direction she had bluffed. Lieutenant Erin Rine was not fooled. She shot a moment later in the right direction but bumped her crossbow on a strut at the last second and missed the shot.

Tyme was now standing above the second small mark on the floor, closer to the center of the stage, and slightly closer to the Czarzina. A few more bolts shot out to thunk dramatically into the floor nearby. More banging sounded from the ceiling as the archers reloaded.

"You said you will not harm me," the Czarzina hissed. "Yet you say you came to kill me! Why should I believe anything you say?"

"Why would I kill you when your reign has already come to an end?" Tyme answered. "You will be tried instead."

Arrows continually flew past Tyme, missing her and striking loudly into the floor, a few ricocheting into the wall. Lieutenant Erin Rine could not sight her crossbow correctly, so she just guessed where she was pointing and shot. The auditorium was mesmerized by Tyme's invincibility to being hit.

The Czarzina was speechless. The audience was whispering Tyme's words, echoing and passing back and forth like a wave through the throng, so that every person in the banquet hall repeated what Tyme had said. *Her reign has come to an end! She will be tried!*

"Silence!" The Czarzina screamed. She felt dizzy, her heart pounded in her chest. Yet another crossbow twanged, and the quarrel whizzed past Tyme's neck into the floor.

"I come to tell the Czarzina how she has been betrayed," Tyme cried out to the audience, and then turned to the Czarzina and added with a bow, "If she cares to hear."

"Tell me who!" the Czarzina demanded.

"There is a web of plots against you," Tyme state loudly. "Your corruption has spread into the Senate, into the Heart and the Hammer Legions, and into the old cities. I was sent to confirm judgment," Tyme said calmly, "that you are beyond redemption."

"Tell me who is behind this!" the Czarzina ordered. She did not stop the crossbow archers; her first concern was her own safety.

Lieutenant Erin Rine continued to blindly shoot. Just a hair too high. The arrow went over the assassin's head.

"General Cata Cara hatches plots against you as we speak. She risks civil war to see you deposed." Tyme did not trust the General, nor her dreams of Empire building. The Ambri Empire had its day and fell apart because of dysfunction and greed. Chasing after past glories by attempting to return to something that had ultimately failed would only fail again. Tyme had no use for going back.

"Captain Targono of the Hammer Legion has spies in the old cities with plans for revolt." He had enlisted Gribono, who had killed Noot. His hands were covered with the blood of innocents already. She sensed that Targono's plans might lead to the most bloodshed of all. More bolts flew past her to strike the floor.

"I was given these knives by still another group," Tyme taunted, "that conspires your demise."

With a quick feint in one direction, which released a few crossbow bolts, a second feint more toward the Czarzina, which drew even more bolts to strike the empty floor, Tyme darted in a third direction. She stopped above the final mark on the stage, further from the Czarzina but much closer to her escape route to the hallway and skyhook. But also closer to Lieutenant Erin Rine.

"I have come to fulfill the prophecy and declare the end of your reign." Tyme stood tall and proclaimed from the *Book of Elders*:

A Bright One shall come unto us
Her sword shall be Flames of Truth
Her shield a Dazzling Crystal
Her Voice a Great Song!

As Tyme spoke Lieutenant Erin Rine shot blindly at her, awkwardly holding the stock away from her shoulder.

"Hear this pronouncement!" Tyme continued. "Czarzina Hana Hama Hala! Your reign has come to an end! You are finished!"

A great murmur rippled back and forth through the auditorium. *Her reign has come to an end! She is finished!"*

Lieutenant Erin Rine reloaded her crossbow and held it out awkwardly.

Tyme reached for the pouch of flash powder in her pocket to blind everyone so she could make her escape.

The Lieutenant pulled the trigger of her crossbow.

Tyme nearly stumbled from the searing force of the bolt's impact on her body. She looked at the quarrel stuck deep into her right side. A patch of dark red blood was already growing around the arrow. Tyme knew from her lessons with Tao Tau and Klew that she had been struck in her liver. 'Twas a lethal wound. She released her grip from the flash powder.

Escape was no longer possible.

Her concept of time suddenly shifted. She ignored the pain and stood tall to speak clearly from the Kabaal Prophecies.

I am the Mother of all Daughters
The Daughter of all Mothers
Divine Daughter
Who fills the world with love and compassion!

The site of Tyme's blood emboldened the Czarzina. "Who else betrays me?" she hissed.

"They will all abandon you," Tyme shook her head sadly as two more arrows flew past. "You have lost everything, and everyone. The offisers. The Legions. Now, at the end, the Senate will finally rise up along with the people!"

Tyme took a breath to gather her strength and cried out. "They will build a new empire, not of stone and steel, but a Divine Empire, inside each heart and soul. Against such a force no tyrant can stand."

Lieutenant Erin Rine shot blindly again but missed.

Tyme closed her eyes and thought about Epoh. How their wedding and their moons together in Karvor had been the best days of their lives, just as she had guessed when insisting they not wait to get married. Those brief moons would be their only moons together.

Now she was leaving him. She realized that he would never be the same.

A sharp stab of pain made her whimper softly. She heard the faint sound of hoof beats. The Czarzina was yelling something, but Tyme was not listening to her words. The sound of the hoof beats was growing, awakening something deep inside of her.

King was coming!

She nearly stumbled as she clutched her body in agony.

King was returning for her!

The hoof beats grew louder and louder, the sound filling her ears. Tyme collapsed with relief into the pool of blood spreading at her feet. Everything was going to be all right!

King would lift her up and carry her away!

PART V

She is the Mother of all Daughters,
the Daughter of all Mothers,
Divine Daughter
Who fills the world with love and compassion!
The Bright One will vanquish the enemies of Light,
and bring Righteousness and Truth to all.

> *Kabaal Prophecies from the Mask of Brilliance*

Blessed is she who comes in the name of Divine. For the glory of Divine will be revealed, and all shall know that the voice of Divine has spoken.

> *Hope the Proclaimer*

A VERY BAD FEELING

Zandero watched the small loop of cord by his foot from the skyhook line running up the back wall of the Empress Auditorium. When Tyme made her escape, she would throw the flash powder, then run off the stage to the hallway, grab the other end of the line and pull tight, eliminating the loop. That was the signal for Zandero to jump from his narrow perch on the limestone cliff and lift Tyme from the floor to the vent skyhook.

Zintowo was standing on the ground to help spot him for the landing, and then to play out the cord to bring Tyme back down to the ground.

They had made estimates of how long it would take before Tyme would reveal herself during the quiet moment before the Listing of the Women's Clans. How long it would take her to confront the Czarzina and call out her evil and corruption.

That amount of time had now passed. But still the loop in the cord by Zandero hung loose. Tyme was not making her escape.

Zintowo began to have a very bad feeling. He heard some indistinct shouting from the front of the building. Suddenly there was a roar of voices as excited people streamed out the auditorium.

Epoh arrived from his lookout. His face in shock. "Some soldiers are coming around the outside of the auditorium above us," he warned the Z's. The guards made their way down the narrow cart path on the side of the building, more interested in talking amongst themselves and trying to figure out what had happened inside, than closely examining the building perimeter. The cord in the air was too thin to see on a dark Moonday night.

When the guards passed, Zandero climbed down the limestone cliff to join Epoh and Jyg on the ground. Zintowo pulled the cord back through the skyhook to fall down the side of the building and cliff so he could retrieve and coil it.

"The Ser Cus never leaves anything behind on the stage," Zintowo said, his voice breaking. "Even when the show goes badly. We will not let them know how she got in. They will never find the skyhook hidden in the vent."

"She never pulled on the other end of the line," Zandero began to tremble and apologize. "I never felt her. She never came out."

"'Tis not your fault," Epoh said numbly. "Something went wrong."

"We need to split up and meet at the Veranda," Klew advised.

The terrible journey seemed to take forever as they tried to walk normally across town and not run and draw attention to themselves. They came through the back fence to reach the Veranda and gathered together in shock.

"Was she not the Bright One?" Jyg asked Epoh in distressed confusion. The possibility of Tyme failing her mission was beyond his comprehension. "She was the Divine Daughter. She had to be! Everything about her was extraordinary!"

Epoh felt so dizzy he had to lie down. He could barely breathe. Barely think. He was falling into a crushing darkness. He tried to tell himself that Tyme was still alive. That somehow, she had saved herself and was now making her way back to the Veranda.

But when Riin Ruel arrived solemnly and shook her head, Epoh knew Tyme was gone. He covered his head with his arms as his body convulsed in sobs. He started reciting the first *Prayer for the Dead*, frantically searching for a lifeline to stop freefalling into despair and anguish. After a few minutes he was able to sit up in a daze and listen to what had happened.

Riin Ruel described Tyme's dramatic appearance. "She was something to behold!" Riin Ruel said in awe. "Even from where I sat in the back of the balcony. She commanded the stage! Proclaiming the end of the Czarzina's reign. Crossbow bolts whizzing past her from all directions! The entire auditorium riveted by her every word, and the whole crowd repeating her words to each other."

"She listed out the coup plotters in the Heart and the Hammer. She prophesied that everyone was abandoning the Czarzina--the Legions, the Senate, the people. And that the Czarzina would be tried."

"Then a crossbow bolt hit her in the side," Riin Ruel faltered in her narration. "She stood tall and said she had come to fulfill the prophecy from the *Book of Elders*:

A Bright One shall come unto us
Her sword shall be Flames of Truth
Her shield a Dazzling Crystal
Her Voice a Great Song!

"She also recited from the *Kabaal Prophecies*," Riin Ruel continued:

I am the Mother of all Daughters,
The Daughter of all Mothers.
Divine Daughter,
Who fills the world with love and compassion!

Riin Ruel took a few moments to compose herself to speak again. "She prophesized a new empire, not of stone and steel, but a Divine Empire, inside each heart and soul." The mystical warrior looked stricken. "And then she collapsed. A luminosity left the stage. I could tell she had passed."

Epoh began to sob again. Klew and Jyg helped him wobble to his room. Riin Ruel went out into the darkness. They all spent the night weeping and wailing in their beds.

WHAT SHOULD
WE DO?

The next morning, they gathered at sunrise on an eastern patio. Riin Ruel arrived with news from the capitol.

"I have never seen the city so abuzz. Everyone is saying the Czarzina's reign has come to an end, even though nothing official has happened and the Senate has not even met. The Legion offisers are all nervous and uncertain about what is happening. Everything is in an uproar!"

"What should we do?" asked Epoh in anguished daze. His whole purpose in life had been taken from him. He had no idea what to do next.

"We can go to the Jawbone Ridge Gang," Jyg suggested. He told them of Delgado's offer. "He said if anything bad should happen, we could count on him for protection and a place to hide."

"I am staying in Ambrit," Riin Ruel told them. "I am not sure what my orders will be."

"We have no need to leave immediately," Klew said to Epoh and Jyg. "Let us take a few days to grieve before we travel. My heart is broken. I can hardly muster the energy to get out of bed."

"What happened to her body?" Epoh asked with a wave of grief crushing his heart.

"We are looking into it," Riin Ruel replied stoically. "We think she was buried in an unmarked criminal's graveyard."

Epoh spent the day crying. And the next day as well. The empty hours of the night were the worst, an unrelenting cruelty that gave no rest but drained what little energy he possessed. At night all his fears and doubts were magnified.

When the sorrow became so deep that he was beginning to lose himself, he was forced to accept what had happened. He had to learn to live with a gaping wound in his being. He was not doing it for himself, but for Tyme, who had made him promise that he would somehow learn to go on.

"Mourn deeply, but then, come back to life," she had told him. "Tao Tau taught me the Great Sorrow is no place to live."

On the third day he was able to briefly come out of his bedroom and eat some food. On the fourth day he went to his desk and took out a few pages of his finest paper and began to write.

News of Tyme's confrontation with the Czarzina spread like lightning through the city, the Legions, and across the Old Empire. The next morning there was no official government announcement or comment about what had happened. The Czarzina had been so traumatized by the events, and anxious for her own safety, that she did not consider her response to the planned coups until late the following day. Then she faced a grim reality.

General Cata Cara was in Pintone. The Czarzina would order her to surrender, of course, but was fearful that she would not comply. Whom could she trust to arrest her? And how? That would require some finesse.

She had no idea who Captain Targono was. When she learned that he was in charge of guarding the silver shipments from the Vanttan mines her worries skyrocketed.

"Our last silver shipment is moons late already!" the Czarzina fretted. "We have to insure the Captain is arrested before the mine sends the shipment to the capitol." This would require strength and resolve. She did not know if she could trust the Hammer Legion soldiers to arrest Targono and his followers, so she ordered a battalion from Ralston Garrison to march to Vargo Garrison to make sure there were no problems arresting Captain Targono and ensuring the safety of the critical silver shipment.

PLANS OF A COUP

Captain Targono was testing his new bridge couplings when a spy courier arrived from Ambrit. He opened the message on the spot. A warrior prophet had appeared during a play at a banquet, had thrown knives, and stood unaffected by a hail of crossbow bolts while proclaiming the reign of the Czarzina had come to an end. Targono thought the story highly amusing.

Then he read that the young woman had also exposed his plans of a coup, and others. The Captain became furious. Who in the seven hells was she? And how did she know anything about him? To be listed together with General Cata Cara was especially insulting. He had no respect for the pious bitch and guessed she would now hesitate or even abandon her coup plans.

He would do otherwise. He had planned to rob the silver shipment and take the wagons as he left. But there was money where he was going, and he would have it soon enough. The important thing was to move quickly. A similar message would have arrived at the Vargo Garrison headquarters. The offisers in charge would worry about arresting him without a battle. Most likely they would call for reinforcements, further delaying any response for a few days. He gathered his sergeants for an emergency meeting.

The Captain opened a saddlebag and took out his engineering book. He removed a packet of plans that Sergeant Kakano had drawn up earlier for the bridges on the old Mining Trail to Thessal. He handed them back to the sergeant, his lead engineer.

"Send out 50 men, a cook wagon with supplies, and seven wagons lightly loaded for fast travel with all the struts and equipment you need to build the first three bridges. I want you to lead a smaller team on daya horses to ride ahead of the wagons and prepare the footings." He pointed to a pile of supplies. "The remainder of the struts that we have here will be stacked high in slower moving wagons coming right behind you."

He turned to Sergeant Vocovo. "Everyone else is to return to the barracks at Vrak pass as fast as possible to resupply." The next morning, everyone gathered at an amphitheater to hear him speak.

"Today I stand before you, ready to embark on a path never taken by a man in all of herstory," he told them. "A path leading to a new Kingdom." He said the word proudly. "As of this moment, I will no longer take orders from the Czarzina in Ambrit, nor the Generals at Vargo Garrison. Nor any other woman!"

A smattering of surprised cheers arose from the soldiers.

"Are you ready to stop taking orders from women?" he asked the group. "Are you ready to have a King whom you can trust to look out for your interests and welfare?"

More shouts of encouragement.

"I have a plan," Targono continued, "a plan that requires boldness and fearlessness, from a small group of dedicated soldiers who are willing to strike out against all the inequality that we have faced our whole lives!" he roared.

A roar of agreement came from the soldiers.

"A plan to take control of our own destiny!"

More whoops and shouts of support.

"Are you with me?" Targono challenged. "Do you wish to be a part of what we can create together?"

The soldiers stood and chanted their approval. "Yes! Yes!"

"Together," Targono shouted, "we will change herstory!"

He told them of his plan to make a road through the

mountains that wagons and horses could go over, building and then dismantling and reusing the bridge struts after they crossed, to move with great speed through improbable canyons. Where they were going, he did not say, but Captain Targono promised them a better life if they would follow him. They all believed.

He sent them out in waves. The first group loaded quickly to move fast with lighter wagons of bridge struts; the following wagons were piled high and the teams of horses strained to pull the heavy loads. Supply wagons, cook wagons and contingents of both mounted and foot soldiers headed out.

The final group had horses pulling wagons of camp supplies, food, chickens, another cook wagon, and a large herd of goats. Following behind was a force of soldiers on foot to ensure no one attacked them from behind as they made their getaway into the mountains of Vanttan.

Captain Targono left behind a small team of men with instructions on how to ambush the late running silver shipment by booby trapping the road and dropping the wagons off an immense cliff into a deep ravine where it would take considerable effort and engineering to recover and collect all the silver again. If Targono could not have the silver, neither would the Czarzina, at least for a few more moons, which was long enough to be critical for her survival.

A BRIGHT ONE

On the fifth morning after Tyme died, everyone met on the Veranda patio. Wiir Waar and the Z's had not left yet and seemed in no hurry to do so. Epoh expressed no desire to move anywhere soon. Nor did Jyg or Klew.

"Something has happened in the capitol," Riin Ruel reported. "A priest started calling Tyme the Bright One. She was arrested by the Czarzina. That has only helped the story spread."

"She was certainly the most inspiring person I have ever known," Klew agreed. "No matter what has happened, I call her the Bright One still."

"Yes," they all agreed, "the Bright One."

"A Bright One," Epoh explained the title she preferred. He had spent the previous day writing about her.

"The giving of her life has greatly magnified her impact," Riin Ruel said with growing awareness. "She is becoming a martyr. And martyrs can greatly inspire and give rise to grand causes for social change."

They all felt ready to perform a memorial ceremony. Epoh read the *Prayers for the Mortal Body* from the *Prayers for the Dead* to help everyone with their grieving and give voice to the hurt and sorrow they were feeling. They took turns telling stories, crying, mournfully chuckling, and giving honor and respect to Tyme. They promised to have a better memorial when they got to Karvor, a celebration of life with laughing and dancing like Tyme would have wanted.

Riin Ruel left while the others discussed what to do next. The Z's were ready to head for Pintone and meet up with the rest of the Ser Cus. Wiir Waar chose to stay longer.

"I have a few things I can do in Ambrit. I will stick around and go with you to Karvor." Her eyes teared up. "You are my connection to her. I am not ready to let her go."

Which set off another round of lamentations and mournful hugs.

In the evening Jyg suggested going out to get some air, stroll around, and maybe even listen to some music. "I need a break from crying," he said.

"Yes," Wiir Waar agreed. "We have got to force ourselves to begin to live again."

The Z's nodded their approval. Klew as well.

"I think that would also be good for me," Epoh joined in, "but I am not sure about the music. Actually," he said at second thought, "I would swing pass the Splendorous Dome and mayhaps listen to some singing or chanting there."

'Twas only a few days until Bright Moonday, which meant the moon was nearly half full and high in the western sky when the sun sank into a dark, reddish-purple haze. The moonlight was strong enough to illuminate the streets. But the lovely views of the city at night offered little condolence.

They walked slowly through the gardens and parks around the Mother Womb. Epoh remembered how he and Tyme had sat meditating and praying together, marveling and enjoying the beautiful scenery. Now everything seemed meaningless and lifeless.

Inside the Womb a group was singing one of Epoh's favorite Glorias. He found a seat in a corner where he could lightly hum and sing under his breath without being heard. Even in the refuge, a man caught singing in the Splendorous Dome of the Divine Womb would be arrested.

When the women in the sanctuary finished singing, Epoh sat with Klew near the statue of Tatano, the first True Warrior, and together they again recited the *Prayers for the Mortal Body*.

Wiir Waar, Jyg and the Z's went out into the gardens to walk in the moonlight. They ambled slowly toward some distant music from a rooftop tavern. As they drew close, they sat on a bench to listen to the band playing and everyone talking and laughing. It all seemed so hollow. None of them felt like going closer. Instead, they sat mute, listening to a crowd having fun, with no desire whatsoever to join in.

THESSON AND TEPU

Captain Targono watched as the last struts to complete the bridge were efficiently pinned into place. The group before him, ready to cross, had waited just long enough to take a few bites from their hardtack and have a drink of water. The wagons they were driving had all the supplies for the next bridge, the last they would need to construct. His army was not far behind.

His engineers and soldiers crossed numerous deep ravines and canyons to reach Thessal in just three days, building triangular framed bridges out of wooden poles capped with interlocking metal eyelets and iron pins. Using four bridge building teams that worked and rotated in sequence, they dismantled each bridge after all were across to use the struts again further ahead. That also ensured that no army could catch up and attack from the rear as the earlier bridges were no longer there.

The Captain left the last two bridges standing. He was through the canyons and no longer needed the struts or so many wagons. They took the horses, saddled them with riding tack, and abandoned all the equipment they no longer needed. The bulk of the force and all the soldiers on foot skirted around Thesson and headed for Tepu.

Targono led a smaller mounted force to Thesson. He had charts showing the layout for the Heart Legion toll stations, guard posts, treasury building, and soldier's barracks. He also had three soldiers dressed with Heart Legion uniforms. That night, his "lieutenant" banged on the door of the guard station demanding to be let in. When the door opened, Targono's fighters stormed in to handily overpower the soldiers. Only two guards were killed and three others injured.

The doors to the barracks were locked and barricaded with the soldiers inside. Targono's army filled the courtyard. He spoke to the imprisoned soldiers.

"I could kill you all, but I will not if you remain calm and stay where you are. We wear Hammer Legion uniforms, but we are no longer Hammer Legion. We are soldiers bound for a new Barbarian Kingdom. If you are ready to follow a man, to be a real soldier, and if you are strong enough to keep up," he challenged them, "come with us to crown me the new King of Karvor!"

His soldiers roared with approval. "To the new King of Karvor!"

A few of the Heart Legion soldiers joined them. But most stared at the renegade Hammer Legion Captain as though he were a madman soon to be crushed by the Heart Legion.

With the treasury cleaned out, Targono led his soldiers down the dry Iridi River Valley. Because his group was mounted, they caught up to the bulk of the army that night. 'Twas fortunately the night after bright Moonday, so travel was very easy the first half of the night. Even after the moon had set, they easily traveled by starlight on the straight and flat Royal Highway to Tepu. They advanced so fast there was no chance that word of their coming could precede them.

Overrunning the Heart Legion compound in Tepu late on the second night did not go so easily. Ten Heart soldiers died and another four were seriously injured. Targono lost two men with a third injured. When he gave his join-with-us speech to the remaining Heart Legion soldiers, only two soldiers enlisted.

"To the new King of Karvor!" they chanted with enthusiasm.

ESCAPE TO KARVOR

The day after the Z's left Ambrit, Epoh told the others he was ready to go to Karvor.

"But first I have to deliver a package," he said. "I have written a long letter, a treatise actually, to the priests at the Splendorous Dome of the Divine Womb, to share Tyme's story. How she is the fulfillment of prophecy." His eyes shone with hope. "A Bright One. A Divine Daughter."

At the Womb he spoke with two shamans and three priests explaining about the document he was delivering. He wanted to make sure a number of people knew about it, so it could not be easily hidden or ignored.

When he returned, the others had the horses saddled, packed, and ready to go. They were all weary of the Veranda, as beautiful as the home was. And weary of being stuck in Ambrit. They all hoped that moving might help lift the oppressive sadness.

The first few days on the road Epoh was very quiet. So was Klew, which encouraged Jyg and Wiir Waar to seek each other if they wanted to be social. They often rode beside each other. And even shared an occasional laugh.

"So, what are you going to do in Karvor?" Wiir Waar asked. "Join the Jawbone Ridge gang?"

"Manser Jygero!" Bones called out in a nobleman's voice. The big raven was standing and riding at that moment on the rump of Jyg's horse.

Jyg shrugged his shoulders. He still did not have an answer.

"You should join the Ser Cus," Wiir Waar encouraged him.

"You are fun. And talented! And you have Bones!"

"Bones!" the raven croaked her name in reply.

"Ah, yes!" Jyg joked. "That is whom you are really after!" He began chuckling. "We will only take Jyg if he brings Bones."

"No," Wiir Waar protested. "You are worthy on your own." Then cracked again, "But do bring Bones!"

"Mayhaps," Jyg laughed. He wanted to say something more but was too self-conscious. He had always admired her and thought of her as older and far beyond any hope or chance for romance. But now that he had grown into a man, three or four decades in age difference seemed less of a barrier. When they danced together at the Cactus Club, he had felt a flame ignite in his heart. That created an awkward problem for him in joining the Ser Cus. But how could he tell her?

They traveled with minimal breaks, riding evenings after the heat, and by the growing moonlight, which they preferred. The cool glow of the moon's light felt like a healing balm to their burned spirits. The lack of color emphasized the patterns and textures across the landscape of rolling hills and fire cactus. They walked as much as they rode. Moving forward physically helped them to move forward mentally, and spiritually as well. They felt themselves rejoining the journey of life.

When they arrived at the Iridi Valley caravansary, they were stunned to find the footprints of an army in the dirt, along with abandoned equipment, wagons, and harnesses. Klew examined a well-made cook wagon.

"This is all Hammer Legion equipment." He grimaced somberly. "I think Captain Targono has passed through with his army. He must have built bridges to get wagons across the deep canyons of the old Mining Trail."

"Tyme had hoped to stop the coups before they began," Epoh said sadly. "And save many lives. But now an army is marching up the Ambri Scout trail toward Karvor."

"Hopefully not against Karvor itself," Klew shook his head. "My guess is Targono will hit the toll booth treasuries. Most likely he has already taken Thesson and Tepu. Now he will take the toll station at Jintiga Bridge. He hopes to move so fast they will have no warning that he is coming."

"Blood and guts!" Bones croaked.

"And we are right behind him," said Klew.

NIGHT DUTY

The last time Gribono reported to Captain Targono in the Vanttan Mountains, the Captain had told him to continue his spying and not move from where he was staying. Obviously, the Captain had something planned for Karvor. Gribono could not imagine what. There was no route to move an army from Vargo Garrison to Tepu across the Dry Hills. The only way to Karvor was through Ralston Garrison and Ambrit.

Except for the old Mining Trail to Thesson, with its missing bridges and numerous detours for single riders only, no shorter way to Karvor existed, not for an army. Gribono thought about Targono always building strange bridges. Was he thinking of taking an army across the deep canyons of old Mining Trail? That many bridges would take far too long to build. He would be attacked from behind by soldiers sent out from the garrison headquarters. By the time he crossed the mountains, the Heart Legion soldiers in Pintone, Karvor, Thesson and Tepu would be alerted to his plans and ready to face him.

When Gribono returned to Karvor, he got together with all his gambling buddies, including Sergeant Etna Nate. She had been growing closer with Captain Wirvimo, who she believed was sympathetic to the Fire. Shamano, the shaman Birjj, had also asked Gribono to investigate Captain Wirvimo.

"There is a power struggle between Captain Wirvimo and Captain Kin Kell," the Sergeant said. Captain Kin Kell was a trusted offiser of General Cata Cara, who suspected Captain Wirvimo was a secret member of the Fire.

"Now, I am getting pulled into it," Etna Nate said with disgust. "Because I have been getting to know Captain Wirvimo, Captain Kin Kell is suspicious of me. She put my squad on night guard duty to keep an eye on us."

None of them knew that Captain Wirvimo was actually a follower of General Cata Cara and had been placed as a spy to infiltrate the ranks of Fire supporters within the Heart Legion. Captain Wirvimo appeared sympathetic to the Fire but was actually gathering information for the General about the leaders of the Fire, their behavior, and their plans.

THE ARMY OF
CAPTAIN TARGONO

When the army of Captain Targono left the dry Iridi Valley and headed up the Ambri Scout trail to Karvor, the lead group contained all the hardest fighters. They did the three-day trip in just over a day. Now 'twas midnight and Targono was overlooking Karvor at last.

When he was young, he had spent three weeks in the city as squire to Captain Gornado, before his mentor fell from grace and they were both exiled to the Hammer Legion. Targono had been entranced by Karvor and had drawn maps marking a number of tunnels he thought could be built to connect key valleys between the narrow ridgelines, greatly increasing mobility across the steep, mountainside city. That map was in his pocket.

"This is when we prove who we are!" he told his soldiers. "Now we pick up the pace to strike fast at the end."

They raced around the outskirts of the city with hardly an incident. Targono had every back street and junction drawn out. Shocked pedestrians cowered at the sight of the large, fast-moving pack of hardened and utterly fearless soldiers and quickly got out of their way. He brought the army to a depression on a hillside above the toll station barracks where they could not be seen. 'Twas now a few hours before dawn, the moon had gone down, and the stars gave little light.

Targono led fifty of his best fighters down the hill toward the compound and the guard house. His fake offiser dressed in a Heart Legion uniform banged on the door. A few moments later a night guard opened the spy hole to see what appeared to be a Heart Legion Lieutenant and two Heart Legion soldiers standing outside. At the fake offiser's command, the night guard unlatched the door.

The three impostor soldiers were barely through the door when the night guard realized his mistake. He was killed as he began to call out a warning. Sergeant Etna Nate and her soldiers rose to fight the armed intruders who were forcing their way into the guard house.

If the sergeant could have had a chance to stop and talk with her attackers, she would have found herself in complete harmony with their mission and motives. She and her guards would have gladly abandoned their posts with the Heart Legion and joined the ranks of the rebel soldiers they were now fighting. Instead, they were swiftly overwhelmed and killed before they could alert any other soldiers in the compound .

The Heart Legion soldiers in the barracks awoke to find themselves prisoners, locked up in their own bunk house. Their entire compound, practice yard, stables and guard house were filled with fierce Hammer Legion mercenaries.

Captain Targono immediately set up an office and command center. He gave addresses he had received from Gribono to small squads of soldiers who were sent out to arrest and capture Major Bayn Baya and other high-ranking offisers who lived off the Heart Legion base. He also sent a note to Gribono himself, telling him to keep spying, keep their relationship secret, and wait a few days before reporting to the new King of Karvor.

Then Targono went out into the compound to speak to his soldiers. "We robbed the toll stations at Thesson and Tepu because we were passing through," he told them. "But we are not leaving here. The money in the treasury is now ours. We are going to add in the money we brought from Tesson and Tepu. And we are going to continue adding money to our coffers by taking over the toll station and the tax collection at

Jintiga Bridge and the Royal Highway to Pintone."

"This is our fort now," the King of Karvor boasted. "We are going to defend it and make it our home."

As the sun came up, Targono sent requests to armorers and blacksmith shops to forge metal caps with eyelets and pins that were smaller than those he had use to build the wagon bridges on the old Mining Trail. He sent out agents to buy loads of long, thin wooden poles. He also sent engineers to scout the southern rim of Jintiga canyon, with instructions for what he planned to build next.

When the Mayor of Karvor heard a group of soldiers had staged a coup at the Heart Legion compound and the toll stations, she assumed 'twas the same group that had contacted her earlier and promised to make her Queen of Tanis --- if she did not intervene with her City Guards.

Soon after, an envoy from the soldiers arrived to speak with the Mayor. The pronouncement was not what she expected, though the content intrigued her, nonetheless.

"I represent the newly crowned King of Karvor," the envoy told her. "King Targono wants to give you the chance to remain Mayor of Karvor. He knows how you have been hamstrung under the Queen of Tanis. You have not been free to do all you would like for Karvor. King Targono would change that. As King, he will be your protector against the Czarzina, against General Cata Cara and the Heart Legion, your protector against all the politicians in Pintone and Ambrit that tax you heavily and yet treat Karvor as an afterthought, while pampering themselves with excess."

"With you as Mayor, and Targono as King," the envoy continued, "Karvor will become the greatest city in all of Ambra. The taxes will no longer be sent to Ambrit. The taxes now belong to the King of Karvor, to pay his soldiers handsomely! Those soldiers would love to spend their money celebrating in your town. The new King offers you not only protection, but an army of well-behaved customers with coin who are eager to do business with your city."

DISTURBING REPORTS

General Cata Cara was in Pintone when she learned of Tyme's dramatic appearance before the Czarzina, dodging crossbow bolts while proclaiming the end of the Czarzina's reign. She was perturbed that the young warrior prophet had also revealed General Cata Cara's plans for a coup, along with others.

The General received the message via one of Major Bayn Baya's special pigeons, the day after it happened. The pigeons in Karvor had all been lost, eaten by Monitor lizards, but there were still birds flying messages from the capitol to her. That gave her plenty of time to seal up the military garrison in Pintone against any force that might come from the Czarzina against her. Her plan was to remain in her stronghold at Pintone Garrison and wait. The Czarzina was obviously weakened and at the end of her reign, if the prophecy was true.

General Cata Cara had been planning a nearly bloodless coup. But if the Czarzina was to fall, why go through with the coup plans? And accept even those few deaths? She would show mercy and find favor with the Senasers, whom she needed for her own plans to come to fruition.

She assumed the Hammer Legion Captain, who was also exposed by the prophet, was planning to take over the silver mines. She considered this fact more worrisome than the outgoing Czarzina. General Cata Cara needed the revenue from the silver mines to pay for her own ambitious plans to create a new Ambri Empire and crown herself Empress.

One week later a pigeon from Ambrit said support for the Czarzina was crumbling fast. The General congratulated herself on the decision to just sit tight and wait for the inevitable.

A few days later, General Cata Cara received disturbing reports by horseback messenger that the Thesson and Tepu toll stations had been robbed by a band of soldiers wearing Hammer Legion uniforms. The group had fled up the Ambri Scout trail toward Karvor. The Captain was on the run!

The General felt relieved that she did not have to worry about the Hammer Legion Captain taking over the silver mines of Vanttan. She sent a company of soldiers after him up the Iridi Valley to seal off his retreat. Then she sent a pigeon to Karvor, alerting Major Bayn Baya to send a band of soldiers out for Targono's capture. She had him from both sides. He would be brought before the Senasers for his crimes. That would show them her quick thinking and effectiveness.

But the next day came the stunning news that the Jintiga toll stations and barracks had been taken over by a man claiming to be the newly crowned King of Karvor. His soldiers wore re-marked Hammer Legion uniforms. And, most incomprehensible of all, reports from merchants stated that everything at the toll stations was running smoothly, the soldiers polite and orderly. She did not receive any report from Major Bayn Baya and had no idea that the Major had already been arrested and jailed by the new King.

General Cata Cara did exactly what King Targono expected. She took a few days to think about her response. She knew her prize was in Ambrit. She did not want to take her eyes off the Czarzina. But she could not ignore the threat of losing the toll stations at Jintiga Bridge. Nor could she ignore the outlandish claims of the rogue Captain Targono.

At last, she ordered her troops to prepare for battle. The number of soldiers she had in her favor would make up for any advantages the Captain held occupying the Legion compound. She would march up the Jintiga Valley and overwhelm his forces. Then she would return victorious to Ambrit, with the Captain in chains, and declare her intent to be Empress.

RETURN TO KARVOR

Epoh and the others were uneasy following behind Captain Targono's army. His actions were the very thing that Tyme had hoped to avoid.

"I am going to see him when we get to Karvor," Klew vowed. "If he is my old friend, mayhaps I can convince him into some kind of armistice."

"Good luck with that," Wiir Waar said skeptically. "I think his days of talking are over."

"I have to try," Klew responded, "I see nothing else before me."

They also discussed when it would be best to have the celebration of life for Tyme. They were arriving a few days before full Moonday. "Why not then?" Wiir Waar said. "Tyme loved moonlight parties."

"Hopefully that will work with Delgado," Jyg said.

Epoh nodded thoughtfully. "I think I will head to the kiva in the Painted Hills we visited on our honeymoon. I want a quiet spot to do some writing until the memorial."

"Are you writing more about Tyme?" Wiir Waar asked.

"Yes." His eyes welled with tears. "She is with me when I write."

When Delgado heard the news from Ambrit of a young woman warrior prophet dodging crossbow bolts and proclaiming the end of the Czarzina's reign, he knew instantly 'twas Tyme. When he heard the woman had been shot and continued her prophecy, he prayed that she made a miraculous escape.

When he learned she did not, Delgado sank into a deep depression. He had been afraid that something like this was going to happen. Despite her death, or mayhaps because of it, some were calling her the Bright One. He believed that himself, that she was special, now more than ever. Others called her the Divine Daughter. He was unsure what that meant.

When Jyg, Klew and Wiir Waar appeared at the Blue Moon, they hugged and cried. Delgado had heard a number of widely varying rumors and reports about what happened at the Empress Auditorium and was anxious to hear a factual version of the events. They told of the planning and preparations to set everything up and get Tyme inside the building. And they repeated Riin Ruel's tale of what had occurred on the stage, Tyme's claim to fulfill prophecy, and her announcing the end of the Czarzina's reign.

"When she was struck by the arrow," Klew marveled, "she stood tall and said she was the Divine Daughter, who fills the world with love and compassion! Her last words were about building a new empire, not of stone and steel, but a Divine Empire inside each heart and soul."

"Her empire *is* inside our hearts and souls," Delgado affirmed. "Yes. She lives on in me. She has changed me."

"She has changed all of us," Jyg agreed solemnly.

"We want to have a celebration of life for her," Wiir Waar said. "Could we do it full Moonday?"

"Perfect," Delgado agreed. "We actually started already." He showed them where the Jawbone Ridge gang had built a shrine, filled with candles, tokens and offerings, including from Fire devotees. "We have been telling stories about her and playing music she liked."

The travelers were exhausted from their journey. Delgado escorted them to a house nearby where he had arranged for them to stay.

"I will probably be around for a week or so," Wiir Waar told him. "I am not ready to perform yet in Pintone. There is no need for me to leave soon."

"I need another week to figure out what I am going to do as well," said Jyg.

"What have you heard about Captain Targono?" Klew asked.

"He calls himself the King of Karvor," Delgado answered. "His army has taken over the Heart Legion compound and barracks, along with the toll stations, which they have been running very smoothly and courteously. He sent out secret squads who arrested most of the Heart Legion offisers who were not living on the base."

The next morning Klew went to the former Heart Legion compound and asked to see Captain Targono.

"You mean the King of Karvor?" the guard corrected him.

"Yes," Klew agreed. "The King of Karvor. We went to the Military Academy together."

"He is busy right now," the guard said dismissively. "Give me your name and I will write it in my book."

"May I wait here at the gate in hopes that he might have a moment to see me?" Klew asked, seeing no other recourse.

"Suit yourself," the guard replied.

Klew sat all day until the heat. He returned to sit outside the gate the next day as well. He did not know that the King of Karvor did not get his message. The King was not even in the compound. He was further down Jintiga Canyon, engineering an ambush.

A CELEBRATION
OF LIFE

Epoh had planned to walk alone back to Karvor for Tyme's celebration by retracing some of their honeymoon route. When Gybeko, Singer, Draktono, Frisoto, and Swindovo told him they also wanted to attend the memorial, he decided to go together.

Then Ozono showed up unannounced to join in with a large group of Canaries, plus a small group of red-dusted men, and a few blue and green colored pigment miners as well. Ozono had been stunned to learn that Tyme had gone up against the Czarzina by herself and chose to die rather than back down against her power and control. Tyme's unwavering bravery and commitment to the cause of justice had astonished him.

Ozono had first thought of her as a pampered, spoiled princess on an expensive horse. She had asked him, *what do you want from me*, when he had confronted her about what he had assumed was her privileged upbringing. Then she had saved the Canary's wagon load of pigment from being stolen. And later came to the kiva to listen and learn about the plight of men in a society where they were less than second class citizens. She had not preached or talked down to them. She had listened intently to everything Draktono had said about the injustice of Ambri law, and given her life to stand up against that oppressive system of inequality.

The group made an unusual parade. Swindovo and Gybeko were in the lead, beating out cadences for walking, and then rhythms for songs on their drums. Singer, Draktono, Frisoto, and Epoh came next, singing Divines as they strode through the Painted Hills. Behind them the colorful groups of pigment miners joined in singing on the easier Praises. They walked silently and proudly in honor when the choir sang more complex Glorias and Hallelujahs.

The music and the support from others were like a healing balm for Epoh's broken heart, making the journey so much more bearable than if he had been by himself. He almost felt joyful. He could feel Tyme's presence. He could hear her laugh in his mind. He could see her adorable, crooked smile when he closed his eyes. Her golden-green eyes looked back at him under her thick and expressive black eyebrows as she watched their procession moving to the beat of the drums.

They arrived at Old Town in the early afternoon and drew crowds along the streets that marveled at their strange appearance. Their magnetism was such that numerous people joined in walking behind them out of respect and support, despite not knowing what they were even about.

When they came to the Blue Moon, they saw that a stage had been built outside on the street with awnings and umbrellas, along with a shrine on each side with larger than life-size statues of Tyme. The ceramic figure on the left showed Tyme holding a flaming sword and a crystal shield. The face looked remarkably like Tyme with her slanted smile and even the beauty mark high on her left cheek. The glazed figure on the right showed her standing in the pose of a True Warrior, with the point of her sword on the ground before her and her hands resting on the hilt.

At the base of the statues was a growing collection of flowers made of colored paper, black candles, red candles, sweet breads, gourds of water, pulque, and mezcal. There were also numerous totems of Tyme with her sword, from hand-size to doll-size, some made of cloth, others of clay, wood, and cactus fiber, bundled and twisted together. Epoh was surprised to see that Gybeko and all the Canaries and dusted miners had made and brought such figures of Tyme, and were now pulling them out of bags and pockets to reverently add to the shrines.

Singer and his companions climbed onto the stage where Swindovo began to drum, and they broke into song. The Canaries and other dusted men took up residence nearby under a group of awnings strung above the street.

Epoh went inside the Blue Moon. Despite the large crowd, he quickly found Jyg and Wiir Waar. Delgado was busy elsewhere.

"How are you doing?" asked Wiir Waar.

"Writing helps me," Epoh said. "I am working on another letter about Tyme." He smiled faintly. "To the Mother Womb in Karvor."

"You were destined to do this," Wiir Waar said with growing realization.

"I believe I was," Epoh agreed. "I have certainly been well prepared. That now gives me strength." He told them about the parade of men from the kiva that had accompanied him with singing and drumming. "They are outside on the stage performing now. Tyme is not being forgotten."

"Let me show you something," Jyg said as he led Epoh to an overflowing shrine inside the Blue Moon built to a Bright One. Here was another figure of Tyme holding a flaming sword and crystal shield, surrounded by a mound of smaller totems representing Tyme with her sword. Circling that were more flowers of colored paper, burning candles, mostly black but also gold and red, bread figures with salt, and gourds of mezcal, wine, and tiny cups of viruna.

Epoh studied the offerings in amazement. "What do the totem figures of Tyme represent?" he asked.

"People in Karvor and the Tanis Mountains make shrines like this after someone dies," Jyg answered. "They make the figures as a sign of respect and think about the person who died as they make them. The totem embodies what that person meant to them."

"Does Tyme represent a warrior to everyone?" Epoh asked,

looking at all the figures holding swords. He was not sure that was what Tyme would have wanted.

"I think she represents the fight for justice," Jyg replied. "Everyone knows she chose not to use her sword in the end. But for some reason people want to put the sword in her hand anyway."

Delgado appeared as they were talking. He gave Epoh a solemn hug. "I heard what you were saying," he told them. "And I had thought the same thing. When I had this statue made, I was thinking of Tyme and her fight with Rocozo in the Blue Moon. But when I ordered the statues outside, I made sure one had Tyme's sword pointing into the ground like a True Warrior. When the celebration is over, I am going to have that statue moved inside and placed permanently on the other side of the stage."

Looking at the shrine, Epoh was amazed by how Tyme's martyrdom had amplified everything about her life. Her actions deeply affected a growing number of people who had not even met her yet were moved and changed by her story.

"I heard about the letter you wrote of Tyme and delivered to the Splendorous Dome of the Divine Womb in Ambrit," Delgado said. "Could you send a similar letter to the Mother Womb in Karvor?"

"I am already working on it," Epoh replied.

When Delgado learned that the shaman from the kiva had walked with Epoh from the Painted Hills for the celebration, he insisted on asking Gybeko to be part of the ceremony. "I asked the shaman from the Old Town Womb to recite from the *Prayers for the Mortal Body*," he said. "Mayhaps Gybeko would like to join him."

Delgado had also arranged for some musicians, but quickly changed plans when he learned that Singer and his group had arrived from the Painted Hills.

"They would be best," Delgado said. "They knew Tyme and walked all day to come and honor her. My musicians will play later when we want dance music."

When the heat ended the crowd in the Blue Moon went outside to join everyone under the awnings. Delgado had also alerted street vendors to come and sell food and drinks.

They began the memorial service as the sun set and the colors of the sky were streaked with flaming orange. Swindovo began parading solemnly through the crowd slowly beating a large drum, with Singer, Draktono, and Frisoto following silently behind. At their rear, Kreoko, the gang member who first met Tyme and had his nose broken, carried a pole above his head with a life size papier-mâché statue of Tyme in the pose of a True Warrior, her sword standing before her with the tip on the ground, her hands resting lightly on the hilt. On their second trip up and down the street the choir shared a simple but haunting hymn of sad lament. They sang it again as they passed through a third time, with the audience singing along.

When they finished, they climbed up on the stage, and Epoh joined them to sing one of the Hallelujahs that Tyme had so loved hearing the men sing at the kiva. When they finished Gybeko came forward and recited from the *Prayers for the Mortal Body*:

Know that you will grieve through your life. You will never forget the loss of a loved one.

But you will learn to live with it. You will heal. You will rebuild yourself around the loss you have suffered. You can be whole again.

Yet you will never be the same. Nor should you be the same. Nor would you want to be the same.

Epoh and the men's choir sang another of the songs that Tyme enjoyed. Then he introduced himself as former Crown Prince of Dayrstad and told of the dreams foretelling Tyme's arrival at Dayr Castle. How she had appeared in the stables, and learned to ride Spike, a notorious mountain ibex, into the high mountains. How she had been trained by Tao Tau, a wise old herb woman, who was her spiritual mentor.

"I was enamored of her from the first moment we met," Epoh smiled at the memories. "The thought of her has sustained me through great perils," he said emotionally, remembering his terrifying days in the underground river. "The thought of her continues to give me strength today," his voice broke. "And the thought of her will give me strength in all the days that follow."

Swindovo began beating his drum, and the men's choir launched into one of the catchy and easy-to-learn Praises that he had composed. The audience sang along.

Klew spoke next. He told the story of Tyme battling Noot with wooden swords and her noble words, *to protect the weak and innocent*, that made him willing to take her as apprentice to the sword. And how quickly she had learned and grown.

"I was witness to her vows to be a True Warrior," Klew said solemnly. "She started as my apprentice, but she became my teacher. She has shown the way of true service and sacrifice."

Jyg talked of meeting Tyme in keep school and teaching her to climb into the rafters in the stables. How they explored the abandoned buildings at Dayr Castle together and had adventures with the Ser Cus. How she had taught him to have a spiritual practice.

Wiir Waar told of her respect and fascination with Tyme from the moment they first met. Getting her dressed up and taking her to her first banquet. "We danced the first song together," Wiir Waar recalled. "We had so much fun. She was always so present and alive."

Delgado told of her dramatic introduction to the Jawbone Ridge gang, her thrashing of Rocozo. "She showed him mercy," he said, "and risked his attack again." He laughed with irony. "She actually apologized about it to me later. She felt like she had lost her temper." The crowd chuckled. "She showed the Czarzina mercy. She was all-powerful, yet full of mercy."

Now Singer sang a dramatic Gloria with Draktono, Frisoto, Swindovo, and Epoh joining in on the chorus.

When they finished Epoh told of the writings from the *Book of Elders* and the *Kabaal Prophecies* regarding a Bright One. How those prophecies had been fulfilled in Tyme. How he had come with Riin Ruel to find her in Karvor.

"Tyme felt honored to be in a position that could change herstory. Now, 'tis up to us to see how deep and long lasting that change will be."

The crowd cheered and hooted.

"She gave her life," Epoh declared. "Her body has passed from our view. But she still lives very much in our hearts. Thank you all for the part you now play in keeping her vision alive."

A few began chanting *Bright One! Bright One!* More of the crowd picked it up.

Wiir Waar came forward again. "She is living on in each of us now. We know that she would want us to cheer for the amazing life she lived," the whole crowd roared their approval, "and our wonderful good fortune to know of her." Another boisterous round of applause. "So, with Tyme forever in our hearts and minds, let us have music, dance, and celebrate all we have been given in life!"

Jyg and Wiir Waar danced together for a number of songs before taking a break. "Have you decided what you are doing yet?" she asked as they sipped their drinks. "I am going back to the Ser Cus in a few days. You are welcome to come along."

"If I bring Bones," Jyg joked.

"Yes," Wiir Waar agreed, acting serious. "That is, with Bones along, of course!"

Jyg's smile faded. "Actually, there is a problem."

"What problem?" Wiir Waar replied with surprise. What could possibly not work?

Jyg had been trying to figure out how to tell her for days. How he could not be with the Ser Cus unless he was also with her. And that, he believed, had no chance of happening.

"I love you," he confessed. "I am afraid you will get tired of me being moonboy after you, then we will be over," he sighed. "I could not stay in the Ser Cus if I was not with you. I will always love you. I could not be around you continually if we were not a couple. That would break my heart."

Wiir Waar was momentarily speechless. A smile spread across her face. "That was the most beautiful thing anyone could say. I have been thinking similar thoughts but now you jumped ahead and declared your romantic intent." She smiled mischievously. "So, I will do the same."

Wiir Waar pushed her chair back, stood up, and then slowly bent to one knee on the floor before him. "Will you marry me?" She took his hands. "Will you be my husband and helpmate?"

Now Jyg was speechless.

"Sorry, I do not have a ring yet," she chortled.

"I would be delighted to marry you," Jyg answered with emotion as he helped her back to her feet so that they could hug.

A few moments later Epoh came over to their table. "What just happened?" he asked. "I saw you on one knee like you were proposing."

"I did!" Wiir Waar said with pride. "He said yes!"

"That is the most wonderful news. We must announce it to the party!"

"No," Wiir Waar shook her head. "We can announce it later. Tonight's celebration is for Tyme."

"Are you kidding?" Epoh replied. "Tyme would insist! She would consider this to be the *very best thing* that could possibly happen at her celebration tonight! Her two best friends-- getting married!"

He gave them a sly smile. "She told me she thought you two would end up together."

"She did?" they echoed in amazement.

"Yes. A number of times."

Late into the night Klew sat thoughtfully watching the crowd when he spotted a familiar face. Gribono mingling in the audience! He thought of telling Epoh or Jyg, but he did not want to dampen their festivities. What would they do anyway?

Klew moved through the crowd and discreetly watched as Gribono stopped occasionally to talk with various people. 'Twas obvious that Targono's spy was checking out exactly what was going on. It appeared as if he had only just arrived, as Klew was able to get up close enough from behind to hear Gribono asking people about Tyme, what had happened earlier in the memorial, and who had spoken.

Gribono had been passing through Old Town heading down the hill toward Karvor proper, when he had come across a fascinating memorial celebration. He was stunned to find out it was for the young warrior prophet who had confronted the Czarzina, dodged a hail of crossbow arrows, exposed the coup plans of both General Cata Cara and Captain Targono, and then finally been killed at the end.

The spy was amazed to find that the young woman, named Tyme, was also the one who beat up the rogue gang leader months ago in Old Town. He thought of Sergeant Etna Nate, who had first heard about the incident, and told him it was a large white warrior woman with red hair who had been responsible.

Gribono did not see Sergeant Etna Nate around. The dead warrior prophet sounded just like the kind of person that Etna Nate would be thrilled to follow. Gribono had not heard from the sergeant for a few days. He figured she was probably still locked up as a prisoner from Targono's takeover of the Heart Legion compound. But she would most likely be out soon, once the King of Karvor found out her true loyalties. Gribono had no idea that she had already been killed by the King she would have been eager to support.

THE NARROWS

General Cata Cara of the Heart Legion left Pintone with a battalion of soldiers for the four-day journey to Jintiga Bridge near Karvor. She was utterly confident that she had more than enough soldiers to completely surround and overwhelm the Legion compound and gain control of the barracks Captain Targono had captured.

Targono, the newly claimed King of Karvor, also believed that a battalion of Heart Legion soldiers could overwhelm and pin down his forces at the former Heart Legion compound by Jintiga Bridge. That was why he planned instead to ambush General Cata Cara's soldiers on their march up the Jintiga Canyon, at the narrows. He thought of the idea centuries earlier, when he first came up the canyon as a squire for Captain Gornado and noted the many large boulders on the canyon rims for an ambush.

Over the last three days, his engineers and workers had created a series of slender hidden walkways and pedestrian bridges along the canyon rim where large rocks could be leveraged and rolled down from high above. Everything was built quickly using a light framework of wooden poles forming triangular struts, with interlocking metal eyelets and pins.

Targono watched the columns of Heart Legion soldiers approach the narrows to determine where General Cata Cara was located. He guessed correctly, she was near the front, out of the dust her army created, feeling confident. Targono made sure she was in the right spot before he attacked.

Forty of his best soldiers scurried down their hidden wooden ladders to cut off any retreat, forming a wall of sword fighters with large shields, and a line of spearmen behind to stab between the shields and kill anyone who threatened to overwhelm the front line.

A larger force, including Targono, dropped down in front of the Legion soldiers. As Targono attacked, the rest of his soldiers, who were much higher on steep scree fields, rolled rocks over the cliffs, which hit other rocks, and showered down a deadly avalanche of stone upon the trapped Legion soldiers, who only had small shields to cower under from the onslaught of rocks that came ricocheting off the walls from every direction.

Targono's men simply held their line to keep the Heart Legion soldiers from escaping the destruction raining down upon them. He let the rocks and stones do most of the maiming, injuring, and killing.

When 'twas over Targono led a group in search of General Cata Cara. She was alive but unconscious. Targono ordered for her to be treated and locked up, along with a few other offisers. He then loudly announced to those without serious injury that they were welcome to come and join his forces.

"I could have killed you all," he told them. "But instead, I only gave you a beating. If you are tired of following women generals who do not know how to fight, I offer you a change of banners. If you are tired of not getting paid, I offer a better salary."

"I am now King of Karvor," he boasted. "Swear allegiance to me if you want to win. If you stay with the Czarzina and her generals, I will not be so merciful the next time we fight."

THE KING OF KARVOR

The morning after Tyme's memorial celebration the group at the apartment came together for breakfast. Wiir Waar and Jyg came out of the same bedroom to the cheers of the Epoh and Klew.

"Any idea when or where you might marry?" Epoh asked.

"Unfortunately, not for almost a decade," Wiir Waar replied. "We want to be married in Karvor, so we have to wait until the next time the Ser Cus returns."

"We want part of the celebration at the Blue Moon," Jyg said. "Will you both still be here?"

"I would not miss it!" Epoh declared. "I will be writing and staying in the caves by the kiva in the Painted Hills. Swing by any time to say hello."

"I hope to be here as well," Klew said without further explanation.

When they finished eating Epoh loaded his pack and said goodbye. "Your wedding will give me something to look forward to," he hugged each one and told them he loved them. Epoh walked to the Trusted Scribe and bought a thick bundle of the very best writing paper, ink, and extra quills. Then he left the city for his hermit cave near the kiva. Gybeko, Singer, the Canaries and others had already left earlier that day.

Later that morning a message came from Delgado. When Wiir Waar, Jyg and Klew arrived at the Blue Moon, they met in a back room.

"I just got word," Delgado informed them with stunned

disbelief. "General Cata Cara was wounded and captured yesterday afternoon in the narrows of Jintiga Canyon. Her soldiers were trapped and pulverized by an avalanche of rocks from high above set off by the King of Karvor."

They all listened solemnly. Klew seemed especially stricken.

"They say a battalion was destroyed," Delgado continued. "Numerous deaths but most just injured. Of the rest, many deserted the Heart Legion to join with the new King."

"This was what I had hoped to stop," Klew said with anguish.

"I do not think anyone can stop it now," Jyg shook his head sadly.

"I have to try again to see Targono," Klew vowed with renewed determination.

"You will be walking into the same situation that Tyme faced," Jyg replied worriedly. "The King of Karvor has not chosen the Noble Path. He will not let anyone sway his intent."

"Nor will I allow anyone to sway my intent," Klew responded. "I am but an apprentice. I follow a Bright One who led by example. Now, I must take my turn to try and stop the bloodshed. She has given me great strength and courage for what lies ahead."

"If you think you have some plan, or some chance to make Targono listen," Wiir Waar said with concern, "then we will not try to change your mind. However, if you follow such a course because of any despair or guilt, then we ask that you reconsider. Tyme would not want you to throw your life away."

"No more than I wanted her to throw her life away!" Klew replied. "Do any of us think that is what happened? That she threw her life away?"

They all shook their heads. "No," Jyg said.

"She died trying to make a difference," Klew said with respect. "We have not yet seen the full effect of her deeds. How far her actions may reach."

"No, we have not," Wiir Waar agreed.

"I must also try to make a difference," Klew nodded with determination and resolve. "And like Tyme, I believe I have some chance to make it out alive. Targono and I were once more than just friends. Mayhaps that will save me."

He hugged each of them and told each one that he loved them. Then he left the Blue Moon in Old Town and walked toward Jintiga Fort to seek audience with the King of Karvor.

When Klew walked up to the fort of the King of Karvor, the guard at the door remembered him and greeted him this time with more respect.

"This way manser," he said as he led Klew into a small room with a table and chairs and a jug of water. "The King wishes to speak with you. I will send word that you are here. Wait here until he calls for you." The guard closed and bolted the door.

'Twas nearly the heat when Klew heard the bolt being drawn and the door opened. He was escorted to an unadorned audience chamber where Targono sat alone. The King did not rise from his chair.

"Klewono," he said guardedly, calling him by his old name. "'Tis you after all."

"Targono," Klew smiled in admiration. "You always said you would make captain. I never got beyond sergeant."

"No captain now," Targono gave a throaty chuckle. "I am the King of Karvor!" He looked at Klew shrewdly. "And you?"

"I bought out my Heart Legion contract centuries ago," Klew answered. "I have been a soldier for King Eyrico of Dayrstad."

"A Barbarian King!" Targono roared with approval. "Like me!"

"King Eyrico strives to follow a Noble Path," Klew answered pointedly. "It has been my honor to serve him."

"Do you serve him now?" Targono asked. "Are you his envoy?"

"I now follow another," Klew said. "A Bright One!"

"The Bright One?" Targono shouted. "You mean the young warrior who died lecturing the Czarzina? What kind of prophet is that?" He barked a laugh. "She was right about one thing, however. The Czarzina's days are numbered!"

"The young woman was a True Warrior," Klew answered, "who gave her life rather than compromise her principals."

"Principals are overrated," Targono sneered. "I learned that when Captain Gornado lost everything after shooting his mouth off about idealistic vows and eternal principals."

"Yes, he did," Klew agreed sadly, "taking you down as well." Targono had been busted from squire to private and transferred to the Hammer Legion when his mentor fell from grace.

"So, who is this Bright One?" the King of Karvor asked, trying not to show his true interest.

Klew knew him better than that. Targono had always been drawn to stories with drama, intrigue, and warrior heroines. Klew told him of the prophetic dreams surrounding Tyme's mysterious arrival at Dayr Castle. Of Riin Ruel, and her search for Tyme. How the young girl had taken the vows of a True Warrior and been his apprentice to the sword.

"Never in my life have I witnessed anyone who learned as fast as she did," Klew marveled. "She was unrivaled with a sword."

"And good at throwing daggers," Targono added with annoyance. "And evading crossbow bolts, for awhile at least. But what does that have to do with me?"

Klew told him about Noot being killed by Gribono, and how they had followed Targono's spy to Karvor. "I also trailed him when he came to report to you at Vrak Pass."

"Gribono!" Targono cursed. "He can get too full of himself. And not nearly so clever as he thought to be trailed by you all the way from Dayr Castle to Vanttan without realizing it."

"I followed him around Karvor as well," Klew said. "And saw him yesterday at the memorial outside the Blue Moon for

Tyme."

"What do you seek?" Targono asked.

"We came to find justice for a murdered stable boy. But now it has become truth and justice for all."

Targono huffed. "Tyme thought exposing me would give some justice for the boy?"

"She exposed you in hopes of stopping a civil war," Klew said. "To stop what happened in Jintiga Canyon."

"Jintiga Canyon was a brilliant engineering and tactical success," Targono boasted with confidence. He was more than a bit annoyed that his old friend was not congratulating him on his victories and cleverness.

"You were always inventing things and building things when we were young,"
Klew smiled and acknowledged fondly.

"And you always had your head in the clouds," Targono recalled. "What are you up to now?"

"To be a Bright One, and a True Warrior," Klew answered. "I plead for an end to the fighting. Enough blood has been shed."

"You come to me as follower and puppet of some enchantress. You plead mercy for a corrupt society filled with prejudice," Targono hissed in anger.

"I plead for a new society without prejudice," Klew answered. "You are King of Karvor. Stop the fighting. Sue for peace with the Senasers. Demand a new Czarzina. Use the position you are in to create something better for everyone."

"I am not stopping now," Targono laughed bitterly. He wanted to brag and share his plan with someone, and who better to tell than Klew?

"I left behind men to ambush the silver shipment out of Vattan and run it off a cliff. It will take months to retrieve the silver and haul it back out. The Heart Legion soldiers are more than a moon behind already in getting paid," the King continued. "When they see how well my soldiers are paid, they will flock to my banner. I am already getting recruits who have left the Legion, and also Fire devotees from the mountains, itching for at fight."

Klew listened without comment.

"I have General Cata Cara, Major Bayn Baya, and other Heart Legion offisers locked up. I was merciful to the Heart Legion soldiers in the Narrows. Give them another month without pay and they will abandon their posts. Then I march on Pintone. Then Dorgon, and Ambrit not long after that. I will be King of Ambra."

"I am pleading with you not to do that," Klew said. "You have already proven to everyone your abilities. Stop now and bargain with them from your position of strength."

"Why stop when I have them right where I want them? The Czarzina, her generals, the whole stinking mess is going to get cleaned out!"

"And the Senasers?" Klew asked.

"The Senasers will be evaluated one by one. The Senate will run the government under my oversight."

"And when you die?" Klew asked. "Do we pick another fighter to lead us like the Hool? Or like the Dark Ages?"

"Get another Czarzina again for all I care," Targono hissed in outrage. He had not yet thought much about that. "I will no longer be bothered by what happens."

"I cannot let you do that," Klew said. "I know you. You always get mad about something at first, but then later you cool down and rethink, and modify your response. Send envoys now to the Senasers to stop further fighting."

"You think I am going to change my mind and lose my anger over this?" Targono roared. He pushed his chair over as he stood. "By the deepest hell. You have no idea how angry I am."

"Do not condemn Heart Legion soldiers to injury and death to assuage your anger," Klew pleaded, "Just to prove once again your superior battle skills?"

"I am going to eliminate all the corrupt and hypocritical rulers so Ambra can start fresh and clean," Targono hissed. "And there is nothing you can do to stop me."

Klew stepped forward to block his way to the door. "I cannot let you leave the room to give such an order. I know you will come to regret it."

"You are not man enough to stop me," Targono said as he drew his sword.

Klew drew his sword as well. He hoped that sparring would calm Targono down. Targono came at him hard and fast. Klew easily deflected the blows. After so much training with Tyme, who was quicker than either of them, Klew had no problem at first defending himself from Targono's blade.

But as the fighting continued Klew began to tire from the sheer force and strength of Targono's attacks. Sparring with Tyme had done little to train Klew against a larger, stronger opponent.

Then Targono bobbled for just a moment, exposing an opening. Klew did not press the attack to cut Targono's sword arm. Klew did not want to win the fight by physical force, he wanted Targono to decide to stop on his own free will.

But when Targono saw Klew hold back, it only insulted and enraged him all the more. He threw himself into the fight with renewed fury. Striking. Striking. Harder. Harder. Klew began to lose his balance. Targono lashed out without any thought of the consequences. Klew tried to block the thrust but was too late. Their blades twisted sharply as he stumbled, and his arm buckled.

Klew felt a blinding pain. He looked down to see Targono's sword, run through his stomach. Targono pulled it out in shocked surprise. Klew dropped his sword and tottered on his feet. He reached out to gently pat Targono's arm.

"I am sorry," he whispered. "I had to try and stop you."

Targono woke from his fury to look at his bloodied sword and then dropped it, as reality began to register.

Klew's legs buckled. Targono half caught him as he was falling. They sunk together slowly to the floor.

"'Twas an accident," Targono stammered with regret.

Klew gasped for breath. "I stayed faithful to you," he said in pained whispers. "I never loved another again."

Targono scrunched up his face and began to cry.

"'Tis okay," Klew consoled him. "I am happy to die in your arms. With you holding me."

"No," Targono choked out. "Do not die."

Klew looked tenderly into his eyes. "You always had a temper," he said with a gentle, quivering smile. "But I know you will do the right thing." With those words Klew took his last breath.

RIIN RUEL

When Riin Ruel met alone with Major Gwen Gail after Tyme's death, the Hilt of the Daggers was devastated and furious at the outcome of their plans. Everything the secretive warrior group had worked for and believed in for millennia, esoteric and arcane teachings passed faithfully from one generation to another, all of their hopes, prayers, and dreams had been snuffed out, broken, and left unfulfilled.

"She did not *Slay the Beast!*" the Hilt of the Daggers seethed. "She did not even *Smite the Beast!* She left the Czarzina, the puppet of the Beast, alive on her throne," Major Gwen Gail said in disgust. "You were wrong! She was not the Bright One at all."

Riin Ruel hung her head. She had all of those same fears herself, and yet, "Tyme's prophecies have taken hold in the city," she reported cautiously. "Many believe the Czarzina will be deposed and tried in a court."

"The goal was far beyond the Czarzina," the Hilt of the Daggers gritted her teeth. "The goal was to battle the Beast and rid the world of evil!"

"I failed in teaching her," Riin Ruel said numbly. "I offer my resignation as Point of the Daggers."

"Your resignation is accepted," the Hilt of the Daggers dismissed her scornfully. "You may leave." The Daggers would resume their search for the Bright One without Riin Ruel. They believed the prophecies had yet to be properly fulfilled.

Czarzina Hana Hama Hala continued to lose her hold on power. Then news arrived of Captain Targono's raiding the treasuries at Thesson and Tepu, overtaking Jintiga Garrison and the bridge toll booths, and declaring himself King of Karvor. The Senasers all abandoned the Czarzina, just as Tyme had foretold. She was arrested by a new Will of the Blades.

While the Daggers expelled Riin Ruel from their group, the Blades, who knew nothing of failed prophecies, had only praise for her actions. The new Will of the Blades promptly re-instated Riin Ruel with high honors in recognition of her finding and bringing the young woman prophet to Ambrit. Stories from the Bright One's life began to circulate through the city, oddly from a letter written by a man to the Splendorous Dome of the Divine Womb.

Then came news of the rockslide ambush, deaths, injuries and defections that decimated a battalion of Heart Legion soldiers at Jintiga Canyon, along with the imprisonment of General Cata Cara, Major Bayn Baya, Captain Kin Kell, and other Heart Legion offisers. The King of Karvor had ruthlessly demonstrated his claim to power.

The Senasers were eager to stop the hostilities. The Ambrit treasury was broke. There was fear of total revolt among the unpaid Legion soldiers. The Senasers voted to send a delegation to the King to acknowledge his control of Jintiga Garrison, Jintiga Bridge, the city of Karvor, and the mountains of Tanis.

Because of her knowledge of Karvor politics, Targono and his spies, and others involved, Riin Ruel was named as special escort and adviser to the leader of the envoy.

REMORSE

Targono lay on the floor with Klew dead in his arms, weeping all through the heat. He continued to seal himself in the room through the evening and the night.

When he emerged the next morning, he looked like a madman. He refused all food. He ordered that Klew be buried with full military honors. A meeting with the Mayor of Karvor was put on hold. The King took to his bed with strict orders that he was not to be disturbed.

Targono could not forget the tender look in Klewono's eyes when he said, *I am happy to die in your arms.* Those words pierced his heart. *With you holding me.* How could he have killed the man he had once loved? The man who had proclaimed to love him still? The man whom he now realized he still loved in return. The remorse overwhelmed him. Especially at night when he was totally unable to sleep. He could not get Klew's words out of his mind. Nor the forgiving look in his eyes.

In his grief, Targono flipped emotions and grew angry when he recalled other parts of their conversation. *You always had a temper* Klewono had reminded him. *But I know you will do the right thing.* Whatever Klewono thought was right. How pretentious! How judgmental! How dare he appear at the last moment and tell Targono what to do?

Why should he give up an opportunity to become King of Ambra? To totally wipe out a corrupt government full of prejudice against men. How was it right to allow such discrimination to go on when he could do something to change it? Why did Klewono have to say those words as he died? Targono was so angry he could not sleep. He spent nights tossing and turning and thrashing in his bed.

Finally, out of utter exhaustion, he at last began to fall asleep, only to have nightmares of their swordfight where he knew he was going to slay Klewono, but he could not stop himself. No matter how he screamed at himself not to do it, he watched repeatedly in horror as he thrust the blade into Klewono's stomach. And then came the sickening realization of what he had done. The anguish and despair overwhelmed him. Over and over again the scene was replayed. A never-ending torment of sorrow and regret.

When the Senasers envoy arrived, Targono was barely functioning and not presentable. One of the King's lieutenants met with the group and offered no explanation why a meeting was not possible that day. The following day the meeting was postponed again while Targono's offisers tried to get him prepared for an interview.

Riin Ruel spent the two days sleuthing around the King's compound and the city of Karvor, trying to figure out what was happening. She learned that there had been a funeral for a soldier that no one seemed to know, yet the soldier had been buried with the highest military honors. After the funeral the King of Karvor had canceled his meeting with the Mayor of Karvor, and the meeting had still not been rescheduled. The King had been in seclusion ever since. Then Riin Ruel discovered, with sadness yet great respect, that the name of the dead soldier was Klewono. Or, as she knew him, Klew.

The next day the Senaser's envoy was finally given an audience with the King. Riin Ruel accompanied the group into a small and inappropriate audience chamber. The King of Karvor sat brooding in his chair. He did not look up when the envoy was announced. Instead, he sat staring at a dark stain on the floor. 'Twas the same room where Targono had killed Klew. He had spent days moping listlessly in the room and had not allowed Klew's blood to be cleaned from the floor.

The envoy introduced herself, but the King made no reply, nor did he acknowledge her presence. He did not appear well. The envoy was uncertain how to proceed.

Riin Ruel studied the stain on the floor as the envoy stammered her introduction. The King was clearly not listening. Riin Ruel realized normal protocol was not working. She boldly stepped before the King to try a different tactic.

"Klewono came to see you," she said, gesturing at the dark stain.

Targono came out of his stupor and gave her a startled look. Suddenly his mind was alert again. "You are the Blade mystic who thinks she found the Bright One," he spat out accusingly. "You are the one Klewono was listening to." The King of Karvor became outraged and frantic. "Get out!" He screamed. "Get out before I have you all killed!"

The envoy and rest of the group scuttled for the door. Riin Ruel did not move.

"Do you think I am afraid of death?" she asked without any sign of concern. A sudden realization touched her. She sensed snippets of his terrible dreams. "You are having nightmares. You cannot sleep."

"Get out!" he shrieked.

"I can help you sleep," she told him confidently. "I can help rid you of your nightmares."

For a moment the King looked like he might rise from his chair and attack her. But he restrained himself and ordered his guards to throw her out of the compound. Riin Ruel was escorted from the fort.

Three days later he sent a message for her. When she arrived, he looked worse than before.

"I can no longer live like this," the King told her desperately. "You must help me! The nightmares are unbearable. Do something before I kill myself!"

NEWS

Epoh was at his writing table in his cave in the Painted Hills when he heard a horse approaching. He came out to find Delgado climbing down from the saddle. Epoh could tell from the look on Delgado's face that he brought unsettling news. Some good news came first.

"Just as Tyme had prophesied," Delgado reported, "the Czarzina has been deposed and is now facing trial."

"Praise Divine," Epoh said with relief. Tyme's death had not been in vain.

"A peace agreement is being signed and you have been requested to help write it."

"How can that be?" Epoh asked in astonishment.

Delgado told him of Targono's ambush in the narrows of Jintiga Canyon and the deaths, injuries, and defections of Heart Legion soldiers. He reiterated Klew's determination to do something to stop the fighting.

"He said he was no longer the teacher, but the student," Delgado quoted Klew's exact words. "He said he followed a Bright One who led by example. Her strength gave him great courage."

Delgado grew somber as he told how Klew and Targono had fought. How Klew had died, and his last words had been of forgiveness. "They had been young lovers at the Military Academy," Delgado revealed.

"Klew was a True Warrior and a Bright One as well!" Epoh whispered in awe.

Delgado nodded his head in amazement. "He said he was

happy to die in Targono's arms."

"How do you know of all of this?"

"Riin Ruel," Delgado answered. "She was reinstated into the Blades with full honors. Because of her knowledge about Targono and his spies, she was named counsel to an envoy from the Senasers to meet with the King of Karvor. They arrived to find Targono had descended into near madness after killing Klew. He was having such terrible nightmares he became suicidal. Riin Ruel nursed him back to health."

"So, Targono is now willing to sign a peace agreement?" Epoh marveled.

"Yes. Riin Ruel wants to write up a Bill of Rights for him to sign. She wants your guidance on a few issues."

"Then I would invite Draktono as well," Epoh suggested. "Targono wants to be the champion of men's rights. Who better to articulate those rights than Draktono?"

A BILL OF RIGHTS

Riin Ruel convinced King Targono that the only way for his nightmares to end was to confess his crimes, which included killing Klewono, along with Heart Legion soldiers at Thesson, Tepu, Jintiga Fort, and of course, the narrows. He must take responsibility for Noot's death, and others he did not know who were nevertheless affected by his actions. He had to hand over General Cata Cara, Mayor Bayn Baya, and other Heart Legion coup plotters to be court-marshaled, release all other prisoners, and move forward with a general amnesty against his foes with a promise of no more killings or reprisals.

"Reconciliation is based on forgiveness," Riin Ruel had told him. "Forgiveness is based on true confession, which must be grounded in penitence, in genuine contrition and sorrow for what you have done. Only then can we start again with a clean slate and new set of laws."

The meeting was held at Jintiga Fort around a big table with King Targono of Karvor, Ser Tapa Tana Tama, the Senaser's special envoy from Ambrit, Riin Ruel as counsel to the envoy, the Mayor of Karvor, Epoh, and Draktono.

The head priest from the Mother Womb in Karvor had been invited but refused to come. She felt the proceedings to be illegal and wanted no part of it, thinking that would only give legitimacy to the rogue claims of an illegitimate Barbarian King. The Queen of Tanis was also invited but did not attend nor send an envoy. She had similar misgivings. They both felt the Senasers were acquiescing to the scoundrel King and abandoning the women of Karvor to an appalling fate.

King Targono had planned to send an invitation to

Shamano, the shaman from the mountains of Birjj, to be a representative of the Fire. King Targono's spy, Gribono, had met Shamano at Dayr Castle, and then again more recently when the shaman had secretly visited Karvor. Since the poisoning and death of the rebel leader, Bokono, the cohesion of the assorted small bands of soldiers throughout the mountains who aligned with the Fire had diminished. Shamano intensified his focus on the corrupted souls of men, and their special need for purification. Was not Bokono's murder further proof of men's fallen nature? Shamano's critical judgments and haranguing diatribes grew more frequent. His humorless lectures became more divisive than unifying.

"Shamano believes women's bodies were first created by Divine from the ether as angelic beings," Gribono reported to the King. "He believes men's bodies were created through worldly passion. Hence, a man's body is more stained and impure. He thinks desire, and struggle for political power, is the problem, not the solution."

"Who else represents the fire?" asked the King in anger.

"The Burnished Man," Gribono replied without hesitation. He described the memorial he had witnessed in Old Town for the warrior prophet who had confronted the Czarzina. And the man who had spoken. Gribono had come late to the event and not heard how Noot's death had triggered Tyme's leaving Dayr Castle. That small piece of information eluded him. Everyone had told him about Tyme's fights with Rocozo, the villainous gang leader, her stopping a pigment wagon robbery, and her dramatic encounter with the Czarzina. Gribono had been impressed by the participation of shaman Gybeko and all the dusted men from the kiva in the Painted Hills, the numerous red candles from Fire devotees, and the outpouring of affection from the Jawbone Ridge gang and people of Old Town. Obviously, the young warrior prophet was held in the highest honor with the groups the King wanted to champion.

"The Burnished Man was highly esteemed by everyone

there," Gribono reported.

"Does he have another name?" the King asked.

"Epoh," Gribono replied, unaware of Tyme or Epoh's connection to him, or to Klew.

Prior to the meeting, Riin Ruel met with the Mayor of Karvor, who had already met with King Targono a few times and felt they could work together. The Mayor told Riin Ruel that she found Targono more reasonable and open to new ideas than the Queen of Tanis had ever been.

"The people of Karvor have never liked their lowland Queen, who knows nothing about their city. On the other hand, having a powerful King, who lets me run the city and whose army lives beside us in their fort," the Mayor smiled as if 'twas obvious. "'Tis very good for business. We are next door. He pays his soldiers generously and they are well-behaved."

"Besides," the Mayor shrugged her shoulders, "none of us has the power to stop him. We all know it. Yet look how accommodating he is. I think he has realized he is happier, and 'tis more profitable to build relationships rather than dictate them."

The biggest concern of the Senasers and the Mayor was to clearly state that the King was not above the law. The King would have clear limits to his power, just like the laws which originally set the boundaries for the Empress of the Ambri Empire. However, the laws governing the rights of citizens in the Ambri Empire had been written just for the rights of women.

Now, both Epoh and Draktono insisted that the new document for the Bill of Rights be written to include not just women, but also men and fifirs, giving everyone the right as full citizens, including the right to a fair trial with a jury.

Draktono also insisted that men be allowed to sing in the Womb. "The wall between the refuge and the sanctuary has to be removed," he boldly told them. "If men are to be treated as equal citizens, they must be allowed in the sanctuary." He did not say anything of the sanctum, nor discuss the gender of Divine. That would have to wait for another day. He realized there was only so much they could change at one time.

Riin Ruel shook her head. "The priests need to be here to give their opinion and vote on this. I am afraid they will never agree."

"They were invited and chose not to attend," King Targono said dismissively.

Ser Tapa Tana Tama, the Senaser's envoy, also raised her voice in protest. "This will set a bad precedent."

King Targono ignored them both. He turned to Draktono and Epoh. "Write down the articles just as you have spoken."

After they had done so, Targono immediately took the Bill of Rights and signed it. "I will abide by what is written," he vowed.

Ser Tapa Tana Tama frowned with worry over the clauses giving equal rights to men and fifirs.

"Take it or leave it," the King threatened. "The document cannot be changed." He turned to Riin Ruel. "You wanted a new, clean slate to start over. This is how we do it. Otherwise, I will go my own way." He handed her the document and the pen.

Riin Ruel hesitated for only a moment before signing. "You are right," she conceded. "We all must make concessions to forge a new and lasting peace."

The Mayor signed next without any complaint.

Ser Tapa Tana Tama shook her head with concern that there might be any misunderstanding. "This document is only for Karvor," she reminded the King before signing. "It has no affect on Ambri law."

"But, as you said," Draktono replied after she had signed, "this sets a precedent." He did not complain that he and

Epoh helped write the document but were not among the signatories. The important thing was what the Bill of Rights would do moving into the future.

Riin Ruel returned to Ambrit with the envoy and helped with the lengthy negotiations to ratify the agreement. Despite the opposition of the priests from the Splendorous Dome of the Divine Womb, who objected to equal rights for all genders, the Senasers and new Czarzina finally signed the document.

Riin Ruel had not used her Yoke to battle demons since she began preparing her body for the poison she would take to escape prison in the Box at Ralston Garrison. She had not been strong enough when leaving Falcana Nunnery. After finding Tyme her total focus had been on training and mentoring the young woman. Now, at last, she was stronger herself and free from all-consuming responsibilities. She could resume her spiritual battles.

She opened a leather pouch and removed her Yoke. Thirteen bones on a string she used for demon hunting. Only two of the demons were still alive. A badly weakened monster in the third hell, and a slightly weakened fiend in the fifth hell, whom she had only ambushed a few times. She fingered that bone, from the little finger of the sword hand of one of killers who had tried to ambush her on her first visit to Dayr Castle.

She had been taught to use the Yoke by the Daggers, who had taken her in when young and trained her in their arcane and mysterious rites. She had never questioned or doubted their cause or beliefs. But now she had been expelled by the Daggers for mistaking Tyme to be the Bright One.

But was it a mistake? She was no longer sure. She was not even sure any more about the Yoke she fingered in her hands. She remembered Tyme's words.

Throwing myself into demon battles in the lowest pits of hell gives demons what they want. They want me, in hell, fighting.

For the first time in her life, Riin Ruel had doubts about the Yoke and what was even happening during her demon battles. She had been so busy instructing Tyme down a different path, she had never stopped to listen and learn from the young woman. It had taken Tyme's death for Riin Ruel to pay attention.

I must leave the Beast behind and turn to love and compassion.

That was the message. Riin Ruel put the strand of little finger bones back into their leather pouch. The following dark Moonday she built a fire and burned the pouch and bones to ash. She promised herself never again to recited any of the *Prayers for the Damned.*

EPOH'S DREAM

Epoh sat at his desk thinking about the letter he had just written. He felt a great responsibility to present things right and true. He had a stack of similar letters he had already written in his satchel.

He had delayed sending them. He was not quite sure why. He wanted to be certain he had included everything that was important to say. The letters were addressed to the Mother Wombs in each of the old cities. Letters which told the story of a Bright One.

That night Epoh went to bed and had a most powerful dream.

Tyme was standing on the Empress Auditorium stage confronting the Czarzina. At first Epoh was watching her from the back of the auditorium, feeling the audience's shock and suspense as Tyme condemned the Czarzina, impervious to the rain of crossbow bolts all around her, then leaping and dodging more arrows as she moved closer.

She stopped to stand tall again and proclaim from the *Book of Elders*:

A Bright One shall come unto us
Her sword shall be Flames of Truth
Her shield a Dazzling Crystal
Her Voice a Great Song!

Surrounded by a continuing volley of arrows, Tyme fearlessly called out the Czarzina's crimes.

But now the dream began to shift into a terrible nightmare, as a part of Epoh knew what was coming, but he was powerless to stop it. He watched helplessly in terror as a crossbow bolt hit Tyme on her right side just under her ribs.

Suddenly, Epoh was inside Tyme as she nearly stumbled but then stood up straight again. He could feel the searing pain. The catch in her breath. The pounding of her heart as she let go of the flash powder in her pocket. She knew she could no longer make it out safely. She would not risk the lives of her friends in a bungled escape.

Epoh saw how her concept of time shifted, and he witnessed the rapid stream of images and events she remembered from her life. So many of their moments together.

Tyme gathered her strength to stand tall and proclaim from the *Kabaal Prophecies*:

I am the Mother of all Daughters
The Daughter of all Mothers
Divine Daughter
Who fills the world with love and compassion!

As the end neared, Epoh saw how Tyme closed her eyes and thought of him. An amazing wave of memories of them together flooded into her mind--from their first meeting at Dayr Castle to their last days in Ambrit. How their wedding and moons together in Karvor had been the best days of their lives, just as she had guessed when insisting they not wait to get married.

Epoh felt her immense sadness at leaving him. Her realization that he would never be the same. She thought of his near drowning in a sacred pool in the Womb of the Earth. How he had become another person, no longer Epohco, but Epoh. Now part of Epoh would die once more and have to be reborn and endure the pain of becoming someone new. Who would he be?

Then Tyme thought of Starai, the acolyte nun who cared for him and nursed him back to health. Starai could help soothe his soul, Tyme realized. She could ease the burden he would carry. Tyme did not want Epoh to be alone.

A sharp stab of pain made her whimper.

Epoh heard with her the faint sound of hoof beats. The Czarzina was yelling but Tyme was no longer listening. The sound of the hoof beats was growing.

King was coming!

The hoof beats grew louder, the sound filling her ears. Tyme collapsed with relief into the pool of blood at her feet. Everything was going to be all right!

King would lift her up and carry her away!

HOPE THE PROCLAIMER

When Epoh woke from his dream, he felt a new purpose in his life. The pain of Tyme's death was still there, but different.

Tyme was right. He would need to become someone new.

Now he knew why he had not sent the letters to all the Mother Wombs. He had not signed them. He had been concerned about revealing that he was a man; that some might not take Tyme's story as seriously if they knew his identity.

But now he understood that reality was the whole point.

He pulled out the letters from his satchel and signed each one with his old name reversed as an anadrome. He was now Hope.

Hope the Proclaimer.

A SER CUS WEDDING

Hope continued living and writing in the caves by the kiva for nearly a decade. Then, unannounced, Jyg and Wiir Waar showed up on horseback one day. The Ser Cus had come back to Karvor, and his two dear friends were getting married in a week on bright Moonday, before performing a week later at the full Moonday festivals.

"We stopped in the Blue Moon and talked with Delgado," Jyg said. "He told us what happened to Klew."

"He died trying to make a difference," Wiir Waar said with respect. "And he succeeded. Delgado told us all about what happened. How King Targono agreed to sign the Bill of Rights that you helped draft."

"Yes," Hope nodded. "'Twas a miraculous turnaround."

"Who would have imagined that both Tyme and Klew would give their lives for their beliefs," Jyg shook his head. "I still cannot believe it happened. I keep thinking she is going to come back. Klew as well."

"She has come back," Hope replied mysteriously. "She helps me when I write. And she has appeared to me in dreams." He told them of his most recent dream about Tyme. What she had been thinking and feeling at the very end. How she had remembered so many of the different moments from all their lives together. And of her thoughts of him becoming someone new. But he did not say anything about Starai. He was not ready.

"Tyme was right," he affirmed. "I am changing. I have decided to take a different name. My pen name is Hope the

Proclaimer." He smiled before adding, "but you can call me Hope."

"Hope," Wiir Waar repeated happily. "I like it."

"So do I," Jyg agreed.

"I think Tyme would approve," Hope said with a knowing grin.

"'Tis good to see you smile," Wiir Waar said before adding, "Hope." They all laughed.

He told them of all the letters he had sent and also about the book he was writing. "I have titled it *A Bright One Chronicles*. 'Tis the story of Tyme's life. We are all included. Everything that happened. The prophecies at the beginning, and at the end."

"That is a beautiful tribute," Wiir Waar said approvingly. "Her story should be told!"

Hope moaned a laugh as tears ran down his cheeks. "I still cry often but they are healing tears. I do not try to stop them." He wiped his eyes so he could see again. "But, enough about me. I want to hear about you. My two best friends--who are getting married!"

"We are so in love," Jyg said with the biggest smile.

"We really appreciate each other," Wiir Waar agreed as they held each other's hand. "All of the time. 'Tis so natural and easy."

They visited the school and the kiva to talk with the others and invite them to the wedding. "We would be honored to have you sing before and after the service," Wiir Waar enthused. "And have Gybeko somehow be a part of the ceremony." He could not marry them, of course. Only a woman priest could perform those rites.

"Come early and visit the Ser Cus tent and meet everyone," Wiir Waar added. "You are welcome to stay and spend the night at our tents after the wedding. That will make it easier for you to walk back the next day. And come see our show the following week."

They returned to Hope's cave where he put the manuscript

he was writing, his pens and extra paper, and his few belongings into his pack. Then he saddled his horse and rode with Wiir Waar and Jyg out of Viridescent Canyon. He did not think he would be coming back to the kiva, but he did not say anything about that yet to the others.

The Ser Cus normally pitched their tents at Skyline Stadium while working in Karvor. Because they were now here first for a celebration, they set up their tents in Old Town close to the Blue Moon. That evening Hope went with Wiir Waar and Jyg to see Delgado, who had offered the couple the use of the Blue Moon and told them he wanted to help with the wedding festivities wherever possible.

Delgado hugged Epoh like a long, lost friend. When he learned that Epoh had changed his name, he was astonished.

"You are Hope the Proclaimer?" Delgado gasped. "Your letter to the Mother Womb of Karvor provoked a much-needed shake-up with the priests. They tried to suppress it, but word got out anyway." Delgado got a proud look on his face and puffed out his chest with comical exaggeration. "I am best friends with Hope the Proclaimer!" he boasted.

They all laughed.

Delgado grew serious again. "The priests at the Mother Womb are also ignoring the new Bill of Rights," he told them. "They say 'tis blasphemous and goes against the laws of Divine. Especially the articles that proclaim men to be treated as equal citizens, and that the walls of the refuge be removed to allow men in the sanctuary."

"We knew 'twas not going to be easy nor fast to make those changes," Hope replied sadly. "We did not expect the transformation to happen immediately."

"No, not everywhere," Delgado agreed. "But," he said with enthusiasm, "your letter got copied and posted on the door of the Womb in Old Town. The shaman reads it aloud daily since most men cannot read. The priest there agrees and has already allowed some holes to be knocked out in the refuge wall and invited men into the back of the sanctuary. She has also invited the shaman to help perform part of the liturgy.

"Let's get married there!" Wiir Waar exclaimed. "Maybe Gybeko can be a part of the ceremony after all. And the men's choir can perform during the service."

They talked for a while about how they could adjust their wedding plans, now that the rules about who could be in the sanctuary had changed. "This will be a wedding like we never imagined," Wiir Waar said with excitement.

When there was a lull in the conversation, Delgado showed them a few changes to the two shrines they had moved inside to honor Tyme. Hope was quick to note that the figure with the flaming sword had more offerings.

"People are drawn to the statue of Tyme showing her power," Delgado noted.

"She did have great power," Hope agreed. "That power is still felt today, magnified by her restraint and sacrifice. I do not want people to forget that."

"Klew certainly did not," Jyg answered solemnly. "He tapped into her power."

Wiir Waar nodded in agreement. "He used the same restraint, sacrifice, and love to confront the King of Karvor."

"That belief led to a new Bill of Rights for government and society," Jyg marveled.

Delgado escorted them back to his private area. "I have a new friend that I am getting to know," he told them hesitantly. "We enjoy similar music. He is also learning to meditate and pray. I have been sharing a few tips with him that Tyme shared with me, for when my mind is wandering out of control."

"Has it helped him?" Hope asked.

"Yes. He likes focusing on the breath and chanting."

"Do we know him?" Jyg asked.

"Yes," Delgado answered cautiously, unsure how they would react. "'Tis Targono, the King of Karvor."

"I think you would be a great influence on him," Hope said approvingly. Then he joked, "Although he might not be good to have around with your smuggling business."

"Smuggling has changed," Delgado answered. "The toll money used to go to Ambrit. Now it stays here in Karvor and pays for better wages for the soldiers, who spend their money in the town." He smiled innocently. "Smuggling is no longer honorable."

Delgado looked at Jyg and asked, "Does it bother you that I have befriended Targono?"

Jyg shook his head. "If Klew and Hope can forgive him, mayhaps I can learn to forgive him." He and Wiir Waar stood up to leave. They had had a long day traveling and were now exhausted. Hope got up to go with them and spend the night at the Ser Cus tent. He turned to Delgado.

"I would like to stay awhile in Karvor after the wedding and the performance," he said. "Could you find me a small, quiet room where I can write and sleep?"

"No problem," Delgado said. "I think I know just the place." He escorted them to the door. "Tomorrow, we have a great band," he reminded them. "You will love the music. Come early! Stay late!"

Hope had a healing week of smiles and laughter with occasional tears. Most evenings he spent with his friends at the Blue Moon. During the day Wiir Waar and Jyg were busy at the Ser Cus tents. Hope spent much of that time writing.

He also enjoyed watching Wiir Waar and Jyg. They always spoke kindly to each other, never interrupted, or spoke over the other. They were attentive without being clingy. 'Twas obvious they loved each other immensely.

Hope delighted in seeing Jyg and Bones train for the routine they were performing for the Ser Cus. Hope also enjoyed seeing the looks of endearment on Wiir Waar's face as she watched them practice.

"Their act is getting better all the time," she praised. "Audiences love them!"

◆ ◆ ◆

The group from the kiva arrived at the Ser Cus tents early before the wedding. After all had been introduced, everyone sat together for drinks and a light snack. Wiir Waar and Jyg told them about the changes that had occurred at the Womb in Old Town and how they would be allowed to sing in the sanctuary itself. They discussed some music options and also how to include Gybeko. Everyone chatted amiably as they got to know one another, and then the kiva group left for the Old Town Womb to work out the exact details of the service with the priest and the shaman.

The wedding ceremony started with little Weethee Wona, dressed in a green Ser Cus outfit and scarves, walking down the aisle daintily throwing out cactus flower petals from a small basket. Then her stocky, but only slightly older brother, Wuleeno came next, also in green, throwing the traditional dried kernels of corn with gusto in every direction.

Lana Pana and Tana Pana followed next in yellow, doing cartwheels and walking on their hands down the aisle. Then Zandero and Zintowo, in orange, doing handstands and flips. When they got to the front they lifted and flipped Weethee and Wuleeno into the air to do one-armed handstands on their heads.

Wana Weer, the Ser of Ceremonies, came next in her high boots and jeweled, multi-colored corset, pulling a rope. "We are the Ser Cus!" she announced proudly. The troupe at the front pulled one end of the rope, while Darvio, the bottom of the mountain, held the far end, suspending the rope the length of the aisle. Wiir Waar's mother, Waar Weer, the Ropewalker, dressed in fluttering and sparkling gold, strode regally across the elevated line.

Narvago, Mam's youngest son and coach for the troupe, wore white as he rolled a large wooden target down the aisle. Behind him ambled giant Darvio. Like little Weethee, he was dressed in green and had a small basket of cactus flowers, which he daintily threw out over the audience, in imitation of the little girl, to great laughter and amusement.

Then came Jyg, dressed in a traditional black shirt and pants with red trim, one arm stretched out holding Bones. "Manser Jygero," the big bird announced in the booming voice of the noble manser he had imitated long ago to learn his first words. "Bring your raven?" Bones questioned, mimicking Panr's high and scratchy voice. Hope and Delgado walked on each side of Jyg as best men, dressed in gray.

Finally, Wiir Waar came down the aisle in a traditional red wedding dress with gold trim, juggling and spinning swords into the air, then catching them with a dramatic flourish. She presented the swords to Mams, her grandmother and greatly respected matriarch of the clan, dressed in blue, who gave her a sheathed set of six, long, throwing knives.

Hope and Delgado rolled the wooden target to the front of the aisle and stood on each side, balancing the disc, while Jyg stood up against it with his eyes open. Wiir Waar began throwing the knives in rapid succession, two by his legs, and two under his arms. At the last second, Jyg closed his eyes as she threw the final knives on each side of his head. The audience erupted into cheers as Wiir Waar abandoned all propriety and ran up the aisle into Jyg's arms.

The ceremony was so much more welcoming than any of them could have imagined a few moons before. Although Gybeko was not a Womb certified shaman, the priest still allowed him to do part of the rites. Because of the Jawbone Ridge gang and the group from the kiva, the sanctuary was filled with more men than women. Singer performed with Swindovo drumming and singing in the backup choir with Draktono, Frisoto and Hope. They also did a few of the new Praises with the whole audience singing along.

Wiir Waar and Jyg wrote their own vows, which were inspired by the vows Tyme and Epoh had made at their wedding. They had asked Hope if that was okay, and he told them he was honored that they would make similar oaths.

To always be honest and true.

To treat each other as equals.

To support and challenge each other to be their best.

To love each other forever.

At the end, Gybeko announced them as wife and husband, instead of woman and husband, as was the custom. Wiir Waar did not put a collar on Jyg.

As the bride and groom came out of the temple, a brass band began playing enthusiastically. Members of the Jawbone Ridge carried the traditional large wedding caricatures on poles overhead: the bride wagging her finger disapprovingly; the groom grimacing and pulling mournfully at his oversized collar. Along the street everyone danced and had small shots of viruna handed out by the Jawbone Ridge gang.

When the music changed the procession slowed and Wiir Waar and Jyg danced together. The crowd gathered in a circle around them chanting with the music, swaying to the rhythm. The giant figures of the bride and groom also bobbed and twisted in unison. When the horns blared and a new song started, the newlyweds and crowd resumed their way up the street.

They stopped first at the Ser Cus tents where Wiir Waar did the courtship dance she had taught to Tyme. Hope cried tears of both sorrow and joy, watching in remembrance of how he had felt during the dance. He noted that Jyg had practiced more and was a better dancer.

Then the Ser Cus women joined Wiir Waar and surrounded Jyg in the traditional marriage dance of the Women's Clan, displaying their power and influence as they accepted Jyg, the new helpmate and husband, who was assured shelter, food, and work in his new family.

Next, Wiir Waar and Jyg danced a slow and romantic song all alone. Finally everybody joined in. When the song ended, Hope had the honor of doing the traditional toast to the bride and groom.

"My two dearest friends in the world have married," he raised his small metal cup of viruna. "I am so thrilled you have found each other. May you fully appreciate and relish your wonderful romance and love, every day of your lives! Your commitment and joy inspire us all."

Thunderous applause.

Everyone went back onto the street, following the band and giant puppets up to the Blue Moon. The celebration and music went on long into the night. Finally, the crowd escorted Wiir Waar and Jyg to the cavort at the Old Town Womb. They had tried to book the much nicer bridal suite at the cavort at the Mother Womb, where Tyme and Epoh had stayed on their wedding night, but the priests had turned down their request. The Mother Womb no longer recognized the validity of marriage ceremonies performed at the Old Town Womb, because they allowed men in the sanctuary and the shaman to perform some of the lesser rites.

The next morning, Wiir Waar and Jyg left their honeymoon suite for a short while to attend an important meeting with Hope and the group from the kiva, who had also spent the night with the Ser Cus. When Wiir Waar and Jyg arrived, they found everyone in the family tent resting on cushions and chatting over the remains of a relaxed breakfast.

Mams, the matriarch, had been talking of the herstory of the Ser Cus. Zintowo and Zandero had shared about their various roles, on stage and off, and what it was like living together in a performing troupe. They also described their traveling schedule and life on the road moving from town to town. All in preparation for what was coming next.

"Jyg and I wanted to thank you again for helping us make our wedding such a special event," Wiir Waar told them. "Everyone in the Ser Cus also wanted to discuss something important with you before you return to the Painted Hills."

Wiir Waar sat down and Mams stood up to speak. "We have all been greatly affected by Tyme's life and death. By the brave choices she made, and the implications for the rest of us to follow her example."

The Ser Cus members nodded their heads somberly.

"Not all of us are called to great sacrifice like Tyme and Klew," Mams continued. "But all of us are called to do *something*, even if 'tis smaller in deed."

More somber head nodding.

"We are Ser Cus," Mams said proudly. "We do not want to change that, nor risk losing that. We can incorporate references to Tyme and her message into our Ser Cus performances and build her a shrine at the entrance of our tent. But we have limits to how much we can do and still remain Ser Cus. Audiences come to see us to be entertained and to forget about their worries. Not to hear preaching."

"However," Mams smiled at the group from the kiva, "you all have no such restrictions. Singing, teaching, and preaching is what you do." She paused for a moment to let her words sink in.

"If some of you wanted to travel with us, we have a smaller tent you can use and pitch next to us. The days when we are not performing, you could feature your own programs and talks."

"Our shows take up only a small amount of the time we are in each town," Wiir Waar told them. "Usually, we are training, preparing for shows, or relaxing. People are always curious and walk past our tents to see what is happening. That would be a perfect opportunity for outreach of another type."

"By putting your tent next to ours," Mams offered, "you could take advantage of the crowds and interest we draw, but still be separate to have your own activities and events. We can offer the opportunity to greatly increase your audience, to spread your message across all of Ambra."

Singer began the short refrain of a Hallelujah that Tyme had loved, and the others from the kiva all joined in the chorus.

"Your offer is very generous," Draktono said when the

refrain ended. "I think Singer has already given his answer." He paused uncertain how to continue. "But my message is not really focused on Tyme as a Bright One. My message is about men's rights, or lack of rights."

"Your message is about a new and more just social order," Hope answered. "That is Tyme's message as well. The focus does not have to be all about her as a Bright One. The focus can be on creating a world that is fairer and more equitable. Those are the things Tyme stood for and believed in."

"There is one other issue," Draktono replied. "We have started a school at the kiva. We have an obligation to our students to continue what we have started. I am unwilling for that to be abandoned."

"Not all of us need to go with the Ser Cus," Gybeko pointed out. "I also have a commitment to the kiva. I can stay and take on more teaching duties."

"I can also stay to teach and sing," Frisoto said to Draktono. "But I think you should reconsider going with them. Gybeko and I can find another teacher for the kiva if we need to, but only you can speak eloquently to larger, educated audiences in the cities. Your talents are not being fully utilized at the kiva. Your skills would be better used speaking to crowds across Ambra."

A BRIGHT ONE
CHRONICLES

Wiir Waar and Jyg savored their week-long honeymoon in Karvor. They danced most nights at the Blue Moon. They also went down the hill to Skyline Street a few times to eat at some unique and romantic places Wiir Waar knew about. And they got dressed up for Wiir Waar to take Jyg for drinks on the top patio of the Plumed Bird and see a show with Rona as one of the dancers. They went backstage afterword to congratulate her on her performance.

Hope wrote in his book and sang at the Old Town Womb with the group that learned some of Swindovo's songs. Hope also joined Jyg and Wiir Waar a few evenings at the Blue Moon and danced with Wiir Waar.

At the end of the week everyone from the kiva came back to Karvor to join Hope in watching the Ser Cus at Skyline Stadium. Hope had not seen them perform since he was a young boy at Dayr Castle. The others had never seen the show. They were all amazed by the extravaganza. The Z's astonishing acrobatics. Wiir Waar's sword juggling and knife throwing. Jyg and Bones were still perfecting their act, astonishing audiences and getting big laughs, even when things did not go as practiced. The ropewalker high across the stadium in the moonlight was dazzling and heart-stopping for the grand finale. Everything was spectacular and awe-inspiring.

Two days after the final performance, the Ser Cus prepared to leave Karvor. Draktono arrived to announce he would join with Singer and Swindovo and follow along.

"Frisoto assured me that the school at the kiva would continue without me," Draktono told them. "He also pointed out that if I went with the Ser Cus, I might be able to inspire men and boys to start similar schools in other towns."

"We will be a much more effective team with you along," Swindovo enthused. They all looked expectantly at Hope.

"I believe I am most effective writing," Hope told them. "I must finish working on my book before I can leave Karvor."

Draktono was stunned by Hope's decision. He had assumed that Hope would go with the Ser Cus for sure.

"These are copies of the letters I wrote to the Wombs in each of the cities," Hope handed Draktono a sealed bundle of manuscripts. "You can read parts of the letters to your audiences each night. That will be like me speaking to them." He also gave Draktono and Wiir Waar each a large purse of coins.

"I sold another gem from the Endless Waste," he told them. "This will pay for any extra expenses you might incur."

"This will pay for our whole tour," Wiir Waar exclaimed when she opened the pouch. "We can buy a bigger and brighter colored tent for our new traveling partners and pay for posters and extra advertising as well."

Hope hugged everyone farewell.

"We will be back in about 14 moons," Wiir Waar said as she and Jyg waved their final goodbyes and followed behind the Ser Cus wagons. Jyg rode Zill, his daya horse, and Wiir Waar rode Cadie, Tyme's horse. Veeda, Klew's horse, which Tyme had ridden when younger in preparation for riding Riips, was donated to the kiva and school, along with a pouch of coins.

Hope the Proclaimer moved into the small room Delgado had found for him. He began writing all day, and sometimes long into the night. He took each finished page of *A Bright One*

Chronicles to the Trusted Scribe to have a team of clerks make 100 copies. Once finished and bound, he planned to give a few copies to the main library in Ambrit, and each of the libraries of the six old cities, and the four Barbarian Kingdoms. He was also going to give books to any of the Wombs that expressed interest, the kivas, and extra books to Draktono and the Ser Cus, to distribute wherever they felt the need. And a book, of course, for Delgado and the Jawbone Ridge gang.

Hope continued to go to the Blue Moon a few nights a week to hear music and chat with Delgado, who frequently asked him about his practice, about prayer techniques, and of the *Kabaal Prophecies*. Delgado was becoming an intermediary between the followers of a Bright One and the Fire, the shamans, and the priests.

One morning when Hope dropped off a few more pages of the book to be copied at the Trusted Scribe, there was an old woman sitting on the bench by the door. As he went to leave, the old woman rose up to speak.

"You are Hope the Proclaimer?" she asked.

"Yes," Hope smiled. The woman had a kind face.

"You were the former Crown Prince Epohco of Dayrstad," the woman stated earnestly.

"Yes," Hope could not imagine how the woman would know such a thing. He found it hard to imagine himself. "It feels like two lifetimes ago."

"I never met you at Dayr Castle," the old woman smiled, "but I have heard so many stories about you." Her eyes twinkled with delight.

Hope gasped. "You are Tao Tau!" He could feel her chuckling as he embraced her. When they let go of each other, they both had tears in their eyes.

"I have read the letter you sent to the Womb in Karvor," Tao Tau informed him, her face radiant. "A Bright One lived among us. I always knew she was special. That was why I came to Dayr Castle. To meet her."

"You dreamed of her as well?" Hope asked in amazement.

"I dreamed I would meet someone important at the castle market," she replied. "Through Manser Fagedo, who bought my healing salve, I was given Tyme as my apprentice."

"You were crucial in the forming of her character," Hope said, his face scrunching with emotion.

"And you have given her a voice!" Tao Tau beamed. "Your words are more powerful than any sword."

"Her actions and faith are what make my words powerful," Hope replied. "I feel her when I write. She guides me still."

"Yes," Tao Tau replied knowingly. "Her power continues to grow."

Epoh nodded his head in agreement. "Are you here to publish your book on your healing salve?" he guessed. "Tyme told me the key ingredient comes from mushrooms."

"A special mold that grows on one type of fungus only," Tao Tau nodded. "The book explains how to grow the fungus, harvest the mold, and create the healing salve. It takes about a decade to get started."

They began meeting a few times a week. Sometimes for meals, sometimes to pray or sing at the Old Town Womb to Swindovo's music, which Tao Tau loved. She also enjoyed going to the Blue Moon and getting to know Delgado, who shared his theories about the healing qualities of certain types of music. Tao Tau was captivated by his stories and thoughts about Tyme. How profoundly the young woman had influenced him and the Jawbone Ridge gang. Tyme had been something different to each person she met.

After a few moons, Tao Tau packed up for Pintone, Dorgon and Ambrit, where she planned to distribute more of her books and give out instructions in her healing techniques. Hope told her he would send her copies of *A Bright One Chronicles* when the book was finished. He had already made some revisions to the first part of the book, after their many conversations, to include more stories of Tyme riding Spike up to Lost Valley with the old herb woman.

"'Twas so very wonderful to see you," Tao Tau smiled

tenderly, holding Hope's face in her hands. "Tyme would be so proud of you." She kissed him on the cheek. He gave her a bag of gold coins to help distribute her healing books and start health clinics.

Hope the Proclaimer finished his first edition of *A Bright One Chronicles* just before the Ser Cus arrived back in Karvor. Wiir Waar and Jyg came to his apartment to let him know they were in town. Hope was excited to hear how their last decade and a half had gone on tour.

"We love being married and working and traveling together," Jyg gushed.

"'Tis definitely way more fun living on the road with Jyg," Wiir Waar agreed happily. "He and Bones are a huge hit, as expected," she added proudly. "Audiences cannot get enough of Bones. He and Jyg are the talk of the Ser Cus."

"Bones definitely loves performing and all the attention," Jyg confirmed. "I am more relaxed now as well." He laughed and shook his head. "I was a bit jittery during our earlier shows. One night, Wiir Waar said to me, 'relax, don't be so nervous.' The very next show I stumbled a little with my introduction. Right away, Bones says to me, *Relax, don't be so nervous.*"

"Twas such a big hit with the audience, now 'tis part of their act every night," Wiir Waar chuckled.

"Bones is learning new words all the time," Jyg reported proudly. "I never know what she is going to say next."

"Draktono, Singer, and Swindovo are also doing well," Wiir Waar informed him. "Their singing and Swindovo's songs draw enthusiastic crowds. Draktono's teachings and readings of your letters have been very successful. He has had a number of shaman and even a few priests come after their shows and to hold long conversations with him about the Bill of Rights and what it means to be a Bright One."

"The clergy and leaders of the smaller neighborhood Wombs seem to be more receptive to what he says than the priests at the main temples," Jyg noted. "Draktono has been asked to speak at a few refuges in smaller Wombs. He has had scribes make more copies of your letters to hand out and has been encouraging the shamans to read them daily out loud, since few men read well."

Hope was thrilled to hear their report. It made his next decision easier.

"Now that you finished your book," Wiir Waar asked, "what do you plan to do next?" It had now been a quarter of a century since Tyme's death.

"Actually, my writing is not finished," Hope confessed. "The book may be an ongoing process." He told them about meeting Tao Tau, and the stories and insights she had shared about Tyme. "I think there is still more of the tale to tell." He was also working on new translations of the *Kabaal Prophecies*, which would help others understand Tyme's beliefs and reasons for her actions.

"Will you stay here to write?" Wiir Waar asked.

Hope took a moment to answer. "I told you about my dream of Tyme at Empress Auditorium. What she was thinking at the end." His eyes grew misty. "How she thought of all of us. And her elation at hearing King's hoofbeats and being taken away."

Wiir Waar and Jyg nodded their heads solemnly.

"She also thought about me becoming someone new," Hope said.

"She told me she did not want you to mourn her for too long," Wiir Waar prodded him, remembering Tyme's exact words. "She said if anything happened to her, she wanted you to live your life and love again."

Hope nodded his head. "Yes. She had specific thoughts at the end about what I should do. But I was not ready yet to share that with you."

"This should be interesting," Wiir Waar said with relish.

"She thought I should go back to the Endless Waste," Hope

said.

Jyg looked shocked with incomprehension.

"Starai," Wiir Waar guessed immediately. "The acolyte nun who saved you."

"Yes," Hope replied. He had to pause for a moment before he could continue. "Tyme thought she would be good for my soul."

Wiir Waar and Jyg listened in amazement.

"I always felt sad about never saying goodbye to her," Hope told them. "Mayhaps that left something unfinished between us."

He also felt there was another reason he needed to go back to the Endless Waste but was unsure what that could be. He remembered shaman Gybeko and Ozono's words about the prophecy of the Burnished Man, who came out of the Endless Waste, but then returned again to the desert.

Hope stayed in Karvor for the next month to be with his friends. He also finished his translations of the *Kabaal Prophecies*, both the *Mask of Splendor* and the *Mask of Brilliance*. His writings opened vast new insights into the prophecies, yet Hope felt they were only rough translations. He now realized he needed to have a much better understanding of Hool to adequately give a complete and full understanding to the texts.

He spent a number of evenings at the new blue and white striped tent where Singer, Swindovo, and Draktono held their events. He joined in their singing and was moved by Draktono's teachings and, of course, the readings of his own letters about a Bright One.

The words he had written were familiar, yet somehow new, when hearing Draktono's stirring proclamations toward a more just and equitable society, and a better understanding and view of what it meant to embrace and follow Divine.

Hope also sang along when the group performed at the

Old Town Womb. His favorite was when they sang at the Blue Moon, and Jyg, Zintowo, Zandero, Delgado, and the Jawbone Ridge gang all joined along.

Full Moonday arrived, along with the Ser Cus performances at Skyline Stadium. Hope enjoyed every bittersweet moment, especially Jyg's performing with Bones. The big, black raven had a growing sense of timing, and knew just how to maximize the laughs and amazement of the audience.

The next few nights after the shows, Hope savored each evening with his friends at the Blue Moon. When the Ser Cus pulled their tents to move once again, Hope packed up as well. Everyone met at the loaded Ser Cus wagons. Hope had said goodbye to Delgado and the Jawbone Ridge gang the night before. Now he walked beside the Ser Cus out of town and across Jintiga Bridge.

When they got to the other side, they all lined up to say farewell. The Ser Cus was heading north up the canyon to Sikes for the Grand Viruna Festival. Hope was heading east to Dayrstad. His final hugs were for Wiir Waar and Jyg.

"Do not say this is a last goodbye," Wiir Waar stopped him when he implied he would not be coming back. "You returned from the Endless Waste once before. Leave open the possibility that you might do so again." She smiled hesitantly. "I would like to meet Starai."

DAYR CASTLE

When King Eyrico learned that his disowned eldest son had returned to Dayr Castle with yet another name change, the King would not allow Hope entry into the Royal Palace, nor even the keep. Hope had to ask Jhoop, the sergeant at arms, to quietly deliver the letter he had written to the priest and shaman at keep Womb, and also to take a copy of *A Bright One Chronicles* to the keep school, and another copy to the royal palace library.

Instead of staying at the Daya Mare, Hope asked Utuno if he could sleep in the bunkhouse room where Tyme had lived. He cried himself to sleep that night lying in her bed but felt better the next morning. Utuno found him before sunrise behind the back corrals at the mountain ibex pen.

"What are you going to do with Spike?" Hope asked.

"I have been meaning to let him go," the stable manser replied. "But I just have not been able to do it. He is my last connection to Tyme." Utuno sighed. "But now that you are here, I think we should do it together."

"Do we just open the gates to the pen and the corrals to let him through?" Hope asked.

"Spike can jump over the corral fences easy enough, but I think we should open the gates anyway just to let him know we are not trying to stop him." Utuno sent Tado, the new stable boy, down the Grand Way to castle gate to warn everyone that Spike was being released and would be coming through most likely in a blaze of speed.

"Would you like to do the honors?" Utuno asked.

"Yes. That would mean very much to me." Hope's eyes

misted and his face filled with emotion.

Spike seemed to sense Hope's surge of feelings. He watched as Hope swung the iron-barred door open. Hope and Utuno slowly backed away from the gate. Spike began walking casually toward the opening. As he came close, he grew cautious, as though it were some trick. When neither Utuno nor Hope made any move to shut the gate, Spike picked up his pace. Just before he reached the opening, he bolted forward and through the gate.

Spike did not race as though being pursued, but instead trotted rapidly with great dignity through the corrals and out the entrance to the stables. Hope and Utuno ran out onto the Grand Way. They watched Spike trot down and around the upper switchback. They saw him again, further down the Grand Way at the lower switchback.

"Go, Spike! Go!" Utuno chanted with glee.

Spike trotted regally out through castle gate as Hope the Proclaimer shouted joyously, "Whoohoo!"

"Whoohoo!" Krugero yelled back from the top of tower one.

After the rejection from his father, the King, Hope had planned to leave Dayr Castle the next day. He had not expected a warm reception from the King, but he had never imagined that his father would not even want to see him or allow him to step foot in the royal palace to see his mother or other family members.

Hope thought about the passage from the *Kabaal Prophecies* saying that prophets were seldom welcome in their home country. He was not a woman prophet, like those in the *Kabaal Prophecies* and the *Book of Elders*, he was just a male proclaimer. Yet the verse seemed to apply to him as well.

Krugero's wave and joyful shout over Spike's release from the top of castle gate reminded Hope that Krugero had been his first Hand, and a best friend to him when he was young. Hope realized he had an obligation to tell others in Dayr Castle more about what had happened to Tyme, and to Klew. He was not the only one in the castle to be heartbroken over their deaths.

In the morning Hope gathered Utuno and the other stable workers to tell them about everything that had happened. He went down to castle gate and talked with Krugero, Anda Dana, and others. He visited with Jhoop and the guards at keep gate. He spent much of the evening talking with the soldiers at the Rusty Sword, including Vrakeno, his second Hand who had tried to force him into being a soldier, and Captain Hanvoro, who had searched in vain for him when he fell into the underground river. Manser Xacano was there, their teacher and philosopher from keep school, along with Manser Undaho, the librarian who had given him the book *Dragons of the Endless Waste*. Jyg's uncle Pio and aunt Whi also came, among so many others whom Hope did not remember by name. He told them about the prophecies being fulfilled. And the power of Tyme's words and actions. By the end of the night, Hope was exhausted. He fell asleep quickly and slept soundly in Tyme's bed all through the night.

The next day he followed the old Scout Trail to the Siren.

The Duke was a miserable and unhappy host. His smuggling business had been ruined by the new King of Karvor. All of his plans for glory in leading the Fire had collapsed, along with his dreams of overthrowing his brother and becoming King of Dayrstad. Hope excused himself early from the Duke's brooding presence at court and left early the next morning.

He rode down the bait and reluctantly exchanged Chia, his faithful daya horse, for two camels and desert supplies in Valhal. It took him only a few days to adjust once again to the heat of the Endless Waste. In less than two weeks he was at the Valley of Invitation, greeting Kaven, the guide who had first taken Riin Ruel to Ezkia Nunnery, who would now escort him as well.

RETURN TO THE NUNNERY

When Nadji Nani, the Abbess of Ezkia Nunnery, saw Hope the Proclaimer she was stunned. The story he told was even more amazing. A Bright One of prophecy had indeed been fulfilled in Tyme, and her example followed by Klew, her sword manser.

"You are a Bright One as well," the abbess declared while she examined the collection of letters he had written to the Wombs and libraries across Ambra along with the book about Tyme. "You are welcome to stay here as long as you wish," she said. "All of us would be honored to hear you speak about what you have seen."

"I would be happy to do so tonight," Hope replied. "These letters and the book are for your library. They will also help answer any questions."

He changed the subject. "Starai?" he asked without further preamble. "How is she?"

"She became a Quiet One. She is living in cave seven at Tonyin Springs. 'Tis only for Quiet Ones."

"I will be a Quiet One," Hope vowed. "I will speak through the words I write."

"Not until after your talk tonight," Nadji Nani reminded him with a smile. She looked at him thoughtfully. "You may stay in cave four," the abbess affirmed. "You have my blessing to see her."

After a three-day walk Hope arrived at Tonyin Springs

before the heat. He hiked to his cave and set out his sparse furnishings, sleeping mat and blanket, food supplies and simple altar. He also had a bundle of manuscripts, a small, folding lap desk, paper, pens and ink. During the heat he retired to a cool alcove in the back of the cave to do his practice and rest.

When the temperature cooled in the early evening, he went to her cave. She was not there. 'Twas swept clean and sparsely furnished. She had a simple altar with candles, prayer beads and her bell. He sat outside to wait at the entrance as the yellow-orange colors of a dramatic sunset blossomed across the sky.

When Starai appeared, she set down the basket of cactus fruits she had been collecting and walked in amazement toward him. He stood up and walked to meet her. Her dazzling white smile contrasted with her rich, black skin, her frizzy hair a halo around her head. They hugged tightly. Both had tears running down their cheeks.

Starai went into her cave and came out with a tablet and piece of chalk. She wrote *I knew*.

Hope pondered those two words. *I knew*. What did she know? That he had to leave the nunnery and try to get back home? That he had to be with Tyme again? Or that he would someday come back? Previously, as Epoh, he would have asked her to explain. But now, as Hope, he did not need more information about how, or why, or when. 'Twas enough to be aware that she *knew*--and that she herself did not need further explanation about his actions.

Starai gave him another hug. Then she wiped the slate clean and wrote again. *I waited*. She looked at him tenderly.

He took her slate, wiped it clean and wrote, *I am in cave four*.

They sat together, silently, holding hands watching the sunset colors in the sky fade to stars and the valley fill with moonlight.

HAVE STORY TO TELL

While Starai read his letters and book, Hope the Proclaimer sat at his lap desk and wrote a letter specially for the priests and nuns of Ezkia Nunnery. Then he began a second letter to the Temple of Bool at Jchow Oasis. He had visited the temple during his few days at the oasis with the grubbers, and fondly remembered their last moonlight night on the rooftop patio looking out over twinkling lanterns and firepots illuminating the desert city. Hope was writing the letter in Hool, and 'twas going slowly.

For the next three moons Starai reread and studied Hope's writings. He now often joined her to work silently nearby in a bright corner at the front of her cave, which had better light than his own. One morning she stopped her studies and sat thinking. At last, she picked up her tablet and wrote.

Not good you are Quiet One. She showed it to Hope and then cleaned the tablet and wrote again. *You have story to tell.*

Hope sat on the floor before his small desk. He smiled and jokingly waved the quill pen in his hand at her. Was it not obvious his pen told the story? He did not need his voice for that.

Starai was not convinced. *We must meet with Abbess* she wrote.

Hope grew solemn. He had adjusted easily to not speaking. He felt cocooned in the calm and peaceful quiet of the hermit caves. Part of him was reluctant to face his own questions about all that was still left undone.

But Starai was adamant.

They left the caves at Tonyin Springs the next morning for the three-day trip back to Ezkia Nunnery. They hiked at a quick pace, but stopped often to enjoy the views or inspect something close, like how the barbs on a vulture feather found beside the trail could split apart and then stick together again. Each evening Starai enjoyed tending a small fire while the sunset colors filled the sky and the temperature in the canyons dropped quickly. They soon arrived at their destination. The Abbess saw them the following day. Starai wrote out her concerns about Hope.

"You are now writing a letter to Jchow Oasis?" Nadji Nani asked him.

He nodded his head.

"You are writing in Hool?" she questioned.

He nodded again.

"How is that going?"

He shook his head. 'Twas proving more difficult than he imagined.

"Why are you a Quiet One?" the Abbess asked.

Hope looked fondly at Starai.

Starai shook her head. She grabbed her tablet and wrote *He does it for me. But I never asked.*

"You need to speak and practice your Hool so you will write better," Nadji Nani said. "Your days of being a Quiet One have passed."

He did not say anything.

The Abbess turned to Starai. "Are you ready to help him?"

She bobbed her head assuredly.

"Your days of being a Quiet One have also passed," the Abbess told her. "You are released from your vow of silence."

Starai smiled happily. "I will help you," she told Hope in Hool.

"I will help you," he repeated her accent and inflections with a smile.

They moved into separate caves with gardens just a short walk from the Nunnery and worked together for more than a decade at the library, teaching Hope to speak Hool more effectively and crafting a new letter that better addressed Hool culture. When 'twas finished they showed it to the Abbess.

"This is much better," Nadji Nani said after reading it. "But the letter will have no validity unless you deliver it yourself. This is not like the letters you were able to send all across Ambra. You are in a different culture now. You will have to deliver the letters in person for them to be read and taken seriously. You must leave the Nunnery to accomplish your task."

Hope looked shocked.

Starai less so. "We can leave bright Moonday and travel by moonlight," she suggested with excitement.

On his hike into Ezkia Nunnery, Hope had left his two camels with Kaven in the Valley of Invitation. On the hike out he was glad to find Kaven still had them.

"Iban and Eban," Hope introduced the camels to Starai, who had never seen a horse or camel and was thrilled about learning to ride and care for an animal. Her delight over the simplest things was a wonderful balm on Hope's heart and soul. She made everything new and interesting.

Each day they stopped for the heat, and then traveled again as the shadows grew long and the sky began to color for another dramatic sunset. This was their favorite part of the day, when the light was golden and the air began to cool. With the growing darkness, the soft moonlight grew in power, until the world was bathed in an eerie void of color that emphasized patterns and compositions across the barren landscape.

Although they talked deeply, they still often used sign language and enjoyed long periods of silence. Hope seldom cried tears of anguish anymore. But his eyes still welled with tears of memory and joy from his previous life.

By the time they got to Jchow Oasis, Hope was as excited

to show Starai the city as she was excited to see it. She never imagined anything so big and complex. The buildings were sculpted and whitewashed walls of mud with graceful archways and domed ceilings. He led her down crooked alleys covered with narrow lattice angled to let in morning light but provide shade during the heat. Near the school and library, they found a modest apartment with three tiny rooms and a moon patio with a great view of the city and shaded oasis gardens in the distance.

"In Hool culture an unmarried woman living with a man is scorned, even if she sleeps in a different room," Starai reminded Hope. "We should have two apartments." They were able to rent another room with a shaded patio nearby for her.

Hope took her to the baths where they were separated, rinsed, and wrapped head to foot in piping hot towels then laid in steam rooms to bake on the stones. They were each given massages and scrubbed with soft, gritty mud, followed by a shocking cold-water rinse and bath. Then they were rewrapped in piping hot towels to lay on the hot stones of the steam room and repeat the process.

When they emerged, they were ravenous. He took her to a shaded plaza where vendors with food carts sold a variety of dishes. Hope chose bland food by Hool standards, while Starai picked more spice. They ate on a stone bench next to one of the many tunnels that lead into the underground city, then followed a similar tunnel on Tailor Street into an subterranean maze of shops and residences, four and five stories deep, accessed by stairs, ladders and carved out passageways. Hope bought simple, well-made clothes in the local style for them both. Next he went to the Temple of Bool and arranged to have a meeting the following week with the head shaman.

That night they sat on Hope's patio with a firepot and paper lanterns, looking out over twinkling patios and flat rooftops across the city. "I remember a similar view like this when I was here before," Hope reminisced, "how beautiful Jchow was at night with all the fires and lights across the city."

He looked affectionately at Starai. He would never have attempted to bring Tyme's story to Jchow Oasis if it had not been for her encouragement, fortitude, and collaboration.

"Do you think the shaman will have a problem if my assistant is an unmarried woman, even if we live separately?" Hope asked.

"No reason to say anything about me to the shaman," she replied.

The next day they went to Roasters, the poor disreputable jumble of buildings on a south-facing hillside that simmered all day in direct sunlight. Stairs and ladders led down into the shops and homes below.

Hope guided Starai to Grubbers Supply, where he asked to speak with Crago. "Tell him I came earlier with Grinst, Horton and Harvig."

Crago had not seen any of his grubber friends in decades. He did, however, have an address for both Horton and Harvig. They went to Horton's house but someone else lived there. Then to Harvig's house, where they had to wait at length at a guardhouse before being escorted inside.

Harvig burst into tears when he saw Hope and gave him an anguished hug.

"Horton was robbed and killed," Harvig informed him. "That money was a curse to him. He could hardly trust anyone. All they wanted was his wealth."

"What about Grinst?" Hope asked.

"I have not seen him in half a century," Harvig said. "He went back into the desert."

Hope introduced Starai and explained what they were doing at Jchow Oasis, and the letter they wanted to deliver to the Temple of Bool. Harvig was entranced with the tale of a Bright One and their quest to share the story with the city's inhabitants. He offered to help in any way he could.

"Starai and I want to translate *A Bright One Chronicles* into Hool," Hope told him. "You could help with that."

"Of course," Harvig answered. "I would be honored. When

do we start?"

They began the next day. Harvig's help was enormous. "This is even more exciting than *Dragons of the Endless Waste!*" Harvig marveled during their work on the first chapter. "And 'tis true! No, once upon a time at the start." They all laughed remembering the story of how Epoh had tried to convince the grubbers that *Dragons of the Endless Waste* was not true because it began with the words *Once upon a time.*

Hope the Proclaimer met a few days later with the shaman from the temple and gave him the letter he had written. Unlike the Womb temples in Ambra, there were no female priests at the Temple of Bool. The shaman politely asked a few questions and promised Hope that he would look at the letter later. They scheduled another appointment for the following week.

They continued to translate *A Bright One Chronicles.* Although Harvig could neither read nor write in Hool, he was quick to orally translate each sentence after Hope read it aloud. The most difficult part was trying to spell out new and unfamiliar words. During breaks they wandered through the oasis talking and chatting with people and practicing their Hool.

Hope could tell that Harvig had been very lonely since Horton's death. He did not seem to have any close friends. And he was less inclined to trust anyone after Horton had been robbed and killed. Harvig was also very self-conscious of the burns to his face and hands from the explosion of the cargo bird. Hope noticed that many Hool stared at him, even with his hands and face hidden behind scarves. Their looks were not of sympathy, but of revulsion.

Hope was disappointed when he returned to the Temple of Bool to find the shaman had canceled the meeting. An assistant informed him the shaman had been called away unexpectedly. Hope was told to come back in a week or so.

During the day they continued working diligently on the book translation. On bright Moonday, Hope and Starai walked through the twisting streets to a busy plaza with food carts and vendors selling trinkets and jewelry. A band was playing and people were dancing in the moonlight.

"Will you teach me to dance?" Starai asked. She had read in Hope's book that Tyme loved to dance.

"Sure," he smiled while continuing to watch the others.

"Now," she gently pushed him.

"Here?" he said with surprise. "I thought you would want to practice alone on our patio first."

"I am ready now," she replied with her eager grin.

They laughed together as she learned a few basic steps. When they took a break Hope looked at Starai thoughtfully, seeing her in a different light. 'Twas now more than four decades since Tyme had died.

"What?" she asked. "You are staring at me."

"Should we get married?" Hope asked.

Starai laughed. "Not, *will* you marry me? Instead, you ask, *should* we get married?"

"Well, should we? It makes sense to talk about it together. Instead of having one or the other of us propose and surprise the other."

"One or the other of us propose?" she questioned.

"By Ambri tradition at Ezkia Nunnery, you propose to me. By Hool tradition, I propose to you."

"Did you think I was getting ready to propose?" she wondered with humor.

He smiled and shrugged his shoulders.

"Are you ready to propose?" she asked.

"Mayhaps," he grinned.

"What brought this on?"

"We want to be sensitive to Hool customs. If getting married will help facilitate the work we are doing, then we should marry."

"Any other reason?" she asked.

"I love you," he answered. "I loved you first as a friend and confidant, and now as a partner and co-worker. You are a wonderful, caring, and giving woman. I want to be your husband.

"Are you ready to love me as my husband?" she asked boldly.

"Yes, I am."

She looked at him tenderly. "I have loved you since I pulled you out of the pool in the Womb of the Earth. I have loved you as a friend. I am ready to love you as your wife."

They bought plain silver wedding rings and were married the next day in the Temple of Bool. An assistant shaman performed the short ceremony. Harvig was the best man and only witness. They went dancing that night and began learning Hool dances so they were not so conspicuous.

Starai moved into Hope's apartment. Harvig began sleeping in her old apartment since it was nearby and easier for the work they were doing together. He often joined them when they went out each evening through the full Moonday festivities. The moonlit plazas and rooftops filled with people eating, drinking, strolling, talking, dancing, and listening to Hool music.

The following week Hope was again turned away without explanation from any meeting with the head shaman at the Temple of Bool, despite the good word promised by the assistant shaman who had married them.

"You said the Womb temples that were the most receptive to your message in Ambra were often the smaller ones at the edges of the cities," Starai reflected when she learned what had happened. "Mayhaps the same would be true here in Jchow Oasis."

"I think you are right," Hope agreed. "I had thought it more effective to go straight to the main temple, but that is obviously not working."

"There is an underground temple near Grubber's Supply at Roasters," Harvig remembered. "Mayhaps you should try there."

Hope could tell Harvig was thinking of something more. "Go on," Hope urged.

"Instead of giving them your letter, I think you should start reading chapters of your book," Harvig suggested. "Hool may not be as interested in theology as in a good adventure story. Tell the story first and let them figure out the implications of what the story means and teaches."

"That is an excellent suggestion," Starai agreed. "Your goal is not to start a new religion. Your goal is to help people see Divine or Bool or whatever name they use for Holy Spirit in a new light, here and now. Your goal is to enrich their day to day lives with love, forgiveness, and service toward others."

"Yes," Hope agreed. "We want to use spirituality to bring people together, not create divisions."

The next day Hope introduced himself differently to the shaman at the Bool temple near Grubber's Supply. He said he was a rousing storyteller and proclaimer of grand and momentous events. The reaction was more favorable.

"What kind of stories?" the shaman asked.

"Stories of a heroic young girl and her friends, filled with adventure, courage, belief, and sacrifice," Hope answered. "Let me read parts of the story to you. If you wish, I can return and share it with others. 'Tis a grand and sweeping tale, with numerous days for the complete telling. If you are not enthralled, you may stop me at any time."

The shaman was intrigued. He invited Hope to return the next day and begin the story again to a larger audience.

Hope, Starai and Harvig continued working on the translation of *A Bright One Chronicles*, eager to stay ahead of the readings that Hope did each day. When Starai met some women who expressed interest in having her narrate the story to their group, she happily agreed.

"I cannot read the story," Harvig lamented, "But I have worked on translating it enough that I can tell the important parts from memory. There is a group of young people who hang out at one of the lower caves. 'Tis okay if I start telling the tale to them while you two are busy elsewhere?"

"Yes, of course," Hope replied.

Their loyal following began to grow. When they finished the tale, they each had requests to start the story again to new audiences. After a few more moons, Hope was asked to tell the tale in the courtyard of the main Temple of Bool. 'Twas his largest audience yet.

When he finished, he was asked to deliver a letter to the shaman whom he had tried to have an appointment with earlier. The shaman made no mention of their earlier meeting, nor did he acknowledge receiving Hope's first letter. Instead, he asked for a "written scholarly explanation," so that he might study the theological implications of *A Bright One Chronicles.*

About a decade later, Hope, Starai and Harvig sat on a rooftop patio watching a molten purple-red sunset turn into a fiery lavender and crimson haze filling the sky. They were in a new part of town, at a music club they had recently heard about, chatting as the band set up.

"Remember when we crossed the Broiled Mountains and looked down into the Valley of Death?" Hope asked Harvig. "How Grinst was convinced there was a trail. Maybe the mythical trail to Horizon."

"Yes," Harvig nodded his head.

"What is Horizon?" asked Starai.

"'Tis a rumored oasis on the other side of the Endless Waste," Hope replied.

"And you were thinking of trying to go there?" Starai intuited.

"No," Hope shook his head. He had not yet realized it himself. "I was just wondering if there really was another city out there. Bigger than Jchow Oasis. And green lands beyond."

"Green lands like you found in the cargo bird book?" Harvig asked.

"Possibly."

The band started playing so Hope and Starai got up to

dance. Starai also danced a few songs with Harvig, who had just started learning. When the band took a break, they resumed talking in the cooling air, watching the waiters light firepots and paper lanterns.

"If there is a trail through the Valley of Death leading to a large city in the desert, I think we should follow it," Starai announced.

"What?" Hope said in shocked surprise. The idea seemed so preposterous he had not even dared consider it.

"Why not? You found Apocalypse. You found the cargo bird. I think you can find Horizon."

"Grinst found Apocalypse," Hope said. "Grinst and a fairy tale from a book led us to the cargo bird. Grinst led the grubbers back to Jchow Oasis."

"Well, you found Ezkia Nunnery. And you led us to Jchow Oasis," Starai said in defense.

"I question whether I have the skills to find the trail across the Valley of Death," Hope said regretfully. "When Grinst tried to point it out I could not see anything."

"Me either," lamented Harvig.

"Mayhaps a more recent group has gone that way," Starai said hopefully, "and left a fresher track."

Neither Hope nor Harvig said anything.

"The shamans at the Temple of Bool have pronounced your letter acceptable for teaching," Starai pointed out. "There are Hool translations of *A Bright One Chronicles* in the libraries and schools. We have done our job and are no longer needed here."

"There is even a puppet show touring the oasis telling the story of a Bright One," Harvig told them in amazement. "I just heard about it today and forgot to mention it."

"That was your goal, was it not?" Starai asked. "For the Hool at Jchow Oasis to take the story and mold it into something of their own. Something to challenge them yet fit their culture?"

"Yes," Hope agreed.

Starai raised her eyebrows. "A new goal would be to go through the Valley of Death to find Horizon."

"We might never return," Hope said.

"We might not want to return," she answered simply.

"Well, we could go have a look," Harvig shrugged his shoulders. "See if someone has recently gone that way and made a better trail."

"Are you willing to give it a try as well?" Hope asked Harvig. "What about your life here in Jchow Oasis? Your big house?"

"Since you two got here," Harvig answered, "my life has turned around. I have purpose again. If you are leaving, I am coming along. I do not care about the big house. 'Tis lonely."

They left Jchow Oasis two days before the next bright Moonday with a large caravan of camels. They stopped to resupply their finances in the Broiled Mountains where they had buried part of their treasure from the cargo bird.

When they got to the top of the ridge that looked into the Valley of Death, Hope and Harvig were able to find and follow a faint track down the dusty and rocky hillside. Starai had been right. Someone had recently gone this way!

They camped that night with gladdened spirits despite the huge cloud of dust that engulfed them and blocked out the moonlight. The next day as the air cleared, they were stunned to see a figure coming up out of the valley. When the person drew closer, both Hope and Harvig began waving. They recognized the fast, loping walk.

"Grinst!" they yelled out in excitement.

He was as happy and excited to see them as they were to see him. Everyone jumped up and down hugging each other. They made camp and excitedly caught up with the news. Grinst had been fascinated with Epoh's story about *Dragons of the Endless Waste*. Now he listened carefully and intently to Hope's story of a Bright One. He also seemed entranced by Starai.

Grinst told them 'twas his trail they had been following down into the Valley of Death. He had gone back and forth searching for the way across. The trail split further along, he told them. One of the forks led out to a trail of skeletons. He had followed the second fork to an overlook that held promise for a way across. He was now coming back to resupply with a couple of camels, food, and water before going any further.

"But with all this!" Grinst gestured at their camp, "We can go now, together!" He teased them about having nine camels. Hope and Starai had a sun awning and medium sized tent with a carpet for a floor, along with other conveniences including a small lap table for writing, a box of paper, quills, and ink, and even a small case of books. Harvig also had a tent and large sun umbrella, along with other extravagances. And Grinst was astounded by the amount of water and food they were carrying.

Yet when Hope suggested they could lighten their load and eat a few of the camels as they traveled, Grinst would not hear of it.

"No, no," he said as he shook his head. "You brought a caravan. We will keep everything. Just in case."

HORIZON

Grinst led their group across the Valley of Death and into the immensity of the Endless Waste. Their well-supplied camel caravan made the worst parts of desert travel more tolerable, made the boring parts more enjoyable, and made the best parts exciting and fun. There was a strange and haunting beauty in the barren terrain, especially during the early morning, evening, and moonlight. They marveled at the new varieties of cactus and sparse desert plants and grasses, and the wildlife living around the scattered seeps and springs they discovered along the way. They saw new types of spiders, scorpions, reptiles, and lizards, along with dust rabbits, meercats, jackals, black goats, sandcats, silver antelope, and even small and thin desert ibex. They also saw burrowing owls, roadrunners, sandgrouse, cactus wrens, ravens, hawks, eagles, and a variety of vultures.

They traveled at a reasonable pace but did not feel any rush. Grinst was happiest out in the middle of the desert with a far-away goal. There were plenty of difficulties and hardships, through heat, wind, and dust storms, across vast regions of dunes, over desolate mountain ranges, and massive, flat and crusted pans of dried-up lakes.

There were also scenic vistas with stunning views of eroded landscapes and strange formations. Deep canyons and valleys. Rocks and dirt of all colors. Moments of immense and breathtaking silence and stillness so profound as to touch their souls.

Seventeen moons later they arrived at Horizon, a vast oasis

of shaded farms and gardens which took more than three days to cross. The vibrancy of all the green plants was like a soothing balm to their spirits. Along with all the smells and moisture in the air. They were amazed by the immensity of the fields, and the gridwork of alleys and paths that allowed access to the patchwork of gardens. They stopped often to buy provisions and eat at food stalls. Everything tasted delicious.

The city itself was built on a mound of soft rock, smaller than Ambrit, but larger in population because of the underground rooms four to five layers deep. The inhabitants spoke a different dialect of Hool, which took the newcomers nearly a decade to learn and polish before they could begin translating *A Bright One Chronicles* into a story the locals could understand.

Once their translation was complete, Hope and Harvig began speaking and narrating the story outside of temples and in underground plazas, anywhere there were groups of people who would listen.

Starai had been inspired when hearing of the puppet group at Jchow Oasis. During their trip across the desert, she wrote and developed a puppet script with stories adapted from *A Bright One Chronicles*. Upon arriving in Horizon, she had a puppet stage built, and a troupe of adorable puppets made. Now, she began doing programs that were entertaining and educational for both kids and adults. Her shows were an instant hit.

"'Tis amazing that stories from the life of a girl and young woman could be so popular in a male-dominated culture and theology like the Hool," Hope marveled.

"Tyme comes from a land where women rule," Starai pointed out, "yet she did not use her power to become Empress and take control. She gave up that to be a servant. That fits into Hool theology of women being a servant."

Epoh shook his head. "That is like the Book of Tatano. The only book written by a man in the *Book of Elders* because it teaches that men should be subservient."

"Tyme followed a man's teachings to be a True Warrior," Starai observed, "Mayhaps young Hool boys will be inspired to follow a woman's example in return."

Grinst remained with them while they were learning the new dialect of Hool, then he followed his urge for adventure further into the desert. There were no stories or legends of any oases east of Horizon. But Grinst was determined to scout everything himself, regardless. Like Hope, he had been captivated by the paintings in the books in the cargo bird, which he still called the dragon, that showed large areas of land covered in green plants in full sunlight. He was determined to find evidence leading to such places.

Hope began to learn of tales from a period long ago with massive sandstorms that had destroyed all the crops, combined with an earthquake that had introduced bad water into many of the wells. That led to a collapse of society, a civil war in Horizon, and a series of large migrations with armies of armed survivors leaving the oasis and heading west in search of new lands. In studying the local history, as herstory was called in the Hool dialect, Hope believed those events occurred when the armies of Hool had come out of the desert and over the Barrier Mountains and into the Ambri Empire.

For the people who chose to stay in Horizon, it had taken millennia for the wells to run clean again, for the farms and fields to be reestablished, and for the population to grow back to its former level.

Hope and Starai had been living in Horizon for nearly five decades when Grinst came back sick from one of his long explorations in the desert. He arrived deathly ill, and they were certain that he was going to die. After two moons, to everyone's surprise, he began to recover. As he grew stronger, he had a realization.

"I do not want to die in Horizon," Grinst told them. "And I do not want to die wandering around in the empty desert further east of here."

"Where do you want to die?" Starai asked.

"In the Sea of Dunes," Grinst answered. "I want to try to find another dragon."

Grint's pronouncement promoted much discussion later that evening with Starai, Hope, and Harvig.

"Do you want to die here in Horizon?" Starai asked Hope.

He sat quietly thinking. The main Temple of Bool had accepted his letters, and the smaller temples had copies as well. There was a growing group of devotees. The library had a number of copies of *A Bright One Chronicles*, as did the University. Three other puppet groups were also giving shows featuring stories about a Bright One. They had accomplished their task of spreading the word about Tyme, and what she stood for. The seeds had all been planted.

"No," Hope said with a growing realization. "I do not want to die here."

"Nor do I," Harvig added.

"Do either of you think you could find your way back across the Endless Waste to Jchow Oasis without Grinst?" Starai asked.

"I would not want to bet my life on it," Hope shook his head, trying to make a joke.

"Then when Grinst gets ready to leave," Starai said resolutely, "we better be ready to go with him."

While they continued to talk, Hope and Starai realized they did not want to stay long at Jchow Oasis.

"I only need to stop and make sure the followers of a Bright One are still growing in numbers," Hope announced. "If everything is fine, I would prefer to continue to Ambra. I am ready to go home at last."

"And I am ready for a new adventure as well," Starai enthused. "I would like to meet everyone I read about in *A*

Bright One Chronicles." She turned to Harvig. "We would love to have you come with us."

"Yes," Harvig was quick to agree. "I am ready for a new land and adventure as well."

Once they were back in the desert, Grinst grew happier and stronger every day. It took 14 moons to return, now that Grinst knew the way, three months faster than their first crossing. After passing through the Valley of Death they climbed back up into the Broiled Mountains. Again they stopped to resupply their finances from the treasure they had cached centuries earlier from the cargo bird.

Then they sadly said goodbye to Grinst and tried not to worry about him going alone to the Sea of Dunes. "I still do not understand how he can find his way anywhere," Hope marveled. "His eyes are so cloudy he can hardly see."

"He has a powerful sixth sense," Starai affirmed. "And if he does have any problems, that is where he wants to die. Be happy for him."

A SURPRISE

A line of camels emerged from a haze of dust blowing across the Endless Waste. Valhal Oasis came into view at the base of the Barrier Mountains below the Siren of Dayrstad.

Hope, Starai and Harvig grinned with anticipation astride their camels, approaching the oasis to trade for daya horses. Neither Starai nor Harvig had ever seen a horse, and they were excited to ride them and learn about their care. Once they sold their camels, desert tents, and gear, they purchased horses, saddles and bags, mountain camping gear, and new Dayrstad clothing. Hope remembered the uproar he had caused previously when he arrived at the Siren dressed in Hool clothes.

After the heat, they delighted in riding up through the luxuriant, green-terraced fields to the Siren, sitting like a polished jewel in the golden evening light, to all appearances a palace with few defenses. But the inside was a fortress, with secret caves and escape routes.

The Duke was no more hospitable than previously. He was confused as to who Hope was, even when Hope repeatedly called himself Epohco. He had no memory of Hope passing through a century earlier on his way into the desert. The Duke was equally baffled by Starai, and alarmed by the burns on Harvig's face and hands. The travelers retired early to their rooms.

The next morning at dawn the trio gathered on a patio to do their practice. After a dusty-orange sunrise, Hope showed the others around the beautiful architecture of the building.

When the Duke finally appeared, they thanked him for the lodging and bid him farewell.

Neither Starai nor Harvig were ready to ride the steep Scout Trail up out of the Siren. They walked their horses the entire way in nervous but enthusiastic awe of the narrow and exposed trail. The normal three-day trip to Dayr Castle took four days. They were amazed by the different cacti, aloes and agaves filling the shady sides of the hills and valleys.

The travelers camped one night in a group of shaggy yucca trees, the next night beside a giant Baobab tree, as big around as a barn with only a few stubby and root-like branches and no leaves on top. A growing crescent moon hung over a majestic ridge of mountains in the western sky.

"'Tis so much more beautiful than I ever imagined," Starai said. Hope felt the same way. He had forgotten how much he loved Dayrstad.

Their first view of Dayr Castle above the rows and patterns of shaded gardens of Dayr Valley was emotional. The approach was surreal for each of them for different reasons. They felt in a dream as they grew close and rode up the hill to the grand and intimidating castle entrance between the massive tower one and tower two at castle gate. Krugero was not standing lookout on top.

Anda Dana, the big, black guard with tattoos on her arms and left side of her face greeted them at the entryway to the tunnel in the wall. She did not recognize Hope. From the near side of the tunnel Krugero came out of the shade of castle gate to examine them closer.

"Epo..." he started to say, then corrected himself. "Hope?" he asked in disbelief. His eyesight was no longer good enough to stand lookout on top of tower one, but the old soldier still recognized the former crown prince.

"Krugero!" Hope quickly dismounted to hug his first Hand as a boy, then mentor and friend as a tween.

"This is Starai, my wife," Hope introduced his companions. "And my friend, Harvig."

"You have returned yet again from the Endless Waste," Krugero proclaimed with eager astonishment, and then he grew solemn. "I regret to inform you that King Eyrico has passed away. Your brother, King Dracoro, now sits on the throne of Dayrstad."

"Please give him word that I am here," Hope replied, "and I request audience to see him and my mother, the queen dowager."

"I will," Krugero answered. He smiled as he fondly patted Hope's shoulder. "There is a surprise for you in the commons." The old guard excitedly motioned for him to ride through castle gate.

When they came out on the other side, Hope had two surprises. The large Mother Womb in the commons that had been sealed up for millennia was now open to the poor and country folk. There were still unrepaired holes in the dome and cracks in the walls, but next to the round, open door was a large statue of Tyme standing in the pose of a True Warrior with the end of her sword on the ground. Approaching closer, Hope could see the wall inside the building between the refuge and the sanctuary had been removed.

Past the temple, the second surprise was the giant yellow and white sun tent of the Ser Cus being set up. Beside it was the orange and white family tent with banners flying on top. Nearby, the blue and white tent of Draktono, Singer, and Swindovo was also up, with another True Warrior statue of Tyme by the entryway. As the travelers advanced, they could hear drumming and singing.

"Get ready to meet your new family," Hope said enthusiastically.

A SHRINE

The reunion was as wonderful as Hope had imagined. Everyone crowded around for introductions and hugs.

Wiir Waar gave Starai a welcoming embrace. "I told Hope to bring you back so we could meet you," she enthused.

"You do not look as weathered as you did last time out of the desert," Jyg joked.

"We were mostly in oases," Hope explained. "When we traveled, we had camels, umbrellas, and plenty of food and water." He could not help but add, "Although we still ate locust patties, kangaroo rats, and hopping mice stew."

"I *hope*," Draktono smiled as he emphasized the word, "that you are going to join us in a Bright One's tent and travel with the Ser Cus."

"A flaming sword of truth!" Bones proclaimed loudly. She had a list of responses whenever she heard someone say *a Bright One.*

"Yes, and we are thrilled to be here with you," Hope replied. "I also want to continue writing, studying, and be a shaman."

"I have a puppet show of a Bright One stories I performed at Horizon Oasis that I want to recreate," Starai announced with excitement.

"Her voice a great song!" Bones called out.

"I get to help with the puppets," Harvig said proudly. He loved the laughter and awe of the kids watching Starai perform. Behind the screen with puppets on his hands, no one would be aware of his scars.

"We can help with music and drumming," Swindovo

offered with enthusiasm. Singer nodded his head, smiling and humming.

They spent the evening and long into the night catching up and telling stories. Jyg and Wiir Waar seemed more in love than ever.

"'Tis wonderful having my husband and best friend with me in the Ser Cus," Wiir Waar gushed as she gave Jyg a hug.

"We give thanks every day for each other," Jyg agreed. "And for our lives. Every day is interesting. And I love performing with Bones."

"The star of the show!" the big raven bragged at the mention of her name.

"You may be the star," Jyg prompted, "but who is the True Warrior?"

"A Bright One!" Bones answered.

Hope was eager to hear of the growing movement to embrace Tyme as a role model and prophet, and as a bridge between the Fire, the kiva movement, and the Womb.

"How did the Mother Womb in the commons open?" Hope asked in amazement. 'And where did the statue of Tyme come from?"

"Since there was no kiva to reclaim in Dayr Valley," Draktono explained, "the Fire devotes took over the building for their ceremonies. The priests complained but King Dracaro would not arrest them. Delgado had the statue made in Karvor and hauled here in a wagon. He wanted to establish a shrine at the castle."

"Did you notice how different Hope is with Starai, than how Epoh was with Tyme?" Wiir Waar asked Jyg when they were alone later.

"Hope is a different person than Epoh," Jyg mused. "'Tis more than just a name change."

"Epoh and Tyme were passionate and demonstrative,

always touching and kissing," Wiir Waar recalled. "Hope and Starai are loving in a different way. Deep, but understated."

"They are a team," Jyg agreed. "But they do not focus on each other. They focus on their common goal."

"Starai is not threatened or jealous of Hope's commitment to Tyme's story, nor envious of the love he will always have for her," Wiir Waar marveled. "There are not many women who could so graciously concede the stage light to her mate's previous wife and lover."

"Not just concede," Jyg noted. "She is in the front row cheering for Tyme's encore. She is as committed to Tyme's story as Hope."

On his last two visits to Dayr Castle, Hope had stayed only a few days amid heart breaking turmoil with the King declaring him outcast and dead. Now his father was gone, his brother was King, and Hope was being escorted to a private audience chamber.

"Your highness," Hope bowed, "Thank you for seeing me."

King Dracaro rose from his throne to give his older brother a warm embrace. "I am sorry our father never forgave you," he said. "I have no such anger or resentment."

"The pain I caused him grieves me still," Hope replied.

"He was too busy blaming you to acknowledge that I was a worthy substitute," Dracaro said ruefully.

"Was he not impressed with your soldier's tournaments? I thought you clever and astute to hold them. King Eyrico always believed me to be inadequate in military training and comradery with the soldiers."

"The tournament brought all the fighters out of the mountains, including the so-called rebels and followers of the Fire," Dracaro recounted. "King Eyrico worried that I gave all the malcontents opportunity to come together and join ranks.

"Did he know his brother, the Duke, was vying for the title

of rebel leader?" Hope asked.

"He admitted it to me on his death bed, when he warned me of Eddarko's treachery."

"And my mother," Hope inquired, "the Queen Dowager?"

"Alive but senile. I am sorry to say she will not even know you."

"I must see her regardless."

After a moment of silence, King Dracaro changed the subject. "I read *A Bright One Chronicles* that you left at the keep library," he said with admiration and patted his hand over his heart. "I was moved to tears. 'Twas like some ancient and grand epic tale. But she was real. She was here, in our castle."

King Dracaro's face lit up upon further reflection. "I danced with Tyme when the Ser Cus performed at the keep. 'Twas the first celebration after moons of grieving over your death. I was shy, and still shaken by your disappearance. But later I thought often about holding on to her and dancing." He grinned sheepishly. "A boyhood crush."

"She was a remarkable person," Hope agreed. "Easy to admire and love."

"You have spread her story across Ambra, and beyond," the King praised him. "I am in awe of you, brother."

They reminisced about Tyme living in the stables, and then talked of the statue of Tyme in front of the Mother Womb.

"The statue represents different things to different people," King Dracaro reported. "Some say the statue defends the Mother Womb. Others say it defies the priests. The shamans claim she breaks down the walls. The Fire says she transcends the boundary between women and men."

The King raised his eyebrows. "What do you think of the Fire? Should I continue letting them occupy the Mother Womb and do their ceremonies?"

"The Fire arose in response to a disrespect for men," Hope replied. "When a group feels disrespected, they can behave in a variety of ways, from lashing out, to internalizing that disregard into deep seated insecurities. Your willingness to let them freely voice their complaints is a strong first step toward any possible reconciliation."

"Do you think reconciliation between the Fire and the priests is possible?"

"We should always work toward reconciliation," Hope answered. "As to whether we see it to fruition during our life, we can only pray."

Hope returned to the palace with Starai to meet King Dracaro and his wife, Queen Maya Maay, who seemed uneasy with her husband's infatuation over a stable girl turned prophet and True Warrior. Hope also introduced Starai to others in the castle, but mostly she kept busy creating her puppet show.

At the stables, Hope helped Utuno make Tyme's former bunkroom into a memorial. And they made Merryleg's stall, which had been nailed shut since the horse's death, into a joint tribute for Noot, who had loved sitting up in the window. They also made a marker to remember Spike in the ibex pen.

Hope was elated to be sleeping in a tent in the commons next to the Ser Cus. He loved spending his days and evenings singing, writing, and talking about Tyme with anyone who stopped by. One night, Jyg led Hope, Starai, Harvig, Wiir Waar and the Z's through the castle exploring abandoned buildings and climbing to the lookouts and vantage points he had taken Tyme when they were young.

Jyg also showed the group where he grew up. His uncle's shop was now called Pio's Pigeons. The *and chickens* part of the name had been dropped. After Jakiko stole and then sold Panr's pigeons to Major Bayn Baya, the Major had used the breed to send numerous messages between Ambrit, Karvor, Pintone, and Ralston Garrison. That success, along with Pio's own messages sent between Dayr Castle and Panr, convinced Jyg's uncle that his special strain of messenger pigeons had been adequately tested and were ready to be sold to the general public. The Czarzina herself had ordered a dovecote of the birds, and so had the Council of Priests, along with a number of wealthy merchants. Panr helped raise the pigeons to fill those orders.

Despite this lucrative increase in business, Pio's uncle, aunt, and cousin still lived behind the shop in the gatehouse to the old mansion. Jyg gave a tour of the dovecotes, including the brick dovecote on the rooftop, which he had been sworn never to speak about when he was young. A pair of guards now patrolled the site night and day.

The rest of the tiered mansion was still locked and sealed. Jyg led them through the servant's passageways up to the third floor where he had lived in the first daughter's bedroom. His private workshop was still intact. They were all impressed with his private clifftop patio looking down over the commons.

The grand finale for the desert travelers was seeing the Ser Cus perform. The show exceeded their expectations, a mesmerizing and thrilling spectacle of physical prowess with tumbling, acrobatics, feats of strength, sword jugging, knife-throwing, and rope-walking. Jyg and Bones were boisterously cheered as the Dayr Castle hometown heroes. After resting a few days and enjoying some relaxed moonlit nights of socializing, everyone packed up and moved on to Birjj.

Jyg entertained everyone again when he took them out to the estate of Nahi Naha Nala, the woman who had bought his gyrfalcon, Zaru, for three gold coins. Jyg had visited the falconer during earlier Ser Cus stays in Birjj, and had joined her in taking Zaru out to hunt for sage grouse. Bones was never brought along as Zaru would have viewed the big raven as prey to kill. Watching Zaru hunt was still exhilarating, but owning such a predatory bird no longer held Jyg's interest. There was room for only one bird in his life and that was Bones.

Karvor held a special place in Hope's heart. 'Twas the colorful city where he and Tyme had found each other and fallen deeper in love. As Tyme had said--the best moons of their lives. To be here was to remember her everywhere.

Jyg and Wiir Waar had already updated Hope and Starai about Delgado, the Blue Moon, and the Jawbone Ridge gang. He and Rona had a baby girl, and Delgado was talking about changing the rules of the gang so that she could be included as she grew older. Delgado had grown even closer to Targono, the King of Karvor, and was a leading advocate for establishing shrines to a Bright One throughout Ambra.

When they first arrived, Delgado showed Hope and Starai the statues of Tyme on each side of the stage in the Blue Moon.

"Every dark Moonday, we clean out the figures, totems, and gifts from the shrines to make room for new offerings," he told them. "The money goes to support the school at the kiva in the Painted Hills."

"The work to build new shrines comes from the Jawbone Ridge gang, and the money comes from the King of Karvor, who also lets us use his wagons and horses. We have constructed shrines across Ambra. In sponsoring shrines to Tyme, the King also honors Klew."

"Who was a Bright One as well," Hope agreed.

"I will tell King Targono that you have returned from the Endless Waste," Delgado said. "He would be interested to see you again. He has read your book. He also appreciated your help with Draktono in drafting the Bill of Rights. The document embodies the highest ideals for a more just and equal society."

"Does Targono sing or drum?" Hope asked. "We must invite him to join us in a Bright One tent for music and theological discussions."

"That might appeal to him," Delgado agreed. "Sometimes he goes out in disguise with only a few guards to observe the city and get a feel for the mood of the people. He has sneaked into the Blue Moon a few times for bands I recommended. Music of the soul, as I call it."

"I want to hear music of the soul," Starai said with interest.

"Yes," Hope agreed. "Let us know which bands we should hear. We can take turns staffing a Bright One tent."

"The band tonight is excellent and will be starting soon," Delgado replied.

"And I can give you a quick lesson on the latest dance," Rona offered. "'Tis easy and lots of fun."

Hope, Starai, and Harvig also went with Singer, Swindovo and Draktono to the kiva of shaman Gybeko in the Painted Hills for a few days. Frisoto was still head of the school, which had five teachers, three drum groups, a men's choir, and a traveling ensemble. Gybeko was interested in Starai's stories of the meditation caves and Quiet Ones at Ezkia Nunnery, and they all enjoyed hearing how she had been taken into a large room full of bowl-shaped bells to find the bell and tone that resonated best within her for her own practice. She hummed the tone. "The bell is still on my altar."

When they returned to the city, Hope, Starai, and Delgado were invited to a meeting with King Targono at his fort by Jintiga Bridge. After greetings and introductions, the King got straight to the point.

"Tyme was buried in an unmarked grave in a cemetery for criminals. Riin Ruel confirmed the exact spot a decade later and people began visiting the site. Only a few at first but then word spread, and more people came and left mementos and offerings."

"I saw the statues and shrines that Delgado had made for Tyme at the Blue Moon," the King explained, "and told him I would pay for a similar shrine to be made and put over her grave in Ambrit."

"Krenoko drove the wagon with the tiles and statue," Delgado interjected proudly. "He was the one who Tyme headbutted in the alley, which led her to meet the Jawbone Ridge gang."

The King resumed his story. "After Czarzina Hana Hama Hala was removed, the next Czarzina, Vana Nava Avan not only agreed to the shrine being erected, but she also talked about putting a roof or even a building over it. As those plans were being drawn, different opinions and ideas began to compete, especially arguments about whether Tyme's body should be dug up and moved to a more appropriate place."

King Targono shook his head in disgust. "Everything stalled. 'Twas all politics of power and greed couched in pretended concerns over what was appropriate and proper. After Czarzina Vana Nava Avan's mysterious and suspicious death, Czarzina Laa Lee Luu was inaugurated by the Senate. The Senasers who had argued to have Tyme's body moved were just stalling until one of their candidates came back into power. Then they began spreading rumors and lies about Tyme."

"They made a big deal about the shrine at the grave being made by the Jawbone Ridge gang," Delgado said in disgust, "and claimed we run a saloon with demon music and a crooked protections racket for a house of prostitution. They profess outrage that Tyme was a gang member, and imply she was an escort and prostitute."

"They also say Tyme's followers are Fire possessed sun worshippers and Barbarians," King Targono added with anger. "They embrace any lie that will discredit her and the movement toward change that she represents. Change to them is a loss of power and influence. Her opponents say they are upholding and fighting for traditional values. But they are really fighting to retain their dominance and control."

"One group labels her harlot, while others a saint," Starai shook her head.

"This is how it has been through history," Hope replied sadly. "An event of great impact occurs. Some people are moved to introspection, growth, and reform, while others are threatened and do everything to deny it."

"Speaking of saint, the priests are distressed over rumors of people praying to Tyme to help guide them on the path to Divine," King Targono revealed. "The practice has been growing in Ambrit."

"Intercessory prayer," Hope mused. "Where souls and spirits mutually help one another on the journey to holiness." He smiled with delight and softly proclaimed, "Saint Tyme!"

"We are interested in what you think should be done with her grave," Delgado said.

"Yes," Hope replied, "I am updating the ending of *A Bright One Chronicles*. Visiting her grave will be the final chapter."

There was a long silence.

"I killed Klew," King Targono said in a flat voice. "I was angry that he expected me to be noble, to be a True Warrior. He saw something better in me, even when I did not see it in myself." He looked at Hope. "Can you ever forgive me?"

"Klew forgave you," Hope reminded him. "I forgive you as well."

"'Twas a terrible thing that I will regret every day for the rest of my life," the King lamented.

"We all miss him," Hope agreed. "And Tyme. They both ignored their fears and strove to set the highest examples of fortitude, integrity, and self-sacrifice. May we all be inspired by their actions and faith."

"Faith does require action," Starai concurred.

"You stopped being a Quiet One soon after Hope returned to Ezkia Nunnery," the King asked Starai. "What inspired your change?"

"Being a Quiet One was about establishing a deep and abiding stillness and connection with Divine. 'Twas also a mirror to the desert in which I lived. Hope exposed me to a wider world where I saw that action was greatly needed. I realized we are the hands and feet of Divine in this world. We are her emissaries. We must be the change that we want to see in the world."

"Focusing only on selfish desires gives fleeting satisfaction," King Targono agreed. "And leaves a profound emptiness. Riin Ruel taught me the healing power of shifting one's focus toward others. And the importance of admitting, acknowledging, and amending past sins and mistakes."

Hope invited the King to come to a Bright One tent to sing and see Draktono.

"Yes," he replied. "I would like that. And visit me again whenever you are in Karvor."

As full Moonday approached, the excitement of the Ser Cus performing at the Skyline Stadium grew to a crescendo. The outside of the grand theater, built on a steep hillside and prow of rock, featured exquisitely carved statues of the Founding Mothers of the Ambri Empire. The audience sat in tiered seats facing the setting sunset colors on the western horizon, while the rising moon behind the spectators illuminated the stage with a glowing light. Despite the declining population of Karvor, the stadium was half full.

Hope, Starai, and Harvig had front row seats. The audience was rapt with attention from the opening acrobatics and gymnastics to the riveting finale with the Ropewalker, high in the dazzling moonlight, on a line strung across the width of the giant stadium. Wiir Waar was marvelous with her sword juggling and knife throwing and commanding stage presence. Yet when the crowd left the stadium after the performance, the name everyone spoke was Bones.

Jyg and Bones interactions were astonishing to watch. The big raven had an ever-growing vocabulary, with so many vocal inflections from different people. She obviously enjoyed making people laugh and fine-tuned her antics to cause greater reactions. Jyg brought Bones into the audience for disbelievers to look closer to see 'twas Bones really talking. Those intimate encounters evoked even more fans and funny stories. Jyg also displayed his rock-climbing skills on the stadium walls and arches, with Bones heckling and landing on perches along the route. Bones also appeared briefly at the start of the Ropewalker's performance to crack a few jokes about her falling and not being able to fly.

When the Ser Cus arrived in Ambrit, a Bright One tent was set up nearby, but Hope and Starai spent most of their stay at Tyme's grave site. She was buried in a military cemetery, behind the area for orphan males born in the Milk, in a sector of shallow plots for criminals. Yet her statue and shrine near the back wall were obvious upon entering the cemetery. A well-trampled path showed the quickest way to her grave.

A mound of glazed tiles with shimmering iridescent colors covered her grave and formed a backdrop to the larger than life-size ceramic statue of Tyme standing in the pose of a True Warrior with the point of her sword on the ground and her hands resting lightly over the pommel at the end of the hilt. Her face was resplendent and lifelike, complete with beauty marks, thick eyebrows, and off-kilter smile.

Thankfully, no one was there when they arrived. Hope wept openly as he drew close. He brushed away the candles and offerings covering the base of the statue so he could lie on the tiles and embrace the grave mound.

Starai backed away to give him privacy.

When he stopped crying, he sat up and motioned for Starai, who also had tears on her cheeks, to come closer.

"I have wanted to visit her grave for so long," Hope said with emotion. 'Twas nearly one and a half centuries since Tyme had died. "I needed that completion. A final release."

"Stay here as much as you want," Starai encouraged.

Hope nodded in agreement. "While we are in Ambrit, let's spend most of our day talking with people who come to her grave and telling them more about her life."

Starai looked up to see people walking through the cemetery toward the shrine.

"Others are coming already," she told him, wiping away the last of his tears.

"Good," Hope smiled with a renewed spirit and sense of purpose. "Now when I think of Tyme, I only feel joy."

CAST OF CHARACTERS

Bayn Baya - Major in Heart Legion with spies and plans for a coop

Bokono - rebel leader of the Fire, poisoned by Duke Eddarko of the Siren

Bones - clever and talkative raven raised by Jyg

Cata Cara - Heart Legion General who plans treason with Major Bayn Baya

Dari Riad - owner of the Dusted Man tavern in the Painted Hills near Karvor

Dracaro - brother to Crown Prince Epohco

Draktono - leader of the apprentices to the Singer

Duke - see below

Eddarko - **Duke of the Siren**, brother to King Eyrico, uncle to Crown Prince Epohco

Epoh - name of form Crown Prince Epohco after near drowning

Etna Nate - sergeant in Heart Legion, plays cards with Gribono

Eyrico - King of Dayrstad and father of Crown Prince Epohco

Frisato - one of the apprentices to the Singer

Gambler – nickname for Gribono

Gribono - the gambler, spy for Captain Targono

Grinst - a tough, old grubber, desert survivalist and scavenger for lost treasure

Grodoro - sent by rebel leader Bokono to infiltrate and kill Singer

Gwen Gail - major at Ambrit Military Academy, covertly new Hilt of the Daggers, the leader of a secret mystical warrior society

Hana Hama Hala - Czarzina that imprisoned Riin Ruel

Harvig - apprentice grubber for lost treasure and former trail worker at Ezkia Nunnery, brother to Horton

Horton - a real grubber, older brother to Harvig, scavenger for lost treasures

Jakiko - set fire to Panr's dovecote and stole her pigeons

Jyg – Tyme's friend, manser of birds, companion of Bones the raven, climber extraordinaire

Klew - soldier of King's Guard who teaches Tyme the sword, full name Klewono

Lana Pana - acrobat, juggler, and bossy tween Ser Cus performer

Lartso - spy for Captain Targono, poisoned with Bokono by Duke Eddarko

Mams - matriarch and leader of the Ser Cus

Narvago - coach and trainer for the Ser Cus

Noot - stable boy at Dayr Castle who is murdered by Gribono

Otovo - rebel from kiva on old trail to Birjj from Karvor

Ozono - leader of Canaries, the yellow powdered miners at Dusted Man tavern

Panr - pigeon breeder, partner with Pio (Jyg's uncle) whose birds are stolen

Pio - uncle to Jyg, owner of Pio's Pigeons and Chickens

Riin Ruel – spiritual warrior and Point of the Daggers, a secret, mystical cabal of demon fighters

Shamano - an influential shaman and Fire devotee from the mountains of Birjj

Shelodo - Manser of Viruna to the King of Sikes, organizes Singer and the apprentices

Singer – young man from Sikes whose earlier visions compels him to sing

Starai - baby girl Riin Ruel tested, later found Epoh near drowned and brought him to Ezkia Nunnery

Swindovo - youngest apprentice to Singer, excellent drummer, updates music with catchy rhythms, beats, and choruses

Tana Pana - young acrobat, juggler, and contortionist Ser Cus performer

Tao Tau - wise old herb woman who mentors Tyme on trips to Lost Valley

Targono - captain in Hammer Legion who plots a coup and send out spies, boyhood friend of Klew from Military Academy in Ambrit

Tatano - the first True Warrior, ended the Dark Ages when he convinced his soldiers to stop fighting for leadership amongst themselves and submit to the will of the Women's Clans, wrote Book of Tatano, only book by a man in the Book of Elders

Tyme - the foundling of Dayr Castle and possible Bright One

Utuno - Manser of King's Stables where Tyme is raised

Vela Vara - Will of the Blades, the leader of the personal guards to the Czarzina who arrests and imprisons Riin Ruell

Weethee Wona - youngest and smallest female Ser Cus performer

Wera Wahn - hilosopher and survivor of failed Ambri expedition who becomes Saint of the Desert and founds Ezkia Nunnery

Wiir Waar - sword juggler and knife thrower in the Ser Cus

Xacano - philosopher and teacher at keep school, counselor to King Eyrico

Zandero - acrobat, tumbler, and juggler for the Ser Cus

Zintowo - finest male acrobat in the Ser Cus and all of Ambra

Z's - nickname for the cousins Zintowo and Zandero of the Ser Cus

GLOSSARY

Adept's pose - for sitting meditation, similar to sitting cross-legged, but with left ankle tight under groin area, and right outer ankle comfortable over left inner ankle or calf, hands relaxed on thigh or knees, palms open or up, which holds the back straight and erect

agavr – worker harvesting agave to make viruna liquor

Ambra - all countries and lands west of the Endless Waste

Ambri - people of the Ambri Empire

Ambri Empire - the great matriarchal civilization that arose from the chaos of the Dark Ages and lasted over six millennium (486 years), but broke apart two and a half millennium ago (200 years)

Attributes - the seven aspects or Attributes of Divine are Spirit, Womb, Love, Compassion, Truth, Justice, and Forgiveness

Beast - the devil, also excessive and uncontrolled male energy

Beatifics - choir songs, prayers, and praises of Divine

billy - a male ibex or goat

Blade - former personal guardians of the Empress now protecting the Czarzina

Book of Elders - the sanctioned holy word and writings about Divine

burner - a rebel follower of the Fire

castle gate - the main entrance into a castle

cavort - the back section of Womb temple for sexual love and fertility

centurion - a person who is 100 moons in age

condition - a thick walled and protected room to escape the heat with cool stone couches or beds to sit and lie upon, can also be any shelter from the afternoon heat, even just a hole dug in the ground to reach cool dirt

Czarzina - woman ruler of Ambrit replacing the Empress after the collapse of the Ambri Empire

Dagger - or Divine Dagger, secret warrior group seeking the Bright One to become Empress of a new Holy Ambri Empire

daya - type of horse bred in Dayrstad for mountain travel

decade - 10 moons or months

Divine - the Ambri name for God, who is female and gave birth to Creation

Divine Council - the women elders who establish and protect the holy doctrines of the faithful

Divine Daggers - secret warrior group seeking the Bright One to become

Empress of a new Holy Ambri Empire

Divine Essence - Holy Spirit

Divine Fire - originally considered an Attribute of Divine, but much later banned by Divine Council and labeled a heretical men's cult or sun cult

Divine Fist - men's warrior group in the Barbarian kingdoms and old cities but not sanctioned in Ambrit

Divine Hand - a politically and religiously sanctioned warrior group for both women and men

Divine practice - a person's spiritual devotions, prayers, meditations, disciplines

Divine Womb - the temple, or the Mother temple

Divines - hymns and liturgical songs, Beatifics, Praises, Glorias, Hallelujahs

eyass - an unfledged (no flight feathers) bird of prey taken from the nest for training by a falconer

familiar - an animal that has an extra-ordinary and special bond with a person

fifir - queer or gender blend sexuality and behavior, with further defined terms:

    fafar - qeer or transgender woman tending toward feminine

    fafor - queer or transgender woman tending toward masculine

    fofar - queer or transgender man tending toward feminine.

    fofor - queer or transgender man tending toward masculine.

Fire - formerly Divine Fire, accused of being a sun cult, often for men only, some shamans believe only the Fire can purify the grievous   taint in men's souls

Fracture Wars – Breakup of Ambri Empire in countries of Ambri, Rhaldor, Tanis, Birjj, Thessal, Vlice, Sikes and Dayrstad.

flaunt - teacher of sexual love and fertility expert who works at the cavort in the Womb temple

gate - entry way or tunnel through a fortified wall

gender terms - see fifir

gesture the womb - a greeting of peace with both hands prayerfully held loosely in front of the chest, forming a womb shape with the hands.

Glorias - traditional choir hymns used in worship glorifying Divine

Glories – short for Glories of Divine on Her Throne, the 23rd through the 50th Prayers for the Dead

grubber - a scavenger for lost treasure in the Endless Waste

hall of Attributes - entrance into Womb temple for both women and men

Hand - a protector, mentor, errand runner and guardian for nobility, also an enforcer

Hallelujahs - exuberant and ecstatic hymns of joy toward Divine

herselves - a group of women

herstory - history

herstorical - historical

herstorian - historian

Hilt of the Dagger - the leader of the Daggers, who seek the Bright One to become Empress of a new Holy Ambri Empire

Kabaal Prophecies – written between the Dark Ages and the rise of the Women's Clans prior to the Ambri Empire

keep - the walled inner most protected area of a castle

kookerboom - a sparse desert tree, no leaves but fleshy fingers at end of a few thick branches after rains

manser - master, male head of trade, or male title of respect

mantle(d) - a climbing term, the move made to get out of a swimming pool or pull up to get on top of a wall if there is no ladder

mark - a person targeted to swindle

marked - someone seen and noticed

Mask of Brilliance- one of two versions of Kabaal Prophecies (17 scrolls)

Mask of Splendor - one of two versions of Kabaal Prophecies (19 scrolls)

mayhaps - maybe, perhaps

meda powder - from medaar plant, used as energy and sustenance when fasting

Milk - slang for Mother's Milk, the orphanage in the Womb temple

milker - a lactating woman, a woman who works at the Mother's Milk

mis - young woman

missin - loose woman, mistress

moon - one month, 29-30 days

moon blood - menstruation

moonboy – a young man to flirt with but not take seriously, a starry-eyed man who thinks he's in love, a young male prostitute

Moonday - first day of the week as follows:

    dark Moonday or Divine Night begins the first day of each month

    bright Moonday starts the second week with evening socializing

full Moonday begins third week with celebrations and festivals

    dim Moonday starts last week of month, dwindling moonlight

moon patio - a east facing patio for maximum enjoyment of early evening moonlight during bright and full moon, and also for receiving the healthy early morning rays of sun just after sunrise

Mother(s) – workers at the Mother's Milk

Mother's Milk - the mostly boys orphanage that is an integral part of every Womb temple

Mother Womb - largest or 1st Womb temple built in a town or city

mun - derogatory term for an adult male

Noble Path - a code of ethical combat behavior espoused by True Warriors

offiser - officer

old cities - cities formerly part of the Ambri Empire that are now all capitols of new countries

Point of the Dagger - the leading enforcer of the secretive Daggers, who seek the Bright One to become Empress of a new Holy Ambri Empire

practice - a person's spiritual devotions, prayers, meditations, disciplines

Praises - simple short, repetitive, and catchy songs praising Divine

Prayers for the Dead – prayers 1 – 19 *Prayers for the Mortal Body*, prayers 20 -22 *The Bridge*, prayers 23 – 50 *The Glories of Divine on Her Throne*, prayers 20, 51 – 52 the *Under Bridge*, prayers 53 - 77 *The Prayers for the Damned*

precurser - precursor

priest - an ordained woman minister of Divine

professer - professor

prophet - a woman who makes Divine predictions and pronouncements

refuge - outermost section of Womb temple for men only

remembrance - the recalling of a dream sparked by seeing someone who is gifted to trigger such events

sanctuary - inner section of Womb temple for women only

sanctum - most holy inner section of Womb temple for menstruating women only

ser - title of respect for women

seremony - ceremony

seremonies - ceremonies

senasers - senators

shaman - a male clergy for men's rites, in the Womb refuge and subordinate to women priests

Siren - fortified decoy castle built by Ambri to delay Hool attacks from the Endless Waste

smear(ed) - climbing term, using surface area friction to stick against the rock when no holds are available

soothser - woman who makes daily life predictions and forecasts

stretching postures – hatha yoga

surge - another name for the power of moon blood, or menstruation

tanche - a loose muslin shirt and baggy pant with tight cuffs around the wrists and ankles

'tis - it is

True Warrior - men who follow Tatano's vows to serve the Women's Clans, protect the weak and innocent, and be morally strong in the way of Divine, which led to the end of the Dark Ages and the birth of the Ambri Empire

'twas - it was

tween - ages between 150 moons (coming of age/12 years) and 200 moons (full adulthood/16 years)

viruna - a fiery and expensive golden liquor from Sikes, known throughout the Ambri Empire

Voice - originally called Peoples Voice, an area for open public forum and discussions on all topics

wait - the period between the first darkness of each night until the rising of the moon, which after the full moon increases nightly by nearly an hour

Will of the Blades - the leader of the Blades, the personal guardians of the Empress who now protected the Czarzina

Womb - a round and domed temple built to honor Divine, also the creative power of Divine

womb - a greeting of peace in a gesture of holding hands prayerful and lightly together in front of the chest

Yoke - ceremony and bone prayer bead connecting a Divine Warrior, who ritually slays an evil person, to take on their sin, and the demon behind the sin

BOOKS IN THIS SERIES

A Bright One Chronicles

An intriguing, coming-of-age, low fantasy adventure about friendship, belief, sacrifice, love, life and death. Captivating characters in a female predominate culture shaped by mysticism and spiritual awakenings.

The Foundling Of Dayr Castle

A girl of prophecy on a black stallion, a boy falconer and a Barbarian Prince share destinies with a deadly female warrior mystic. But not happily ever after.

Death Of Innocence

The Ser Cus arrives at Dayr Castle and Tyme meets Wiir Waar, her new friend and mentor in sword juggling, knife throwing, court etiquette and dance.

The Way Of The World

In Karvor, the polychrome city of potters, artists, song and dance, Tyme has a surprising encounter with the Jawbone Ridge gang.

A Bright One

Tyme and Epoh reunite at last in the colorful, artistic,

gambling city of Karvor. Tyme and Epoh reunite at last in the colorful, artistic, gambling city of Karvor. The intrigue and suspense grow as they strive to control their destinies in the final book of the series.

BOOKS BY THIS AUTHOR

The Road Of Dreams: A Two-Year Bicycling And Hiking Adventure Around The World

Follow the unforgettable exploits of seasoned travelers Bruce Junek and Tass Thacker on their 26-month around-the-world bicycle trip.

They crossed four continents through sweltering temperatures and winter snowstorms--punctuated by 42 flats.

This deeply personal travel book is also the story of an inner journey with a compelling message: Recognize what you value most in life, and pursue it.

Andes To The Amazon: Seven Journeys In Mexico, Central And South America

Join Bruce and Tass on seven wild and exotic trips south of the border.
* Bicycling through Central and South America
* Kayaking and swimming with whales in Baja
* Hiking through cloud forests in Costa Rica
* Snorkeling with penguins in the Galapagos Islands
* Traveling by dugout canoe in the Amazon Basin

Available from the author at imagesoftheworld.com

ABOUT THE AUTHOR

B Burgess Junek

Bruce Burgess Junek has traveled and bicycled with his wife, Tass Thacker, in more than 50 countries. In 1987 the two photographers created Images of the World to share the stories of their continuing adventures. Two million students have seen their educational school assembly slide presentations, along with adult audiences at festivals and cultural events.

A Bright One Chronicles is rich with influences from their many journeys, including bicycling through the Kalahari, Sahara and Gobi deserts. Their pilgrimages to sacred shrines and temples around the world celebrates the universal longing to find meaning in life through personal practice, spiritual beliefs and mystical teachings.

Bruce has written two travel narratives, The Road of Dreams and Andes to the Amazon, a rock-climbing guidebook, and created the documentary feature film Bruce & Tass Bicycle China. They still travel and are now enthralled with salsa dancing.

www.ImagesOfTheWorld.com   iow@hills.net
Instagram & TikTok @ bbjunek / Facebook - Bruce Junek